To
Don
Happy Reading
Meredith Campbell
4/21/01

Righteous Warriors

by Meredith Campbell

Righteous Warriors

Printed in the USA

Published by Two Trails Publishing
120 S. Main Street
Independence MO 64050

Marketed under Caroline Books
Rocky Medley; Graphic Cover Art
Reflections Printing; Cover Manufacture

Righteous Warriors

Franny slumped on the bottom step gagging on her tears and gasping from the smoke. Then her mind shouted. You dare not just sit here, Frances Margaret. You must find Josiah! You must find Josiah!

She took off her wrap, tore out the sleeve, and tied this over her nose and mouth. It helped to filter out some of the smoke but did nothing to keep it out of her eyes. Stinging tears making it nearly impossible to see. Wearing only her nightdress, she edged her way down the back stairs. Almost to the bottom she spied the door leading out into the back yard and the porch. Tiny flames from the outside nibbled around the frame and little fiery fingers poked beneath the solid oak.

Praying the fire would not burn through the door until she had searched the pantry, she stepped down and stumbled over his body. Josiah lay face down, unconscious, bleeding from a wound on the back of his head, and barely breathed. "Oh, Josiah," she sobbed and pulled at his arms and legs, "please, please wake up!" There was no way she could carry him.

She swore, using curses she often thought but never uttered and ended her tantrum with, "Damn you! Wake up! I didn't come all this way only to have us both burn to death"

As her lungs burned from the fumes and her eyes continued to water from the smoke, she kept shaking him. When, at last, his eyes opened.... Suddenly the back door burst into flames and a gust of fire whooshed into the kitchen.. Consuming all in its path, as the flames bore down upon them.

ACKNOWLEDGMENTS

Any writer of historical fiction can attest to the fact that their books couldn't be written without eons of research and the help of many people. I am of no exception.

In Jefferson City, John Viessman, the graphic arts specialist with the Missouri Department of Natural Resources allowed me to monopolize his time, his private library, and his office for a week while he showed me early images of Jefferson City. Also in Jefferson City, Professor Antonio Holland at Lincoln University pointed the way to the collections of documents, papers, and letters about free Negroes in the city at the time of Civil War. Other helpful commentators and guides were Attorney Robert Hawkins III and Professor Gary Kremer of William Wood College.

Retired Detective Mark Schrieber gave information regarding the State Penitentiary located in Jefferson City since the 1830's. Police Corporal Jerry W. Jeffries, Jefferson City Police Department historian and author of *From Hog Alley to the State House* provided me with information regarding policing the city during that era. Fire department historian, Tim Young, described in vivid detail how the Jefferson City Fire Department answered a fire call.

Special consideration goes to Executive Director of the Cavalry Museum at Fort Riley, Kansas. Major Terry Van Meter (RT) spent several hours discussing Civil War cavalry with me and later sent me field records that helped to pinpoint the exact location of the 4th cavalry during the conflicts at Dug Springs and Wilson's Creek.

When I showed up, unannounced outside Jefferson Barracks outside St. Louis on a rainy January morning, I discovered the museum was normally closed that time of the year. However, when he learned that I was researching for the book, the curator of the Jefferson Barracks Historic Site, Marc E. Kollbaum, graciously accommodated me and gave me a personally guided tour. Later, he sent me photographs and documents that spoke of the life of this active Civil War post.

At Fort Leavenworth the museum tour and an especially helpful rare book library staff helped me understand 1860's life there. Diane B. Jacob, archivist at Virginia Military Institute gladly sent me material about cadet life during the 1850's.

Another word about librarians: At Lincoln University in Jefferson City, Miss Im with humor and patience took my numerous telephone calls and helped me find valuable material. The staff at the Thomas Jefferson Public Library in Jefferson City went out of their way to help me find rare books on the history of the city and of Cole County. State archivists researched and sent me documents pertaining to marriage and divorce laws of the period. The State Historical Society of Missouri in Columbia house state newspapers that have survived and the staff went out of its was to help me glean through these to find relevant material. In Colorado, librarian, Molly Otto at Trinidad State College helped me maneuver the inter-library loan system. Which brought me Dino A. Burgioni's definitive work, *Civil War in Missouri As Seen From The Capital City*.

For help on steam boating on the Missouri I turned to Bob Massengale in Jefferson City and then to the Sons and Daughters of Pioneer Rivermen. At their convention in Marietta, Ohio, Alan L. Bates, author of *The Western Rivers; Steam Boating Cyclopaedium*, spent several hours with me patiently going over the intricacies of the side-wheelers and stern-wheelers that plied up and down the Missouri.

Finally, Joanne Chiles Eakin, Missouri historian and author of *The Little Gods; Union Provost Marshals in Missouri 1861-1865*, read the manuscript in progress and noted the changes needed for historical accuracy. Her advice and encouragement were invaluable.

And lastly, I want to give a special thank you to my editor and friend, Glenda A. Bixler. I am essentially a lazy writer, not used to discipline. Glenda kept me on deadline and prodded me to keep going even when I wanted to quit.

Meredith   Campbell

Dedication

I dedicate this novel to my dear husband, Jack, who endorsed my solo venture into Missouri to do research around the state. He listened patiently while I monopolized every conversation outlining plot moves and character development, and encouraged me even when he suffered through first-draft readings, usually read aloud by me.

Meredith

PROLOGUE

May 1856

11PM on the 24th, Pottawatomie Creek
Kansas Territory

On he crept, groping his way through the woods with six other men trailing after him, four of them his sons, and all of them armed with pistols and razor-sharp broadswords. Blinded by insanity, his eyes glittered in a ravaged face. The fog shrouded moonlight catching his mane of flowing white hair and beard, tall, gaunt John Brown stole through the dark, intent upon one objective - to kill his enemies and the enemies of God.

Anyone misled enough to have taken "Captain" Brown to court became the abolitionist's enemy, and a German settler, "Dutch" Henry Sherman, had accused him of stealing 24 head of cattle and 2 horses. Tonight, the radical anti-slaver would wreak vengeance against the accuser - his personal enemy.

God's enemies lived along the creek, near the German. Pro slavery, these men wanted Kansas to join the Union as a slave state, and for holding such a design, they too must die. Slavery, as sin, sent a stench to the nostrils of a wrathful God. The Lord God Almighty, in His Holy Writ said, "Without the shedding of blood there is no remission of sins" a fact that he reminded his family of twelve living children from two wives.

Through the night, the killers came, a party of righteous avengers, with death drumming in every step and without a shred of mercy in their souls.

"Pa, wake up! The dogs is barkn' somethin fierce." Fourteen-year-old Hy Wilcox stood in the almost pitch blackness of the two-room log cabin and shook his father out of a weary sleep.

Jeremiah Wilcox, farmer and recent settler on Pottawatomie Creek, groaned, but woke up when his son shook him, reached to the gun rack nailed on the wall above the bed for his .40 steel-mounted Lancaster rifle.

Growling for his son to "keep it dark," he waved Hy away from the oil lamp and waited until he could see in the darkness. Faint shimmers of moonlight wiggled between the unchinked logs and through the tiny open hole in the cabin wall that served as a window.

As he pulled on his boots and canvas work pants, he saw that his son shouldered the 28-gauge squirrel rifle and crouched by the open window. A premonition made him hiss, "Run off the stock into the woods so's they kin get theirselves lost, and you do the same. Git yourself hid in them woods, yonder, an' don' let me ketch you out, 'til what ere happens, happens, and is done for. And be quiet about it. You hear?"

Pa stood at the window gripping his 45-inch barrel with the full stock of black walnut. A pistol shot broke the stillness. It sounded like it came from down the creek, over by the Doyle cabin. One shriek - then all was silent again, except for the terrifying hacking noises, of flesh and bone being ripped apart by something heavy and sharp, a similar sound heard when a man butchered an animal.

Hy had not obeyed. "Didn't you hear me, Boy?"

"But, Pa, I'm man enough--"

Jeremiahs reflex, a backhand across the face, cut the boy off. "I said move! Now! You heard them screams!"

Holding his jaw, Hy left through the lone door. Jeremiah listened to the soft sounds of his son clicking to the team of oxen and the two saddle horses they had brought with them then heard the animals and boy move through the undergrowth behind the cabin into the woods.

When the only sound was the dogs going crazy, he breathed a sigh of relief. His son would most likely live out the night. But, would he?

Wilcox listened. Presently, over the barking, he heard a shout, a gunshot, and the strange, butchering sounds again at the cabin of the Franklin County prosecuting attorney, Allen Wilkinson. Before long, he heard men whooping and laughing and walking his way.

The southerner from Missouri decided that defending his home and castle would probably only get him dead. So he obeyed his own order. He fled to the woods, and ran as far as he could, taking only a minute to let his beagle hunting dogs out of their pen so they could run ahead of him into the black, terrifying night.

Perched on a laurel branch over his head, a contentious jay woke him before the sun had crossed the horizon. In the pristine wooded grove of mid-spring Kansas, a baby squirrel scampered up a scrub-oak. Thornberry thickets grew around him, purple milkweed bunched beneath newly leafed lindens and maples, while here and there huddled wild flowers - daisies, buttercups, and bluebells. On any other morning he would have luxuriated in the primitive beauty and mild air, charmed by the spring-songs of birds and insects. But sleeping on the cool, damp ground had made him stiff, and when he remembered last night, terror, again, gripped his innards. He sat up too fast, reaching for his rifle, and wrenched his back.

A rustle in the bushes alerted Wilcox and he cradled the Lancaster, but it was only his dog, Dugan. The hound saw his master was awake, ran up wagging a white tail, and tried to lick his face, but the beagles white muzzle dripped with blood. The dog shied away from Wilcox's outstretched hand and ran back into the bushes. With head held high, Dugan soon returned and dropped his find at his master's feet.

"What you got there, boy ?" Wilcox demanded, but

5

the dog sat back on his haunches watching while Wilcox bent over the savaged flesh.

In the early dawn light, he couldn't be sure of what he saw, so he poked at it with a stick, examined it closer, suddenly recognized it.

"A thumb!" he screamed, jerking backwards, almost tripping over a tree root. "Done come from somebody's hand!" At that moment, the tan bitch, Molly, sauntered out of the brambles carrying a half-chewed human arm bone.

Insane with fear and shouting oaths to the heavens, he drove the yelping dogs into the bushes. Then, fearing the hideous things lying silent and bloody at the toe of his boot, he couldn't take his eyes off them.

When Hy walked from behind the maples into the clearing, swinging two plump squirrels over his shoulder, he found his father, standing stock-still, barely breathing, and staring transfixed. "Want some squirrel for breakfast, Pa?" He spoke before he realized what had captured his father's attention. But after the young hunter got a gander at the bloodied flesh, he decided he wasn't hungry after all.

Praying the danger had passed but afraid of what they would find, the two walked back to the nascent community on the creek, alive with buzzing insects and bird song, but eerily silent to the sounds of human life. By now, with the sun poking into the sky, the men-folk should have been outside, harnessing teams to the plow. The women-folk should have been calling for wood or water as they prepared breakfast. The Doyle boys, close to Hy's age, should have been outside at their chores and helping their father.

But at the Doyle's they heard only weeping. Mrs. Doyle stood in her yard, staring at the clump of woods behind her cabin and wringing her plump hands while tears rolled unchecked down her cheeks. Struggling with his own tears, stood ten-year-old Johnny, her youngest son.

When Mahala Doyle saw them, she nearly collapsed from relief and her words lapsed into guttural moans. Nevertheless, the Wilcoxes understood that late in the night several men claiming to be from the United States Army - one of them John Brown - had knocked at her door. After learning that her husband didn't care one way or the other about slavery, the men had taken Doyle and his two oldest sons, William, aged 17, and Drury, aged 15 - "prisoners." They even tried to hustle little Johnny outside. But upon hearing Mrs. Doyle plead for the child, Brown relented and allowed him to stay with his mother. Brown then had warned her to stay inside. After the intruders led her husband and sons into the woods, she never saw them again.

Following her pointing finger, Wilcox and Hy hurried to the thickets that lay several yards to the rear of the cabin. Carnage, Wilcox decided, did not begin to describe what they found. James Doyle, Mahala's husband, had been shot in the head, his hands and manhood cut off. Beside him lay the dismembered bodies of the two boys, their bodies hacked to bits. In the warm May morning blowflies were already assaulting the putrefying flesh strewn around the gory clearing.

Hy immediately vomited behind the blood-spattered trunk of an oak. To keep down his own bile, Wilcox gulped air with so much force that he made himself dizzy and sat on a miraculously unbloodied stump.

Then, behind them, came a wrenching cry from Mahala who had followed them to the killing scene. Somehow, with promises of immediate Christian burial and vowing to avenge this savage crime, Wilcox managed to get the hysterical widow and her sobbing child back to the Doyle cabin.

Lying in the road some distance south of his cabin, his body mutilated like the others, they discovered Louise Wilkinson's attorney-husband. Wilcox found Mrs. Wilkinson bed-ridden with measles and surrounded by her young children. He listened as she told a story similar to the one told by Mahala Doyle.

"Twas the dogs that woke us. And I heard them footsteps. Walkin' slow they was and a big, bushy-headed man passed by the window." Mrs. Wilkinson began to cry.

But she regained her self-control, dabbed at the tears streaming down her measles-pocked face, and continued her story. "Then, come a knock at the door and a man calls out, *"I'm lookin' for Dutch Henry. Can you tell me how I might find his place?"* Then, Allen, he answers back, tells him how to cross over the ford, yonder. But they won't leave us be." The tears came afresh. "They just keep a-hollerin' for Allen to come out and show them the way."

Again, she struggled for composure before she spoke. "But I warned him not to open the door. My insides was a-tellin' me that these men were up to skullduggery. And Allen listened to me. But it didn't do no good for they broke open the door!"

"My God," Wilcox murmured, glancing at Hy who stood like stone staring at the woman. "What happened next, ma'am," Wilcox asked softly, dreading to hear the rest of the story.

"Well there we all be in the bed, the children is scared to death and I'm burnin' up with fever. It makes no never mind to them. They shout at Allen, askin' him about whether he's for the Free-soilers or not."

"What did Mr. Wilkinson say, Ma'am?

"He says that he's agin' the Northern Free-Soil Party. Then, soon as Allen spoke them words, the bushy-headed man with a beard orders my husband to get up and get dressed and says that he's their prisoner."

"Did they touch you or the young'ens?" Wilcox took a deep breath, felt the vomit start up his gorge again.

"No, Mr. Wilcox, they didn't, but they might as well

had. I done begged that man to let Allen stay with me 'cause I was so sick and couldn't care for myself. But he says to me, real cold, 'Call on your neighbors and if they can't take care of you, it matters not.' That's what he said."

Wilcox let her cry for a moment. Then, "Go on, Mrs. Wilkinson."

"They didn't even give my husband time to put on his boots. You'd think they'd of showed more respect for him, being the local postmaster and a member of the territory's legislature as he was. Led him right outside into the wet grass without his boots."

The oldest Wilkinson child, eight-year old Tim blurted. "Later, they come back and stole two saddles and said they was takin' Paw to a prison camp."

The widow put her arm around her son to comfort him as much as to quiet him, added, "When the men had all gone I thought I heard Allen's voice calling out to me, but when I stepped to the door and listened to the night, it was silent."

Promising to send help back, Wilcox and Hy walked a mile south and forded Pottawatomie Creek "Dutch Henry's" crossing to check on the James Harris family. They found Harris alive.

"Yes, Sir, I'm breathin' today only because I said I was a Free Soiler, like Brown. 'Course I ain't, but somethin' tole me I better agree with him." He invited them to look inside his ransacked cabin. Mrs. Harris and their little one were trying to set the place to rights.

"The son-of-a---" Harris broke off, rubbed his hand over his thinning hair, nodded towards his wife and child, and motioned Wilcox and Hy outside. When they stepped to the porch, he whispered, "She's real upset; you can imagine."

Wilcox nodded.

"The son-of-a-bitch," Harris spoke low so that his

9

wife wouldn't hear him. "Didn't even bother to knock. We's all asleep in the bed, and next thing I knowed here was Old Brown and his gang wavin' sabres and pistols in my face. Then they ask me to give 'um my Bowie knife and my two old Hawken rifles." His voice rose for emphasis, "And then, they tears the place up a-lookin' for powder and ball for the rifles and rouse up Dutch Bill, sleepin' like a baby up in the loft." Harris stopped, shook his head, remembering.

"What'd they do then?"

"Well, Wilcox, that's the damnedest thing I ever saw." He looked up at Jeremiah, his face contorted with the horror of the tale. "You recall as how Dutch Bill, Henry's brother had taken board with us?"

Wilcox nodded. The image of the big, slow-talkin' German rose before him.

"Without speakin' a word to him, they jest marched him outside." He wiped his mouth with the back of his hand and darted a look over to the creek bank a few yards from the house. "I found him like that not too long ago."

Dutch Bill Sherman's body had suffered the same barbarisms as the others, only it appeared that he had put up a fight. His skull had been split open, his chest ripped apart, and one hand cut off.

"Peter and Henry up in Lawrence on business?" Wilcox asked about Bill's brothers. Harris affirmed this with a nod. Silently, the two men and the boy gazed at the corpse long enough to note that the flies marched in formation across the mutilated flesh.

"Strange, ain't it," Harris broke the silence, "Brown come here on purpose to kill Henry and Henry ain't here. So his little brother gets it, instead."

After the burials, after the women had been given over to the care of their families called in from Missouri and Tennessee, after the captain and a company of the newly formed First Cavalry from Fort Leavenworth had

10

come and gone, Jeremiah and Hy hitched up the team of oxen to the Conestoga wagon. They tied the two saddle horses to the rear and, with the dogs roaming along behind, drove over Dutch Henry's Crossing.

As they rode past, Henry stepped to the door of his cabin and called to them. "Vell, goot-bye. Where you go?" he asked.

"Back to Missouri, to Cole County outside of Jefferson City. My wife - his mother," Wilcox jerked a thumb at the pale, skinny boy beside him, "is buried there. 'Taint nothin' short of hell itself could make me stay here."

"Don't blame you." Henry frowned, as if sorry to see them go.

"You ain't leavin'?" Wilcox squinted into the morning sun, anxious to be on his way, thinking. If it hadn't been for the damned Dutchman, shootin' off his mouth 'bout Brown in the first place, none of this probably would have happened. Hell, everybody knowed Old Brown was crazy, just like the rest of' his kin who had gone and died raving lunatics.

"*Nein*. Been here since '47. Too long here to leave."

Wilcox nodded, clicked to the team of oxen, and set off for their journey back to Missouri-back to the peace of home.

1861

CHAPTER ONE

April

Tuesday the 16^(th)

The buzzing of a newborn April fly broke the absolute silence in the Missouri legislature's chamber room. Looking grim and dressed in a black frock coat and brown trowsers, the cause for bated breath and hushed voices addressed his audience.

"As you know, four days ago the Confederacy forced the surrender of Fort Sumter in Charleston harbor. Consequently, the newly elected president of the United States has declared war against those states that have chosen to leave the oppression of the federal government in Washington City. Lincoln has called for 75,000 men to come forward to fight to preserve his personal fiefdom. But, my friends, as I said at my inaugural address in December, 'Missouri must consult her own interests and the interest of the whole country by a timely declaration to stand by her sister slave owning states in whose wrong she participated and with those institutions and people she sympathized.'"

Hearty applause allowed the Governor of Missouri to wipe the perspiration from his balding forehead and oval face and sip from a glass of water placed on the speaker's podium. Pocketing his handkerchief in his brocade vest, he continued in a voice stentorian from practice and raspy from overuse.

"Abraham Lincoln has requested that Missouri furnish enough of her sons to fill four infantry regiments to fight against our southern sisters. And I have said, No!" Again applause violated the stillness of the hall.

"Gentlemen…and ladies," he nodded towards the men and women seated in the visitor's gallery overlooking the legislative chamber and made a special bow towards Mayor Ewing's wife and her friend, Mrs. Parsons, sitting in the front row. From the prominent to the lowborn, half of Jefferson City had jammed in to hear the Governor's response to Abe Lincoln as presented to the Missouri legislature.

"…. To the minion of the radical, black Republicans and abolitionists I have written the following:" Cleb Jackson drew himself up to his full six feet, puffed out his thin chest and held up a letter-sized document so all could see it. He began to read. "There can be, I apprehend, no doubt that these men are intended to form a part of the President's army to make war upon the people of the seceded states. Your requisition, in my judgment, is illegal."

"Yes," came a low voice from the legislature floor.

"…. Unconstitutional…."

"Hear, hear," said another voice, a decibel louder.

"…. and revolutionary in its objects,…."

Someone began to applaud.

"…. inhuman and diabolical and cannot be complied with…."

Others began to clap. A whistle of approval came from the gallery. The governor raised his voice.

"…. Not a man will the State of Missouri furnish to carry out such an unholy crusade!"

By the time Jackson put down the letter the floor of the legislature and the gallery above it had erupted into pandemonium. Mrs. Ewing dabbed at her eyes, and called out, "Thank God, for a man like Claiborne Jackson, with strength in his soul and courage in his heart." More cheering and "hurrahs" greeted her remarks.

"Did you hear that, Franny? " At nineteen, Hy Wilcox believed that he had just witnessed and heard a

13

miracle. He yelped a cheer, shook hands and slapped the men around him on their backs, and cheered some more. "Honey," he poked the arm of his silent companion, a pretty girl still in her teens with ungovernable curls the color of fire and autumn gold. She smiled up at him but demonstrated none of his enthusiasm. "Did you hear old Jackson's sassy answer to Abe Lincoln?"

An old gentleman in a rumpled suit and black cravat shook Hy's hand and nodded to Franny. "Well, Son, reckon you won't be drafted into the army after all?" And he patted Hy on the back.

"No, Sir! But, that don't mean I ain't fightin.' I'm joinin' with the South, soon as I can." The man smiled, his cheeks puffing out like a squirrel's, nodded to Franny again, and moved away.

"What do you mean, Hy Wilcox, about joining as soon as you can?" The girl did not smile.

He sat down and held her hands in his. How could he make her understand? He couldn't, he knew. But he'd try. "Sweetheart," he began, avoiding her angry gaze. Usually a soft misty green, her eyes always turned the color of hard jade when she got upset with him. By the tone in her voice he knew this to be one of those times. He choked, searching for the exact words to convey his need to fight. But she didn't give him a chance to find them.

"Oh, yes indeedy!" She blurted, but softly, not wishing to draw stares. "You're going to leave your pa to run his farm all by himself, are you? You said you wanted to marry me. Sounds more like you want to run off and be a soldier, instead." She stood up and drew her spring shawl about her shoulders. The paisley brought out the color of her eyes and the bloom in her cheeks.

"If you please, escort me home, Mr. Wilcox."

His face reddened with fury because this girl whom he happened to love with all his heart seemed to be so contrary. "Goat-headed" her ma, said about her. And for

14

once, Hy agreed about something with his future mother-in-law. Irish immigrant, the widow Deidre Moone, Franny's mother, ran a hotel and a boarding house that catered to legislators and their families, drummers peddling their wares in Jefferson City, and newspapermen. She and Hy had clashed many times on the subjects of slavery and union. She hated the former and loved the latter. He believed slavery had been ordained by God and despised a Federal government that would interfere.

Without a word, he guided his petite sweetheart stiffly through the crowd, down the steps and onto Main Street. Outside, the sunny warmth of the afternoon foretold spring. Early crocus and iris's bloomed from the gardens around the Capitol. New buds broke through on the yellow forsythia bushes and a white dogwood arrayed its beauty on the front lawn. But Hy's turmoil prevented him from enjoying the day and when he looked, Franny's scowl told him the same story.

Maybe he could find a way to do both - fight and farm. He'd join up and fight a little, then come on home and help Pa around the place. And Franny would be at home, waiting for him. They walked the block to Jefferson Street in silence before Hy spoke, addressing the top of her green felt bonnet that barely came to his shoulder. "Are you very mad at me, Pet? Cause if'n you are, you got no need to be. I'm still gonna farm with Pa. We can still get married."

"Do you promise me?" Frowning, she stopped at the corner and faced him.

He noticed that tendrils of fiery hair had escaped the bonnet's confines and curled around her oval face. She hated her hair because it wouldn't tame and always complained because it wouldn't lay smooth like other women's. He loved it. Seeing it awry like this made her even more dear to him. Then he saw the tears shimmering in her eyes. At once, remorse filled him; to think she, the prettiest girl in Jefferson City, cared so much about him,

15

and he took her hands without thought of what gossip might ensue.

"God Almighty! Honey, I'm sorry. I didn't mean to start you cryin'. Of course, I promise you...I..." he lowered his voice, "I love you."

Hy came to her the next day, three hours before supper, and told her his plans. At that hour most genteel women napped, but Franny sat, wide awake, on the wrought iron bench in Erin House's backyard rose garden. She wore one of her prettiest dresses, a thin cotton print of tiny spring flowers against a pale green background. But she might as well have been wearing a burlap tarp for all the notice he took of her. Instead, up and down he paced, waving his arms and talking so fast she barely understood him. She wanted her beau quiet, sitting beside her, holding her hand and playing with her curls, making future wedding plans, but she knew he couldn't do any of those things. He seemed too agitated, too prickly. So she watched him, calmly, waiting for him to catch his breath.

"Yep, Jackson's put out a call to take over the Liberty Arsenal! A camp of soldier's instruction is being' set up in Independence, and Cap'n Henry Routt - he was in the regular army but quit to fight on the South's side. Anyway, he wants as many men as he can get to he'p him storm the arsenal." He emphasized "storm," relishing the idea of plundering the United States ordnance depot in Liberty, Missouri by force. He stopped pacing, folded his arms, and grinned at her.

"But, you just told me that the call came for men from Clay, Jackson, and Lafayette Counties. They're all west of here, at least a hundred miles," she said lightly and met his grin with a demure smile, hoping her resentment didn't show at this latest idea of his for a lark.

"I know, Sweetheart, but me, Buster, and Horton, wanna go over and join in. Anyhow, what's to hurt if Cole

16

County men like us help out? "

She realized it useless to try and further discourage him. His hazel eyes shown with anticipation and his square, honest features betrayed the joy at his prospects of going. Every nerve, every muscle seemed pulled taunt with the itch to pursue this adventure.

Still, "But, what if you get hurt, killed even?" Franny made a tear escape her eye, and with the white lace-trimmed hanky she held in her hand, daintily dabbed at her cheek.

"Aw, honey," he swooped down beside her, took a furtive look to the back porch to see if anyone observed them, and scooped her into his arms. He kissed her. But to her, the kiss seemed hurried and perfunctory, as though he only wanted to pacify her before he rode off to his real love, his first love, being a soldier. She wiggled free.

"And what about your pa? What does he think about you goin'? " She pouted and folded her arms.

"He wants me to go. Tole me so, this mornin.' Said he wished he could go too." His voice dropped a notch and he became serious. "You know, Franny, Pa hates Yankees 'bout as much as he hates the damn "Dutch" and he's all for this war. Ever since we done got back from Kansas…." Almost as though someone or something had locked shut his mouth, he abruptly stopped talking, looked away, and seemed to stare at the rose bushes that soon would be filled with blood red blooms.

After he sat rigid and silent, staring for several minutes, Franny wondered if something ailed him and reached over and lightly touched his arm. "Hy ?" she whispered.

"Off!" he yelled, forcibly shrugging away her touch, "Leave me be!" Then he buried his face in his hands.

This side of Hy came as a surprise and his violent reaction to her timid and loving touch alarmed her. She might as well have put her hand on a wounded wolf. They had sat alone in the garden and, suddenly, she sensed a black unease around Hy Wilcox, her friend, and her beau. So black she suddenly wanted the safety inside Erin House. She rose to leave.

But he grabbed her arm before she took the first step and she almost screamed. His quiet voice stopped her. "Wait, please." His eyes were wet. "Please," he repeated softly when she tugged trying to get free. He stood up, ran his hand through his sandy, lank hair, and put his arms around her waist. Still unsure of him, she held herself stiff while she allowed him to hold her and nuzzle her hair. Then when he seemed to be his old self she relaxed against him.

"Something happened back in Kansas…" he paused and looked away and Franny feared he'd erupt again with her in his arms. But, he exhaled deeply and turned towards her again, "and it don't do nobody no good to talk about it. It's done. It's over. Mebbe someday I'll tell you about it." Kissing her lightly on the forehead, he released her.

"Well, pray for me, darlin' and I'll be back just fine. Expect me back Tuesday night." Slamming his black slouch on his head, he turned and walked away, leaving her standing alone in the back yard. Not until she heard his horse take off at a gallop did she realize that he had avoided her gaze the whole time she had been in his embrace.

Friday the 19th-Saturday the 20th

His nerves tight as telegraph wire strung on a pole, Hy suddenly agreed with Franny. Along with Buster Cowles and Horton Davies he should have stayed at home where they belonged. If they had, instead of traipsing around on this dark night, they wouldn't be sitting on their horses on this strange road courting a bullet, right now.

They had stopped because of spotting a group of horses bunched in shadowy darkness beneath the willow trees lining the bank of the Missouri River. Like black sentinels, the trees seemed to put up a silent guard in the still, moonstruck night.

"Hold up," Hy whispered. He had halted his chestnut mare in the middle of the road, saw that he was a perfect target in the direct moonlight and rode to the side by a ditch where a clump of bushes threw over him a pall of ghostly lace. "Stay low."

His friends pulled along side him and watched the dozen or so mounts tied beneath the trees ahead. From the ramuda they heard the nicker of horses and the low voices of men. Hy called out just loud enough to be heard," "Excuse us, gentlemen. We're lookin' fer the Hippo Rio. He had gotten the "sign" from Captain Routt the day before.

Silence from beneath the black trees, from the motionless forms beside the road. For several minutes no one spoke. No one seemed to breathe. Frozen—the boys waited, statues on horses carved in ice.

"Flag Mitto, here." A deep, bass voice from the sentinel trees gave the counter sign.

They had met up with the party of men recruited by Captain Routt to ford the Missouri River here at Sibley, six miles below Independence. For the next hour they waited in the dark for others to join them while the low talk of these "secesh" farmers, all southern sympathizers, swirled around them. Some expressed the hope that Missouri could remain neutral while others claimed that leaving the north and joining with the Confederacy was the only way to save the state from being overrun with "slave-stealin' Yankee trash."

"Well, now," a slow talking voice interjected, "I remember from '56 on them Kansas Jayhawkers comin' over to Jackson County and pretty near burnin' us all out and stealin' our darkies."

"I'm afraid it's gonna start up agin," growled the bass voice in the darkness.

19

"Hell, it ain't never really stopped! Why, jest the other day I heard tell of a fella...." The rumbling voice seemed older than the speaker. But, although fascinated, Hy deliberately turned his mind away from the stories of atrocities done to the people of Jackson county at the hands of Kansas jayhawkers. He could have told his own tale of horror if he wanted to, but he didn't. For if he did he knew he'd start to blubber and then what would these solid, Missouri men think of him?

Eventually the bass voice gave the order to cross the river. The water splashed cold and black against his legs and arms. His belly growled from hunger because he hadn't eaten since early that morning. But then, Hy believed it was only right to go into war - empty. It made a man's thinkin' sharper. In his belt tucked a model '51 Navy Colt revolver and across the pommel of his saddle lay his old squirrel rifle. He knew the rifle couldn't do much damage, that the 36-caliber Navy packed more of a lethal punch, yet he carried the rifle of his childhood more for good luck.

On the other side of the river they traveled to Independence and met Captain Routt and the rest of the command, around 200 men. Many of the men brought their wagons to haul off the ordnance supplies they intended to steal. Only it wasn't much of an army Hy observed. Rowdy and disorganized, many of the men had been pulling at the jug.

But Hy didn't say anything. In fact he had barely spoken only his name and where he was from since joining these men. Buster and Horton were as equally quiet, and he knew his childhood friends well enough to know they were just as scared.

A panoply, the sky shimmered with stars and the moon cast a murky glow. It lit the way of Routt's mounted "army", following the wagons on their way to "take the Arsenal," to show Abe Lincoln that "Missouri ain't gonna fight the south."

Orange dawn streaked the sky when suddenly from the valley floor appeared the hamlet of Liberty, Missouri. The arsenal stood near by and only one ordnance sergeant was on duty. The Federals hadn't reinforced it, thank God. At this news, Hy and his friends breathed much easier.

By ten o'clock on this bright Saturday morning, jeering, shouting men had shouldered into the depot yard. Intermittent gunfire followed yells, and curses added to the dusty melee. Hy's eyes stung and watered from the gun smoke and the glare of the sun. The crowd seemed to be a murderous entity unto itself, seething, undulating, and becoming increasingly angry.

The blue-wool uniform of the ordnance sergeant appeared at the doorway. Obviously, he had been expecting this, had been wiring St. Louis head-quarters for days, begging for reinforcements. But, none had rushed to his aid, and so he stood alone, facing the riled mob while his clerk cowered in the office. The sergeant's round, middle-aged face looked weary, his pale hands shook, but his firm voice pleaded, "Boys, go on home, now. Don't y'all be doin' nothin' foolish." Perspiration crept from beneath his forage cap and he took it off to mop his brow with a stained kerchief, revealing damp thinning gray hair.

Someone shot off another round, creating more smoke to mix with the dust and the sun's blinding glare. Whoops and curses ensued and the mindless rabble surged forward. Quickly, the ordnance sergeant ducked back inside and hid in the office with his clerk while the looters set about emptying the stores. The three friends pulled down the Stars and Stripes and ran up a Rebel flag on the pole in front of the building before they turned to help load up the munitions that belonged to the U S Army.

They laid box after box of black gunpowder into the back of a buckboard and helped load up forty crated muskets and carbines. Someone had dropped a box and shattered the wooden top, causing the new carbines inside to send up a gleaming temptation.

"Reckon we can take one fer ourselves," Buster admired the Sharps carbine, checking its cartridge chamber and sighting through it.

"Sure beats bejeezus out of my old squirrel rifle," Hy hefted one from the box and examined the walnut stock, adding, "A .52 caliber--it's supposed to be accurate up to 600 yards and can fire 10 rounds per minute." He knew he would take it with him, but would continue to carry his old squirrel gun.

Horton helped himself to one of the carbines. Mahogany hair falling in his eyes, he admired the stock and cocked the hammer.

"Hey, you boys from Cole County!" Captain Routt yelled, "Leave them guns in the box. We're a gonna distribute these arms to the volunteer units in the surrounding counties !" Routt looked hot but official in the navy wool coat of his Mexican War uniform, buttoned to his chin and in his old style high crowned black officer's hat. He still wore his old company's insignia - Company C, 2nd U.S. Infantry.

Horton let his carbine clatter back into the wooden gun crate, but Buster and Hy held on to theirs. "Sir," Hy made his tone respectful, " We believe we've earned a gun of our own."

"And I'd say those boys are correct, Captain." The deep baritone came from a stranger a full head taller than the rangy Captain Routt and fully six inches taller than Hy. He approached them and Hy saw the flat pentagonal features and coppery skin that suggested Indian blood. But the grey-blue eyes were those of a white man.

"Don't you agree, Captain Routt?" The half -breed smiled down at the wiry figure that could do nothing but stand speechless and stare up at the giant. He wore cavalry issue pants of blue-grey kersey and a non-regulation red flannel shirt under a deerskin vest. His military bearing said he was a soldier, yet something about him signaled he wasn't. Instantly, Hy Wilcox experienced the paradox of wanting to run screaming in terror at the sight of this enormous man while at the same time wanting to get as close to him as possible and learn. But learn what?

At last the commander of the mob that had just plundered a facility belonging to the United States Government realized he had a tongue. "Well, we had planned to give the cannons, ammunition, and small weapons to the militias of Jackson, Clay, and Lafayette Counties--" The weak response trailed off. The tall man's smile showed teeth, even and very white, the smile relaxed. But the eyes were rattlesnake wary and Hy noticed they didn't blink.

" . . .But now that you've called it to my attention, I suppose you're correct, Sir." Captain Routt cleared his throat and coughed into his hand.

"Good, knowing you to be the fair man that you are, I reckoned you'd see the sense of it." The stranger nodded towards Hy and the others. "Grab your guns, boys, and follow me." He tipped his wide-brimmed black felt to the Captain, "Thank you, Sir, and allow me to introduce myself. I'm Captain Jacques Verboise, former guide and scout with the First Cavalry. At your service, Sir." Verboise stuck out a hand. Routt suddenly remembered his manners and offered his handshake, to disappear in Verboise's bear-sized paw.

When out of ear-shot Buster chortled, "Didja see how the old Cap'n just stared and stared after us, like his eyes was glued on our backsides?" The tall, square-bodied boy laughed and leapt about, knocking Horton on the shoulder and giving Hy a sock in the arm.

"He weren't lookin' at us, he be wonderin' who you are, Mister." Hy squinted at the silver-haired pigtail hanging down the back of the mountain leading them to

23

where the horses were tied. He had the carbine and this pleased him, but his concern lay with the man called Verboise and the reason he had commanded them to follow.

When Verboise didn't say anything, Hy stopped, motioning for his friends to do the same. The boys halted in the middle of the village street. Except for a barking dog following them, the town seemed deserted until finally Hy noticed a timid face peek from behind the closed curtains of a window. "We're beholden' to you, Mister, but we ain't goin' nowhere with you 'til you tell us what you want with us."

"You'll be in my army." Verboise turned around and grinned at the three skeptical faces. "You'll learn how to be real soldiers under my command and we'll fight the Federals our way. They can't be defeated in the field; there's too many of 'um and they're too well armed. But they can be defeated in other ways."

"So, you believe Missouri will have to fight?" Hy's gaze darted from Buster to Horton and back to Verboise.

"I know Missouri will have to fight." Verboise took a step towards the three boys and seemed to realize they were frightened of him. He nonchalantly shrugged his shoulders and put his hands in his pockets. A slow smile spread across his face. To Hy the mannerism only half succeeded in making the man less menacing.

"But, everybody says, the war'll be over by Christmas," Buster yawned but caught himself. It'd been a tension filled, long two days, and all of the boys were tired. Nevertheless, they knew they had to be as alert as ever. At any moment a cavalry unit, having gotten wind of the caper at the Liberty Arsenal, could come galloping into town. Or they should stay awake for no other reason than the man at least half again over six feet who blocked their way.

Suddenly, Verboise hunched down over his long legs

in the dirt beside the road and motioned for them to join him. Lower to the ground, their leader didn't seem to be as formidable. Hy glanced at Buster who eyed Horton. Both boys waited for Hy to make the decision as to what they would do. A nod from him brought all three boys squatting down around Verboise.

"The war won't be over by Christmas," Verboise gazed into the distance as though viewing the future, "It will be long and very bloody and many men will die."

"Aw, come on! How can you know that?"

"My friend," he faced Hy's challenge, "I know the tempers that rage on each side. I have ridden with their military and with ours. I know what great resolve they have and I know the quality of their armaments."

"Hell, everybody knows that one southern boy can whip five Yankees." Horton smirked and fell off his heels. Crouching this way was new to him, and he couldn't do it for long.

"That may be true for now, but give them time and they will become superior." Excitement broke the stranger's somber tone, "You see, boys, that is why we must strike now, today, this instant. We must keep them from becoming so strong that they can overtake us. By striking now, we may be able to defeat them.

"And you want us to be in your army?" Hy could not believe this. He had never been outstanding in anything in his entire life and as far as he knew neither had Horton nor Buster. He asked, "Why us? We're just plain fellows from Cole County. Farmers."

"Precisely. You're worthy men. I watched you raise up the Confed flag and then work like bees loading up the ordnance supplies. And nobody told you what to do. You just did it. And when it comes down to having to defend your farms and your homes you'll fight like sore-tail bears and be mean as rattlesnakes. We'll work well together." Verboise stood up and extended his hand to Hy. "Come, you still have much to learn."

"What?" Hy accepted the assistance and stood as did Buster and Horton.

"What have we got to learn?" He repeated.

Over his shoulder Verboise replied, "How to be killers."

Tuesday the 23rd, Fort Smith, Arkansas

The staccato notes of the bugler's call, "boots and saddles," meant that First Lieutenant Josiah Scarborough had about 20 minutes to wind up loose ends before the call to mount up and march out sounded. He ran a hand through thick, unruly black hair in an unsuccessful attempt to make it stay tucked under his forage cap, and looked over at the sergeant hovering in the doorway.

"Brady, see to the men's packs and girths. Oh,and Brady…" The veteran sergeant paused, removed his cap, and scratched the bald spot at the top of his head. "Make sure that my camp chest gets put in with the officers' baggage, this time."

The emphasis upon "officers" alluded to the lieutenant's camp chest lost nearly a week before Brady found it packed among the enlisted men's gear. Both men grinned and when Brady did, his enormous gray moustache lifted at both corners.

The newly commissioned officer waited until Sergeant Brady made a bow-legged exit from headquarters, looked casually about to make sure any of the brass weren't watching, then began his brisk walk over to the far side of the parade field. As he walked he scowled, thinking about the humiliation his regiment would soon undertake. "Let it be noted," he muttered "that tonight, the heretofore undefeated United States First Cavalry surrendered the command at Fort Smith Arkansas. Take heed also, we gave it to the Rebs without even a raised sabre in protest." Although he understood why regimental commander

26

Emory had given the order to evacuate, it still made him furious. Just like it did when he had heard about the undisputed takeover of the U.S. arsenal at Liberty in God-forsaken Missouri.

Emory judged rightly, he conceded. To preserve the safety of the troops they had to leave without a fight. Arkansas teetered on the fence ready to fall into the arms of the South at any moment, and Fort Smith swam in a sea surrounded by war-shark secessionists. Also, during the past month the Rebs had stolen all the supplies of food and ammunition being shipped down the Arkansas River to Fort Smith. Only 30 days' supplies remained. And if that didn't seem reason enough for high-tailing it out of there, gossip said that 5000 maddened Secesh encamped just a day's march away. With barely 300 men in the two companies of the First they wouldn't stand a chance against those odds.

Scarborough swallowed the bile that arose when he thought about surrendering without any fight at all and observed the scene around him. No doubt about it, the army packed for flight. All about him men loaded wagons for the march-north. Carrying sacks and barrels of what was left of the fodder, feed, and rations, soldiers hurried between the quartermaster's depot and the wagons. Men saddled their horses and filled their canteens.

Over at the ordnance depot a half-dozen loaded ammunition wagons lined up in a standoff. A recalcitrant mule caused the problem. The driver couldn't get the stubborn animal to move out of the way to let another mule pass. From the depths of the jam-up came a rising chorus of ear-splitting, blue-fire cussing. The lieutenant laughed and watched, unseen, for a moment, noting that no rank above corporal supervised. He knew he should straighten out the mess. Instead, he ducked around an empty ambulance and kept on going.

Aware of time slipping away, he picked up his pace

and stayed concealed by avoiding the glowing bonfires built around the esplanade. It wouldn't do for him to be seen. Or, sure enough, somebody would have something for him to do. And he had to say goodbye.

He saw her, standing alone near a wagon piled with wooden wash tubs and scrub boards. Ah yes, in many ways he would miss this gal. She had made it her discrete business to love a man properly without asking too much of him. But such were the fortunes of war and who knew what lay ahead. Anyway, she already had begun to bore him. Nevertheless, she had been good to him and the least he could do was give her a fond goodbye.

A camp laundress, Patsy had been widowed four years ago when her sergeant husband met the misfortune of taking a Cheyenne arrow in the chest and falling off his horse. Along with the other laundresses Patsy had been ordered to travel with the quartermaster by steamer to Jefferson Barracks outside of headquarters in Saint Louis. The First cavalry had been ordered to Fort Washita, 160 miles southwest of Fort Smith, and from there to Fort Leavenworth, Kansas.

The sorrowful, moon face framed by dark hair pulled into a knot at the nape of her neck, looked up at him, her dark eyes made darker by the night and the flickering bonfires. "Joey, looks like you an' me is goin' in opposite directions." A tear coursed down her cheek.

A million times he had asked her not to call him "Joey." Well, it made no difference now, so he put his arms around her sturdy waist and drew her head onto his chest. "Oh, it's not the end of the world, Sugar. I'll catch up to you." He had no intention of seeing his paramour of two months again.

"Is it true that 10,000 rebel Texans will take Fort Smith soon?" She raised her head, fear registering in the frown of her brow.

She exaggerated to the extreme, as usual, and that too

28

made no difference now. "Don't know how many, but there's enough of 'um that we have to skedaddle. Make's me madder than hell, though."

"Just like you to wanna stay and fight." Her hair against his chest smelled sweaty and unclean and he wished for a speedy end to this. Then, the bugle called "assembly," and he said, "I've gotta go. Gimme a kiss, goodbye."

Like an exploding dam, the woman's tears burst all over him. "Joey, take me with you. I can put on a uniform so's nobody'll know I'm not a man. I kin ride as good as any trooper, an' I kin shoot, too." Patsy held a tight grip around his neck, which became uncomfortable because of his over six-foot, plus, height. Worse, she meant it.

He tried gently to disengage but she clung to him all the more. "You know I can't take you," he chuckled, kidding her, hoping she'd laugh too and say she was joking. But the steady unsmiling gaze that met his told him he had been right the first time; deadly serious she was.

On the other side of the parade ground he heard the sergeants bawling out the order for the men to prepare to mount their horses.

"Please, Joey. Please."

Her desperate tone of voice and hold around his neck annoyed him no end. Even as he firmly removed her arms and held her hands so that she couldn't grab him again, she rattled on. Dropping her voice a notch, attempting to sound seductive, she licked her lips. "I kin be yore bunky."

The thought of her sharing his tent did present a tantalizing possibility. But, regardless of her round, warm body, he knew that within 24 hours her incessant, uninformed chatter would drive him up the ass of his horse. Besides, Patsy's snail-moving brain would probably get her discovered within 24 hours. Then, he would be cashiered out of the U.S. Cavalry, court-martialed, kicked out, and afterwards, to go - where?

But he would be as kind as possible - no sense in a fellow being harsh with a woman who had been so willing to share herself with him. "No, honey," he said softly, "it's impossible, just too rough and dangerous, and I'd never forgive myself if you got hurt."

"I never tole nobody 'cept my Arthur that I loved him, but I'm tellin' you, now, I love you, I do. It's them blue eyes of yorn. First time I seen 'um, I knew I loved you." Tears streaked her face and she gripped his hands.

Hers felt rough and strong, made so by years of scrubbing with yellow, lye soap; of rinsing and wringing out shirts and socks and drawers belonging to the men of the First Cavalry. He imagined her in her rude quarters waking up on many a morning seeing the same underwear and socks on the floor beside her bed. He also imagined the owners of this clothing lying in bed beside her.

He was sorry he had come to say farewell; had misread her from the beginning; had thought this Venus to be, if not an outright whore, at least an occasional one. Hell, maybe so - maybe not. He'd be more careful in the future. "I don't know what to say, Patsy. I'm....I'm flattered." He finally stammered, too embarrassed to say more. She stopped crying. He noticed how her hands had grown cold to his touch, and her eyes, also grown cold, gazed up at him.

"*Flattered*? Is that all you kin say to me? What kind of man are you to trifle with a girl like you done me, smiling them pretty dimples and using all that fancy talk, the way you done? Just so's you can get around me." She pushed him away. "I done give up a lot of...." She paused, swallowed, picked her words too carefully… "suitors fer you. I changed a lot of my ways 'cause of you."

Patsy jerked further away from him, pulling her shawl tight around her fleshy shoulders and drawing up as tall as her five feet four would allow. "Well, get on with ya, then. I ain't beggin'." But, as he turned to go, she caught his

30

arm and said wistfully, "You'll remember me, won't cha?"

"Dead right I will, Patsy. You were good to me." With that he tenderly kissed the forehead of the proud woman who had failed one more time, he guessed, to find the man who would make her his and his alone.

Feeling a bit ashamed of himself, Lieutenant Scarborough held her for a fraction longer, then without looking back, sprinted across the parade field to his waiting mount and the long, weary ride north to Fort Leavenworth, just across the river from the Missouri border.

In the warm April sun a half-dozen unconcerned Rhode Island hens pecked in the Wilcox's weedy farmyard around a dozen men and boys standing stiffly at ease. The feet of each man held a natural stance while his right arm curved behind him into the small of his back. And, although he might have been perspiring, no man dared wipe the sweat from his brow or take his eyes off Captain Jacques Verboise when he was instructing the company - the men and boys scrounged together since the return from Liberty. He spoke slowly, pausing for emphasis, hands at his sides, face expressionless, eyes unblinking, and caught each man in the eye. "Never face an enemy with the idea of only knocking him out. Chances are, gentlemen, he will repay your kindness by killing you."

Mesmerized, Hy listened, and realized this fierce man had entranced him from the moment he met him. For the entire trip back to Jeff City from Liberty he had soaked in every word Verboise uttered, astounded at the stories he'd told. Watching him now exhort the company, Hy recalled that story.

Spawned from a Belgian fur-trapper and a Pawnee squaw Verboise had traveled between dual worlds, gleaning a white man's book learning while mastering the physical skills of the warrior. As a youth he captured and rode bareback the wild mustangs roaming the prairies and

31

canyons of the west. When the war with Mexico broke out in '46, and he had come home to find his farm pillaged, his wife and two children butchered by Santa Ana's soldiers, he joined the United States mounted Dragoons as a scout. During the war he had been wounded while carrying four injured men to safety at Vera Cruz. For this show of bravery he had been breveted as a second lieutenant. When the First U.S. Cavalry had been formed in '55 at Fort Leavenworth, he transferred there. He trained new recruits, tracked, scouted, and enjoyed the collegial life of an officer - until Pottawatomie.

Sickened by the stories brought back to Fort Leavenworth by the company of First Cavalry detailed to investigate the Pottawatomie massacre, Verboise had asked for a personal mission of hand-picked men to go after John Brown. He waited over a year for the final permission papers to arrive. Finally, at the end of '57, eighteen months after the massacre, Colonel Sumner, commanding the First Cavalry at the time, told him the war department had turned down his offer.

"I just turned in my uniform, collected my pay owed me and said *'Adios*! ''

"Why ?" The three boys had chorused simultaneously.

"Because the U.S. Army didn't do a damn thing about it. The deaths of those five innocents cried out for revenge."

"And you wanted to do this yourself ?" Hy had asked.

"Of course. I wanted to bring John Brown to the hanging he deserved. That's when I heard of the Kickapoo Rangers." Then he had laughed and added, "They carried hatchets as well as guns. I'm half-Indian and swinging a tomahawk comes natural to me. I reckoned I'd fit right in."

The Kickapoo Rangers had been formed to wreak revenge upon free-staters and abolitionists for the deaths of the pro-slavery men who died at Pottawatomie Creek.

32

For the next three years Verboise had helped the Rangers achieve retribution ten times over. With them he plundered and burned and murdered without so much as a twinge of conscience.

By early '60 he knew the pro-slavery people had lost; Kansas would come in as a free state. Too many people, financed by northeastern abolitionist societies, had poured into the state. And although the Rangers stuffed ballot boxes, burned out whole villages, and murdered at will, bit by bit the consensus of the people sided with the free-state political party of Governor Robinson. Jacques Verboise returned "home" to the First Cavalry. He stayed until Fort Sumter and left again, to once more cast his lot with the South.

How proud Hy had been to bring the Ranger home, introduce him to Pa and to the other secesh-minded men in his neighborhood. To show his appreciation the Captain made Hy his sergeant. If Hy could recruit a dozen more, he'd make him the company's lieutenant.

When the Captain had told about his own anger over Pottawatomie, Hy had yearned to tell his memories about the place. But the day they left, Pa ordered that he never mention it and he never had. Even now, five years later and a man, Hy felt bound by the order of silence. And so Verboise never heard Hy's story about finding the flesh of dismembered bodies putrefying in the sun and crawling with maggots. He closed his eyes against the horrifying memory and turned his full attention back to his commanding officer.

The Captain was pausing, allowing his remarks to soak in on the men a moment, and continued, "A fight was never won by defensive action. This is not a cheap saloon brawl I'm talking about. Hand to hand combat is a matter of life and death. To kill, you must attack with all your strength and seek the place on the man's body that is most vulnerable and is open to a killing attack."

"Excuse me, Cap'n," one of the older men raised his hand, " but I got to find me a privy...."

The half-breed's icy, dead stare cut off the laughter rippling through the lines. Verboise had been interrupted, and by a most unsoldierly comment. "Sergeant, escort this soldier from the ranks. Show him where the sinks are."

"Yes Sir!" Hy saluted and marched a portly farmer at double quick time to the privy behind the Wilcox farmhouse. While he waited for the man to emerge, Hy paced, cracked his knuckles, and grew angrier by the second. At last the farmer came out, buttoning up the fly of his canvas overalls. He barely got the top one buttoned before Hy had him slammed up against the privy door.

"What you doin', Boy?" The man's eyes bulged with surprise and the veins stood out on his winter whitened neck. When Hy waved his Bowie knife beneath the man's nose, he tried to scream, but Hy's hand clamped over his mouth.

"Look, you son-of-a-bitch," Hy whispered, trying to imitate Verboise's quiet menacing tone, "Only reason the Cap'n let you take a piss is so's you wouldn't wet yore drawers when I teach you a lesson. If'n you ever do that again, I will gut you like a fish and throw yore body to the hogs."

The farmer's sour odor and fast blinking eyes bespoke of fear.

Hy reflected on what he was doing. *This is the first time in my life that I threatened to kill somebody. And it had to go and be Mr. Biddle. A good neighbor to Pa and me - known him for years. Bought a horse off him last summer. Took supper a time or two with him and his missus and ate warm gingerbread 'til I was tick-full and ready to explode.* And the young man almost lost his nerve.

Instead he snarled, "You want to ride with us, Private Biddle?"

34

Biddle had served in the Mexican War and recognized the need for army discipline, although Hy's brand seemed a bit extreme. Yet, he exhaled then shook his head, yes.

"Then you damn well hold yore water 'til the Cap'n says we is dismissed." Hy raised his voice slightly; "Do you hear me, old man?" When Biddle again nodded, Hy released him, but continued to stand close enough and several inches taller so that his lips nearly brushed the man's forehead. Finally, Hy stepped an inch backward, and slipped his knife into the back of his waist belt.

Biddle withdrew from his pocket a soil-stained kerchief and whined, "But he done had us standing out there most the mornin'," He mopped his sweating face and red-rimmed gray eyes before he said, "And--"

"--Hesh up yore mouth or I'll hesh it up for ya. If you're goin' to be a soldier then you jest have to take it. What you goin' to do, you old prick, get in the middle of a ruckus with the enemy an' say, 'ah pardon me, boys, but I got to piss. Wait the war for me.'? "

When Hy returned to the company, again marching Biddle at double quick, the men still stood, formed up at ease. Captain Verboise strode up and down and talked without emotion. "Screaming when you attack has two purposes. First, it will frighten your enemy and second, it will cause you to take a deep breath. This breath will give you more oxygen and strength." He motioned to Horton standing at perfect rest and paying rapt attention.

"Corporal Davies."

Horton stepped forward and saluted. "Show the men the natural weapons our bodies can be."

Then he looked at Buster, sweating and red faced beneath the sun's glare but maintaining a soldierly appearance, "Private Cowles."

Buster stepped forward and saluted smartly.

"Demonstrate defensive action against these natural body weapons."

Suddenly, Horton sprang upon Buster, who had four inches height on him. Horton's loud piercing scream startled the bigger boy who ducked in time to avoid Horton's hand, turned flat to become a knife-edge, the fingers folded at the second joint. The two circled each other, seemingly, the bitterest of enemies. Finally, Buster rushed his old friend aiming to hit him in the chin with the heel of his hand, but Horton danced away. Buster screamed and used his boot to trip Horton who went flying into the dirt. But Horton got up at once, lunged towards Buster, and kneed him in the groin. Buster held his privates and howled in pain. At this, some of the men murmured at the brutality implied in the fight. One remarked "taint fair, below the belt line."

And Verboise held up his hands. "Cease. Davies, Cowles as you were. Thank you, men." He waited a moment while Horton helped Buster stagger into formation and took his own place in the line. Then, he turned an evil sneer upon Chester McDonald, 17 years old, and tow headed as a baby.

" What isn't fair, Private McDonald?"

" Well, you seen 'um. Hell, ole Horton there, he…"

"Corporal Davies, to you, Private McDonald," Verboise corrected.

"Oh, that's right. You done tole us that…. Well, the way I reckon is that Corporal Davies shouldn't a hit him in the… uh…privates that way, Sir."

" And why not? "

"They's been friends since they sucked their mammy's titties, Cap'n, an' everybody knows they don' wanna kill each other. I jest figure, it weren't necessary." The commanding officer flicked an eyelash at Hy who stood to the side of the front line of six men. "Chess" McDonald stood on the end of the second line. Without warning, or even a yell, Hy walked over and nonchalantly kneed the boy in his groin.

At once, Private McDonald rolled on the ground, his hands bunching the contents behind the fly of his jeans and screeching in pain. "Now, kill him, Sergeant." Verboise hadn't changed expression or raised his voice.

Only for a heart beat did Hy waver, then, he saluted, "Yes Sir."

He pulled his Bowie, putting it to the boy's throat, and held Chess down with his knee. But although McDonald's face had gone crimson with pain, the boy tried to grin at the old friend ready to slash his jugular. "Ah come on, Hy, what you doin'? You been knowin' me since you first beat me up when I was in the third grade an' you was in the fifth."

Hy slid the blade across his former schoolmate's throat, lightly to be sure, but enough to draw a scratch and bring blood. He decided that tormenting Chess McDonald was grand fun but warned himself, *I best not grin. Capt'ns lookin' at me with that fish eye of his'n.* Suddenly, he wondered if he could really kill Chess if he was the enemy?

"Hey, what you doin', Hy Wilcox?" Chess wailed, "You gonna murder me in front a all these people?" His voice showed pure terror and his pale, blue eyes watered. A tear rolled down one cheek. Hy's stare never left the boy's eyes, but he sensed the other men standing silent, nervous, and unsure of what to do or how to react. Feet shuffled on the yard's hard brown earth. Hats came off, dirty kerchiefs wiped perspiring faces, and hands ran through hair. Eyes darted from face to face and stole sidelong glances at the Captain who studied not poor Chess crying and begging for his life, but instead observed the sergeant. Verboise seemed to be taking the measure of his subaltern trying to determine if Hy Wilcox would, indeed, be capable of slitting an old friend's throat - on an order.

Hy ran feathery strokes of the blade back and forth

across McDonald's throat a few more times, causing more hairline cuts, more blood to flow, and the victim to sob out loud.

Finally, Verboise ended the torture that had seemed like an hour, but in reality had been five minutes. He walked over, stood beside Chess, and looked down at the weeping boy for a moment, then he murmured, "Now, what was it you were saying about something being unfair, Private McDonald?"

Verboise nodded to the sergeant and Hy sprang off, quickly belting his knife. When he stood, he saluted the Captain who ignored him and focused on Chess McDonald. "McDonald, tell these men assembled how unfair it might be to assault an enemy's privates? Then tell us how such an action can be useful?"

Shaking from his ordeal, the blonde boy with the face of a cherub and the neck of the guillotined, stood up. He held his kerchief to his bloody throat and blushed to his scalp when he realized he had soiled himself. In a voice so low as to be almost inaudible he began. " If he's the..."

"Speak up, private, we can't hear you," Verboise barked.

Obviously uncomfortable, his water running down his leg and his under drawers filled with waste, he said more loudly this time, "If'n he's the enemy, then it ain't unfair. Cause he'll kill me sure as anythin' if'n I don' get him first."

"Tell us, Private McDonald, is it easier to immobilize a man and thence to kill him if his manhood has been struck?"

" Yes, Sir." McDonald kept his eyes on the ground.

"And are not our purposes here to learn how to kill the enemy without hesitation or qualm?"

"Yes, Sir." He whispered, then spoke again, louder, "Yes SIR!"

Verboise's coppery skin creased in a smile but on him

38

it looked horrible. He looked meaner than ever.

"Excellent, Private McDonald. Before you are dismissed, tell me, who is the enemy? "

"The Yankees."

"Are they all?"

McDonald's child-like eyes looked up, puzzled. "Sir? Is there somebody else?" The Captain surveyed the knot of men, for they had all fallen out of formation because of the moment's tension. "Can anyone else answer this question?" Everybody looked blank, when, suddenly, Buster stepped forward.

"And all their friends, Sir."

"And who are their friends?"

Again, Buster answered like a proud grade schooler reciting for his teacher.

"Them lop-eared, nigger lovin' Dutch, an' anybody else who ain't for the South, Sir."

"You mean just soldiers in uniform, of course, Cowles?"

"No, Sir, civilians, too, 'cause they help the Yankees. Like I said, Sir, anybody who ain't fer the South, ain't fer Missouri, and our job is to teach 'um a lesson."

"Meaning women and children, too?" The gray, flat eyes dared any man who squirmed at the question to speak up.

When Buster didn't answer immediately, the dead eyes riveted on him. Finally the boy with a mother and five younger sisters at home said, "No Sir, not women an' children," and he finished softly, "...not 'less they deserves it."

That night Franny sat on the edge of her mother's bed and listened to the rippling brogue. Even after 15 years in Missouri, the voice behind the black, Japanese dressing screen conjured up images of green moors, white chalk cliffs, bright blue sky, thatched roofs and stone cottages, of clog dancers, scones and potato stew - of Ireland. Franny could almost smell the burning peat fires of the old country when her mother's brogue thickened, as it tended to in the evening.

"Are ye listenin', girl? I said, 'tis fer a week, only, Otto and me will be gone ta St. Louis. 'Tis some layin' in of some necessities I must do before this rebellion makes everything dear and hard ta come by."

Franny mumbled that she had heard and lay back on the feather bed. When Deidre Moone emerged from behind the screen swaddled in a blue flannel wrap, the sullen 17 year-old raised up on an elbow. She watched her mother methodically brush her long, wavy hair, once a golden red like hers. Lately, though, Franny had noticed the streaks of white edging through red giving her mother's hair a dusty patina. Dusty and old, that would be her fate. She'd be gray-headed like Ma and die an old maid, she silently fumed, if her mother persisted in forbidding her to have a serious beau. At the moment, Hy Wilcox - slaver or not-presented himself as the front-running swain.

As though hypnotized Franny watched her mother's arm strokes move up and down, up and down. Finally, she sat on the edge of the bed, waiting for the right moment. Unable to contain herself any longer, she burst out with "Ma, Hy Wilcox wants to marry me."

When her mother never missed a beat and didn't respond Franny started again, "Ma, I know you heard me," and rushed ahead. "Now, you can't say he's not 'good enough' for me or that I 'don't know him well enough' like you said about the others. His Pa has one of the prettiest farms in Cole County and you've known Hy since we went to school together."

The lack of response from the face in the mirror maddened her. "Mother, are you listening? Remember, how he always walked me from school, then be under foot

40

until you had to shoo him home?"

"No," and the response didn't mean a failed memory.

"But, Ma, I'm old enough--"

"No, old enough ye ain't!" Her small round face set in stone, Dee paused, thinking, her arm uplifted, waiting to be commanded for the down stroke of the brush. "Anywise," she resumed brushing her hair, "the Wilcoxes is slavers and Secesh."

"So what! So is most everybody in the county." Franny's disgusted tone matched her face and she said, "unless they're "Dutch."

"Shame on ye, child, as good as Otto Zimmer's been to the likes of us." She scowled at Franny through the mirror and shook the hairbrush for silence. "And again, don't be callin' Otto "Dutch" when ye know 'tis Germany he's from. Besides, they come over on the boat, same as us an' don't ye never forget it."

As though Franny ever could. She had been too young to remember the 'coming.' But her mother constantly reminded her of their flight from the land and about the trip on the *Queen Isadora*. She never failed to speak of a fine lady, widow of an Irish Lord, who had treated her mother like a sister. Deidre had become the Godmother to the woman's son. Only a few years older than herself, Franny supposedly had adored him, but try as she might, she now blanked on his memory. The familiar story tumbled around in her head. And, if her mother launched into retelling it tonight, she knew she'd scream.

"What if he swore not to have slaves? Would you like Hy then?" Franny hoped she sounded respectful. It wouldn't do to upset her mother even more.

Exhaling in disgust and arching her eyebrows, Dee stared at her daughter through the mirror of her vanity. For a moment she brushed her hair in long fluid strokes without speaking. Then, instead of answering Franny's question, she asked one of her own. "I suppose, now, ye know where the boy be on Saturday last?"

"I reckon he was at the farm with his paw," Franny lied.

"Ye know very well, he weren't 'at the farm with his paw' and I suspects ye know where he were."

Of course, Franny knew what he had been doing - raiding the Federal Arsenal. She hadn't wanted him to go, but he believed he must. But how had her mother known Hy was there?

"It's not fair that you don't like Hy just because he disagrees with you about secession." Franny hugged her arms to her bosom and pouted.

"Taint the only reason I don' want the lad around ya." Still frowning at her image in the mirror, Dee brushed and counted for several strokes. Suddenly, the older woman's ruddy cheeks broke into a smile as though she had decided to treat the whole affair as a simple case of girlish crush. She laid the hairbrush down and eased onto the bed beside her daughter, her Irish brogue rippling softly. "Naow darlin' ya know how I feel about that boy-o. He's got the wild eye."

"But Ma, he's not really wild." Franny paused, trying to come up with something, anything to defend Hy. "He just gets excited about things."

"No, dear, I don' want him courtin' ya an' that's all there is to it." Sitting beside her unhappy child, her tone softened and she took Franny's hand in hers. "Ah, me darlin' girl, fer sure, ye'll fin' the right lad who'll do more fer ye than the Wilcox boy." She stood, then, yawned, and pecked Franny's cheek. "Go along with ye. Best be gettin' yerself ta bed. We're feedin' 23 guests in the mornin'."

Erin House sat on High Street within a block of the state's Capitol designed like a Grecian temple and the pride of the state. With Governor Jackson issuing calls for more militia and more sessions of the legislature, the small, red brick hotel bulged to capacity. Business had never been better. Even so, feeding that number for breakfast would be hectic indeed.

But the girl didn't go to bed. Instead, she sat in the dark on a black horsehair divan, waiting for her mother to go to sleep. She bided in the small parlor of the hotel's apartment that she shared with her mother and 15-year-old cousin Clay. From his room off the parlor she heard light snores. Now, if only her ma would go to sleep.

In the eerie silence, she mulled over their current situation. She had grown up with Clay in Erin House. Lately, he'd been acting like Hy; all fired up about the war and rarin' to fight. Behavior, Dee met with a stern frown and a lecture on loyalty to the Union. But Clay believed in the Secesh cause as much as Hy or she or anyone they knew in the city. Only immigrants like Ma and Otto Zimmer, her ma's advisor and her best friend's father, loud-mouthed about being for Lincoln and the Union.

A nostalgic longing for Sigrid Zimmer swept over her. Dee had taken "Sigi" into Erin House because her mother had died in the cholera outbreak in '51 and the child's father, Otto, had worked on the railroad. A year after his wife died, Otto took over The Royal Flush, an elegant gaming house and saloon, located in the city's better class business district. And, although settled at last and living in town, Otto hadn't wanted his daughter raised in a gambling house. Thus, Sigi boarded at Erin House and Dee Moone raised her. Sharing a room, the little girls of the same age had confided their souls to one another. But when Sigi became old enough to keep house, the child of the Chinese mother and the German railroad boss had moved in with her father.

In the street a wagon rattled past. A sound like crying infants came from the cats caterwauling down the block. If she closed her eyes she could pretend to be a child again, safe, and happy and no war to contend with. Although she leaned towards the south's right to leave a government they hated, she knew she had not a radical bone in her body. And giving all "for the cause" as some said they would do, did not appeal to her. Whoever won-- won. She didn't much care. Anyway, didn't everybody say it would all be over by Christmas?

But what if it wasn't ? She knotted her hands in her lap and contemplated what her life might be like if the war lasted a long time. One thing she knew, she'd probably have to wait to get married because all the eligible men would be off fighting. And by the time a long war ended, she'd probably be too old to catch a man. Then, she'd be stuck at Erin House with Ma, forever. "Dammit," she whispered to herself, "Ma never listens. She finds something wrong with all of 'um."

Ever since she had come home from Mrs. Osborn's Female Academy last December, her mother had discouraged every man who hinted of an interest in her daughter. And there had been many. For, after three years of uninspiring study, she had returned home from Virginia a rare beauty. The drummer from Chicago, who sold hardware, had called her " a true Hibernian flower."

But, her mother would not allow her "Hibernian flower" to bloom. Every potential beau had a flaw immediately perceptible to Deidre Moone. He was either in possession of a "grog-temper," full "of the blarney" or "too dry;" not "learned enough" or "too bookish;" or had a "wild-eye," like Hy. Her mother seemed never satisfied.

One day last month, Hy Wilcox had brought his paw's rig into town to get a new wheel and happened to spot her, window shopping down High Street. Over coffee at the Capitol Oyster House they had become reacquainted. Ever since, she had slipped around Ma to see him and pretended they were only good friends.

Suddenly, the light beneath the bedroom door snuffed out. This signaled Franny that her mother was ready to go to sleep. She counted slowly to one thousand but waited for 20 more counts. Then she tiptoed out of the apartment, closed the door so quietly it didn't even whisper, and walked through the silent, dark house.

On the back porch rocking in the bent wicker rocker she heard the horse walk into the back yard.

"Hy," she whispered, peering out into the dark.

"It's me."

In less than a heartbeat the girl flew from the porch into the arms of her sweetheart. Hand in hand they strolled to the back flower garden, delighted in the sweet smells of early spring, the soft, moonless night, and in each other. Entwined, they sat on the wrought iron bench and he rapidly told her about the arsenal raid and everything that had happened to him over the last few days, and about Verboise. His apparent idolization of the "Cap'n" irritated her and some of the things Hy told her about the man, frightened her. But, it didn't matter. Once they were married, he'd get over this radical preoccupation with killing Yankees and "freeing Missouri."

When he had finally ceased to glorify Jacques Verboise, she told him of Ma's flat refusal to consider his proposal of marriage.

"Doggone it, honey," the boy said gently, "I want us to get married." He had moved a little apart from her on the narrow bench so she corrected that by snuggling next to him and kissing his ear. Before he could think about it, she positioned herself so that his hand brushed against her generous bosom. Soon his lips were nuzzling her neck and his fingers fumbling at her bodice.

Allowing her beau to undo the fastenings at her throat and run his hands over her breasts, she sat thinking. In the past when Hy had gotten too familiar, Franny quelled his ardor. But tonight would be different. Purposely, she had worn neither corset nor hoop under her skirts. These trappings interfered with the serious business of lovers. And tonight, Franny meant to be very serious, indeed.

45

Tonight she'd permit him to taste of her just a wee bit more than usual, have him in fever, sweating and panting, and begging her to let him make love to her before she stopped him. It didn't pay a girl to allow a man his total pleasure before the wedding. After exploring beneath her chemise Hy moved beneath her skirts and pulled at the tie of her underpinnings. In his haste to get them loosened, he only succeeded in knotting the slender ribbon. He cursed and yanked to no avail and she giggled. This only intensified his passion. Breathing heavily, perspiring, frantic with desire he tugged until the ribbon broke. With a sharp inhale Hy timidly moved his hands into forbidden territory. When he did she decided now was the time to stop him. The time had come to be serious with Mr. Hy Wilcox. While waiting for him tonight, Franny had reflected on her mother's reasons for rejecting this suitor as she had all the others. In a snap she determined her fate. She smacked his hands and sat up, ignoring his entreaties and shoving him away.

"Yes, Hy, I want to marry you, too." Once again, he fondled her body and tried to kiss her breast. But she wiggled seductively just out of his grasp, making him clutch at her all that much more. "But if you are to marry me," she grunted, trying to push aside his weight, "we're goin' to have to run off to do it."

"You mean, elope?" He stopped kissing her, removed his hands from her clothing, sat upright, and spoke the word 'elope' as though it were one not used in polite company.

"Are you afraid, Hy?"

Both sat on the bench and faced one another. While his breathing slowed, her lover wiped his dripping face with a kerchief. The partially hidden moon cast a half-shadow and she could see his eyes, big and dark, filled with moonlight and lust - and hesitation.

"Well, no, but doggone it, we talked about bein' mar-

46

ried in St. Peter's and you in a pretty white dress, and all, I just figured that's what you'd want. Yore maw will come around, directly. We can wait."

"Ha!" Franny laughed softly. "I've never seen Ma change her mind about anything. And if you want to marry me, then we'll just have to up and do it."

She stroked his face and he grabbed her wrist, kissing it, passionately. Hoping she sounded reasonable and perhaps a little resigned, she sighed and said, "Sometimes, we don't get all of what we want, only a part of it. Reckon I'll just have to do without my church wedding and gettin' blessed by the priest, at least at first. You can join the church and he'll bless us later on. We can keep it a secret until then."

"A secret? " Hy blurted and started to rise.

To keep her mystified lover from yelling out anything else, Franny pulled him back and put her hand on his mouth. The poor boy seemed flummoxed. Well, so be it.

"Yes, a secret! We don't want any trouble. Now, here's how we can do this. Mr. Zimmer and Ma will be in St. Louis--"

While she laid out the plan, Franny gave him good reason to want to wed her as soon as possible.

CHAPTER 2
May

Sunday the 5th

Scarborough wanted action. He yearned for a rip-snorting, hard charge into the enemy's ranks, dispersing the rebel scoundrels once and for all. When the U.S. First cavalry was 25 miles out from Fort Smith, he thought he might get his wish.

Captain Sturges had not only sneaked out the back gate but also had taken 56 mule teams pulling wagons loaded to the canvas. What powder they hadn't been able to take, they threw in the river. The day after they had left, the conquering Confederate commander sent a squad of 40 men to summon the First to surrender - a squad his company could have taken with ease, and Josiah had hoped for at least a skirmish. Instead, Unflappable Sturges had taken the Rebel squad captive and marched on. But, within 24 hours the prisoners had been paroled and sent home.

Next, at Fort Washita it looked like a little set-to might erupt. Lieutenant Colonel Emory, a regiment of infantry, and four more companies of cavalry from Forts Cobb and Arbuckle had met them there. Harris, The pitiful, little half-breed governor of the Indian Nation had come to Washita and insisted on their surrender. Tall, elegant Emory had threatened him with the guardhouse. Eschewing this, with his slovenly "army" of around 50 men Harris had slunk back onto the prairie.

Then, two days ago, he thought for sure they'd see a fight. Instead, the capture of 250 Texans, had turned out to be as vigorous as a Sunday school party and as polite as a lady's tea. When Corporal Sanders rode up on a lathered mare telling him to prepare "for action - order from

Lieutenant Colonel Emory" - Josiah almost shouted for happiness. The corporal told him that Old Possum and Beaver, Delaware Indians scouting for the First had spotted around 250 horsemen tagging close to the rear of the civilian train. These were Texas Confederate General Ben McCulloch's advance guard. Emory wanted them stopped.

When Josiah's mount fell in beside Sturges, the Indian scouts rode up, reported, "The Texans are cooking their dinners. But nobody's watching their horses." Old Possum grinned, showing age and tobacco colored teeth. "Like squaws, they care only for their cooking." The Indian closed his heavy lidded eyes and rumbled a chuckle from his bare chest.

Priming himself for the assault against these rebels, aching to scream the yell stuck in his throat, Josiah snarled orders as though his men faced Jeff Davis's entire Rebel army - 100, 000 strong.

But instead of a hot, little fight, Sturges had ordered the first lieutenant's men to quietly ride their mounts between the cooking fires of the Texans and their horses tethered to graze. Both horses and men had been captured without a shot fired, a curse uttered, a man bruised, or an animal injured. Then, because the Texas colonel commanding had been a grain contractor that everybody knew and was chummy with, everybody stood around jawing and laughing like a war for the nation's soul had never been declared. Also, Emory knew that his army couldn't feed the 250 captured while traveling the long journey to Fort Leavenworth, so he had paroled them all back to their homes and allowed them to take their horses. But they took them less a few hairs. Thanks to Scarborough and his action-starved men who had been angry as hell, they got their revenge.

"Dammit, Lieutenant, that ain't right."

"Orders is orders, you know that, Brady."

49

"The boys is sore-pissed."

"So am I."

"Them Texans jist ain't gonna go home peaceable an' stay there."

"I know that, too."

"Twill not be me to stop our boys from doin' what they-'re a - doin'."

"What're they doing?"

"Shavin' tails."

"Not cuttin' 'um off are they?"

"No, fer Jeez an' the Mother's sake, it won't hurt the horse none, just make him look funny."

And the newly commissioned Lieutenant and the veteran Sergeant had both walked into the grove to take a smoke and lament the outcome of the day. Naturally, they stood so that neither of them could see the troopers of Company B manicuring the hairs out of the tails of the Texans' horses.

The only exciting thing Scarborough had done since his company had made the midnight skedaddle out of Fort Smith had been to bring down a buffalo to share with the whole company. The vast prairie 80 miles south of the Kansas border, where the army rested for noon dinner, hosted immense herds of buffalo. These shaggy beasts migrated from the south to the north every year and this year - minus one-they walked with the U. S. First Cavalry.

With eyes half-closed, back against a well leafed poplar, long legs stretched out before him, Josiah smelled the lingering aroma of roasted buffalo meat, listened to the gurgle of the Washita River and thought about the dullness of this march. Even reflections upon the assorted civilians tagging along in the rear of the column could not excite him.

At another time such individuals, 150 strong, black and white, men, and women of dubious character, might have enticed him. He'd have gotten up a game of poker with one of the crooked gamblers who thought palming an ace the way to win. Surely, buy some whisky off one of the sutlers. Maybe even find him a woman for a night or so. For a moment's flicker he wished he'd encouraged Patsy to join the civilian train. Parrot brained she might be, but she knew how to take care of his restlessness. But after looking over the scruffy pack of whores and refugees fleeing the Confederates, the bored lieutenant thought better of it. Besides, he was broke. The men hadn't seen the paymaster for over four months.

He yawned. His meal of roasted buffalo and coffee settled in his stomach. But it did little to assuage the sense of futility he felt about this march. And so, remembering, Josiah rested against the tree on this bright, golden day. Around him a million cicadas sent up their eerie crackling noise, the sound of a million insect wings rubbing together. Day and night, they never stopped. The grasshoppers had come this spring in abundance, in their seventeen-year cycle. One of the creatures hopped on his boot. Fascinated, he watched its antennae waving and the bluish green body a good six inches long appearing to clean itself with its front legs. Shaking the insect off his foot he noticed that his messmate ignored them.

Second Lieutenant Clarence O'Shay raised the little pinky of this right hand and dunked a hardtack cracker into a tin cup of thick, black coffee. Wrinkling his nose, he watched the cup come alive with weevils. After months of subsisting on army issue hardtack, the little devils swarmed frantically in the hot brew trying to avoid being drowned or scalded to death. Disgusted, the young man grunted, tossed the cup's offensive contents in the grass behind him, and turned unhappy hazel eyes on Josiah.

O'Shay's effete distaste at the quality of the rations amused Josiah.

He grinned, and as much as his New York City twang allowed, drawled, "I've heard that cracker-worms can keep

51

a man alive for days, in a pinch."

"You won't catch me eating that swill." With a flourish, O'Shay wiped his hands and mouth with an immaculate, linen handkerchief and abruptly changed the subject. "I still can't believe Lieutenant Colonel Emory left Charley Campbell in charge of Fort Arbuckle to surrender it to the Rebels."

"What you got against Campbell?" Scarborough really didn't give a damn, except this fledgling irritated him. Although both men were within a year of each other's age, Josiah felt centuries older. Fresh out of the Academy, Clarence O'Shay had complained about everything since joining Company B. For some reason known only to God and Captain Sturges, the youth with the pomaded red hair and scraggly red goatee had been assigned to the hardened Indian fighters and become Scarborough's shadow. And inevitably, he managed to say or do something that irked Scarborough to his socks.

"As unlikely a partner as ever could be," the first lieutenant fumed one night and passed the bottle of *Jim Beam* whiskey to his best friend in the regiment. First Sergeant Oliver Brady, 25 years Josiah's senior, with even more years in field experience, sputtered whisky when he laughed.

"Hell, I can't talk to you, you're drunk." Josiah glared at Brady. Yet, this was the man who understood him. A skinny, pugnacious, 17-year-old, on the run from the New York City police, Josiah had recruited into the newly formed regiment of First Cavalry and met Brady. Brady had also been the first one to see through the anger and the pain and spot the well-educated, genteel young man underneath.

"Remember the man I put ya beside when ya first come into the regiment?"

Josiah remembered, all too well - Jacques Verboise, the halfbreed with the evil eye and a ready fist.

"All peppery, ya were, a chip on yer shoulder the size of a walnut log. I had to make a horse soldier out of ya. I figured if ya rode with somebody like Verboise, he'd learn ya good to keep yer fists to yer self and yer mouth closed long enough to listen."

Josiah grinned in spite of the still raw memory. Not many men were bigger than he, or so he'd thought until he had met the giant scout who towered over him by half a foot. "That wasn't fair, Brady, what you did, puttin' me with him."

"Well, a-now, what do yer suppose the new lieutenant is sayin' about you?"

"What do you mean? I'm a perfect gentleman with our latest West Point wonder child."

"Aargh, yer, that's true. But I hear ya when ya think I don't, givin' him side lessons on how to stay on his horse." And the sergeant had laughed until the tears rolled his cheeks and his face turned crimson. Even the bald spot peeping from under the silver crown of his head turned red.

"What!" With mocked umbrage Josiah had stood. "Tis fer certain I can't very well bark a command at him, can I?" Then, he marched a few steps, squared his corner, and returned, facing his old sergeant and coming to attention. All of this was done rather shakily for they had nearly depleted the bottle of whiskey. In a voice trying to sound most officer-like Scarborough had ordered, "Mr O'Shay, grip your mount with your knees. Do not tug and pull at the reins. Do not slump in the saddle like a sack of wet flour. Do not lurch to one side then the other. Do not stick your feet straight out at the sides."

Throughout this tirade, Josiah had kept his face firm, his jaw squared, and his head up, allowing not one iota of frivolity to show. But before he was half-though, Sergeant Brady had collapsed in his campchair, bellowing with mirth and holding his sides. After he'd calmed himself,

Brady remarked, "Mebbe Cap'n Sturges wants ta keep us Irish all together. That's why 'tis the young lieutenant you got. We Irish stick together like flies on shit."

And now, here was O'Shay. As Irish as they came and showing more round-eyed surprise than disdain that Scarborough didn't immediately see the point about Campbell. O'Shay replied, "Did you just ask me, what was wrong with Charley Campbell? Why, he's only a first sergeant in the infantry." When his partner didn't immediately agree he added, "Surely, you of all people should know that a man well schooled in military tactics is better at handling matters of that sort."

"Why should I know that?" Scarborough sat upright, opened wide his sleep - drugged eyes and gave this simpleton his full attention.

Flustered, O'Shay blushed, "Well, you…Oh, I forgot, you didn't graduate from the Academy." He fixed Scarborough with a condescending look. Then rushed on, "But you seem well educated…anyway," he stammered, "By the way, where did you matriculate for your upper schooling?"

"Here and there." Scarborough replied evenly. Vague and taciturn - almost rude - certainly, but he wasn't about to give this Irish Mick from Chicago a hint of his past.

He remembered, at fourteen being the youngest cadet to ever qualify for Virginia Military Academy and before that he had made top honors in every class at John Bowie Strange's Military School in Albermarle, Virginia. His horsemanship when he had first come into the regiment had been the major thing that had given him away.

"Come on, lad, tell old Brady who ya are, really."

When he hadn't answered, Brady had looked over at Verboise silently observing the 17-year-old Private Scarborough with half-closed eyes.

"What the hell do you----" was all he got out of his mouth before the blow to his ear damned near deafened him. And he had turned on the big half-breed with all the fury of a cornered animal.

"Lieutenant Scarborough, I asked from where you came. Where is your home?" O'Shay waited for an answer.

The hairs on the back of his neck prickled, a sure sign he was growing angry, and he pinned O'Shay with his eyes. But he answered without emotion. "Back east." In his reply he heard an echo of the terse, flat way Verboise often had responded to annoying people. And that had been five years ago.

Obviously non-pulsed at his fellow officer's reticence, O'Shay leaned back, one elbow on the grass after checking it first to make sure it wasn't where he had thrown his wormy coffee, and tried one last time to break through Scarborough's reserve. "Family?"

"No," then to offset his rising temper Scarborough quickly redirected the conversation and asked sarcastically, "Maybe you think Emory should have put you in charge of surrendering Arbuckel? You think that your own vast knowledge of military tactics and field experience is superior to Charlie Campbell's?"

"But surrender, Sir, is done between officers and gentlemen," O'Shay smiled, happy to change the subject and oblivious to the sarcasm.

"Really? I always thought surrender happened between enemies - the winner and the loser." Scarborough paused, then, "You talk about knowledge - Charlie Campbell has over 20 years soldering. That's experience. I'll take experience, over officer's book-learning anytime. And so will the men." Scarborough had raised his voice. Troopers eating, napping, and smoking around them, turned to stare.

"I don't think I like your tone, Sir." O'Shay rose, sat

upright, his eyes blinking in astonishment that this officer would take issue with him.

"I don't give a damn if you 'like' my tone, you'll hear me out." At that moment Josiah would have given his soul to have the other man throw a first punch. "Do you really believe, these men take your orders because of your exalted knowledge of military tactics? Hell no! They take orders from officers like you because they know they must or stand punishment.

O'Shay moved to rise, but Scarborough's iron grip kept him seated.

"And let me give you some advice you never learned up at the Point. Old timers like Charlie Campbell run the army. If you want to get something done, ask your sergeant. If you need something and can't procure it, ask your sergeant. If you want to know the truth about the ranks under your command, ask your sergeant."

Pleased with himself, Scarborough relaxed his grip, leaned back, and in the same fake New York City drawl, said "Yep I reckon Lieutenant Colonel Emory should have left you back at Arbuckle. After all, you have such an extensive knowledge of military tactics. And surrendering United States property to treasonable enemies is really a game, nothing more than one gentleman taking the sword of the other."

"You really are, insufferable," O'Shay sputtered.

Unfazed, Scarborough asked brightly, "Mr. O'Shay, did you know that when we marched from Arbuckle, the First Cavalry took all the ordnance supplies?" He paused as one would with a child or a student to see if they understood. Then asked, "You do know what I mean, don't you? We took all the weapons and powder." Scarborough knew he sounded patronizing and the second lieutenant's sour glance confirmed it.

"That meant Sergeant Campbell had to face 2,000 riled Texans with only his personal sidearm. He might as well have been carrying a slingshot. Could you have done that, Mr. O'Shay?"

"I resent your inference that I am a coward, Sir!" O'Shay puckered his mouth as he always did when angry, which he usually was, and his fat red lips reminded Scarborough of a tulip.

"And I resent your slur on an intelligent, praise worthy soldier." Feigning indifference when he said this, Scarborough observed the men around them pretending not to overhear. Of course the troopers had eavesdropped. On this perfect, golden day on the banks of a pleasant river, their stomachs full and time given to smoke, write a letter or nap, the rank and file of Company B had heard and enjoyed every minute of the exchange. And not too long ago being in the ranks himself, naturally, Scarborough knew this.

"So, Sir, I will conclude my 'insufferable' remarks," Josiah bobbed a mock bow and grinned, "By saying that neither the piece of paper a commission is written on or any war-college education will ever make a man fit to officer. As for bein' a gentleman? That's not likely, either."

Clearly enraged, the West Pointer stiffened, a retort on his ruby lips, but Josiah stood. "Come, on, time to mount up." He called over to Brady, pretending sleep beneath a tree down the riverbank. "Sergeant Brady, give the order!"

When O'Shay stood his ground, glaring at him in a most ungentlemanly fashion, Josiah asked lightly, "Do you know where your horse is, Mr. O'Shay?"

The officer commanding Hy's militia company literally terrified her. So tall stood Jacques Verboise that she feared she might develop a crick in her neck trying to look up at him. And his eyes the color of sleet and cold rain, following her around the kitchen as she helped Aunt

Sukey prepare the men dinner, unnerved her to the point that she dropped two dishes, shattering them on the floor. No man old, young, black, white, sane or insane had ever looked at her the way he did, she thought. His frozen eyes, a deadman's eyes, chilled her blood. He made her feel that she didn't exist, dismissed her as one would an annoying mosquito. And people slapped them dead; didn't they?

She knew that buttery charm dripped from her mouth, and in her green checked dimity frock with the lace-trimmed bertha, her voluptuous figure and dainty waist showed to best advantage. Even her hair did right the day she went out to Pa Wilcox's to meet the Captain and tell Hy's father of their marriage. Normally, her hair too curly-wild to smooth down in a neat bun beneath a net, she had worn sausage curls held back by a grosgrain tie. Beneath her flower and ribbon-trimmed bonnet four little curls, two on each side wiggled enchantingly at her neck. Experience had taught her that most males thought she looked good enough to eat. Except for Captain Verboise.

Aunt Sukey, that's what everybody called the Wilcox colored woman, from habit spoke little but uttered nary a word when Verboise entered the kitchen. There, the two women worked to get up a noon dinner of boiled ham, biscuits, gravy, and apple pie. It hadn't surprised her when she overheard the men in the next room arguing after dinner, arguing over her.

"But Paw, we is suppose to get married, tonight!"

"I said, no, an' I means it!"

"Well, hell, I'm old enough to make my own decisions."

"Wilcox," Verboise entered the discussion, "your father is right. Leave the girl alone. Now is not the time to get married. We have a war to fight."

"Cap'n Verboise, I truly respects yore opinion, but I figure if'n we marry now, then I won't be worryin' about it an' I'll be able to fight even better."

She smiled to herself when she heard Hy give this reason. She had given it to him. But his Paw, hmm, now that was a puzzlement, indeed. To herself she wondered. *Why would Mr. Wilcox sound like he objected to having me for a daughter-in-law?* She searched her memory to determine if she had said or done anything to offend the elder Wilcox, came up with nothing, shrugged her shoulders, remembered that everybody knew Hy's father was dour and looked on the gloomy side of things.

He was also known around Jefferson City as a reticent, dirty and disheveled sort of man. None the less, widower Wilcox had once produced a miracle from the scrabbly soil he had inherited from his father. In the past the Wilcox farm of over 300 acres had bloomed with fine grade hemp, corn, fruits, and vegetables. Yes, indeedy, she thought, smiling again to herself, she'd be very content to be married to the farm's heir. When she turned of age and Ma couldn't make her get an annulment, she'd be pleased as cream pie to tell everybody she was Mrs. Hy Wilcox.

A dim memory prevailed from her childhood. When she had been four or five years old Jeremiah Wilcox called on Ma a lot. Then one day Sigrid Zimmer had moved in and her father Otto had been around as often as he could. During this time, Jeremiah had stopped coming around. One day, if she thought of it again, she'd ask Ma why Mr. Wilcox had stopped taking dinner at Erin House.

"Captain Verboise, do I have your permission, then?" Hy asked. It sounded to her that the men were now out in the yard, still debating whether or not he should marry. She bit her lip to keep from yelling at them that Hy Wilcox should marry whom and when he chose and didn't need anybody's permission. But when she looked up from the dish she was drying, she caught Aunt Sukey staring at her. And her wrinkled, tan face showed only sorrow. "What? What is it Aunt Sukey?"

"You is too innocent to know, chile." And the old

woman looked away.

"To know what? What should I know?"

"You is marryin' into the wrong family."

Stunned, for she had never imagined the faithful servant would have such an attitude. As far as she or anyone else knew, Wilcox treated Aunt Sukey well. She had been Hy's nurse when Mrs. Wilcox had developed the milk leg and died not too long after Hy's birth.

All Franny could do was stutter, "Why, why do you say that?"

"The apple don't fall far from de tree. An' de seed grows its own."

She didn't have a chance to question further for just then Hy with Buster and Horton at his heels came laughing and stomping into the kitchen. She hadn't heard the other two ride up, but it made no difference. She barely had time to tie on her bonnet and say goodbye to Aunt Sukey before Hy scooped her into his arms and whisked her out the door. Paw was nowhere to be seen when Hy bundled her into the two-seater buggy and yelled for Patrick Henry, the chestnut gilding to "Git on."

As they drove down the drive, only the strange giant standing emotionless on the porch gazed after them. He thought he recognized the boy's problem. The little piece of fluff had teased him into such a state of arousal that if he didn't have her he'd burst. So let him vent his lust for a day. He'd come back, ready to learn, and he, Captain Jacques Verboise would be willing to teach.

Watching the dust of the carriage, he stood musing, remembering. His own control over his desires hadn't occurred easily or early. In his case women had presented more of a danger to manly control than did sleep, food, or water. Sometimes the urge was uncontrollable.

He closed his eyes, scented the spring air, thought he felt his Nina nearby as his mind recalled their innocent happiness. And, as always, when he tried to hold on to their young life together, his thoughts jerked back to that horrible day—the day he had returned home to find his Nina and their two small children slaughtered by rogue soldiers from Santa Ana's army.

Although only in his early twenties, he pledged himself to remain ever faithful to his dead wife. To the soulless stars, he had vowed that no woman would ever lie in his arms again. No woman's lips would ever touch his again. From the depths of his grief, Verboise had spoken what had over the years become his mantra. Watching the young couple drive away, he whispered it again, "Like the proud eagles of the mountains I, too, shall remain faithful and true to my dead love."

He could well see why Hy Wilcox was smitten. The girl's coquettish ways and pouty lips could stir any man not strong enough to resist. But, he thought, the boy headed for certain disaster with her. He'd never hold her. Marriage was no guarantee. Not only was the girl more intelligent than Wilcox, she was also too desirable to other men. Before long she would be unfaithful, and jealousy would devour him.

Let it happen. Then, once over the initial rage and agony, Hy Wilcox would be the stronger for it. Verboise knew his sergeant wasn't ready yet. He couldn't kill just for killing's sake. But, after that redheaded firecracker exploded his heart, he'd be raring to kill and kill again, if for no other reason than to get revenge.

Thoughts milling in his head like grist flying in the wind, Verboise felt the need for a walk. Walking about Wilcox's untended farm had served lately to help him focus, streamline his motives, determine his next strike.

Normally a man of iron resolve, today, he found himself consumed with thoughts of passion and hoped he wasn't going to have one of those torturous bouts of desire that at times plagued him. As he had aged, thankfully, these "episodes" as he called them, had decreased. But occasionally his thoughts filled yet with images, and smells, the touch and sounds of women--soft hair, silken skin, lips, breasts, hips, the scents of rose, lavender and gardenias, the quiet rustle of skirts, hands fondling yielded flesh, and the passionate cries of ecstasy at climax.

Trying to move his thoughts into another direction, Verboise bent down and scooped up a bit of the rich black loam that covered most of the Wilcox farm and wondered why the man didn't farm it. A small field of corn and patches of vegetables were all that grew. But when he straightened up and continued walking, once again desires of the flesh still preyed upon his mind.

Some months ago arousal had come upon him. As usual at these occurrences he entered into his dream-life and made contact with his dead Nina in the world of Spirits. Her shining dark hair flowing and dark eyes smiling, she welcomed him to her side. Around her an aura of light reached out and engulfed him until he too became a part of her light. His children walked at her hand and he spent time in play with them before caressing his lovely Nina. Over sun filled meadows and beside shady creeks the little family frolicked, joyous to be rejoined. Recalling this pleasure, he stopped at the stand of hickory, maple, and sycamore trees skirting the back of the property, closed his eyes, and breathed deeply allowing the verdant spring to fill his nostrils, its harmony fill his soul.

When at last he opened his eyes and turned back towards the house, he decided it was time to pick up again something he had neglected over the past few months. He would read, meditate, and tonight, return to Nina.

Although raised a Roman Catholic he had become a devotee of the second century stoic philosopher, Marcus Aurelius. He had carried *The Meditations* in his saddlebags so long that the cover was ragged and the pages loose. Reading a page or two before he went to sleep helped to offset nighttime desires and helped him to see how Nina though in the Spirit world could still be alive to him in his dreams. Aurelius taught that death is as natural as birth. All in the world is rational and orderly and that the human soul is only another form of matter. Hence, Nina in spirit had become tangible to him in body.

The stoic also taught him that the wise man obtains virtue by reason alone, remaining indifferent to pleasure, pain, and emotions. So, Verboise prided himself on going weeks without food, days without water or sleep. In the hottest weather, he frequently wore woolen trowsers and jacket, like today. In the freezing winter, he often went barefooted and bare chested, and wore the lightest of canvas pants. Sometimes he'd light a match and stick his finger in the flame to see how long he could roast it before sufficient pain struck. Since riding away from the graves of his wife and children, he had spent his life making himself into a virtuous man.

A virtuous man able to kill with a righteous heart.

Evening, of the 5th

A tiny wisp of a woman attired in nightclothes, Mrs. Horace Olmstead remained seated stiffly at the pump organ in the parlor of the Methodist parsonage. Dressed only in his wrapper and carpet slippers, the Reverend Horace Olmstead stood before the young couple and intoned the final words of the marriage ceremony.

"I now pronounce you man and wife. What God hath joined together let not man put asunder. You may kiss the bride." He closed his Service Book and yawned.

Hy Ebenezer Wilcox bent to give Frances Margaret Moone a chaste kiss.

As the couple's lips touched, Horton waved his Navy Colt in the direction of Mrs. Olmstead and bellowed, "Play Ma'am. Ain't you supposed to play somethin'?"

Without thinking the terrified woman's hands hit the

keys and squawking discord filled the room. But, pumping with all her strength, she managed to get the opening strains of Mendelssohn's *Wedding Recessional* out of the wheezy old organ.

The sleepy Methodist Pastor of Wardsville and his nervous wife had retired early. Only to be awakened from a sound sleep by the feel of Colt revolvers pressed to their heads. Behind the guns grinned the faces of the witnesses while, behind these boys the couple wishing to marry had engaged in a shameful display of giggling affection. Thus, roused from his bed, given no time to dress appropriately, his dear wife pushed into the parlor and told to play "some music for weddins'," the unhappy cleric grumpily wrote the names of the bride and groom in his parish register. The next time he went up to Jefferson City he would record these names at the county courthouse. A sly thought occurred to him. What if he didn't record the names at the courthouse? Then this vulgar pair would not be legally married.

But, no, he inwardly sighed. Then he would be a party to propagating fornication and he'd have to answer to God for that. Even devils like this bunch of yahoos, deserved the rites of Holy Matrimony.

In the flicker of the oil lamps, along side the signatures of the bride and groom the witnesses scrawled theirs names and Wilcox tossed him a gold piece. He caught it. Usually, as the minister officiating, he received fifty cents, at most a dollar, or two, depending upon who was marrying. Incredulous, he tested the coin between his teeth. How could an ill-dressed farmer boy like Wilcox come upon so much money? But he didn't ask; for sure enough, it was a five-dollar half-eagle. Suddenly, the evening reveille seemed worthwhile, and he hoped the smile on his lips mirrored the gratitude he held in his heart.

"Sorry about the joke, Parson," the groom smiled,

slapped on his slouch hat. "We'd never have shot you." He chuckled and noticed Mrs. Olmstead sitting on the organ bench. Seeing Her face white with fear and a tear trickling down her cheek, the boy turned contrite, "And you too, Ma'am, we was just funnin'. We didn't mean to rile y'all up, none." Whispering, he asked Horace, "Alright if'n I give yore Missus some-thin' fer playing the music?"

"She would appreciate it, I'm sure," he said and beamed when the groom placed a half-eagle in his startled wife's hand. When the woman just sat and stared at the coin, Horace said gently..,

"Mrs. Olmstead, say thank you."

Yipping and hollering, Buster and Horton raced ahead on their horses into the cool spring night, awash in moonlight set amid uncountable stars. And Hy, one arm around Franny, the other hand holding the reins, had whipped up Patrick Henry into a near gallop. The wind streaked behind them, through the rolling country of hard maples, cedars, and red bud trees, dark shadows in the night. The rhythmic hammering of horses' hooves pounded the dirt road and they didn't slow down until they reached the city, an hour later.

With her mother and Otto Zimmer in St. Louis, Franny had been set in charge of Erin House. About 10 O' clock the marriage party and she arrived back at the hotel with no one the wiser of where they had been or why. As far as Clay knew she had spent the day at the Wilcox place, returned to Erin House in the afternoon to supervise supper, and gone out again with Hy and his friends. His curly auburn hair bent over the receipt book, the boy looked up and broke his round baby face into a smile when she burst in the door.

With the guests of Erin House snoring in their beds and the coloreds long asleep in the hotel's annex next door, the wedding party scrounged bread, cold ham, and lemon cake from the kitchen and broke open a bottle of champagne. Of course, she had to let Clay in on the secret of her wedding to Hy. She knew he'd say nothing to Ma. Clay looked up to Hy and would never do or say anything to curry his disfavor. Lately, Ma had all but sat on and hog-tied her nephew to keep him from running out and joining Verboise's militia.

Franny yawned. The day had been long and tomorrow would be longer. The hotel was packed to the rafters with guests. The only spare, a third floor closet room, waited to be rented. Wedding night or not she would have to get to bed. Besides, everybody seemed to be half-drunk and overly full and she couldn't bear to hear the men talk of nothing but the war, the war, the war.

"We're tryin' to keep the Yankees out of Missouri," Hy talked with his mouth full of sandwich and gesticulated with his left hand.

"Will Missouri go out with the South?" asked Clay, looking first at Hy then at Buster and Horton, all of whom, making lusty inroads on the ham and cake.

"Don' know. All I see is more an' more of Lincoln's army invadin' Missouri." Hy answered.

"We's gonna wind up a-fightin'" Buster said solemnly. "Verboise says, we's bound too. The government done sent a Cap'n Lyon, a real old tough bird from the regular army, to take over the United States arsenal in Saint Louis."

"Ain't that where we're goin' tomorrow?" Horton stopped eating long enough to ask.

Buster and Hy nodded and Clay said, "Well, I under-stand what you're a-tryin' to do. Wish I could join y'all at the militia camp." Wistfully, Clay eyed Hy who chewed his ham sandwich and said nothing.

"Gotta grow some more, little cousin," Buster said with a mouth full of cake.

Clay ignored the remark. He turned to Hy, "I can

ride and shoot a gun pretty good. I know I could if y'all let me come with you."

"Oh, for heavens sake, Clay, just hush." Franny was sick to death of hearing this talk, especially about them leaving tomorrow. She had hoped Hy would spend at least one day with her. So she pulled her mouth into a straight line, like she always did when angry, and said, "Can't you see Hy doesn't want you in the militia, yet."

"It's ok, honey," he winked at Franny sitting next to him at the long, board table, "I like his spirit."

And so the talk swirled on - of Camp Jackson in Saint Louis, commanded by General Frost, where Verboise was taking his "company, Troop G" to join the other state militia. About 600 men were expected to gather for drill, discipline, and military games. A yearly event for the state reserves, this year seemed particularly charged with excitement because of the war. That Hy seemed anxious to go irked her. Finally, she slipped away, unnoticed she thought, and made her way into her bedroom, closed the door, kicked off her shoes, scrambled out of hoops and corset, and flopped at once onto her clean bed.

My, but that felt good and she sighed from the sheer comfort as she settled into her feather mattress. For a blessed moment, alone in her pretty green and pink papered room with the white lace coverlet and her porcelain-faced dolls from her childhood neatly placed on their shelf over her bed, she felt secure. But, the peace broke too soon with a soft knock at her door.

"Hy, oh, what you want?" Half-asleep, she yawned, smiled when she opened the door, added without thinking, "Hadn't you best be getting' on home?" He had left the apartment door open. She overheard Clay telling Horton and Buster that he'd let them sleep upstairs on the third floor in the closet room for the night.

Hy lounged against the door jam and stared down at her. A slow smile crossed his face. "Well," he said, "you gonna let me come in----" he cleared his throat, "----wife?"

When dawn curled a finger around her green draperies, it found her furious with Hy Wilcox and kicking herself 90 times and 90 times again for marrying him. He had consummated their union with little of the ardor earlier expressed on the wrought iron bench. Lying awake afterwards listening to him snore certainly had not impressed her. Neither had he when he woke her from a sound sleep and repeated his clumsy performance. She had tried to forestall him, but he had been rather rough with her and insisted he had "waited too long." So, she had done her duty by him as his wife.

Other than from the veiled references made in the romances she read, that Ma called "trash," she had no prior teaching or understanding of the married side of life. She only knew that last night she had found -unpleasant. He had been less acquiescent and more demanding and hurried than she cared for. In fact, she would have been just as happy to continue their teasing love-play on the wrought iron bench and never let him have his way with her. But, she knew she was being foolish. A wife's first duty meant she lay with her husband, as he had quickly reminded her.

However, and this puzzled her, if one were supposed to feel ecstasy from the touch of their sweetheart, then why hadn't she? The believer of that myth had never spent a wedding night with Hy Wilcox. She lay on her stomach, stark naked with only the light sheet over her behind while Hy stroked her back. For a minute she thought he might regain his old romantic self.

"Come on sugar," he pleaded, "don't be mad at me 'cause I got to go."

"I don't care."

"Yes, you do. You're mad as all get out. I can tell." He kissed her ear and ran his hands through her hair. "I love you," he whispered and bent to turn her face towards

68

him so he could kiss her.

That was the first time in days he had told her that he loved her. She turned towards him, her mouth parted for a kiss. He barely grazed her lips when a loud knock shattered the moment.

"Come on lover boy, we got to git, if'n we're to meet the Cap'n before the train leaves."

"Don't go!" she sat up on one elbow allowing him to see her naked breast but she might as well have been showing him prunes for at the knock he leaped out of bed and now buttoned his trowsers.

"Got to, Pet." He frowned and sat on the edge of the bed frantically pulling on one of his boots. "You still not gonna tell yore ma, we's married?"

"We've been over this, Hy, you know I have to keep it secret." She turned her face away from him and stared at the green velvet drape covering the window. "For awhile, anyway. I'm not of legal age and wedding' night or not, she'd be sore enough to make me get an annulment."

He didn't say anything, and she heard him still tugging at the boot. Either his feet had grown or he'd gotten the pair too small. Grunting with effort he asked, "So I reckon, you won't be stayin' at the farm with Pa, then?"

The thoughts of sharing the isolated Wilcox farm with Hy's father did not appeal to her. Who in the name of heaven would she talk to with Hy gone for a soldier? She said, "No, not yet anyway. I don't want to tell Ma."

He got the boot on. "Oh, almost forgot, Clay's goin' with us."

Nudity forgotten, as though struck with a whip, she sat bolt up in bed. "What? And what am I to tell Ma?"

"Just tell her he done run off to the war, that's all." He tugged on the other boot.

"I will do no such thing, Hy Wilcox! And I forbid

you to take him with you."

He rammed his foot into the boot and stood up, stamping his feet to get the blood flowing in his toes and laughed. "Forbid me? What you talkin' about, Wife? The boy wants to go. I say let him go. Verboise'll either make him or break him. And if he quits he'll come runnin' home to his Aunty Dee faster than a mosquito dives fer blood."

"He will not go with you!" She scrambled out of bed, threw on her wrapper, and started calling Clay's name before she reached the door.

Hy caught her, penned her to him. Even stronger than it had been last night, at seven o'clock in the morning she shrank from his body's stale, sweaty odor.

"He's goin' Franny, an' there's nothin' you nor me can say to him. Don't you think I tried?"

Unable to break from his arms, frustrated and angry, she started to cry. "For the love of God, Hy, he's only 15 years old! And Ma will kill me if she thinks I encouraged him or allowed him to go."

"There were nothin' you could a-done to stop him. If'n he don't join up with us, he'll find another unit. They're formin' faster than fleas hatch on a dirty hound. An' don't you think it's better if he be with us, with me to watch out for him?" He put his arms around her to console her and patted her lightly on her shoulder as she wept.

"But, what if he should get hurt?" She raised a tear stained face to this strange man in her bedroom who called her, "Wife," and who had claimed her last night as his own.

"Nothin' to fear, honey."

He smiled down at her. In his eye she read assurance and contentment. Well, at least he was startin' the day with a happy heart. She only wished she could say the same for herself.

"I'll watch over him. I promise. He'll get back safe an' sound."

Without saying another word, he pecked her on the cheek and sailed out the door.

She stayed in her room the entire time the boys were yelling back and forth about getting breakfast with Verboise and what Clay should pack. Before he left, Clay knocked at her door. By now she was fully dressed for a day's work at Erin House. But she didn't open her door.

"Franny," her cousin called, "I'm a-goin' with Hy, now."

"Yes, I know." She called back through the closed door.

"Just tell, Aunt Dee...."

"I know what to say." Suddenly, she was weary and just wanted the leave taking to be over and the house astir only with paying guests.

"Well... bye then."

"Bye." She sat on the bed, watching the closed door, wondering if she might at least give her cousin a hug or some last minute instructions on being careful. But she didn't. Instead, she sat glum, sniffing back tears, feeling disappointment and anger tighten her belly and ball her fists.

She heard the door to the street close. Suddenly, the hotel settled into the genteel stir brought about by the goings and comings of mature guests. Only echoes remained of the noisy stomping and shouting brought on by four raucous boys - boys going off to war.

And Hy Wilcox had not returned to the room to give her a last goodbye kiss.

Friday the 10th

At midnight Franny stood over the ledger reco73ciling the weeks accounts. With both Ma and Clay gone and being alone in the apartment she hadn't been able to sleep. And so, after tossing in her bed for what seemed like hours, she decided to use the time. Also, the silence that prevailed through the hotel pleased her. No worrisome guest with a complaint or a question could interrupt her mental calculations. She was staring at Monday's assets and debits when what seemed like every bell in town suddenly shattered the cherished calm, and a boarder, a state legislator, burst into the lobby from the street. He shook with anger.

"What on earth... Can you tell me what's goin' on, Sir?" Franny called out to him, but she hadn't been quick enough. For he ignored her and immediately headed for the stairs. "Please, Mr. Gottsberg, pray tell me if you would please, why are the bells ringing so?" However, Franny found herself talking to Gottsberg's generous rump as he heaved himself to his room and muttered unchristian oaths.

"Not now, Miss," he yelled over his shoulder. "I must return to the House chamber." He disappeared into the gloom of the second landing.

Dressed only in her nightdress, covered with a wrapper and chaste shawl, she dared not venture outside. At the window she saw horsemen galloping up and down the street and yelling something unintelligible. Pouring out into the street, the girls from the sporting hotel two doors down shrieked with laughter.

They had carried with them their glasses of spirits and raised these to each horseman who thundered past. Beside them stood the usual motley crowd of drunken males and drifters who frequented the place. These hooted and cheered, shot off their pistols, and clasped their hands over their ears pretending to block out the din of the bells.

Afraid she'd be spotted watching them, Franny turned away in disgust. Yet, she longed to know what was going on. Within five minutes after he had lumbered up the stairs, the legislator flew back down carrying a leather bag. He stopped only long enough to blurt out the news. "We've just got word that Frank Blair, Captain Lyon, and

72

the Dutch have seized Camp Jackson. And that Lyon with 2000 Federal troops is coming here to arrest Governor Jackson, the legislature, and all state officers." He slammed the door behind him.

Awakened from slumber, by now many of the guests had come down to the lobby and for the rest of the night they kept watch with her, expecting at any moment a column of horned Yankees with cloven hooves to march down the street. Tycee arose and made sure everybody had enough coffee and warm biscuits with applesauce to keep them fortified in case of an invasion.

Elderly Colonel Potter, a permanent boarder, waved his antique sword in the air, swearing, "Now, ladies, there's no need to be frightened of a few Federal soldiers. The Governor deserves arrest, as does his treasonable government. If the army come here, I'll reassure them of Erin House's loyalty to the Union and not one hair on any female head will be harmed." He had retired from soldering and moved into Erin House eight years ago and had been like a grandfather to her, or at least, as she might imagine what a grandfather would be, having none of her own.

"But I'm frightened, Colonel Potter." She peered up at him and noticed the smile lines around his eyes and mouth.

His arm went around her and he pulled her head to his broad shoulder. "And why, child?"

"Hy Wilcox and Clay are at Camp Jackson. Remember? They went off with that Captain Verboise on Monday morning."

"Captain Lyon has taken the Camp Jackson men prisoners. He's Regular Army and will treat them fairly, not to fret, dear." He smiled and patted her hair but she took only partial comfort in his words. And for the rest of vigil she kept her fears locked within herself.

When by morning the rumor had not become reality,

some when back to bed, including the Colonel, and some began their daily routines, content that no great evil was to befall Jefferson City. But Franny couldn't shake the feeling that Clay and Hy had been hurt during the capture of Camp Jackson.

As usual, clogging mud and deep ruts slowed the way of carriages and wagons passing on High Street, while shoppers either strolled or hurried up and down the sidewalk. A few gathered in bunches talking about the incursion and arrest that never happened. At 11:00 on this Saturday morning the sun shone down full, and borne on a light river breeze smells from the tannery blew into the city.

Jeremiah Wilcox sniffed the air, thought, *bad as usual*. The tannery hadn't been the only smell that offended his nostrils. It was the combined odors of the town. Burning hides mixed with wood smoke, tobacco, and human sweat masked by rose water perfume and Florida Water aftershave. Adding to the aroma, a pile of fly-packed dung reposed in the gutter. He decided that if it weren't for the way the dang place smelled, his trips into the city would be near perfect.

And, as usual, sure as day followed night, with the coming of spring, here he was, as he'd been for years. The *Wilcox Farm* produce wagon parked at the corner of Madison and High Streets, he'd sell his homegrown produce and gossip with the customers.

On this busy Saturday morning, pretty near a week since Verboise's boys left for Camp Jackson, the girl stood at his produce wagon. He'd hoped for years that one-day Dee herself would come to the wagon, maybe talk with him a spell. But she always sent one of those free nigrahs of hers. At least today Dee Moone's little daughter had walked the block, made her first visit from Erin House. He knew, if her ma had been around she'd never have let the

74

girl come. But here she was, near to cryin' and wantin' to talk about the excitement last night in town and the riot in Saint Louis, yesterday.

"I heard tell, it were a pretty bad scramble," he said, eyeing her, noting that her eyes were the same misty green as her mother's. "Twenty-eight folks kilt—no Jeff. City folk nor none of our boys, though," he hurried to add when he saw her chin tremble.

She exhaled, "Thank God. My cousin Clay went with Hy and Captain Verboise. My mother and Mr. Otto Zimmer were there, too. Do you know what started the riot?"

At Zimmer's name he paused, feeling his hatred for the man boil in his stomach, finally said. "Seems like after only five days of drillin' and marchin' that Yankee Captain- reckon he's a gen'ral by now - ordered General Frost's surrender. Robinson on the ferry this morning said that a few days before, the Yankee had snuck around the camp dressed up like an old woman selling eggs. He saw some cannons and ammunition, figured Frost was gonna try and seize the United States arsenal in Saint Louis. So, gave him only 30 minutes to decide."

"After everybody realized they was surrounded by 7,000 damn Dutchmen, all Federal troops," he spit tobacco juice at the curb, continued, "they reckoned they'd better agree. So less than 700 innocent, Missouri boys was rounded up and marched through the city streets. They was takin' 'um to the United States arsenal." He put lettuce in her basket before he went on with his story.

He noticed the quiet way she waited for him, thought: *Sweet, real mannerly. Got a fancy education in Virginia, Hy said. Too bad for Hy, she's smarter'n him. He won't be able to tame her. I never could tame her ma, neither.*

"You understand," he said, now gathering radishes. "They was marchin' with guns and bayonets at their backs. No weapons of their own. All guns surrendered to the

Yankees." He stopped, wiped the sweat from his face with his kerchief. "All along the way," he went on, "the crowds was lined up on the sidewalk. And they is cheering our Militia and most was waving' Rebel flags. All at onst, somebody threw a stone and fired off a pistol and then Old Nick broke out." He finished putting the radishes in her basket and turned towards the onions.

"Twenty-eight people killed?"

He liked the way her pretty little face turned up at him, the way she hung on his every word. Made him feel important. He realized it had been a long, long time since a woman had made him feel important. Her mother had in the beginning, before she had slapped him across the face and sent him away. Before she had taken up with that damn Dutchy, Zimmer.

At these thoughts he felt the sourness again and said with more rancor than he intended, "Yep," he put the onions in the basket, "and two of 'um, daughter, was young'ens kilt - a little girl, twelve years old."

He watched her depart, noted the tiny waist, the sway of her skirts, and remembered she had flinched when he had called her "daughter." At that moment, he knew she didn't love his son.

On Sunday, Franny stole into Saint Peter's when mass was over and lit a candle, asking God to send her mother, Otto, and Clay home safely. Then she remembered as an afterthought, Hy. This made her feel more ashamed. For not only had she contracted a clandestine marriage that she knew Father Walsh would not approve, but also she realized she cared little for her husband. Poor Hy, she thought, You deserve better. What a fool I have been. She whispered, "And no way exists that can undo the wrong I have done." The tears flowed hot and silent down her face. To her way of thinking, she had no right to ask anything of God.

By some miracle on Monday her prayers were answered. Everybody came home - Dee, giving Clay the backside of her tongue every five minutes.

"Me wee nephew, ya are, an' too young ta be thinkin' of fightin'. Imagine meself surrounded by a shoutin' mob throwin' bottles and stones and people waving knives and pistols around. And there you be, marchin' proud as a peacock ye are, down the middle of the street. Ah, the shame of it all, the disgrace. Arrested--me own nephew was. Why, ye might have been killed! Now, 'tis the lung fever ye'll probably come down with from sleepin' on the arsenal's cold, stone floor all night. An' look at yer, all skinny and pale. Chile, 'tis Ireland I'll be a-shippin' ya back to, if'n ya tries to run off for a soldier again."

Clay only smiled, ducked his head, and kept on polishing an old rifle he'd found somewhere. "I ain't from Ireland, Aunt Dee. I was born here," he said, breaking into a full grin.

"Well, I'll make ye an honorary citizen, if'n I have too," Dee countered, never missing a beat. "And you stop shinin' them gums at me when I speak to you. Grinning like a Finnigan, ye are."

"Yes Ma'am," he said and laughed out loud.

At this, Dee stalked out of the apartment to tend to hotel business, and Franny laughed until she hiccuped.

"She's really angry, you know," Franny said, wiped tears from eyes and suddenly got serious. "And she has every right to be. Honestly Clay, what ever did you think you'd accomplish by going to Camp Jackson with Hy?"

"Learnin' how to be a soldier," He wrapped the gun's ramrod in a rag and ran it down the inside of the barrel as he spoke.

"Did you?"

"Suppose so." He looked up, faced her, "I learned the manual of arms, marchin', how to carry and take care of my rifle, more marchin.'" He chuckled.

77

So mild, so young, yet so confident, he seemed. Different from the bullied boy and slavish follower, who left with Hy, he had returned home completely in charge of himself, like a man, all grown up, she admitted to herself.

"What happened to you?"

"Nothin' 'cept I sniffed them Yankees up close and they smell bad." He made a face trying to be funny, failed to hide the deep anger behind the levity. She waited.

"After Verboise come and told us to strike tents and stack arms, we was all lined up and marched down the street. At first, the Federals put us in the center, while they marched on the outsides in two files. But, they put us in the way of the rocks when they started in to come and when the bullets started to flyin' they marched us on the outside of the line." He worked his jaw as he spoke and returned to the task of cleaning his gun. "Then when we gets to the arsenal, with nary a blanket between us, they make us sleep on the stone floor. And in the mornin' not even a cup of cold coffee, did any of us get. Cold water, instead, and a biscuit so hard I couldn't eat it. But that ain't all." He paused, became transfixed with working and cleaning the trigger mechanism.

"Well?" she asked after a silence.

"Next mornin', before they let us go, they make every jack man of us agree to a loyalty oath, sayin' we'd never take up arms against the United States again." His black look, so unlike him, made her recoil. "And, we ain't never took up no arms against the United States. So they had no cause to make us sign that piece of paper."

"Ma said you signed it."

"Had to, or I'd still be in there. Verboise told us it weren't gonna mean much, though, 'cause we signed it, "under duress," he called it."

"That must have been humiliating." Yes, she thought, I can see you passed an uncomfortable night and your

78

pride is hurt, "But," she said, "I don't see why you're so all-fired angry. You make the Federals sound like monsters."

His young face seemed to age 20 years. He laid the gun aside, said, "Franny, when them stones started to whizzin' by us, some of them soldiers fired right into the crowd. Only after the soldiers shot somebody did we hear comin' from the crowd the report of a pistol." He shook his fist. " That's how them young'ens come to be killed."

She couldn't believe what she just heard. American soldiers fired on civilian Americans because some hoodlum threw a stone.

On Friday morning Dee discovered Clay gone again. She raved and ranted, threatened to go to Richmond, to the Confederacy's President, Jeff Davis, lowered her sights and blamed Hy, but he sincerely disavowed all knowledge of the boy's whereabouts. Only Franny knew when and why Clay had left, but she didn't know where. And she certainly wasn't going to divulge to Ma that she had practically given her "wee cousin," a send off.

He had left last night. After everyone else had gone to bed and she had banked the parlor and the dining room fires, she caught Clay sneaking out of the apartment. In the flicker of the oil lamps lit in the hallway, she saw a blanket slung over his shoulder, a canteen dangling from his pack, and the now gleaming ancient rifle in his hand. She saw something else too, something that sent a shiver through her body. Tucked in his belt she recognized a Navy Colt revolver, the same kind that Captain Verboise, Hy, and several of the gang members carried.

She stopped him, heard her mother's voice when she demanded, "Just where do you think you're off to, Cousin?"

Instead of a blurted answer in his old cowed stammer, Clay met his cousin's frown with a lazy smile. At that moment with eyes dark as the Missouri and wide as the Mississippi, he had reminded her of a wise deer.

"I'm goin' to find my company," he said quietly, but pride and determination wrote itself all over his bearing. He pulled himself up to his full height, a few inches taller than she, and stared her down until she had dropped her eyes.

"Are you leaving a note, at least?

"And what would I put in it? You can tell her good-bye for me."

He turned to go but she clutched his arm, "But, what will I say, and besides, don't you want to be with Hy's boys?

"No." He stared at his work boots, then, faced her, "That Captain Verboise, he gives me the willies. Anyway, if'n I was to join up with him, that'd be the first place Aunt Dee would go to look for me and haul me back here."

He was right. She thought, He's so calm and still so young. On impulse she had pulled him to her and kissed him on the forehead. When she released him she choked on her tears, said, "Just let me know where you are. And please, dear Clay, like a younger brother you've been to me. Don't be..." She paused, searching for the word, exhaled, said,..." brave."

With one raised eyebrow, a quizzical look passed over his face, then he understood, nodded. He'd take no reckless chances with his life. The hotel door to the street closed behind him and he was gone.

The day after her cousin left Hy paid an afternoon visit, suffered Dee's interrogation, then sat with Franny on the back porch. In rocking chairs, both sipped lemonade and enjoyed the warm breeze floating up from the river bringing the odors of steamboats, hides, coal-oil - smells of the river.

"We've got to clear them Federals out," Hy said. "That means we've got to go after the Union men in Cole

County - course, most of them is "Dutch." He spat in the dirt.

So much like his pa, she thought, asked, "How are you going to go after them?"

"Well, let's just say, the boys will be pretty busy come most nights," and refused to say more about the matter.

Something disturbed her, the way he said this, his eyes sly and squinted, a sarcastic smile playing over his mouth. He too, had returned home, changed. She had never known Hy Wilcox to be "mean," as a bully is mean. But, now, he talked of "gettin' revenge," strutted around cracking his knuckles and threatening to "burn out the county if necessary." When he didn't visit her on Sunday afternoon she breathed a sigh of relief.

Sunday the 19th, midnight

Instead of visiting his bride of two weeks, that afternoon he had drilling tactics with the rest of the boys. Now Hy Wilcox loped his horse beside Verboise and observed the countryside's unholy glow beneath the full moon. Demonic shadows seemed to reach out to him from trees, bent and gnarled along the rutted road. Strange shapes appeared to jump into the bushes when he rode near. With yellow, insane eyes, old John Brown's face leered at him from every dark recess of the road.

Don't think about that, he ordered himself. It's all craziness. I must do my job. I am a soldier, now. John Brown is dead. He rehearsed this speech to himself, tried to breathe in the muggy night air. Just up ahead, around the curve, he'd strike his first blow in the county for Missouri's freedom. Wasn't Verboise always callin' um "righteous Missouri men?' His cause was righteous, was a true *holy* cause. But, his mind jeered, If that's true then why is the night around you seem so godless?

Presently, the gang rode up the pathway to the sleeping, farmhouse. At once, three mongrel dogs barked and rushed out from beneath the front porch. Kicking off the dogs, Hy knocked at the front door, waited, rapped again with the butt of his Navy. Behind him in the yard the rest of the boys had dismounted and crouched down to remain unseen. Two men scurried off towards the barn to run off the stock and light a torch. Verboise sat mounted in the shadows of a big oak tree in the front yard. And the dogs continued to bark.

From inside the house Hy heard mumbled curses. Even in German, a curse sounded like a curse. "Vas is der?" the voice hollered.

"Open the door," Hy called out, "I..." His voice faltered, "... Need help."

A scrambling with the locks, then the door flew open. A tall, stout farmer in nightdress and wrapper, holding high a lantern, stood framed in the doorway.

Without another word Hy rushed the man, hit him with his gun, and tore through the door. On his heels came the rest of the gang. By now the woman had come down the stairs and three small children followed her. Hy refused to look at her, as Verboise had taught him. Besides, she babbled and cried in German, and he didn't understand a thing she said. But he got her drift. Her tears and pleas may have come from an alien tongue, but their intent was all too human. But, he justified himself, thought *she shouldn't be in Missouri.*

"In here," Buster called out, "Here's the pretties." He held up a German mantle clock and two porcelain figurines. He started to smash them into the stone fireplace.

"No, Cowles!" Verboise stopped his arm. "They're valuable. Give them to me."

When Hy had finished searching the house for anything of value - money, clothes, jewelry - he went outside to set the torch. From the lump he had given him he could still hear the man moaning and the woman crying, even over the barking of the dogs.

Horton pushed the family into the front yard, still in their nightclothes. Before Hy fired the house he let the woman go back inside and get a few blankets for the children. Thinking about it later he wondered if maybe he shouldn't have revealed a kindness; for while being bustled into the yard, the farmer protested, turned on Horton who held a gun on him.

But Horton hit him, sent the German to the dirt from the blow he had given him. When he came around, Horton allowed the man to hitch up a rickety old wagon to a horse, half-dead from age, and load up his weeping wife and sobbing children. By the firelight from their home and barn going up in flames the wagon clattered out of the yard. Two of the dogs rode in the wagon with the immigrants. Verboise had shot the other one.

Several days later she confronted Hy. Under his nose she waved the newspaper, the story of the immigrant family on the front page.

"Hy is this what Verboise has you boys doing?" He didn't look at her, played with a stone at the toe of his boot. Then, the truth came to her. They were sitting on the wrought iron bench in the back yard whispering so as not to be overheard

"What if we was?" He caught her eye then, his smoldering with anger, almost daring her to speak.

I will not let him intimidate me she thought, said pertly, "Well, I wouldn't like it at all, if you were involved with anything like that, because," she had taken his hand, "because I'm afraid you'll be hurt."

"You're not put out with me?"

"Well, no, not exactly," she chose her next words very carefully, had feared he might erupt into one of his moody, temper fits. "But, is all that violence against those

83

people really necessary?"

"It's necessary, if'n we are to get the Union army out of Missouri." His response had been whispered in a tone so fierce she shrank back. He must have seen her recoil and had softened, "But, honey, look.... It's only temporary. Verboise's gonna get us in with the regular militia, any day now."

"I just hope Ma doesn't find out. It wouldn't do if she learned you were defending your Confederate beliefs by committing acts of theft and arson. She'd run you off with Otto's shot gun."

"Zimmer," he muttered, "another damn Dutchy." He turned on her. "I reckon I best warn you. There's talk about yore Ma and Zimmer. He's a loud mouth, always defendin' Lincoln and now that yore Ma has put up that damn Federal flag in the hotel lobby, she's being mentioned for...." He gulped, pushed on, ".... for revenge."

"What?" She couldn't believe she heard him correctly.

"I said---"

"---I heard you!" Now she was the one to glare. "So help me, God, Hy Wilcox, if you so much as lay a finger on Ma, or this hotel, I'll.... I'll shoot you myself." She rose abruptly from the bench and if Opal hadn't been hanging clothes in the yard just then, Franny would have smacked Hy's face.

Opal was the daughter of Tycee the best cook in Cole County. Years ago Ma had advertised for a cook. Tycee's owner had rented her out to Dee, himself keeping Tycee's wages. But Dee had paid the walnut colored woman a little "gravy money" each month that didn't get reported to the owner. In time, Tycee had made enough "gravy" to buy her and her two daughter's freedom.

"Well, she barely tolerates me coming around, and seeing that damn flag every time I come to see you gets me

84

madder than hell." He jerked her arm, made her sit back down, suddenly grinned, and caressed her hand. "But, I told the boys that you was my wife and whether I likes it or not, yore ma was my wife's mother, so I got to respect that." When she sat stone-faced, glaring at him, he laughed, "Oh come on, I was only joshin'."

"No you weren't. You wouldn't joke about somethin' like that. Not in these times."

"Oh, come on, now, I was. Come on; give us a pretty smile" He chucked her under the chin, said, "Besides, you don't know how to shoot a gun, and you couldn't kill yore own husband."

He started to kiss her, when she stopped him. "Don't." She nodded towards Opal, reminded him they were not alone. To allow the intimacy of a public kiss would be most improper, especially from one who was supposed to be only "a beau." Just then Tycee and Ruby, her younger daughter, took seats on the back porch to shell peas and Toby came whistling out of the livery stable.

Dee Moone had found him, a starving five-year-old abandoned by his mother, and hiding in the livery stable. After no one came forward to claim him, against the advice of everyone, she had not sold him off. Instead, she had raised him, and contrary to state law that made it a crime to teach Negroes how to read, she had educated him. When he turned 18, two years ago, she had freed him. But Toby elected to stay at Erin House and help run the place. Dee found him indispensable and paid him a handsome salary.

Next to Sigi Zimmer, Toby was Franny's best friend in the entire world. She knew he disapproved of Hy, even possibly suspected that more was afoot with this "beau" than she pretended. So when Toby came out of the livery stable she jerked herself to the other side of the bench, a movement witnessed by Toby's sharp glance.

"What you lookin' at, boy?" Hy snarled, bristling the

moment he saw the black man.

Toby nodded a greeting and ducked back inside the stable.

"I wish you hadn't of done that," she fussed, still feeling prickly because of his so-called jest.

"Damn, uppity nigrah, of yours." He glared at the retreating back. "Damn it all, Franny, if I even know why I married you. What with a damn Dutchy hangin' around yore ma, and her with her Union flag a-hitting me in the eye the minute I step inside the door, and them free coloreds on the place, it's all I can do to come visit you." He breathed into her ear, whispering even more softly, "But I keep hopin' that maybe, I can see my wife alone." With one eye on Opal at the clothesline and observing that Tycee and Ruby seemed to be fixated upon their chore, he drew her to him and tried, again, to kiss her.

"I said, don't," she pulled away. "You know, we have to act like we're just courtin' and you're just my beau. You kissin' me out here like this wouldn't look right."

"I might be able to come around in the evenin' when we're not ridin'." He murmured, "we could sit outside in the dark like we done before we married."

The thought of his hands on her made her skin crawl. She whispered, "No, Ma's up all hours, roamin' around the hotel, checkin' on this or that. The truth is she's afraid she'll be asleep if Clay should come back home in the night." She frowned, rose, said, "Come inside with me and sit in the parlor."

"But, sugar," he pleaded, "I want you." He whined, his voice tinged with anger, "We're married. I've got my rights."

Franny led him inside, into the parlor where old Colonel Potter, a veteran of the War of 1812, dozed beside the fire.

She settled herself beside the open window to catch

the light as she sewed on a new dress she was making. Although, Hy still looked unhappy, she had turned the conversation to his pa. "Did you ride in with him this morning?"

"Yep," he sat on the brocade couch and stared at her. She guessed he was still thinking about her - *that* way -but she refused to speak of it.

"What does he think about Captain Verboise stayin' at your place?"

"He thinks it's a good idea." He, sighed, seemed resigned that she would hold him at arms length as she had ever since he'd been back from St. Louis, asked as a parting thought on the issue, "Are we ever gonna be able to be man and wife, Franny? How long are you not goin' to tell yore Ma we is married?"

"Hush!" She glanced at the snoring Colonel, his hands over his pudgy stomach.

"Hell, he's sleepin'. Answer me!"

"Soon." She fought for an excuse, a reason, anything. Got her answer, said hurriedly, "When she's not so frantic about Clay's leaving - when I'm old enough.... Oh, for heavens sakes, Hy Wilcox, don't badger me. Now is not the time. There is a war on. You seem to have forgotten," she hoped she sounded stern.

At first, she thought he'd leave, so restless did he become. Flying off the couch, pacing the room, cracking his knuckles, he didn't speak for some time. At last he sat back down and his manner had totally changed. It never ceased to amaze her, how he could swing from one mood to another from one minute to the next.

He sat watching her sew with his hands relaxed in his lap, then out of the blue blurted, "Wanna help us?"

Never giving his question any real thought she answered quickly, her mouth full of pins and her response sounded like "How me?"

Furtively, he looked about, saw only Colonel Potter

87

still asleep, and leaned his body near. Whispered, "Verboise thinks you could help us. And I reckon you could."

Something about the way he mentioned his captain rattled her. Ever since the day of her wedding, she had thought the man looked upon her as a nuisance. She took the pins from her mouth but didn't answer. While she pushed the pins one by one into the pincushion at hand, he said, "Might help change some wrong ideas about you folks here at Erin House if'n you did."

Immediately she got his drift. Thought, So, that was it. I help the gang and they call off any plan of hurting Ma or Erin House. At first, the thought that Hy felt he needed to bargain with her made her so angry she almost ran from the room. Reflection, though, brought the hope that instead, he may be trying to warn her.

Breathing deeply to calm herself, she became aware that for the first time, she truly feared him, feared his gang, feared Captain Verboise. Thought, God only knew what they are capable of. She dared to ask, "Hy, please tell me the truth. Are we in danger here at Erin House?"

"Let's just say, honey," he peered at the Colonel, whispered, "If'n somebody should get the notion that your Ma was serious 'bout her political affections - and not just some old woman actin' the fool, like I done tried to explain to some folks - then I couldn't say what they might do."

"I see." Her voice choked and she put her head in her hands and cried. Through her tears she said, "You've made her out to be a fool, an idiot, because she believes in the Union. Hy, you are…." She broke off, wiping her eyes.

At once he knelt on the floor beside her. "Franny, I'm sorry, I didn't mean no disrespect to yore ma. I just had to come up with something when Verboise asked me about her."

"Verboise?" She sniffed, "Now, you're tellin' me that

he wants me to do something to help y'all, and if I do he'll leave us alone?"

"Oh, it ain't exactly like that. He just needs a pretty girl to set a trap for us, and he suggested that you might be that girl." He stroked her hair, said hoarsely, "and you are mighty pretty, indeed."

"What would I do?" She moved to avoid his hand.

"Just wave at a boat on the river."

Early the following Sunday morning she faced her mother. "Ma, I'll only be gone for a few hours. Sigrid needs me to help her with her new spring frock. We haven't had anytime together since all this war business started. Besides, you and Mr. Zimmer always go for a drive on Sunday after Mass and everybody else around here always goes somewhere."

Dee stood just inside Franny's bedroom door, arms folded across her chest, brow knotted in worry. "I suppose, takin' me for a drive, Otto could do without today. Then, 'tis be here I will if'n your wee cousin should come back."

"---- Oh Hidee Ho! Ma, he's not wee and he's not comin' back, at least not any time soon." She cut her mother off, but smiled. "You know Governor Jackson has called for 50,000 men to fight the Federal army. Clay's probably with a militia group." Franny pinned on her straw skimmer and examined her reflection in the mirror. "Besides, if you weren't so goat-headed you'd be proud of him."

"Aye, but he's too young and he's gone for a soldier, fightin' on the wrong side!" She threw up her hands in the gesture meaning surrender, "But what can I do?" To herself added, "Sure, a goin' after him, I should." She watched Franny for a moment smoothing her flyaway curls under the hat and offered one last objection to her departure. "Tis riffraff, the streets are filled with. What with all the men pourin' into the city, to join up an' all.

89

Mind yerself."

"I'll be fine, Ma. Everybody in town knows me and if I have a problem, I'll just holler," she reassured, "and look at the time, not even eight o'clock. It's too early for the riffraff to be awake, yet."

Twenty minutes later Franny arrived at the Zimmer home, in "Germantown," a few blocks south west of the hotel. On his way out Otto greeted Franny, glad to see her. "On der way to see your mother," said the huge German with pale blue eyes that had never met a stranger. With a balding head and a comfortable paunch, he carried with him an aura of buoyant strength. Since she had been five years old, Otto Zimmer had been friend, surrogate father, and she wondered lately, if also her mother's lover. As her dalliance with Hy had become more intimate, she had become aware of the subtle nuances of romance between her mother and the well-to-do Bavarian immigrant.

"Sigri and I'll just sew and talk. Later, we'll go to the park and hear the band play. Will you stay at Erin House for supper?" she asked, hoped he'd say yes.

"*Ja*, sure. As long as your mother will let me stay," he winked and strode out the door, seeming to leave the room only half-alive.

China Sigrid Zimmer and Franny Moone - as different in appearance and temperament as any two girls could be. People often remarked on the oddity of their friendship. Yet, each girl regarded the other as her dearest confidant, as close as a sister. Curvaceous Franny an inch or two above five feet; slender Sigrid nearly three inches taller. Franny fought daily with the red curly mop she inherited; Sigrid's long, silky smooth black hair lay easily in a loose bun at the nape of her elegant neck. Poor Franny contended with a raft of light freckles across her high cheekbones and nose; unblemished was Sigrid's ivory skin. Opinion held that in Sigrid Zimmer, the blending of

90

Aryan blue eyes surrounded by Chinese features had created the most exotic looking young woman in the city.

Today Sigrid's eyes sparkled with devilish excitement. When she smiled they scrunched up at the corners—little crinkles with blue jewels at their centers. Just as when she and Sigrid had been children, Franny was drawing reserved, shy Sigrid into something she knew she shouldn't be doing.

"So, you're meeting Hy Wilcox? Oh, that's so romantically wicked!" Sigrid squealed with glee when she was sure her father had lumbered down the porch stairs.

"Yes. He wants me to visit with his pa and some other relatives I haven't met yet. I'd love to include you, but I need you in case Ma gets suspicious." Feeling a twinge of conscience, Franny hugged her best friend. Not even Sigrid knew she and Hy had secretly married.

"It's too bad your mother doesn't like him. I think he's very respectable,"

Franny tucked a stray curl beneath her hat. "Oh you know Ma; she's so pro-Lincoln that she hates anybody who isn't." Taking Sigrid's hands in hers she admonished, "Remember, I've been with you every minute."

Sigrid nodded, delighted to conspire for the sake of "romance." Then, pecking her "cover" on the cheek, Franny flew out the door.

The Wilcox rig was parked at the corner of Sigrid's street, and Hy waited to help her into the carriage. Because of the early hour, not a soul stirred within the quiet neighborhood. No one saw her enter the carriage and drive away towards the Saint Louis road. Today she would strike a blow for Missouri's independence. Today she would exercise her loyalty towards the Southern cause. Today, she would wave at a boat.

Verboise watched the girl alight from the Wilcox buggy. She had courage, he had to give her that much. His eyes played over her figure and he compared her to his

Nina, something he hadn't done to a woman in years. He realized where his mind was leading him and cut the thoughts off at once, surprised that after this length of time he could still harbor such urges. By the time Hy brought her to him he had regained his rigid control.

"Sir, my wife is here for your orders." His lieutenant saluted, stood proud and iron-faced beside the girl with hair of golden fire and eyes of misty green.

He hadn't really expected her to agree, but here she was, and he caught himself staring at her. But she stared back, never wavering, craning her neck up to meet his gaze. Neither did she simper or smile as some women did in his presence, or exhibit nervousness or fear. Gone was the coquette he had met nearly a month ago. Before him stood a serious young lady ready to go to war.

"Take off your hat," he barked.

Without comment she took it off.

"Loosen your hair."

She unpinned her hair, allowed the ringlets to flow around her shoulders, over her bodice. Her beauty stunned him. Thought, *She could have had Prince Albert if she'd met him before Victoria had. Instead, this pretty child chose the bumpkin farm boy, Hy Wilcox. Why?*

"Stay the way you are. I will give you further instructions when we get to the bluff." He turned to the farm boy lieutenant, "Prepare the men to mount up."

"Yes Sir."

Hy obeyed at once and left them standing in the Wilcox yard. Around the pair milled the gang's other men, cinching saddles, checking their guns and ammunition. Curious glances darted their way but not one dared ask why Hy Wilcox's wife was there, with her hat off, and her hair flaming down her back. Or why, their commander seemed transfixed by this female. They knew better than to question him.

"All the men will be on horseback. You will follow

in the carriage. Can you handle the rig by yourself?"

"Yes."

That was all she said. Most women would have immediately protested, pointed out the inconvenience of a woman dressed in her Sunday clothing handling the reins of a carriage alone. Or she would have whined that her white gloves might get soiled. Or insisted that one of the men drive the rig for her. Or - something. But she did not. Instead, she answered him the way he would have answered - taciturn, to the point.

"Are you afraid?" At the question he thought he saw her eyelash flicker and she exhaled before she answered, but she never dropped her gaze.

"Yes," she said and bit her lower lip, "but I'll get over it."

This made him smile. Not much did. He thought, *what an incredible woman she is. If I can teach her how to shoot a revolver, but, no. That can wait.*

"You amaze me, Mrs. Wilcox. You speak the truth. Fear holds us all, but not many admit it. Come, I will escort you to the porch where you may rest in the shade while we prepare to go." He took her elbow to lead her across the yard and noticed how delicate the bones in her arm felt to his touch.

Fifteen miles upriver from Jefferson City, on a bluff overlooking the river, Franny stood, waited, watched. At high water from spring melt and run off, the Missouri's color was a deep, muddy brown, almost black. Thick stands of maples, sycamores, and black willows lined the banks. The odors of spring filled the mild air, borne in on a river breeze. Beneath the oily river smell, she caught the scents of dogwood, shag bark hickory, redbud trees and wild roses. Then she saw it.

The passenger packet, *White Star* rounded the bend, ran at mid-channel.

Franny jumped up and down, called out to the little

side-wheeler, waved her hat in the air. She continued this until the boat's master waved back from the steamer's bow, and the whistle gave a merry little toot signaling that in the bright sunshine he saw her. For a heartbeat she felt sorrow for the boat and its captain, wanted to yell a warning. Then she remembered her resolve. Like Hy, she was now a soldier, following orders.

She stayed atop the bluff smiling at the ship's master until the boat touched the bank, then she ran to a grove of trees where she had hidden the Wilcox two-seater. Her heart thumped in her chest, cold sweat ran down her back. Getting away was all that mattered. Coming out from the Wilcox farm the aging bay gelding pulling the rig had responded well to her light touch on the reins. But, when, panting, she ran up to the carriage and threw herself on the rig's seat, he snorted and rolled his eye. When she slapped the reins, jerked them hard, the horse reared and dashed off at a gallop. Not until they were off the bluff and on the hard packed road headed for the Wilcox Farm did she get the horse under control. And like the wind, panic whistled in her ear until the carriage clattered into the Wilcox farmyard.

As soon as the boat touched the bank, Verboise's men jumped on her main deck, bow, and stern. As practiced, the raiders swarmed all three levels of the little packet, depredations occurring simultaneously. Hy made sure Farmer Biddle oversaw the stokers and immigrant crew of German and Irish roustabouts. These men worked the main deck, fired the wood-eating furnace and boilers, loaded and unloaded cargo. He figured, rightly, they'd give the gang little trouble. The crew seemed to welcome the chance to sit down, even if their hands were on top of their heads and two scowling marauders stood over them with cocked and loaded pistols.

Half-dozen free Negroes, "gold on the hoof," according to Verboise, were part of the crew. Regardless of any freedom-giving manumission papers they might show, Verboise told Biddle to march the "darkies" to Bonnot's Mill where they would be jailed until resold.

At the third level, Verboise locked the good-hearted captain in the wheelhouse with the pilot, the clerk, and the engineer, after relieving these gentlemen of their wallets and robbing the boat's safe.

The rest of the gang sprinted up the stairs to the second level, to the passenger decks. The boiler deck held the main and passenger cabins. These opened out upon the narrow promenade. The roof of the boiler deck, the hurricane deck, gave passengers the opportunity to sit or stand in the open breeze. In the center of this deck, stairs led up to the pilothouse and cabins for the captain and the relief pilot. When seen from afar, the boat resembled a layer cake, with the three decks piled upon the other. The main cabin held card tables and barroom and doubled as dining room. Hy placed Horton in charge of rounding up all the passengers and herding them onto the boiler deck. Then, while all the male passengers turned out their pockets and handed over their valuables, Hy led Buster and Li'l Chess McDonald on a lightening run to the saloon.

Something was wrong with Hy. A queer numbness invaded his feet and hands as he moved towards the saloon. He was perspiring yet shivered with cold. He chided himself, What had he expected - to stay in "training" forever? He knew from the outset that this day would come.

He had gotten over his squeamishness at burning down the homes of the damn Dutch farmers hadn't he? After all, the immigrants were all Lincoln lovers, weren't they? So let them gather up what his gang didn't take and skedaddle to the nearest army post so the Federal army could give them victuals, right? He could even look away when their women and children cried and begged. Even chuckled to see the men, filled with impotent rage and fear unable to stop the destruction of their homes. He might have had to rough up a few who tried to fight back, but he hadn't killed anybody. Not yet anyway.

Today, Verboise ordered him to kill men. Men who have given him no personal reason. But, being a partisan soldier meant that he would, eventually, have to shoot a man who hasn't drawn on him first. He would have to kill without compunction or thought.

In the second before he knew he must give the order to kill, Hy glanced at the two men beside him. Toughened up from that first day when he had sobbed for mercy and shit his drawers, Chess McDonald had made him proud. The cold glint from McDonald's Colt, cocked to spew death at his command, matched the cold gleam in the boy's eye as he readied his aim. Buster's usual faint smile broadened to a satanic smirk, and he steadied his pistol on the door, ready to blaze away when they threw it open.

From inside the main cabin Hy heard loud laughter, smelled the thick smoke from cigars and pipes. So quiet, so quick had the take over of the *White Star* been that the card players were unaware the boat was under attack. Hy wondered, *am I the only one of us to draw back from murder? For murder it is, thoughtless, unprovoked, unless you see all Federals as enemies and thereby to be murdered on sight.*

Verboise had spent hours drumming into their heads that the target was the enemy, not a human being. He had said something else, too. *Don't lose your head through anger or fear. A partisan's worst enemies are his emotions. Watch your opponent's actions, try to guess what his next move will be, and prevent him from making it.* It beat a tattoo through his mind as he burst through the saloon door, firing at every blue uniform in sight.

One lieutenant about to take a sip of his whiskey slumped over the table, a bullet through his head, his glass spilling brownish liquid over his cards. A captain dove under a table, drew his pistol, got off a shot, and hit McDonald in the shoulder before Buster fired low and the captain's brains sprayed over the floor. Several Federals, caught without personal side arms, jumped out of the line of fire, stood with their hands up, pleaded for mercy, begged to be taken prisoner. Without hesitation Hy drilled them down. Verboise had no time for prisoners.

In less than five minutes the massacre was over. Civilians cringed beneath tables and behind the bar with the barkeep. A bullet skimming his scalp had grazed a heavy-set man and he howled in pain. Thirteen Federal officers and enlisted men lay dead.

Over the room's haze engendered by the gun smoke silence fell. Hy surveyed the carnage, a carnage that mocked the bright elegance of the saloon. From the chandelier, grander than anything Hy had ever seen, gleamed a hundred candles. Intensified and shattered into myriad points of light, the glass picked up the glow from each candle. A bullet had struck the gilt-edged mirror hanging behind the bar. Shards of glass had flown everywhere, spilling over the floor and bar. Larger pieces stubbornly clung in the frame and reflected the blood of the dead staining the polished oak tables and floor. Strange, he thought, remorse neither wracked him; nor glee tickled his heart. He felt nothing. Empty. Tugging at him was only a void that threatened to suck him into eternal darkness. Looking at the dead bodies, he suddenly wondered *did John Brown feel this way after Pottawatomie?*

McDonald's hit was only a flesh wound. He helped Buster line up the civilians, methodically commanded each one to "turn out yore pockets."

"Who are you boys?" Dared to ask an older, wiry man wearing a coarse tweed jacket and a worker's billed cap. He handed over a gold pocket watch and a five-dollar gold piece.

Buster was about to respond when Verboise walked into the saloon. He surveyed the dead soldiers, noted the civilians, asked, "Which of you favor Jeff Davis?"

Silence from the line gave Verboise's answer. Finally, a man stepped forward. "I do, Sir." Both tone and proud stance proclaimed the man's defiance.

Verboise eyed him, a cynical curl to his lip, his finger stroking the trigger of his gun. Finally he nodded, said "Thank you, Sir. Be assured your contribution today will go to serve the Confederate cause." He eyed the others, asked, "Is there anyone else?"

Two more stepped forward, not as defiant. Again Verboise saluted them. Three remain undeclared. Verboise said, "Then, I can assume the rest of you support the Lincoln government."

"Yes, Sir! I do!" He was the one grazed in the head, fat, expensively dressed, red faced, had the look of a lover of whiskey. "I am an attorney at law from Lawrence, Kansas and believe the Constitution of the United States is the most glorious document ever written by human hands. This rebellion is illegal, unconstitutional and----"

Verboise's shot didn't allow him to finish what was tuning up to be a dandy defense of Unionist's beliefs, in Hy's opinion. The attorney crumpled to the floor, blood staining the carpet and his silk cravat. This time, the bullet found its mark.

Of the two men left in line, one immediately declared himself a "conditional secesh. I just want to be left alone." Dressed in canvas pants and jacket and a felt slouch hat, he appeared to be a farmer from up river.

"Not good enough, friend." But Verboise studied him, knew many in the state took his view, asked, " How far would you go to assure your neutrality."

The farmer blinked, unsure of the question, then, "I wouldn't lift a finger to help the Unionists and I won't

98

fight ag'in my neighbors and don't want my boys to join up on either side." He straightened up as tall as he could, coming to the guerrilla's chest.

Verboise grunted, said. "That your contribution today will go to our southern sisters to fight the Union aggression within their borders is acceptable to you?"

"I reckon so, since you put it that way," answered the farmer.

Verboise stared the man in the eye until he moved to the last one to state his political position. It was the man who had asked who they were just before Verboise entered the saloon.

The bandy-legged man with a handsome gray mustache returned Verboise's unblinking stare.

Like Goliath towering over David, Verboise trained his revolver on the man, and with his eyes examined his features one by one. Finally, he said, "I know you, Sir."

"Well, now, 'Tis a poor sight ya got for knowin' this old Mick, Sir." He answered, grinned, showing tobacco-stained teeth.

"Take off your cap," Verboise ordered.

"Beg pardon, Sir, but I'm a wee bit shy of showin' off me ugly baldness," he said, winked. But when Verboise gestured with his pistol, the man quickly doffed his cap and ran a hand over a graying bald spot.

"Sergeant Brady," Verboise exhales the name.

"Aye," Brady crinkled his watery blue eyes and smiled.

"You were riding with the First Cavalry the last I knew of you. Has that changed?"

"Yep, retired out after 40 years, mind you. This here war's gonna get too hot, ain't it now, for this old soldier? Me sister and her man in Saint Louis wants me to come and spend out me days with them. Don't that beat all?"

Verboise wavered, uncertain. It was the first time Hy had ever seen this fierce commander appear undecided.

99

Finally, he decided. "I must kill you, old friend. You know that."

"Ya wouldn't shoot an unarmed man, now?" Still seemingly unafraid, Brady opened his coat, showed he carried no weapons, said, "Now, come on, Lad, what would yer be wantin' to shoot old Brady, for?"

Hy had never thought of Verboise as a "lad." But next to this old-timer he supposed he was.

"I must do what I must, Brady. I always have. You know who I am and too much about me, and although you've left the regiment you're still a Union man." Verboise raised the gun's barrel.

Brady put his hand on the barrel, pulled it down, grinned, said, "Sure, an' I remember many a good chuckle, an' even a wee tear or two have we had. Oh, by the way, remember that lad from New York? 'Twas the skinny one. All mouth, he had, and a real scrapper. He's become a bloomin' first lieutenant, don't cha know. Now, then, aren't ya done up proud to know that ya made a rattlin' good cavalry officer outta him?"

"Scarborough didn't want to come with me when I left. I could have made an even better soldier out of him."

"Aye, you could if anyone." Not intimidated at all, Brady talked to Verboise as though they had run into each other in the Town Square instead of in a barroom where 14 men lay dead. His tone was soft, almost conspiratorial, and for anyone else but Verboise, thoroughly disarming. Hy half expected the old man to take the captain's arm, suggest they down a glass together while in the saloon.

He leaned into Verboise, whispered, "What in the name O' the maker have ye got yourself into, man?"

"You know why I left. You should know what I am doing."

"Aye, I think I might have an' idea. But, tis not me you need to be a-fearin'. Besides, what would Nina say if she saw yer now? Ya always said she was watchin' from

100

above, all the time."

It was as though a light turned off, or on, Hy couldn't decide which. Verboise stood transfixed, gazed at Brady, put a hand on his shoulder, said, "It's war, old friend." Then, he turned his face away. Though he wouldn't swear to it, Hy thought he saw a tear.

Just as suddenly as he had turned away, Verboise faced back, once more in control, leveled his revolver on Brady, barked to Hy, "Take the civilians to the boiler deck with the others."

The second of attention diverted to Hy was all Brady needed. Before Verboise could shoot, Brady, spun his body completely around in a blur of speed, came back, kicked Verboise's revolver across the room, and ducked behind a table. Awed by the maneuver, still, Hy fired his own gun at Brady, missed, fired again. The bullet hit Brady's arm, but by now, the old soldier had bobbed and weaved his way through the saloon door.

Giving chase didn't apprehend Brady. No sooner was Hy out the door after him, then he heard a splash at stern and saw the small, muscular body, flailing the water and furiously trying to stay afloat. When he appeared to sink beneath the boat, Verboise turned away. Hy thought it odd that his chief made no effort to find Brady in the water and make sure he was dead, although Hy and several others offered to go in after him.

Falling into war, that's what Missouri was doin', the widow Moone decided. From her parlor window she watched the state militia march and drill up and down High Street in front of Erin House. Thought, 'Twas the whole state sinkin', like a stubborn man in quick sand refusin' the rope of help. Sure, the Federal General Nathaniel Lyon possessed as much charm as thistle burr, but hadn't Lincoln pledged to be fair to Missouri?

Draped across the balcony of the sportin' house down

the block she saw a Confederate flag. Thought of the governor of Missouri and became furious when she did. 'Twas all his fault, that traitor, Cleb Jackson, plottin' to turn the state over to the South ever since takin' the governor's office, he was.

With sorrow, she watched the boys and men shoulder their muskets, perform the manual of arms, and march by fours to the sound of a trilling fife and the beat of a bass drum. They reminded her of Clay, gone over ten days. She thought *right this very minute, more than likely, me wee nephew is drillin'--only the sainted Mother knows where.* A deep sigh escaped her. The pain of not knowing Clay's whereabouts clutched at her heart and a tear strayed down one cheek. But, she thought, I've only me ill tempered self to blame.

She pulled out the hanky she always kept tucked up her sleeve, dabbed at her eyes, remembered. 'Twas Clay had trembled to hear the Banshee howlin' in the night when a babe. But after St. Louis, the boy seemed different. Quieter he was more in possession of himself. She chastised herself, *but ya didn't want ta see it, old woman, didn't want to admit that, overnight, 'twas a man me nephew had grown to and no longer was scared by the midnight winds.*

"With no thanks to his father, even if he was me own brother," Dee grumped still watching the soldiers drilling from her window. She remembered how from near infancy she had raised Clay Monihan. His blessed mother dying' givin' birth to a stillborn girl. Six months later his father dyin' of the drink. Fell into the river, he did, and drowned. Thought, *just like Missouri's gonna do for sure, drown in a sea of blood.*

"Made the lad miserable, I did," she muttered to herself and wiped another tear from her eye. Thought, 'Twas me damnable tongue. Always jawing at him. She sniffled into the hanky, her tears breaking out in earnest.

102

"Pardon, Madam," the address from the short, rotund man standing in the parlor's doorway broke into her thoughts. He watched her closely. "I have observed your distress these few moments past, may I offer myself to be of service?"

One of the new legislators boarding from Saint Louis, St. Charles county, she had forgotten the name but recognized him. Dabbing at her eyes, Dee attempted a smile, "Oh, mercy, Sir, but you give me poor self such a startle."

She motioned for him to sit on the brocade sofa while she sat nearby in a matching chair. As she rattled on about her fears for Clay she waved the perfumed hanky in front of her face as though it were a fan. When she had finished the legislator pulled at his gray whiskers, and mused upon his landlady's predicament.

"Hmm, that is distressing. Fifteen did you say?"

"Yes, still just a boy." She sighed and noticed the mustard stain on the legislator's cravat. Suddenly, his name popped into her head - Gottsberg, a lawyer. So quiet he had been, she barely had noticed his presence over the past week.

"Well, perhaps he will be found out and turned out. Then he'll have to come home." Gottsberg smiled to reassure her.

"Found out? What's to be found out?"

"He's underage."

Dee stared at him waiting for him to finish his thought.

"A lad must be eighteen," he emphasized, "and in some units of the army he must be twenty - one years of age before they will recruit him. Did you not know that, Madam?"

She hadn't known that information.

When Franny learned that 14 men had been gunned

down on the *White Star* she had waited until she was finally alone, gone into her bedroom, and become hysterical. She wailed to herself, "I, only I am to blame. I lured the little boat and ultimately, those poor men to their deaths." She cried out to God to forgive her. Thought seriously of confessing all to Jeff City's Constable Rhodes then remembered that if she did, the gang would probably retaliate by hurting Ma and maybe burning down the hotel.

When Hy Wilcox arrived for a visit the next day, after she had seen the account in the newspaper, it was all she could do to control her rage. Whispering in the back yard on the iron bench, again with the staff going and coming, she had lashed out at Hy.

"What if they realize that I'm the red-headed girl that lured the boat to shore?" She twisted her hanky, dabbed at her eyes.

"Sugar, there's plenty of redhaired females in Missouri. None as pretty as you though." He leaned close enough to nibble on her ear.

"Stop it," she hissed, "How could you murder 14 men the way you did?"

"Honey, they weren't men, they was Yankee soldiers, in uniforms. We's at war and Yankees are the enemy. Besides," he swallowed, continued, his voice as smooth as honey, "I didn't kill nobody." When she only stared, not believing him he said, "Honest, see, cross my heart." And he made the sign of the cross on his chest.

He finally left, leaving her with a bleak sense of shame and a shaky feeling of assurance that they would not be caught. Except for Verboise, other descriptions of the men had been sketchy and general. They could have fit anybody, any farmer, any youth in Cole County. Nevertheless, she fairly jumped with delight when Ma said to her after breakfast the next morning, "We're huntin' yer wee cousin, today."

She couldn't think of anything else she wanted to do

more, at that time, then to get out of Jeff City.

"I thought you'd be poutin' and complainin' but you're actin' all eager to go." Ma eyed her suspiciously. "Ah, I see," she exhaled, " wantin' to get away from that damnable Hy Wilcox, are ya? Well, good you should, child. Now, come along and pack. 'Tis Sigrid I've called to come around and keep things runnin' smooth while we're gone. She and Toby and the girls will do just fine. A' course, Otto will be lookin' in daily."

CHAPTER THREE
June

Wednesday the 12th 2:30 A.M.

With Dee and Franny away Sigrid and her father occupied the apartment. For several days all ran well. The hotel stayed filled with legislators and drummers selling everything from shoes to saddles. Then, while the moon still hung above Jefferson City, Sigrid awakened from a sound sleep to hear someone trying to beat down the hotel's front door. At first she thought it was a dream. But when pulled from sleep, she realized what it was she heard and became terrified.

"Papa!" She called out to her father asleep in Clay's room. He'd closed up the *Royal* around midnight and hadn't been asleep long. Racing into his room she shook him awake.

Pulling on wrappers the two converged in the hallway with Toby who also had heard the commotion. In his nightshirt, Toby held up the lamp and waited for a nod from Otto before he lifted the heavy bar locking the door.

From the open door the faceless voice came loud and urgent. "Yes, awaken all state representatives that board here, please, and do it now! The governor and General Price got back from Saint Louis about half hour ago and they are calling a special session of the legislature at the Capitol. General Lyon has declared war on the state of Missouri."

Sigrid felt a surge of fear tingle through her fingers and toes. Nonetheless, she asked, "May we offer you some hot tea, sir?"

"Can't ma'am. Thank you kindly, anyway. There's only me and three others calling at every lodging-house in town." He hurried away and Sigrid rattled off the names and rooms of those legislators that currently slept beneath Dee Moone's roof and ate her food. "And don't forget Mr. Gottsberg," Sigrid called after Toby already sprinting up the stairs to sound the alarm.

"I go, too." Otto said, stumping back to the apartment to get dressed.

"But, Papa, you're not a state legislator."

"*Truden* daughter, but I'm a city alderman. I go to find out."

Sigrid went into the kitchen to set the coffee to boil. But already, Tycee had put the kettle on and was laying out cold cornbread spread with peach jam.

"This is frightening," Sigrid said and helped lay out the cornbread. "Ever since Governor Jackson defied the president's order to send troops, the legislature has been in an uproar."

"I heard there's been fist-fights and de mens is comin' to chamber carryin' rifles and pistols," said Tycee, dark eyes wide with excitement and turbaned head nodding for emphasis.

"Well, I'm not surprised," Sigrid said, sadness welling up like a mushroom in her chest. "When you have planters wanting to secede, poor farmers wanting to stay loyal, and everybody else praying we can stay neutral - it's a wonder no one's been killed yet."

"Dat's true, Miss Sigrid. I just pray de good Lord stays off de war. Mrs. Dee, she say, it's a-gonna be a blood-bath, if'n it comes."

"And I'm so afraid she's right, Tycee." Unbidden, a tear trickled down Sigrid's cheek. Spontaneously, both women hugged one another, wept over what both prayed would not happen, but knew in their hearts would come with bitterness and death.

By the time the water for coffee boiled, Otto had dressed and the lawmakers had clamored down the stairs. They wiped sleep from their eyes and pulled on coats as the women handed each man a tin of hot coffee and a napkin of cornbread and jam to take with him.

Returning to bed seemed impossible, so Sigrid gathered in the kitchen with Toby and Tycee to drink coffee, eat cold cornbread -to keep a vigil - to pray.

By dawn the men were back, grim faced and frightened. Without a word the legislators rushed up the stairs to their rooms. But Otto and Gottsberg stopped their debate to report to the three, solemn faces hovering in the lobby.

Before Otto could open his mouth an angry Gottsberg said, "Lyon turned down Jackson's offer that if Federal troops were kept out of Missouri, then the state would stay in the Union but remain neutral. As I stand here now, Lyon is preparing to attack this city. Jackson and Price are going to flee with the State Documents and the State Seal. He will establish a new capital somewhere else in the state. He also urged all government officials to leave at once, or face arrest by the United States government." He must have noticed Sigrid's stricken look for he paused, said more softly. "I am sorry, Miss Sigrid, how rude of me to upset you so. Please tell Mrs. Moone that I have enjoyed my stay here very much and I do hope she is able to apprehend her young nephew. " He made a courtly bow and hurried up the stairs behind the others to start packing.

"It's true then," Sigrid searched her father's face. "The meeting Lyon had with the governor, General Price and those other men at the Planter's House came to naught?".

"Ja, child," Otto said, pulled her to him and allowed her to weep on his chest. Looking at Toby and Tycee over her head he continued, "He give Jackson and Price one hour to leave town. Stormed out of room. Said, he'd see every man, woman, and *kinder* kilt in Missouri before he give up right to protect Federal property."

Wiping at her eyes with her apron, Tycee took Toby's

arm and returned with him to the kitchen.

Within the hour Erin House could rent seven empty rooms, vacated by state legislators, hurrying to get out of town and back to their homes as swiftly as possible. The Yankees were coming.

In the street, a man galloped by on horseback shouting and firing his pistol into the air.

Like ghosts the men on horseback came up out of the dawn fog at the beginning of the rise to the Gasconade Bridge. Thirty miles east of Jefferson City, each man rode a horse that a cavalryman would prize - sleek bodied, fast, a "present" to the man from various Unionist farmers living in the area. And, each rider carried a doubled barreled shot gun laid across his saddle's pommel. Holstered in the belt around his waist hung at least two revolvers, the favorite being the 36 caliber Colt revolving pistol.

The mist hung in the air. It would rain any minute. Hy pulled his kerchief tighter around his neck and his wide-brimmed black felt down further over his brow. Beneath his rump the piebald's gentle gait swayed him back and forth in the saddle, swayed so easy that sometimes the motion rocked him to sleep as he rode. But not now, tonight he had a job to do.

Captain Verboise raised his hand, signaled for the dozen men with him to stop. "Before we fire her, we have to make sure we are not observed." He half-turned in his saddle, nodded to the boy bringing up the rear, "Horton, see if we need to clear the bridge, first."

"Yes, Sir," and Horton disappeared into the cotton-like fog.

"Wilcox," he motioned for Hy to ride forward to join him. When Hy's mount pulled along side, Verboise asked in a voice only Hy could hear, "Did your wife have any comment regarding the *White Star*?

For a moment Hy's mind blanked. He remembered her asking if he had killed all those men. He also, remembered he'd lied to her. The first time, he had ever told Franny an untruth. Said, "Well, she didn't take to the killin's much."

Verboise grunted, said softly, "Understandable. She's only a woman. Women don't understand the need to kill like soldiers do."

"Yes, Sir." Hy answered.

"Can you trust her to keep her mouth shut?"

An odd question, Hy thought, answered, "I suppose so, Sir."

"*Suppose* so?"

"I mean," he stammered, "yes, Sir. I hope she will."

Verboise turned in his saddle and fully faced him, said "*Hope* so?" Around the mixed breed, Hy saw the swirling fog, giving him the appearance of a large, dark, shrike, a haunted spirit with burning eyes and a hard mouth.

Then, Hy got the captain's true message, realized that he had gotten his Franny into something that might bode ill for her and all that was dear to her. And there was no way to get her out. Slipping into the monotone he noticed he had been using lately, Hy hesitated for a fraction of a second before he replied emphatically, "Yes, Sir. I know she will."

Verboise's gaze never wavered from Hy's face. "You still sound unsure."

"No Sir," Hy swallowed, "I mean, yes she will."

"Of course, you know if she told anyone she'd only implicate herself." He sounded off-handed, turned away, gazed into the fog.

"She knows that, sir."

"And we wouldn't want her to implicate herself, would we, Wilcox? Such implications could hurt the hotel her mother owns, keep her from renting to all those

Federals sure to swarm over the city now that our good governor is fleeing his post."

He said this last about Jackson running away with bitterness. Hy knew Verboise had talked to the governor within two hours after converging the legislature, that General Price had accepted Verboise's offer of help and had asked him to do certain things. He also knew that the job at hand wasn't much to the captain's liking, but Sterling Price had ordered it, so it would be done. The Captain would have preferred making a stand in Jefferson City against Lyon's German army. But unable to raise enough troops Price, Jackson, and 3,000 raw soldiers had skedaddled west.

In the past Verboise had hinted of possible harm coming to the Union-loving widow Moone, but this was the first time Franny's name had come up in the same vein. He shivered. "She's not going to implicate herself, Sir."

"Are you sure of that, Wilcox?" Verboise still stared into the fog.

"I'll make sure, Sir."

The captain's head snapped around, faced him again, bored his gaze into him, "Good, man, Wilcox. See that you speak to her about it." Then he moved the corners of his mouth up, showing small, white teeth, said, "Pretty little wife you have there, Wilcox - smart too. Maybe she can be of use to us another time. Her mother is Unionist, but she *is* thoroughly Secesh?"

Hy felt like the wind had been knocked out of him and he swallowed before he answered. "Yes, Sir. Completely loyal to the cause, she'll help us."

Saying nothing more, Verboise turned to watch the fog for Horton's return.

Soon, Horton returned. By then, the misting rain had stopped and the sun fought to shine from behind clouds still gray and laden with unshed moisture.

"All clear, Sir," he reported, his spurs jangling as he

rode up to Verboise and saluted.

The bridge burners hurriedly gathered brush, placed this beneath the structure's driest parts, and poured turpentine over its entire length.

After too many attempts to count because of the wood being wet, the bridge finally burst into a decent blaze that sent oily, black smoke into the morning sky.

From the backs of their horses the men silently watched it burn for a moment, satisfied with a job well done. Then, they turned away at Verboise's command. The day's work had just begun. Next came the Osage River Bridge. They'd have to ride hard to get there before the normal morning traffic would make the burning of the bridge an exercise in first frightening off the wayfarers. After that, Li'l Chess McDonald would shimmy up a telegraph pole and cut the wires to all lines headed west. Lyon might yet take Jefferson City, but he would find transportation and communication difficult.

Thursday the 13th 3:00 p.m.

Twelve miles east from Kansas City, on the high open road leading to Independence, Missouri, Lieutenant Josiah Scarborough signaled for the company to halt. They'd rest and water the horses beneath the shade of the abundant jack oaks and maples growing along the little stream. Finding shade, he slid from the back of his sorrel and noticed his new first sergeant ordering the men. He felt the ache again and thought, *I miss Brady. Sanders will work out. But right now, I miss the old man.*

And he remembered: the regiment reaching the first post office anyone had seen in a month - Emporia Kansas, 150 miles southwest of Fort Leavenworth.- Brady receiving a letter from his sister in Saint Louis - Brady telling him he's retiring - Brady's leave taking, the old man happy as hell to hang up his saddle, inviting him to Saint Louis "sometime" to meet his sister and her family.

And then he was gone, racing ahead of the company to get to Leavenworth, muster out officially, and take a boat down river. For days afterwards Josiah felt rudderless, and now he realized how much he had leaned on the veteran.

He sat back beneath a tree and unstoppled his canteen, thought, *This is one of those days I wish I were just an enlisted man again.* Being a commissioned officer wasn't all what it was cracked up to be. He smiled to himself and thought, *But the pay raise with the extras thrown in nearing seventy a month, is very nice, indeed.*

Since the two weeks he had been back at Leavenworth, he had done nothing but chase rebels. Today was no exception. The Colonel had ordered his company to go along with Captain Stanley who at this instant parleyed with Captain Edmonds Holloway, commander of over 600 wild, raw rebels encamped at Rock Creek, a mile west. Josiah's orders were to guard the crossroad while Stanley and his aides rode into the rebel camp under a flag of truce to ask the commander what his intentions were towards the Federal government.

In Josiah's opinion, Holloway was a deserter. He was still listed on active duty as a captain with the eighth infantry in the United States army. Instead of allowing Holloway the dignity of a discussion the renegade officer should be hauled in for court martial and shot for treason. But with Brady gone, he didn't have a trusted confidant. So, he kept his opinions to himself.

Letting the thought go he watched his men, his tired men. They watered their horses in the stream, flopped beneath the trees, glad to be out of the merciless sun if even for a few minutes. Telling signs of fatigue showed in the lines around their eyes and mouth, and in the hollowness of their cheeks. Worse, a pervasive malaise seemed to have settled on their spirits like road dust had on their faces. Since they had got in from the long march from Fort Smith, post command hadn't given one trooper more than a 12-hour pass, including himself. "Request denied. We need you," the colonel had said. Scarborough hadn't been flattered.

However, the two things he most desired had come about. First, he had rid himself of O'Shay. Deciding that infantry instead of cavalry could best suit his talents, the neophyte had transferred out of the First cavalry to a newly formed volunteer infantry regiment from his hometown, Chicago, under Colonel James Mulligan. Second, Josiah and his company had seen some real action, at last. In the dead of night, they had chased back across the river and captured 200 rebels bent on taking Kansas City.

Sergeant Sanders, still mounted, called to him, "Lieutenant, there's a carriage coming hard from the west." He squinted into the glare of the sun, said, "Looks like two women, Lieutenant."

Josiah finished taking a long pull from his canteen, corked it, and turned a tired eye to the fast approaching buggy. The sergeant was right. He swore beneath his breath, thought, I don't have time for any foolishness from a couple of women, said, "You're on your horse. Stop 'um. I'll be there."

He mounted the stallion and by the time he ambled onto the road, Sanders had stopped the two-wheeled shay. He couldn't imagine why a pair of ladies would be out on these roads, in these times, alone. Surely, they had heard of the drunken barbecue going on in the rebel camp near by, knew the Federal cavalry was posted there, ready for a fight if necessary. Before he approached the carriage, Scarborough heard the thick brogue engaged in argument with Sanders.

"Tis me rights, Sonny to drive on any road of me choosin.' " The woman seemed angry and being made more so by her inability to control the skittish young bay pulling at the traces.

"Sergeant, hold her horse," ordered Scarborough, riding over to the woman's side of the carriage.

Sanders dismounted, stood in front of the filly, held the harness, and stroked the horse's nose.

"What's the matter, Ma'am?" Scarborough asked, observed that she was middle-aged, neatly dressed, wore a dark blue sunbonnet and a Union Eagle pin on the lapel of her duster. The other woman he couldn't describe except that she appeared small beneath the large, gray woolen cloak that covered her from head to foot. It gave her a nunnish air. She stared at her hands, knotted in her lap, and he sensed her discomfort.

"Well, an' who might ye be, me han'some laddie?" The matron cocked an eye at him and smiled.

Too weary to pass aimless chitchat with these two, a little shocked by her forthright manner and reference to his appearance, he heard the stiffness in his voice, replied, "I'm Lieutenant Scarborough, Ma'am. I do not advise that you use this road." Irritating she was, but she intrigued him, too. Her round Irish face and distinct brogue reminded him of someone he once knew or his own mother, gone nearly ten years.

The woman seemed startled at the mention of his name, started to ask him something, but at that moment the other one beside her turned and looked directly at him. He didn't hear the question; for he was staring into the prettiest pair of misty green eyes he had ever seen. Poking from beneath the cape around her slender face were tendrils of golden-red curls, the color of autumn.

She spoke to the older woman, "I told you, Ma, we couldn't come this way," then turned to him, said without smiling, "We're sorry, Lieutenant. They told us in Westport there might be trouble on this road."

"That's right Ma'am," he muttered, wished the girl would take off the cloak so he could get a better look at her.

"Why are you two out here, anyway?" He asked the question as his eyes swept the interior of the carriage. Couldn't be too careful, he knew. These Missouri gals were mostly Secesh and treacherous, every last one of them, even the ones wearing Union pins.

"We've come to bring me nephew home," The one green eyes called Ma said. "He's run off. Joined-up with the southern army, he has, an' the boy-o ain't old enough. Tis' half crazy with worry, I am, so we come out to look for the wee lad an' take him home."

He heard the answer, but the girl under the cloak drew his attention. As though she had read his mind, while the one had been speaking, the girl had murmured a complaint about the heat of the afternoon and removed her cloak. When she pulled the hood back, she unintentionally loosened her snood and masses of curls the color of fire fell over her shoulders and bosom. Beneath the buttoned bodice of her dress strained high, ample breasts.

For a fraction of a second he wondered how it would feel to lose himself in that fire, allow its heat to burn his face with passion, smell its fragrance. He wondered to himself, What would her perfume be, Rose? Lavender? - How would it feel to cup those ripe breasts while I kissed her soft, white neck, undressed her and ran my hands over the rest of her body? Then he happened to glance at Sanders who also gaped wistfully at this incredibly beautiful, probably very expensive girl.

Expensive, had he thought? Of course, that's who they were. When he put the older gal's forward, direct manner together with the girl's comeliness, the answer was obvious: they were whores. High toned, to be sure, but whores none the less. He grinned, relaxed in the saddle, felt the tiredness ebb away and decided he'd ask for a furlough again. This time he'd get it.

Coughing from one of the men resting beneath the

trees drew his attention. He saw that most of them had seen the girl remove her cape and now stood, watching the women in the carriage. He allowed himself once more to stare at the girl, who tried unsuccessfully to pin up her hair.

With effort he jerked his mind and his eyes back to "Ma." She was still talking about how loyal she was to Lincoln, but that her nephew was a rebel.

"You say he's with the Rebel army, Ma' am?" He laughed, let the sarcasm drawl through his words, "Well, you've got the wrong army, and I'm not about to let you two through these lines." Looking at the girl, he thought, *unless, little honey, you'd like to discuss it with me, privately.*

"Why, pray tell, won't you let us through?" the girl asked. She returned his stare, her eyes growing more angry, changing color to a very deep green.

"Because, ma'am, I told you; it is too dangerous for ladies like yourselves. There's a rough camp of soldiers encamped along Rock Creek." No need to tell these women about the talk going on there or why he was here. Yet, he couldn't help himself. Knew he sounded arbitrary, and so he found himself leering like a horny baboon.

"Well, I think my mother and I should be allowed to make that judgement, Sir." Defiantly, she pursed her lips, upturned her chin and he caught the hint of freckles splayed across her nose. These enchanted him.

Oh, my, yes, she is riled; he thought, and *will you look at the challenge in those eyes. Look at that stubborn little chin. God, she'd be a hot handful.* He grinned all the more and shifted in his saddle. Beneath him the sorrel stomped hooves and shook mane to get the flies off his neck and legs. *Come on Scarborough,* he prodded himself, *think of some reason to detain her. You've got a bottle of whisky in your saddlebag. Maybe, if you offered her a drink she'd stay, sit under the tree with you. You can find*

117

somebody for Ma to entertain.

Then, he sighed, realized the futility of this fantasy, forced himself to concentrate on the business at hand, turned to the older woman, said, "I'm sorry, ma'am, I can't allow you to do that."

"But 'tis the camp down the road we might be awantin' to go to. Me dear nephew might be there." The woman shook her head, emphatically, "Now, move aside, young man, or tis to President Lincoln, I'll be reportin' ya." She clicked to the horse, but the filly didn't respond. She seemed content to have her nose patted by Sanders.

Scarborough reached for the reins, said, "I mean it, ma'am. I cant' let you ladies through there. And it's highly unlikely that your nephew is there."

Evidently piqued, the girl turned on the woman, said, "Oh, Ma, let's just go back. We don't want to tangle with the United States army," she finished her statement with a sarcastic toss of her gorgeous curls.

"Excellent suggestion, ma'am," he said at once and relaxed the reins. The woman jerked them back into her hands, scowled, clicked to the horse. But, he held up his hand again to stop her.

"Before you do turn this buggy around and head back, tell me your names and where you're from." He hoped he sounded military.

"An' why would the likes of you be wantin' ta know that?" The woman frowned up at him.

Quick, why, Scarborough? Think. "For my report, ma'am," he lied. "The government wants to know the names and place of abode of all travelers on this road."

"Umph," the woman sniffed, "If ye must know, Moone is our name." She jerked her head towards the girl, "This is me daughter Frances. We run Erin House in Jefferson City."

When she said their names he felt a click in his head, but didn't stop to think about it. He laughed outright at the

118

old gal's euphemism to describe her relationship to the girl and figured there was no need to ask what kind of establishment Erin House was; he thought he knew.

At his nod Sanders moved aside. The woman attempted to turn the carriage around, shouted, "Tis a peace lovin' hard workin' woman, I am, tryin' to stay alive an' lookin' for me wee nephew. An' I don' need you to be tellin' me where and where not I can travel. This is America!" She hurled at him and clicked at the horse.

However, if she had meant her last remark to be a parting shot filled with haughty sass and dire warnings, it missed its mark. The horse would not budge. The young filly didn't want to leave Sanders' warm hand or the brown sugar he had been slipping her. And, the horse moved closer to the sergeant and rubbed her nose on his pocket.

Scarborough watched the woman click her tongue and slap the reins, but the horse would not turn. The more she persisted the more stubborn became the animal and the more anger flamed up her cheeks. She muttered a Gaelic curse that he remembered hearing from his childhood. By now the girl sat with her arms folded and her head in one hand, her embarrassment acute and obvious.

He heard the men begin to laugh, glanced at Sanders, enjoying the spectacle as much as he, and decided to let her struggle a bit longer. Chuckling, he thought, *I have never seen it to fail; a woman has no idea how to pick out a good horse.* Finally, said, "Seems my sergeant has made a friend, ma'am. Sergeant Sanders, turn this horse - I mean-*mule* around for the ladies.

Sanders got the animal pointed back towards Westport, and with a deep sigh of desire for the girl, Scarborough watched them pull away. Then, he blushed from hairline to boot-toe; for just as the women pulled off, the girl leaned half-out of the buggy and blew him a kiss. As they picked up speed and her curls caught the breeze, he heard her shout "Come on by and visit us!"

Behind him the men whistled and howled with laughter. "Sounds like an invitation, Lieutenant."

"Shut-up, Sanders" but Josiah grinned and tried to remember what the Devil had the woman said their name was.

"An' what does ya think you're a-doin' Frances Margaret Moone?" Dee yanked her hoyden back inside the carriage. "You're too old to be actin' that way, for the love of Mary!"

Collapsing in helpless giggles Franny said, "I know...." caught her breath, "I know, but, I just had to do something. He was soooo serious." And she laughed in fits until her eyes watered.

Unmoved by her daughter's wit Dee barked, "Well, ye acted like a trollop uncoverin' yerself the way ye did an' then yellin' at the man to come see us. Mother O' heaven, I pray he never does. No wonder the lad was eyein' ya like he was."

They rode in silence, hearing only the rumbling of the carriage wheels on the hard packed dirt road while Franny collected herself. Dee, stern faced, mumbled to herself, and struggled to keep the horse from pulling the carriage to the side of the road to eat the sweet grass. The afternoon sun had crossed the meridian, the air growing cooler by the minute.

Franny put on her cloak, said, "Ma, can we stop looking for Clay now? We've been all over Jackson county and this western part of Missouri trying to find him. All we've done for the last week is make utter fools of ourselves."

"No," her mother stated flatly, her jaw cast in iron.

"Tis in that camp by Rock Creek he is and we're goin' back there, tomorrow."

Although Clay had promised, he hadn't gotten word to her, not yet anyway, and here she and Ma were skylarkin' around the state looking for him. Because of the gathering armies around Independence and Kansas City, Ma had decided that Clay had fled there. Without incident, they had steamboated up river to Westport Landing near Independence. The *Charlotte Bell*, had been a drab little side-wheeler with filthy accommodations and greasy food. In some ways it had reminded Franny of the *White Star*. At each bend in the river she half-expected a guerrilla gang to burst out of the bushes and start firing at the boat. If they had, she figured, it would have served her right. That such an event could occur became more possible, daily, as the news carried stories of other steamers waylaid by thieves and murderers.

At Westport Landing they had hired the rig and filly, said to have been specially broken so that ladies could handle her. What a joke! It was all Ma could do to keep the damn horse from veering off the road to eat the grass growing in the ditches.

Determined, like Clay was, that's what my mother is, she thought. Like a stone wall, invincible, unchangeable, immovable. As far as Franny was concerned of all her mother's unlovely qualities this goat-headedness seemed the most objectionable. That was probably why her mother had never remarried. No man would have her.

Franny's mind flashed on Otto Zimmer and her mother. A sly smile crossed her face, and she turned a sloe eye upon her parent, said, "Mother, you and Mr. Zimmer have been keeping company for ever so long. Has he asked you to marry him, yet?"

"What!" Dee's shock at the question out of the blue almost made her drop the reins. "What's that you'd be askin' your own mother?"

Franny giggled, then remembered her question about Mr. Wilcox. "Well, if you choose not to tell me about Mr. Zimmer, then what about Mr. Wilcox. I remember when I was a little girl he------ "

Slap! Too quick, moved Dee's hand along side Franny's cheek for her to duck, and the blow surprised more than hurt.

"Hush up your mouth, child. Me friendship with Mr. Zimmer, or that filthy Wilcox, ain't none of your business. What ya ought to be thinkin' about is ways we can find me wee nephew, your cousin." Her head bobbed for emphasis, her bonnet moving from the force of the motion. Then, determined to keep the horse in the middle of the road, she settled back, glaring occasionally at Franny.

Chastened, Franny kept a discreet silence, but her mind wouldn't let Pa Wilcox go. Ma's reaction had been unexpected and extreme, even for her. Obviously, something happened between them to cause her mother such anger. What had she called him - *filthy?* Yes indeedy, he was that.

That day at his wagon she had been repulsed by his person - the stained, yellowed moustache that drooped over his upper lip, the sweat-stained flannel shirt, the greasy suspenders, his dirty trowsers, all three apparel the color of Missouri river silt. His streaked hair and skin pallor the same gray as his eyes.

She remembered the stench arising from his unbathed body and the whisky she knew he guzzled on the sly. About her father-in-law, it seemed, swirled an air of decay. She wondered if the farm reflected this same decline. When was the last time she had really looked at the Wilcox farm? Not since a child, before Hy had started courting her. Then, it had been a hard-worked farm with over 100 slaves. The last time she had been there, the only bond servant she had seen had been Aunt Sukey in the kitchen. What happened to all the field hands?

She sighed; the last day at the farm had been her wedding day. My wedding day, she thought and felt self-reproach tighten her chest, again. But she pushed it away. She wouldn't think about it. What was done, was done.

Married is married and it was until death, or so the preacher had said. When she was able to tell Ma, take her place as Hy's wife, and move to the farm, she'd get that place in shape and Pa Wilcox, too, or she wasn't Dee Moone's daughter. And in time, she and Hy would straighten out their differences. Vowing thus, to herself Franny didn't hear her mother.

"Can't ye hear me, Child, or so moon-struck are ya by the blue-eyed Lieutenant that ye don' know what's goin' on around ya?" Dee poked her day dreaming daughter with a sharp nudge of her elbow. Franny was jerked back to the jolting carriage, the hot, dusty, road, to her mother's voice.

"I'm sorry, Ma. And noooo I was not thinking about him. You know I don't like Yankees."

"Can ye be a-tellin' me if ya remember what it was he called himself?"

Franny thought, drew a blank, replied, "No, I don't remember."

While taking breakfast at their hotel in Westport Landing the next day, they heard about the take over of Jefferson City and the fight that had broken out at Rock Creek.

"Yes, ma'am," the old man who had ridden in late last night continued telling his news. "During Captain Stanley's and commander Holloway's meetin', somebody started shootin'. I was in Independence when it broke out and heard the rattlin' of musket fire, 'long with near everybody else in town."

It must have happened soon after that lieutenant told us to turn around and go back, Franny thought to herself and wondered if he had been in the fighting. But the old farmer was still talking.

"Yep, a bunch of us rode on out there and saw some of the battle. We seen the rebels, drunk as dogs, firing on their own men, if you can believe that."

Shocked, silent faces of the other guests met this last

remark. He paused, sipped his coffee, enjoying every minute of being the teller of the tale. "Wounded 17 of their own men and kilt three of their officers, one of them Holloway."

"That's a loss to the Confederate cause," rumbled a portly lawyer from Lexington, "and a boon for Lyon, who has just taken over the capital."

Ma exploded. " What's that yer a-sayin'?"

When he told her the news about Jefferson City's take over by 2000 Federal troops Ma began raging. "Holy Mary, bad enough at Rock Creek me own wee nephew might ha' been, but in Jefferson City, me hotel, me livelihood is." She started to rise, fell back into her chair and turned beet red. "I must send a telegram and see how stands the place and me dear friends a-runnin' it. Then, me girl and me will set out for Rock Creek and find me nephew." This time resolve made her spring from her chair.

But the lawyer gently restrained her. "You can't do that, madam. The telegraph wires are cut down. There are no messages getting in or out of there at this time. I heard the news as I was leaving Lexington and it came through by the last wire received at the telegraph office."

Wringing her napkin in her hands, Ma burst into tears. Attempted consolation from the two gentlemen dining with them had little effect, and Franny found herself hustling her mother back to their room.

Whereas her mother wept and openly despaired, Franny stayed outwardly calm. But fear, at first wearing tiny slippers, soon stomped through her head in boots as she reflected upon the news about the Federal army taking over her city. In some ways she felt violated, and anger surged through her body. Clamping tight her jaw until it hurt, she thought, *How dare they. Jefferson City may be the dullest city on the face of the earth; everybody says so. But, it is peaceful and clean and my home.*

She remembered what Hy and Clay had said about the surly attitudes of some of the soldiers who had taken them prisoner and wondered if these Federal soldiers would also be mean and oppressive with the town's folk? *Oh, Clay, where are you? And Hy, what will you do, now?* Her mind reeled and she fought back tears. *Maybe you'll quit being a nightrider, and join the real Confederate army, or better, just stay home and farm with your Pa.*

By noon, Ma felt well enough to seek out Clay. Ignoring warnings of harm that might befall them, they left Westport Landing for Independence and the Rock Creek area in the same rented carriage drawn by the filly. This time, rather than drive themselves, fearing the roads would be filled with stragglers and scoundrels, they hired a driver. The man reeked of whisky and his age prevented him from swinging himself into the carriage with any alacrity. But he holstered a revolver on his hip and seemed to know how to handle the filly, and so into the two-seater squeezed Franny between her mother and the smelly old driver.

Driving out the Westport Road, they were nearing the intersection where they had encountered the blue-eyed lieutenant, yesterday. Franny found herself fantasizing that he might still be there, his men lounging beneath the trees, his big horse blocking the road. For an instant she almost hoped he was. Then she cleared her head and saw instead what was left of a still smoldering mill.

The driver let fly a stream of tobacco juice before he jerked his head in the mill's direction, said, "Pitcher's Mill, over yonder. Reckon the Federal's done fired it on their way back to Kansas City. Reckon they needed to do somethin' to make up for one of their men bein' wounded and two horses gettin' kilt." No one else spoke as the carriage clattered past the burned out hulk of blackened timbers.

They made the turn north onto the Independence

Road and almost at once began to notice the signs of yesterday's battle. The dirt road showed the scarring of what seemed like hundreds of horses. A farmer's rail fence had been torn down. Some of the trees beside the road were broken and riddled with musketry fire. *One wounded? Maybe the lieutenant had been in the fight and hurt.* She hoped not. She also hoped he hadn't been the one who had burned down the mill. When she caught herself again thinking about the Federal officer, she purposely turned her mind elsewhere and spoke to the driver. "Things seem calm enough, today."

"An' well they might me, Missy. All of Holloway's men, or what's left of 'um, done skedaddled last night to the Big Blue River, a good seven miles east a here. Colonel Weightman's commanding now. And early this mornin', just afore I rode out to go over to the landin', Cap'n Prince, commander over to Fort Leavenworth, done brung an army of cavalry, infantry, and two cannons into Independence lookin' for the Rock Creek rebels. Real sour like he marched around the square a few times, muskets gleaming and set to fire. Even his fifer and drummer boy was along. Must a marched in 300 men to the tune a *Yankee Doodle.*"

To Franny's annoyance, Ma insisted the driver turn the carriage into the lane that had led to Holloway's central camp. At the deserted campsite they stopped and without getting out of the carriage observed the rubbish left behind. Worn out shoes and unwanted clothing, cast-off cooking gear, piles of old flour sacks and papers, blackened ground rings where campfires had been, and a number of empty whiskey bottles littered the area. The stenches from human refuse, yesterday's charred barbecue, musketry, and campfire hung in the air. Except for the bird-song that greeted them, silence prevailed whereas 24 hours ago a pitched battle had prevailed here.

"Beg pardon, ma'am," the driver spit another trail of

tobacco juice, "but I don't get the why of bein' here. I'd like to be gettin' on down the last couple a miles to Independence to be gettin' my supper and---"

"--- Oh hush," Ma turned on him, her face stern, her eyes watering. "Ye'll be paid, proper an' in time ta stuff yer gullet. Help me down."

"Ma, why are you getting out of the carriage? He's right---"

"---An' you hush up, too, Franny. I'm checkin' the clothin' that's piled up here ta see if any of it's yer cousin's. Didn't ya hear me, man, I said ta help me down."

He swore under his breath and slowly swung his scrawny frame to the ground. He said as he stomped around to Ma's carriage side, "Ain't no business a mine, ma'am, but I wouldn't be a touchin' them dirty drawers and shirts, if'n were me. Probably catch you a good dose a graybacks, if'n you do." He stood with his hand out to help her down.

"What are ya talkin' 'bout—*graybacks.*" Ma took his hand and lowered herself out of the carriage.

"Lice, ma'am. All soldiers carries 'um."

Ma only circled the piles of orphaned clothing, prodded at them with a stick, called for Franny to do the same. But Franny refused and stayed seated, fuming to herself that just like she had before the lieutenant, now before this whiskey soaked old reprobate who stood grinning like a mule eating briars, Ma was making herself look the fool.

Ere long, Ma tired of the exercise, sighed sadly, and returned to the carriage. Without a word, her head held high, she received the drivers proffered hand and took her place next to Franny. Arriving in Independence without further incident they learned that the wounded had been taken to various homes on the outskirts of town and none of them carried the name of Clay Monihan.

Thursday the 20th

"The hell you say." Unable to understand how anyone calling himself a soldier could engage in cold bloodied murder, Josiah gaped at the post commander's aide, a captain of the second infantry. The report of the raid on the *White Star* lay in an official communication on top of the captain's desk.

"That's right, fourteen men gunned down without mercy or a chance to even draw a weapon." The captain sat down and spread his hands palm down over his writing tablet. "Now, I've got to write their mothers and widows."

"I'm sorry, Sir. They were all good men." Josiah fell silent, respecting the dead. The men who died had been from the captain's regiment of second infantry who came in from Fort Kearny a month before his own regiment arrived. Most of them had earned a furlough or were mustering out, going home. But he had not known any of them well, so wondered why the captain had asked him to come around to his office after supper.

"Somebody else was on that same boat from your regiment - your old sergeant."

"Brady?"

"The very same. I've no news of him. His name appears as a passenger but doesn't appear among the dead and, apparently, he didn't reach St. Louis when the boat finally docked there. His sister sent a letter of inquiry to the Colonel."

Josiah left headquarters and walked the short block to buy the bottle of Bininger's *1849 Reserve* waiting for him at Fort Leavenworth's sutler. For nearly 20 years the official post trader had sold everything from pins to pies to every man garrisoned there. Although most post commanders permitted no hard liquor sold on the premises, the sutler always seemed to manage to have a few bottles of mellow bourbon tucked back in a dark corner. For this, the many drinking officers at

Leavenworth were eternally grateful.

A western sky still carried the fading footprints of the sun; yet, in another quarter of an hour the bugler would sound taps. So he quickened his step and contemplated the massacre. *So, Brady had been on that boat, too. It seemed that the shooters purposely chose Union soldiers and Union loyalists for target practice. Thank God Brady didn't betray himself. Well, tonight, old Sarge, I'll drink to your continued health, wherever you are.*

"Lieutenant Scarborough?" The orderly from the wire office approached him just as Josiah had left the sutler's stone house and was concealing the bottle of whiskey inside his jacket. The soldier handed him a telegram, saluted, said, "The telegraph line east has just been reopened, Sir." He didn't start back to the telegraph office, instead, loitered a short distance away, watched, waited. No one ever received a wire unless it was bad news. Josiah saw the man was curious, said, "It's ok, corporal, I can handle whatever it says. If it needs a reply I'll come over to the office." Embarrassed, the man saluted again and started on his way.

But Josiah didn't open it immediately. He turned it over several times, reading the outside of the message, examining the fold, trying to figure out who in the name of Jesus would be sending him a telegram. The only ones who might have remotely known where he might be and cared enough to send a telegram were women he had met over his years in the cavalry. But these usually wrote him long, loving letters, hinting that he should marry them.

Then, his blood turned to ice. *What if New York has finally caught up with me? But why the telegram? Could it be a warning--from whom? If so, I'll run again. Desert if need be. Head for Old Mexico, where I should have gone in the first place. I'll not swing from the gallows for Seamus Finn's murder. That mother's mistake deserved to die.*

129

Immediately he pushed away the image of the Irishman, bleeding and dying from a bullet Josiah had put through his chest. He lay on the stairs leading to the saloon's back room. In that room five years ago, 17-year-old Josiah Scarborough, alias, "Joe the Blarney" had found that Finn had stolen his money belt with the $300 he had scrimped to save. He also pushed away the battered, bloody face of Willie Collins, come with him to rob Finn, but now, from the beating Josiah had given him, lying unconscious on the floor beside the open safe with Josiah's gun in his hand.

Josiah walked back to his bachelor's quarters, a small sitting room and bedroom at its rear with its windows covered by thick curtains. Sitting in the row of officer's quarters facing the parade grounds, and surrounded by shade trees, it befitted perfectly a young junior officer like himself - one who might discretely entertain a member of the fair sex in his rooms.

Upon reaching his quarters he uncorked the whiskey and poured himself a jigger, gulped it down and poured himself another, then a third. He liked the way it went down smooth and set his stomach aglow. After the third, he contemplated drinking the whole bottle, thought better of it--no use getting snooted before he read the damn thing. With resolution, he stoppled the bottle and set it on his bookshelf behind a new volume of *United States Army Regulations*. But it peeked out from behind the book, so he placed it behind his dog-eared copy of *Shakespeare*.

Sitting on his camp bed, he pulled off his boots and leaned on the cot with one elbow to again examine the unopened message. *All right Scarborough, let's get it over with*, he thought and ripped it open.

One glance and he sat upright on the bed.

Verboise done the White Star. Stop. *I got away*. Stop. *Got a ball in me arm*. Stop. *In Jeff City*. Stop—*Brady*. Stop.

At once, Josiah roused the captain and showed him the telegram. Within the hour, the colonel's sleepy aide admitted him into the Post Commander's office. Fifteen minutes into the conversation Colonel Miles was offering him a special assignment, a detail to Jefferson City. Josiah wasn't sure he wanted it -Brady or no Brady.

"You're a valuable company officer, Scarborough, a natural leader of men. All your superior officers speak highly of you. We believe you to be the man to catch this Verboise scoundrel. And also, see what you can do for former Sergeant Brady. A fine dedicated soldier, he will testify against Verboise at the hearing."

Hiding the hatred he felt for Verboise, Josiah answered evenly, "I remember him, Sir."

No need to go into detail with the colonel. Scarborough remembered the vicious bastard, all right. The six months he had spent with the giant half-breed had been an ongoing exercise in dodging hard-fisted blows, being bucked and gagged, standing unfair guard duty, and ignoring insults. Once, he had ordered Scarborough tied to a wagon wheel and flogged 39 times with a snake skin whip. If Brady hadn't stepped in at stroke 26, when he'd passed out, he'd probably be dead. His back still carried the scars. The only thing his "trainer" had taught him was how *not* to treat a new recruit, even one as unruly as he had been. Breaking a man's spirit did not make him a soldier. Josiah had refused to be broken, and, so, Verboise had hated him. Then, couldn't understand why the kid he had brutalized with such loving care hadn't wanted to ride out with him when he left.

"Precisely my point. You know how he thinks. Major-General McCellan, commanding the new five state military department, has ordered that we stop this guerrilla action around Missouri's capital. Now, we know who to apprehend. Verboise is operating as a partisan ranger, destroying Federal property, and committing depredations upon loyal Union men and their families. He is probably responsible for cutting the telegraph wires and blowing the Gasconade and Osage River Bridges before Lyon took Jefferson City. He is a *guerrilla*." He made a face and said the word as though he had just stepped into horse droppings. "Hunting him down is within our military jurisdiction."

The graying eyebrows puckered in a frown as the colonel continued, "If he's able to commandeer a boat and murder with impunity fourteen officers and men of the regular army, Sir, then he's mustered a sizeable force." He gave Josiah the glare he intended for Verboise and waited for Josiah to acknowledge the statement.

"Yes, Sir." Josiah answered quickly, realizing that he had stood with his tongue glued to the roof of his mouth and his mouth gaping open while the colonel had been speaking. Watching the Colonel present this idea, Josiah was struck with the thought that he was trying to get him to volunteer for this operation.

Instead Josiah suggested, "The Rebs around here might attack Kansas City again, Sir."

"True, but we have enough force to offset that, we think. Jim Lane is raising an army of Kansas volunteers to defend the state should an assault occur."

Josiah shuddered to hear Lane's name. For the five years after the slaughter at Pottawatomie Creek, the skinny, fire-tongued, senator from Kansas had joined in with James Montgomery, a teacher and backwoods preacher, and Charles Jennison, a medical doctor. These three ardent abolitionists had taken up where John Brown had left off and hated pro-slavery Missouri. Alone or in concert with each other, riding out of the night, armed and sometimes masked, they led in the border war between Kansas and Missouri - a warfare that poured death and suffering upon innocent Missourians. Nothing was past them - rape, arson, thievery, or murder. At one point

Josiah's company had been called out to put a stop to their excesses. So accomplished a horse thief had been Jennison that across the Midwest horse traders used the argument *out of Missouri by Jennison* to clinch the sale of a good, yet, non-pedigreed horse.

Josiah knew in his gut that with Lane's prominence and new army connections he'd hook up with his friends and once again wage vicious warfare on innocent civilians. *Only, this time*, Josiah thought, *the unholy trio will be wearing blue uniforms. Verboise fights for the grey. It makes no difference; Verboise-Lane, Lane-Verboise, both seem to ride the same Apocalyptic horses named—Murder and Mayhem.*

But habit kept these thoughts silent and from being reflected on his face. Instead he offered, "Yes, Sir, I've heard Lane's cavalry is untrained and undisciplined - men who caused the border troubles a few years ago. They're a pretty rough bunch, under Doc Jennison."

The colonel demonstrated that he had missed Josiah's point, when he said, "That too is true, Scarborough. But the cavalry has its ways." He smiled, stuck out his hand, which surprised Josiah. "You'll be a big help. Report to Colonel Henry Borenstein. He's got three, four companies of raw troops. He's started fortifications around the city and started drilling the Home Guard to go after Verboise but they're no match for him. Lyon put Borenstein in charge when he left there over a week ago to chase after Jackson and Price.

Chase after Jackson and Price.... Again Josiah found his mind drifted. Just a few days ago, Lyon had met up with and engaged the untested Rebel troops at Boonville, less than 50 miles from Leavenworth, yet not one man from the post had been ordered out to help the cocky red-head. Of medium height and wiry build, even before his meteoric rise from lowly captain of the 2nd infantry to brigadier general he had evidenced a New Englander's

133

Puritan disdain for anything southern. And he seemed to hate Missourians. Now Lyon stalled in Boonville awaiting transportation while Jackson and Price raced to meet up with the Rebel Ben McCulloch at the Arkansas border.

The colonel's voice brought back his attention. "You'll be able to recruit a force there large enough to go after Verboise, a scourge on the county around the capital city and a disgrace to the First Cavalry."

As he pumped Josiah's hand he said as though saving the best for the last, "Oh, and I've applied to Secretary of War Cameron for your upgrade to Captain. Congratulations *Captain* Scarborough." With the colonel's last words Josiah's interest in chasing a bushwhacker rose one hundred percent.

Another half-hour of palaver to discuss the reports that Josiah would file and the recruiting procedures he would follow. Another half-hour and he had packed, ready to catch the morning steamer going down river. If the boat ran at night and didn't have to stop too often to take on wood, passengers, and cargo, he'd be in Jefferson City within two-three days. Then, he'd get the furlough he deserved. A working furlough, but one that would allow him to find Brady and look up that red-haired fancy-gal. Hadn't the one called *Ma* said they ran a hotel there? Then, the name of their place flashed before him--*Erin House*. He chuckled, imagining the kind of sporting house that hotel might be.

Dee finally agreed to stop searching for Clay and for one week, she had lain in her hotel bed at Westport Landing, coughing, filled with quinsy, claiming she was "a-dyin." For a week, Franny had nursed her ailing mother, bringing her warm broth and teas and reading the newspapers to her. Because of the cut wires, not until yesterday were they able to send Otto a telegram. His reply indicated that both city and hotel still stood, indeed,

134

flourished.

"But, what else could I expect the man to say?" Dee fumed, shaking the telegram in Franny's direction. "Sure he wouldn't be wantin' to tell me the true state of things. Wouldn't want to upset me!" She reread it for the umpteenth time, Franny thought, before looking up again, smiling to herself and exclaiming, "Ah, 'tis a sweet, sweet man, that Otto Zimmer, wouldn't tell me if the buildin' was a-fallin' down if it thundered 'round his ears." Then, with more energy than Franny had seen her mother exert in days, Dee hopped from the bed and immediately began pulling on her clothing. "Now, get packed, girl. We're takin' the first boat we can back home."

Aboard the *Damsel,* Captain LeCroix gave Dee and Franny a cubbyhole for a cabin. They received a cabin situated in the portion of the boat reserved for women - on the far stern end behind the boiler deck. Like all cabins it had two doors - one leading to a ladies' sitting room and the other to the outside deck promenade. Furnishings consisted of a wooden washstand holding a basin and pitcher, with a chamber pot discretely hidden beneath the stand. Bunks hung on one wall, one upper, and one lower. The larger, lower bunk supposedly could sleep two but was still so small, it would have done well to accommodate a child. This ended the "comforts" found on the *Damsel.*

It appeared to be as squalid, and the foods just as unpalatable, as the packet they had traveled upriver on. When dinnertime arrived, neither felt hungry enough to brave the greasy fare of fried pork and lima beans. Instead, they remained in their cabin munching on cornbread and brandied cherries they had brought with them. For supper, Dee sent Franny out for tea and biscuits.

She left through the door opening into the ladies sitting room. The little carpeted parlor furnished a place where all women passengers could sit, chat, sew, and read without being bothered by unwanted masculine attentions. From where the floral carpeting lay to where it stopped at a black velvet curtain signaled that no uninvited male dared to enter the chamber from the main cabin or he risked being thrown overboard by the crew.

Supper had been over for an hour. However, when she pushed aside the curtain she had a full view of the main cabin and she saw the porter, a German immigrant, lounging near the card players at the far end. She waited until he noticed her then beckoned, gave him the order, then said, "You can give them to me on the deck. I'll wait outside our cabin door," and she slipped the man two-bits.

"I'd be glad to bring the tea and biscuits to your cabin, Miss."

"No, I prefer the fresh air." With that Franny headed for the passageway leading outside to the boiler deck.

Mesmerized, Franny leaned over the railing and watched the passing shoreline, as the boat seemed to skim the top of the river. Two little pickannie's waved to her from the bank. She waved back, laughing as one of them jumped up and down in high excitement.

Relaxed, she breathed deeply of the air alive with the smells of summer and of the boat. Beneath the pungent aroma of the wood burning in the boat's furnaces to make steam, the breeze carried the fainter odors of late blooming dogwoods, hickory trees, and wild roses.

The paddle wheel threw up a foamy spray as it spanked the water and throughout the boat the pipes breathed with steam. From the engine room on the bottom deck, came a clanging and banging as the system engaged, valves opened and closed, and giant pistons surged back and forth, driving the paddle wheel. Now and then a crewman would call out the depth of the water. He had to yell over the din to make himself heard to the pilot, sitting like God almighty on his throne in the pilothouse atop the boat.

At last they were going home. The thought cheered Franny although she knew she would have to deal with Hy again. She would also have to face her fears of being punished for being involved in the *White Star's* ambush. And she knew in her bones that Hy Wilcox had lied to her. He had killed those men. She remembered him telling her, once, that "Verboise always calls on me to do the important work."

But she refused to let herself get fussed now. The sun, an hour from setting, cast a pink glow over the water. Everything around her seemed enchanted - the summer, the riverbank, and the little boat-and wrapped in this magical cocoon she felt protected from harm.

The porter came with a tea service, the plate of biscuits, and a tub of apple butter. She had wandered nearly to the end of the deck. Now, with tray well in hand, she turned to hurry back to her cabin and bumped into a man.

"Oh...the Tea! Excuse..."

"Well, hello," he said.

Barely glancing up at the tall figure blocking her path, Franny said hurriedly, "Oh, pardon me, Sir," and tried to move around him. But he didn't move aside. This time she looked up into his face, and noticed merry, blue eyes, surrounded by the kind of thick, dark lashes most women would give their souls to own. If he hadn't been in civilian clothing she would have sworn he was the lieutenant who refused to allow Ma to go to the Rebel camp. Her mouth gaped opened in surprise. She quickly closed it, gained her self-composure. "I'm sorry, Sir, if I looked so startled. You resemble someone I encountered recently." And she again made to move past him.

He still didn't budge. His form seemed to loom over her, and he grinned, showing double dimples on each side of his mouth. "Perhaps, I am that very one, Ma'am." The timbre of his soft baritone carried a lazy half-promise; it's slight northeastern inflection tantalized and teased.

Altogether, it was a quite pleasant voice, she decided, one that had sent a momentary *zing* down her tailbone.

However, she said primly, "No, Sir, you are not," and refused to look at him, instead, looking straight before her at his loose, silk tie. She thought him to be one of those impudent river flirts about whom Ma had warned her. One who would strike up a conversation, unbidden, with any woman aboard ship. As icily as could be, she said, "I would ask you, Sir, to please remove yourself so that I may pass."

"But we have encountered one another, just recently, Ma'am. I am the soldier you met on the road to Rock Creek."

Her head jerked up and she studied his face. He seemed familiar; the dimpled grin was, anyway.

"But -" she stammered, glanced down his long, wiry body, taking in his gold brocade waistcoat, the tie, the sack coat of good quality black broadcloth, the wide-brimmed soft felt hat, impeccably blocked - he looked like a prosperous planter or merchant. "The man I met wore a Federal officer's uniform."

"Yes, I have one of those." He peered down at her, and she could see he was amused. "But I didn't want to wear it on this trip. Too many outlaws are taking deadly aim at boys in blue these days." He leaned a bit closer. "Would you talk to me if I was wearing my uniform?"

Her mind flashed on the *White Star*, and for a half-second she closed her eyes to regain her equilibrium. Yes, indeedy, here stood the lieutenant that had turned them back to Westport Landing. And, thankfully so, she thought. Purposely ignoring his question, she said formally, "We owe you our thanks, Sir, my mother and I. If you hadn't sent us back to town when you did we might have been caught in the thick of the battle that broke out shortly after we left you."

138

"Always a good idea to take a soldier's advice," he murmured. Then he lapsed into silence, but moved until his face almost touched hers and she caught a hint of whisky on his breath. He stopped grinning and solemnly moved his eyes slowly over her features the way an artist might. Then, to himself, said, "You're younger than I thought you were."

Fury overtook her and she felt herself blush. "I really must get this food back to our cabin. My mother's unwell. If you'll excuse me--"

Still, he barred her way as though he hadn't heard her. His eyes moved to her lips and were moving towards her bodice when she raised her voice, "Really, Sir, you are staring at me in a most insulting way. And I must give this food to my mother. Now, if you do not move aside, I will call for help!"

He muttered, *"It is the east, and Juliet is the sun."* Then, before she could ask what it was he said, his eyes caught hers and he asked in a pointed whisper, "Do you always throw kisses to strange men and invite them to visit you?"

She reddened and struggled not to drop the tray. Suddenly, the thought struck her, *He thinks I'm loose, he must. How could he not? Oh my God!*

At that moment, pushing along the narrow deck, the Captain interrupted them. "Excuse me," he sang out, "Sorry to bother you folks. Good evening, Mr. Scarborough, Miss Moone," he nodded to them both, "hope y'all are comfortable? How's your mother feeling, Miss Moone?"

"Fair to middling, thank you, Captain LeCroix," replied Franny and as Scarborough stepped back to let him pass she darted through the opening. "Good night gentlemen," she called over her shoulder scurrying away as quickly as she could.

"Ma!" she rushed into the cabin, "Guess who I just

ran into?" And she babbled on in high excitement while she laid out the tea and biscuits on the wash stand. Finally she finished her tale with "And, you know, he remembered I had blown him that kiss. Dear God, I am so humiliated." She sat next to her mother's feet and bit into a biscuit slathered with applebutter.

Sitting upright, Dee laughed, "Well-an'-a-day, I told ya not to be showin' yourself that way." She laughed again then turned suddenly grave. "Did he have anything to say about the fight at Rock Creek?"

"He never mentioned it."

"Gracious Child, 'tis the most important event since we left home that happened to us and you say he never mentioned it? Long enough it took ya to get back here. What all was you two talkin' about all this time?"

A knock came from the door, deck-side.

"Who might ye be?" Dee called out.

"Josiah Scarborough, Ma'am."

Franny recognized his voice and went cold to hot to cold, all in half a second. She eyed the cabin's exit into the ladies' sitting room but knew Ma would have a conniption fit if she tried to bolt.

"An' how can we help you, Sir?" Dee asked, making no movement to open the door.

"I heard you were ill and wondered if there was anything I might be able to do for you."

Dee sighed, "Open the door, Franny. We might as well be polite."

"But, Ma, he's a perfect stranger," Franny hissed.

"Let him in, I tell ya. The engine's making such a racket I can't understand what he's a-sayin'. I want to hear his last name again."

Reluctantly, Franny opened the door. He held his hat in his hands now and she saw he had a mass of unruly, soot-black hair that tried to curl over his broad forehead and looked as though it needed a good combing.

Obviously, he wore none of the greasy pomaden that most men did. He winked at her and smiled over the top of her head at Dee.

"There's not much room, Lad, but you're welcome. We're having a bit of tea and biscuit; come in and join us."

"No thank you, Ma'am. I don't wish to discomfort you ladies, and these cabins are intolerable, even for midgets." He remained outside.

But, Dee beckoned, insisting, "No, no, I want ya in here. 'Tis something I must ask ya. Franny, close the door."

On command, he ducked through the doorway and stepped inside, immediately filling the room with his size.

Seated on the bunk Dee asked, "Now, boy-o, tell me what yer name be again."

"When you met me I was first lieutenant. Now I'm Captain Josiah Scarborough, at your service, Ma'am." He gave a courtly nod to simulate the full bow that the cabin's size wouldn't permit.

At once Dee shot from the bunk, seemingly completely recovered, and stood in front of him, scrutinizing his face, the same way he had done Franny's earlier. Only, she had to rear her head back to look up in his eyes, for like her daughter, she came barely to his chest.

He chuckled, grinned, raised one eyebrow, said with a laugh, "Well, Ma'am do I pass inspection?" His eyes wandered back to Franny who huddled at one end of the berth.

"Aye, that ye do." Then Dee mumbled, "Spittin' image, ye are." Dee folded her arms over her chest and sat down slowly. She had gone white and seemed to be holding her breath. Franny noticed a tic playing around Ma's left cheek.

"Where are ye from, then, Captain?" Dee asked.

Franny recognized the look. With her mouth set in a

straight line and her eyes drilling through him, Dee reminded her daughter of a small bulldog, tenaciously hanging on to something until it got satisfaction. But not on her life could Franny understand her mother's reaction. It was embarrassing. No one but her mother would pepper a stranger with personal questions the way her mother was doing now. Franny stared at her hands, but the tension in the room drew her eyes back to him. He hesitated, a momentary look of sadness crossed his face, then he showed his dimples, again, said, "from New York City, Ma'am."

"No," Dee said impatiently, "before then, where was ye from, yer mother?"

"Ireland."

"And would that be from County Westmeath?"

"Yes," he whispered, and the look on his face went from cavalier to penitent and Franny saw his eyes brighten with tears. He and Ma gazed at the other with eyes, relentless and unswerving.

"Scarborough Hall." Dee breathed the name - the hallowed name of the place she had bent Franny's ear about - so often that Franny had long ago ignored and forgotten her reminiscences. As though daring not to ask, Dee began, "And ye would be the son of --"

"Lord and Lady Peter Scarborough, fourth Earl of Athlone," he finished in a stunned whisper. "My mother's name was Caitlin."

To Franny's amazement her mother, who she always thought of as being made of iron, burst into quivering sobs and embraced this tall stranger dwarfing their cabin. Tears streamed down his face, too, and through her tears Dee said, "Me Godson, ye are lad, me own dear cousin's child."

Josiah had seen them board at Westport Landing, the girl, her strawberry gold ringlets poking askew from beneath a straw bonnet. The older woman hadn't look well, leaned on the girl's arm, and held a handkerchief to her nose. Seeing them board the *Damsel* surprised him. He thought they would have been back in Jefferson City by now. Amused, he watched them dicker with LeCroix, saw the women insist they have a private cabin, then argue over the price.

He'd hoped to speak to the redhead during the day, and was disappointed when the two had kept to themselves in their cabin during the noon meal. But after eating the greasy pork, gravy, and the stale biscuits, Josiah couldn't much blame them. Camp rations couldn't be worse.

After lunch he roamed the boiler deck and the hurricane deck above it, hoping to see her. Then, back inside the main cabin, the saloon, he'd snoozed in a chair, keeping one eye on the curtained partition, separating the men's from the women's side. He'd willed the curtains to part and she to emerge. It would look ungentlemanly to boldly seek her out, even if she was what he thought she was.

Frustrated, around four o'clock he'd wandered over to one of the card tables in session, had two short whiskies, and won a few hands of draw poker. All the while, he kept watch on the black velvet separation.

When the women still didn't come out for supper, he'd gotten worried. What if they holed up in the cabin for the entire trip to Jefferson City? He began to think that, perhaps, he should tell LeCroix or the porter that the ladies in cabin E hadn't emerged since boarding. Maybe the older woman was seriously stricken, the girl unsure of what to do, afraid to call on someone. He was about to be the hero of this fanciful drama and search out LeCroix when the girl stepped out into the main cabin.

For not a moment could he take his eyes off her. The unruly locks, she had tucked into a knot at the base of her neck the best she could. Still, naughty wisps escaped, curled around her face and over her neck, and glowed from the late afternoon sun filtering into the large room. And, she had thrown on a lacy shawl that defined her slender shoulders and rippled over her breasts. Thoughts of bedding her brought his poker game to an end and he followed her outside to await an opportunity to speak to her. He already was thinking he might get her to come back to his cabin with him, discretely of course.

But, when she had bumped into him her youth, circumspect manner, and obvious disdain for his attentions puzzled him. Gone were the challenging eyes, the saucy spirit, and the flirtatious ways with which she had left him on the road. He wondered if she acted this way because she was on the *Damsel* and the old woman was truly sick.

Then, she'd run away, back to her cabin. But LeCroix had mentioned the other woman's health, so propriety now allowed him to knock at their door and make inquiry.

As he held his Auntie Dee to his chest and let his tears flow with hers, he realized why she had seemed so familiar that day on the road, why the strange click in his head when he had heard her name. *How long has it been since you've seen her, he asked himself, 15, 16 years and you barely six years old? And that gorgeous little morsel you've been stalking for reasons impure is the daughter of your own Godmother and also a distant cousin. She's also the one whose life you saved when aboard ship.*

Memories engulfed him-his mother and he, in the dead of night, running from the fire at Scarborough Hall, someone else running away with them. It had been Auntie Dee and Baby Franny. They'd made their way to port and got on a tall ship, under sail. The ship had fascinated him and he heard himself telling his mother, "I want to be a sailor when I grow up." He'd hung around the tars so much, he made a nuisance of himself, and his mother had scolded him. Because of her wealth Lady Scarborough had been able to buy first class accommodations for them all. No dirty steerage class, with bad water and scant provisions for them. On the firstclass deck he had frolicked away the days as the ship made its way across the Atlantic. Then had come the storm.

As Josiah now held his arms around his long lost relative, weeping for joy, his mind catapulted him back.

Waves are washing over the decks. I was to stay in the cabin with the baby. But the baby isn't there. "Where's the baby, Joe? Where's Franny?" Mother is asking. Auntie Dee is crying. I dart out the door and onto the deck before the women can stop me.

On the deserted deck the baby is playing in the rain. Her mop of red curls frames her face and she stoops down amid the ropes while waves crash and break within arm's length of her. I call to her but she doesn't hear me and she's oblivious to the waves getting stronger, reaching out for her. Suddenly, she looks up, sees me, laughs. When I start for her, she runs away playing her game of catch-me-if-you-can. She runs towards the ship's railing. There is enough space between the bottom rail and the wooden deck for a two-year-old to slip under, to slide into the sea. She is looking over her shoulder, urging me to chase her, chortling, not looking where she is going.

The ship pitches to and fro, first one side and then the other. As she reaches the railing it lurches and she slips. But I hurl myself upon her. Big for my age, I pin her down with my own body. Beneath me, she is crying while I grip the railing with both hands. I feel the crush of the icy waves, but hang on with fingers growing numb with the cold. Then, when I fear I can hang on no longer, there are strong men's arms lifting us up, carrying us back to our mothers.

Shortly, on chairs pulled from the main cabin, they sat on the hurricane deck, talked, sipped tea, and ate jam tarts Dee had thought to pack in the food chest. "'Tis steaming ahead for Jefferson City, we are, instead of tying

145

up for the night. We'll be home by day after tomorrow."
She offered him the last of the tarts.

He took it, glad to have something good to eat this day. "We've got a master pilot. LeCroix says the man can tell by the way the moonlight streams over the water if there's a snag in the river bottom."

"So how is your dear mother, lad?" Dee asked after a bit. "For shame, I never learned her address and 'tis a pity she never wrote me."

The sun setting on the river sent a patina over the mud -colored waters. One side of her face was caught in this glow and the other shadowed, making difficult to see Dee's expression. But through her voice Josiah sensed her genuine concern. And he had expected, eventually, to face this question. Still, when it came, it caught him off guard. What could he say - certainly not the truth. To spare her, he lied, "Mother died when I was 12 of a burst appendix."

"Oh, so sorry I am to hear that." She patted his hand.

"She couldn't write because she lost the information you'd given her about where you were going. Someone stole Mother's money belt and all our trunks after you two got on the canal boat for Albany. All she remembered about where you were headed was that you were going out west to meet your brother." This much, at least, was dead truth.

"Stolen! Good Lord! What did you do, boy?"

Are you going to lie again, Scarborough? Of course. Does she really need to know how we nearly starved to death, begging for food on the city streets? Of the stinking piles of garbage and offal that characterized the Five Points neighborhood mother's circumstances forced us to live in? Of the "Irish boarding house," the filthy tenement, to which dock "runners" had first lured us? How, with a family of five we'd shared a basement one room until

146

Seamus Finn had thrown us out on the streets? Make it uncomplicated, Scarborough. If you tell too much she might stumble upon the truth about mother's death.

"Mother contacted Mr. Sean Lalor—"

"--Did she naow?" Dee broke in, surprise and a touch of alarm in her voice.

"So, you knew him too?" Josiah acknowledged. Something about Dee's startled reaction tickled a premonition he didn't want to face.

"Yes, that I did." Dee said, eyeing him briefly before she continued, 'Twas the year before you was born he came to Scarborough Hall and bought some horses from Lord Peter."

"Right you are," he said keeping his tone level, feeling the excitement build in him. "Wasn't he from Athlone, too?"

"Aye. Grew up in the village. Poor as a rat, he was." She answered so softly he had difficulty hearing her over the churning paddle wheel.

When she offered nothing else, he continued, "I guess he got tired of Irish poverty because when he immigrated over here he got rich." He waited for Dee to say more. She didn't. Instead, her gaze swept the river that shimmered in the fast setting sun.

"Anyway," he said after an interval, "he gave mother and me money from the winnings accrued from the stallion and his off-spring. Said he'd never owned a successful racer until he bred Lord Peter's champion stud. He paid for my education."

"And well he should," he thought he heard Dee mutter, but before he could ask her to explain the remark she asked, "Where is he now?"

"Died of heart failure when I was sixteen. I had one more year at VMI to finish."

"And did ya finish?" She was looking at the river again.

147

"No, I joined the cavalry." End of story, his mind warned. No need to tell her the rest.

Telling about his life, even sketchy and half-true, had caused his shoulder blades to tighten and his neck to feel stiff. His whole body ached from taut nerves and muscles. A sip of whiskey would taste mighty good, right about now, he decided, and almost excused himself to go after one. But chose a cigar to ease his tension, instead.

He held the Corona up in the silent gesture that asked the ladies in his company if they minded if he smoked, got their approval, and struck a match. Concentrating on the cigar helped his hands stop shaking. The tobacco in his lungs helped calm his nerves. He hadn't given that much information about himself to anybody, even Brady, since he'd left New York

"Sean Lalor, ye say?" Dee whispered, then went suddenly pensive, and he thought she bit her lip. But she quickly recovered, smiled, said, "If me address you'd known, you could have finished off a-growin' up here, being the big brother to me head-strong nephew and me wayward child." She, grinned, nodded at Franny who hadn't taken her eyes off him but had remained unsmiling, and church-mouse still.

"If I had I'd probably be a Reb, today." He laughed and blew a smoke ring, relieved that Dee had changed the subject. He raked the girl with his eyes.

"Now, go along with ya. I wouldn't have *let* ya be one." Dee laughed and playfully slapped his hand.

"That didn't stop Clay, did it Ma?" Franny broke her silence.

Ignoring Franny's question and looking chagrined Dee asked, "Honestly, now can ye forgive her for her high-spirited ways when we first met ya?"

He guessed she referred to the kiss Franny blew him and the invitation to visit. Not willing to disclose that at the time he had thought them both a pair of trampled

148

blossoms, he decided to make a joke of it. "I don't know, Aunt Dee." he chuckled.

But when Dee alluded to her daughter's indiscretion, Franny abruptly turned to gaze at the river. Josiah felt like she had left them. Darkness had fallen by now. Light came from the few oil lamps hung on deck and a dim, cloud-cloaked moon. Lulled by the steady chugging engine and the *schlclop, schlclop* of the paddle wheel, a few other passengers dozed. Only in the saloon could they hear voices not their own -some playing cards, others getting quite drunk, and another breaking into song. *"It may be for years and it may be foreverrrrr; then why art thou silent, Kathleen Mavourneen?"* The song lamented the silence of a girl in the face of her lover's departure to sail across the ocean.

That's how far away the girl seemed to him, now. And why her silence? He couldn't see her face for the shadows, so said lightly, "I would have come by your hotel, for sure when I got to Jefferson City. Wouldn't have wanted to miss out on any of that good Irish home cooking. Of course, I was glad when I saw you two board." *You tease, now, Scarborough,* he chided himself. *Two hours ago, you were glad because you were thinking of other things.*

So his baby cousin had grown up to be a beauty. He took in the alabaster skin, the fiery, wayward curls, the rounded breasts and slender waist and doubted if her mother appreciated just how much of a temptress Franny was to men.

"Ya hear that, girl? What if he hadn't been me godson and yer cousin? What if he had come, a strange soldier to Jefferson City expecting to meet ya there?"

"Oh, Ma, let it lay," she murmured, still unwilling to look at either of them. Then, showing an abrupt change of manner, suddenly tossed her curls and gave him a sassy look, "I would have enjoyed you coming to Jefferson City very much, cousin, -" she paused, then, "-and making your acquaintance, that is," she finished demurely and burst out in lady-like giggles.

He laughed with her, and teased "If I'd known what a vexation you'd be to your mother when you grew up, I'd have let you drown."

They all laughed and bantered and became reacquainted until the fog set in on deck and it grew chilly. Later, in his own cabin, lying kitty-corned on the too short bunk with his feet hanging off the ends, he reflected on this sudden happenstance.

Feelings of desire for Franny intruded upon those of profound gratitude for finding Aunt Dee. She and Franny were the only real family he had left. Obviously, he could no longer pursue this kinswoman with the same intentions he had earlier. Only a cad of the lowest sort would do that

Yet, he wondered if she were drawn to him. Other officers had joked with him about his ability to attract women, and he supposed he'd been as successful with the fair sex as most chaps. But Franny was different; he didn't feel as confident. Certainly, a girl like her would have a sweetheart, a dozen probably, all in eager pursuit and with honorable intentions.

He blushed, feeling shame wash over him as the waves of the sea had done long ago. What an idiot he'd been, leering and winking, locking her on the deck so she couldn't pass. Since meeting her today nothing in her manner or speech had given him cause to think that she was remotely interested in his flirtations or anything but a lady. He got up, raised the wick on the small oil lamp in its sconce beside the door, removed a flask from his coat pocket, unstopped it, and let the whisky burn down his throat. He took two swallows before capping the flask and putting it away.

The whisky didn't help, for he flopped back on the bunk and continued to think of his beguiling cousin.

Sighing deeply, lamenting the possibility that he would have to let this seductress go by, he drifted into sleep. But even in his dreams the girl was there, laughing at him, and beckoning to him to follow her.

CHAPTER FOUR
July

Tuesday the 2nd, Wilcox Farm

"Scarborough! Did you say his name was *Captain* Josiah Scarborough, Mr. Wilcox?"

"That I did, Captain Verboise. With a nest of Yankee officers, boardin' at Erin House he's with my daughter-in-law and her high-hattin' mother." Pa rocked back in his chair, lit his pipe, and watched his guest. "Is that a concern to you?"

"Why is he here? Did you find out if he had a specific reason for coming to Jefferson City? There's no cavalry unit here, not yet anyway, and he's a cavalry man."

"You know this fella?" Pa was sort of tickled to see the *great* Captain Verboise, who his son seemed to follow after like a pet dog, appear to be in a stew over this new boarder at Erin House. Hell, as far as he was concerned all them Yankee vermin swarmin' into town looked and acted the same. Smelled the same too. Made no never mind if this one was Franny's relative or not. Dee's Godson...well, well. Proved how bad pennies always turned up didn't it? He smiled to himself. It wouldn't do to let on to Verboise how funny his consternation seemed.

"I do. We rode together in the First Cavalry a few years back." On Verboise's face settled a scowl that Pa recognized as meaning the news had unsettled him.

"Franny only said he was here to help train raw recruits. Seemed real taken with him, too."

"What you mean, Paw?" said Hy, listening from the porch's top step. He laid his whittling stick beside him. "What did you mean when you said she was 'taken' with him?"

My, but didn't his news from town cause a stir. First the mighty captain and now his lovesick son. Wilcox chuckled, "Oh, 'tweren't nothin', boy. That ornery little piece of fluff you call 'wife' spoke highly of him."

"How *highly?*"

"--Did you say you met him, today?" Verboise cut in.

"Yep, come down to the wagon with Franny. Carried the basket of parsnips she bought back to the hotel for 'er." He paused, waited, smiled sadistically, "put his arm 'round 'er, too."

"*What?*" "Hy jumped up spilling wood shaving down the front of his trowsers.

Seeming to take no notice of his son's growing misery, Wilcox continued, his voice as smooth as butter. "She was a-sashayin' back to that fire trap hotel of her ma's when she stepped off the curb, nearly getting herself run over by an ordnance wagon." He pulled at the pipe, let the smoke out slow, before he added, "Them's the biggest wagons I ever saw. Why I heard tell they carry pretty nar' on to 1000 pounds of ammunition at a time. Wonder the mules can pull 'um." He fell silent. Pretending to be oblivious to the two pairs of eyes riveted upon him, both for different reasons.

He puffed on the pipe again, gazed out at the yard, noted the chickens. Thought about how he might lay in a dozen more. 'Specially now, since Verboise's boys had been bringing him the loot they stole to sell on the St Louis black market.

"Well?" Hy asked.

"Huh?" Pa acted as though Hy's question had pulled him from a trance.

"His arm, Paw!" Hy exploded, "You said he done put his arm 'round 'er."

Verboise hushed his young lieutenant with a curt look and addressed Wilcox, "More importantly, sir, I want to know if he said anything to you, at all. Did he speak to

153

you?"

He ignored his son, turned to Verboise. "Well, I don't rightly remember if he spoke to me or not. I reckon he did. I let him shake my hand, anyway."

Verboise gave a snort of disgust and abruptly left the porch. He pushed past Hy and walked swiftly to his horse, a big chestnut stallion saddled and tethered beneath the jack oak in the front yard. He mounted and without a word, galloped away towards the road leading to town.

When dust trailed after Verboise's horse, Paw Wilcox glanced at his son, saw rage written over his face. He smirked, "She shore looked pretty, today, Son." He knew Hy hadn't been with his wife since their wedding night and it delighted him no end to see him suffer. The boy should have taken his advice in the first place and not married the little strumpet. "Had on a silky green dress that--"

"Shut up, Paw!" Hy thundered. "I want you to tell me about him and his god damn arm."

On the dusty four mile trek into Jefferson City Verboise contemplated the fact that his former trainee was in town. Worse, he was staying at Erin House and he had to know why on both counts. The stallion he whipped into a gallop and by dark the horseman arrived at the first guard post.

Verboise slipped past the sleeping sentry, frowned at the lax behavior, and walked his horse through the city streets. No one stopped him. No one asked to see a pass or ask for a code word. Unmolested, he rode to Hog Ally. In the shadow of the Capitol dome the ally ran parallel between High and Main street and behind Erin House. He tethered his horse at the mouth of the dim lane and began walking.

Several wild pigs rooted about the shadows in the garbage -hence the name. Coarse laughter drifted from the number of gambling dives, brothels, and grog shops that lined the way. Several men lay in stages of intoxication in the doorways. One lay with his head in the lap of a blowsy older woman who looked up when she spied Verboise.

She called after him as he passed by, "Hello, big man, wanna go ta heaven fer a dollar?" He paid her no attention, heard her drunken cackle behind him, and strode to the Kentucky the last saloon on the end.

To the little black boy sitting in the dirt in front of the saloon he growled, "Find Brush. I'll be in back."

No lack of business since the Federals got to town, he noted, feeling the disgust rise in his throat like it did every time he confronted the world's debauchery. The smell of whisky, cheap perfume, and cigar smoke assaulted his nostrils, and a wall of solid blue uniforms blocked his way. However, when taking in the size of the man quietly saying, "Excuse me, let me pass, please," the wall quickly parted.

Verboise waited nearly 15 minutes before Brush Arbor entered the storeroom where he sat at a small table with one lamp flickering in its center. Before him was a map of the state and a cup of coffee. "Why did you keep me waiting?" he glared at the girl with raven hair to her waist and black eyes that held nothing but contempt for the world around her.

"What the hell do you care, for? I was busy." She poured herself into the chair across from him and held out her palm. "Men pay for my time, Chief, even time *wasted* in conversation." Her low cut gown revealed lush, touchable curves that were the most sought after in town. Since he had met her through old man Wilcox, he presumed that Hy's father had frequently found them.

Once, she had offered herself to him-free. She had said she never had screwed a man as tall as himself, and wanted to see if his height was any indication of his manhood. When he had indicated that her body was of no

155

interest to him, she had laughed and made disparaging remarks about his virility.

These, he ignored. She had been born in Leavenworth, Kansas, the child of a prostitute who had conceived her while working an evangelical church meeting. The meeting had been held in the field next to a small country church, too small to hold the overflow crowd that came from miles around to hear the travelling evangelist. He stayed for three days, preaching at evening and day services, exhorting folks to forsake the Devil or be assured of eternal hell-fire. To keep the sun off the listeners, the men made a shelter of brush laid on top of poles and this they called a "brush arbor." Brush's mother had named her daughter after the place of conception. Brush didn't say if she had been conceived before, after, or during a service. A brother served as a telegraph orderly at Fort Leavenworth. His sympathies also lay with the south, but, unlike him, Brush's loyalties came with a price.

Tonight, Verboise put a coin in her palm, ordered her a bottle of whisky, asked, "A Captain Josiah Scarborough lives at Erin House. What do you know about him?"

"Describe him." Brush sipped the whiskey. When he did she said, "Oh him," and smiled into her glass.

"You know him, all ready?"

"He's been in once or twice." Then she gave Verboise a sarcastic grin, "Why do you care about him?"

"Why is he in town?"

"He's a Federal soldier, why else?" With this she threw back her head and laughed.

When she did, Verboise gripped her hand so tightly that the girl stopped laughing and struggled to get free. "I can easily break it; don't mock me," he said, his voice a monotone, and released her.

"I don't know why he's here. Trainin' troops or some-thin' like that." She rubbed her hand with the other one. Verboise's grip had hurt.

"That's absurd and you know it. Borenstein's Hessians, *Die Schwarze Garde,* speak mostly German. Why would an Irishman be sent to a city to train troops who spoke German or only limited English?"

She frowned up at him and he could tell she hated him. That didn't matter. What mattered was getting answers from her. He reached for her again but she jerked away, said quickly, "He's on orders here."

Now that was interesting. "Upon whose?"

"Jesus, Chief, how the hell should I know. He don't confide in me, you know. He just comes in with this old man and sometimes with a few other officers. They have a couple of drinks and..." she let her voice drift off and shrugged her smooth white shoulders.

"This old man. Who is he?"

"Sweet Jesus, but you're curious as to my customers. A girl like me has to be discrete."

Her sly smile infuriated him but she sat too far back for him to reach her. After a pause, she said, "I might be persuaded to unseal my lips." She held up the coin he had given her and motioned for another.

When he put the half-eagle on the table before him she said, "Name is Brady. He's old but cute, real funny. He quit the army."

So he didn't drown beneath the White Star, after all. Verboise thought and settled back in his chair. Things were beginning to make sense. "What do they talk about?"

She snatched up the coin, said, "Drinkin' and the war, mostly."

"Have you heard them mention my name?"

She stared at him a good minute or so before she asked, "Why?"

"Because, I want to know." The woman deliberately provoked him, but he allowed her to do so. Frequently, she played this game with him, only tonight he felt edgier than usual and was in no mood for it. He stood and started for

157

her, but her sneer stopped him.

"Hurt me again, Chief, and I'll scream and 100 ring-a-ling alligators will come in here and twist your half-breed balls off. You're big, you're dangerous, and you might even maim a few. But in the end, even you ain't no match fer the number of rarin'-to-go boys drinkin' in my saloon tonight."

After glaring at her for a full minute, Verboise sat down, took a sip of coffee, and subdued his emotions. Now, was not the time to call attention to himself by starting a brawl in the Kentucky saloon.

"That's better," she said, patting his arm but quickly pulling back her hand. "Calm down. You come in here, spittin' out questions 'bout chaps I hardly know." She settled back in her chair and drained her glass, winked, said, "But, I'm sure plannin' on gettin' cozy with that Captain Scarborough."

He cared nothing for knowing with whom she did or did not bed. "Just find out the real reason he's here and why he's staying at Erin House."

"Oh, I know that all ready. Widow Moone is his aunt or somethin' and she invited him there."

Could it be just coincidence? Still, "and the girl, Franny. Does he have much to do with her?"

"How am I supposed to know that? She's his cousin, ain't she? She lives there too, don't she? I don't know what you mean?" She waved her empty glass in front of him. "Be a gent fer a change and pour me another whiskey."

Eventually, Brush agreed to get Scarborough's information. What orders did he have? What did Brady have to do with them? Her brother, a corporal in the telegraph office would be able to find out. Then Verboise would know for certain. Then he could act.

Thursday the 4th--Erin House

"Says here in the *Examiner* Lyon's stopped all river traffic on the Missouri." Colonel Potter squinted at the newspaper, held so far away at arms length that it almost lay folded in his plate of eggs. "The *John Warner's* to be a gunboat and cruise the river. It will capture or blow out of the water any river craft that is transporting enemy troops. More gun boats will be put into service by the Federal government" He fell silent, mumbling the rest of the story to himself.

"And what else does it have to say?" Brady poured gravy over his biscuits and leaned over to see the article for himself.

"Well, if you'll kindly remove yourself from my plate, my good man, I'll read it to you"

"And if you'd put yer glasses on, you could read the dang thing without first bathin' it in yer eggs!"

Josiah grinned to himself. This morning was beginning like the others Brady had been in residence at Erin House. He had found Brady near to losing his arm and languishing in the city hospital, a two story white limestone on Cherry, by the state penitentiary. He had learned that the dank, evil-smelling place had gone up when the penitentiary was built in the '30's to isolate infectious disease cases. When a person was sent to the hospital, he expected to die there.

His former sergeant he had brought "home" to Erin House to recuperate from the nasty bullet he had taken while fleeing the *White Star*. Not only had the wound become septic but the infection had spread up his arm. But, with decent food, spotless surroundings, and the poultices of heat and herbs Tycee used, the limb was healing, the redness, and swelling disappearing. It looked as though Brady not only might live, but keep his arm after all.

"It says here, Sergeant Brady, that Colonel John D. Stevenson will be in command of the river from St.

Charles to Kansas City and will maintain posts at Boonville, and Jefferson City. How can one man maintain discipline with such a vast territory to command?" Potter glanced over at his breakfast partner, grunted in disgust to see Brady hunched over his plate and shoveling in his food.

"Never heard of the man," Brady retorted with his mouth full of eggs and biscuits.

I dare say, Sergeant Brady, please observe the common courtesy of not talking with your mouth full. You are no longer eating in a Cavalry mess tent."

Without stopping for Brady to comment, Potter continued reading,

"He is with the 7th Regiment, Missouri Volunteers. Not only will he have command of the entire river, but will also field troops in the countryside to scout the surrounding country, gain information of hostile parties and break them up. Hmm," he looked up, caught Josiah's eye, said, "We certainly need something done around here to stop all these depredations against honest Union men."

It amused Josiah to see the two old veterans sparring with each other and agreed with Potter, "Indeed, we do, Sir." But the story had caught his interest. "Does the newspaper say anything about the kind of troops he'll use for the scouts on land or when this command will begin?"

"Not a word, Sir. I presume command will start soon and the troops will be fairly raw. Most of the men coming into the army are a great deal more fresh than when I was campaigning. Also, a man wasn't considered field-worthy until he'd had at least six months training under his belt."

"Ah go along, with ya, now, Colonel," Brady scoffed. "Ya know and I know that ain't true. Many a lad got hustled into the corps, a musket shoved in his hand and told to get out there and shoot the enemy before the enemy shot him." Brady wiped his mouth with his napkin and took a swallow of coffee.

Unnoticed, Josiah pushed back his chair, murmured, "Gentlemen, if you'll excuse me," and edged away. He left his breakfast companions heatedly debating the merits and demerits of military training before the Mexican War.

From across the room and equally as loud, laughter erupted from the oak table that sat twelve. The conversation swirled around the Independence Day Celebrations the city planned for late afternoon and the fireworks display at sunset. At the table several young officers from Borenstein's regiment vied with each other for favorable glances from the two young females seated side by side. Masterpieces of feminine pulchritude, Josiah decided, Sigrid and Franny were trying to decide who among the youths should accompany them to the celebrations. The girls giggled at everything any one said. Listening, he stood aside, drinking a cup of coffee.

He eyed Sigrid, noted the elegance of her posture, her serenity, her Eurasian beauty. Among the admirers she seemed to favor Lieutenant Gus Werner. Josiah found him to be a stable, good-hearted, and fun-loving German-American who was one of the few who knew how to ride a horse. He had been delighted that the men of the new company he was forming had voted in Gus to be the First Lieutenant. Although Josiah knew little about Otto Zimmer, Gus had sought his advice about how to approach Sigrid's father.

As though he should know! Great Scott, up until recently he hadn't sought out the sort of women that had fathers around to approach. He wondered why he wasn't attracted to Sigrid instead of to the tempestuous redhead. If he were in the market for a wife, then Miss Zimmer would be ideal. But he wasn't looking for a wife, not today anyway.

Today - in fact at that very moment - he was supposed to be at headquarters meeting with Borenstein to discuss the overall organization of the new company. Moreover,

Independence Day or not, he would have his new recruits on the field this morning drilling and learning tactics in unmounted horsemanship. He had told no one but Borenstein and Brady - not Aunt Dee, not Franny -about his mission. He dared trust nobody - even these kinswomen. Colonel Miles had warned him that the town crawled with Secesh, and until he was sure, everyone he met was a suspect.

Secesh or not, as usual, Franny drew his attention. Although she sat as demurely as her friend, hands folded quietly before her, most of her hair this morning tucked neatly beneath a snood, she gave off sparks. She might as well have been dancing a jig on the table, skirts lifted, and shouting for all the world to hear. Composed and lady-like she appeared, yet he sensed beneath the smooth crust lay a volcano of molten fire. He glanced at the other men, wondered if they sensed the same thing.

He saw they did by their glittering eyes, wolfish smiles, and fastidious dress - the way every morning they risked reprimand for tardiness to duty. Thanks to Dee confiding in him as though he was the "older brother," he knew that many of them had sought out the girls, inviting them for walks, talks, and carriage rides. Two had given them small gifts of candy and lace. Franny had eaten so many German chocolates at once that she had made herself sick.

One had even spoken to Dee about seeking Franny's hand in marriage. Of medium height and square build, Borenstein's aide stood slightly to Franny's left with his hand resting in a proprietary manner on the back of her chair. Every now and then Franny would gaze up at him and smile. Watching them, Josiah flushed with sudden anger.

Dee had discouraged the suitor. Well mannered, educated, ambitious, the lieutenant was from a moneyed family in St. Louis. Josiah supposed women might find him attractive in a blond, Germanic way. But Dee had said, "I'll not be havin' me only daughter wed a soldier-boy." Her remark had irked him when spoken and still rankled today, and he couldn't figure out why.

Without waiting further to catch Franny's eye, he set down his cup and briskly walked away.

Breakfast over, the officers finally gone to their posts, the girls rested in the apartment parlor. Meal times had become exhausting, yet, heady affairs. And with Sigrid to share the work of serving and hostessing, it was all the more fun. The jollification of Erin House may have been due to the dozen or so Yankee officers quartering there, but Franny didn't care. For a glorious change, the dining room rang with music and laughter so much so that sometimes she had to pinch herself to remember that they were the enemy.

For the whole time she had been back from the western counties, she had flirted and giggled, and moments actually occurred when she hadn't felt married. When she did remember Hy Wilcox, headache and melancholia overtook her. Not a sign of her husband since her return. She figured, if he really wanted to see her, he could have pretended to the sentries that he was just a farmer riding to town with his Paw to help sell vegetables. When she did see him, Franny thought, she'd give him a piece of her tongue for neglecting her.

Or would she? She couldn't decide. Perhaps, she was better off not to have him under foot all the time, pestering her for.... She didn't want to think about it. Right now, she'd enjoy the Yankees' attentions, giggle with Sigrid over this one and that one, and forget Hy Wilcox existed. At least she'd try.

As soon as the three of them had left the boat and walked in the front door, they saw the new borders were mostly Federal officers. This pleased Dee, excited Franny, and caused Josiah to move right in. Because of his rank

163

and experience he immediately assumed a relaxed leadership over the other officers billeted there. Within two days his charm had mesmerized the Zimmer family, the coloreds, and the other day even Paw Wilcox shook his hand.

Franny knew Josiah Scarborough watched her. He watched her all the time. Sometimes she'd catch him staring at her, the way he had on the boat and on the road near Rock Creek. However, since discovering they were remotely related he had been a model of decorum and kept his distance. This behavior disappointed her. More than any of the others, she wanted him to flirt with her.

"Your cousin Josiah seemed a bit put out this morning. He left in a hurry. My word, Franny, but he's the handsomest man I've ever seen!" Sigrid nearly swooned when she had first met him.

"Suppose he is? That means he's had women all over him, all the time. A man like that *is not* good husband material." Franny smoothed her green cotton frock and sat back in the Boston rocker.

"But how can you resist him? Besides, I think he's got a real spark for you." On the davenport Sigrid lounged back, moving beneath her head a pillow embroidered with a spring nymph dancing amid vines. The nymph's golden hair entwined around the vine until one couldn't distinguish between the sprite's hair and the vine. Sometimes Sigrid possessed this sylph-like quality, like now as she lay back and rhapsodized about Josiah Scarborough.

Franny blushed to her heels. If Sigrid saw it, then had Paw Wilcox? There she had been racing back to the hotel, not watching where she was walking, when she had stepped in front of the ordnance wagon. But, Josiah had pulled her back to safety with his arm around her waist, had kept it there a moment past the time propriety allowed. Then he had given her a squeeze. Right out there on the street in front of God and everybody in Jefferson City. Right out there in front of Paw Wilcox, who probably couldn't wait to gallop home and report it to Hy.

"Oh, I don't think so, Sigrid. I think he's just a tease. Josiah treats me like a little sister." True, he had acted brotherly - other than those moments she had caught him staring at her and the arm-around-the-waist-squeeze. Neither of them had admitted noticing it. "I think," Franny continued, "any woman would have a difficult time holding his interest for long. He'd tire of me within a year."

"Hmmm, I don't know. I think he wants to be your sweetheart." Shrieking with laughter, Sigrid ducked beneath the pillow while Franny threw its mate and every other pillow in the room at her friend.

Friday, the 5ᵗʰ, three o'clock in the morning
Baby Franny plays with the rope. Waves wash over the ship, inching closer with each thrust, but they are putting out a fire. Flames run the length of the mast and sails billow with orange tongues of fire. The ship is on fire.

The dream, again, recurring as far back as she could remember. Only, this time instead of sea spray it was filled with smoke and Franny sat bolt up in bed, her eyes still closed. When she opened them she saw a conflagration outside the window dancing its shadow upon her bedroom wall. By now Sigrid was awake. Coughing from acrid smoke filling their lungs, both screamed simultaneously for Dee Moone.

"Mama!" ---"Aunt Dee!"

Panic threw them out of bed and into their wrappers. Tycee's daughter, Opal, ran into the apartment, her words tumbling over each other in an incoherent scream. "Miss Franny, Mis' Dee, Miss Sigrid—we is burnin' to the groun' y'all git up. The whole place be on fire!"

It appeared as if the entire back of the hotel had gone up in flames. Soon, the smoke would be so thick they couldn't see. Dee quickly began gathering up documents and deeds, ordered Franny to get keepsakes they had brought from Ireland. She opened the little safe she kept beside her bed and managed to stuff her wrapper pockets with money and bank notes before the smoke forced her from the bedroom.

In the lobby voices from the boarders floated down the stairs. Josiah's face appeared above them at the banister rail. "Franny? Aunt Dee?" he called down. He was buttoning his shirt and tucking it in his pants as he spoke. He spied Toby. "Get the women out of here. Have you called the volunteers yet?"

"Yes Sir! Ruby be runnin' all the way to the court house."

"Good! Gather all the buckets and water containers you can." He disappeared into the gloom of the upstairs hallway. Franny heard him bellow an order about the third floor.

"Josiah!" Dee yelled up at him. She shook off Toby's hand and tried to run up the stairs. "You come back here!"

"It's awright Mis' Dee. He's just helpin' to get the peoples awake. He'll be awright. You come along with Toby, now." His voice, soft, as though talking to a child, he nevertheless clutched her arm, refusing to let go.

"But me godson, He's got to come, now!" Dee's hysteria made her seem ten times stronger than normal, and it was all Franny, Toby, and Sigrid could do to pull the woman from the hotel into the street.

Once outside, they huddled together and heard the deep gong of the bell on top of the courthouse at the corner of Monroe and High Streets, two long blocks away. Heard for ten miles around, the bell summoned Jefferson City's volunteer firemen.

From St. Louis four German women with their seven

children had followed their husbands, who served with Borenstein. Boarding on the third floor, they now scurried out the door. Handkerchiefs over their mouths, coughing, the women carried what little baggage they retrieved before the soldiers helped them to evacuate. Following the women and children, the Federal officers spilled into the street. Except for Josiah.

"Where's me godson?" Dee screamed. Tears ran down her cheeks and with her disheveled hair tumbling about her face contorted with panic, Franny thought her mother looked like a wild banshee from the Irish moors. Before she could stop her, Dee ran to Gus Werner. Bent double coughing, the man couldn't answer quickly enough for Dee. So, she began beating on his arm, demanding to know, "Where is Josiah Scarborough? Where is Captain Scarborough? Where is he? Why ain't he out here with you? Where's me godson?"

Choking with every word, Werner finally gasped, "He's looking for the Colonel and Sergeant Brady. They're not here."

"What you mean, not here? 'Tis by nine o'clock every night the old gentleman goes to his rest. As for Brady, an Irishman he is and only the devil knows."

Sigrid and Franny stood at her side, their arms around the heaving shoulders. Tears streamed down Sigrid's face, but she appeared her usual serene self. Franny, however, felt no calm. If she didn't have to restrain her mother, Franny feared she too would panic.

"Yes, Ma'am. But they're not here." Lieutenant Werner finally got his wind and his voice back. He extended his arm to Dee. "Come, Mrs. Moone, stand back from the hotel. Look at your girls," he glanced at Franny and caught Sigrid's eye. "See how worried they are about you."

When the volunteer firemen arrived, Franny noticed that some came with nightshirts tucked inside their trowsers. Nearly 75 men came rushing on foot down High Street dragging the hand pump and the hose wagon after them. Soliciting the help of the officers and other bystanders, the firemen connected the hose to the underground cistern and began pumping. Arc after arc of water fell on the blaze coming from the back of the hotel.

Otto Zimmer often referred to Franny as his "other daughter." So when he jumped from his carriage and took Dee and his "two girls" in his huge arms, Franny's butterflies subsided - but not for long. She watched the front door, anxious to see Josiah's tall, handsome figure bounding towards them. Surely, he would come. Why hadn't he? When they had been there long enough for flames to spurt over the roof top at the rear of the building, and he had not joined them, she knew something was wrong. Her mother had fainted. Otto and their friends were either busy trying to awaken her or help the firemen. Gus had thrown a blanket around Sigrid's shoulders and stood engrossed, soothing her. Unnoticed, Franny slipped away. She ran towards the hotel, keeping to the dark and stumbled into the side door off the driveway, to be met at once by gagging, blinding smoke.

"Josiah!" She called. Continuing to call out his name, she made her way into the lobby, so dense with searing smoke she almost fainted. Seeing no flames, however, she started up the stairs. Suddenly, from behind a rough hand grabbed her around the waist, yanking her back down the stairs. She swerved her head around and saw a wet kerchief over a nose.

"Hy Wilcox!"

"Damn you, Franny," he growled, and he brandished a revolver beneath her nose. "You ain't supposed to be in here. Whyn't you outside with the rest of them women?"

Speechless with shock she could only stare. He held her pinned to the wall at the bottom of the stairs.

"Oh, ain't talkin' to your husband, are you, Wife?

168

Well, this here is the news for you today." He breathed in her ear and gripped her so hard she could barely breathe, difficult anyway because of the smoke filling the room. "This is only a warnin'. Ain't nothin' much burnt 'cept them nigger quarters and the stable. You tell yore maw to quit goin' 'round town and sayin' the South's cause is the Devil's own. And you, *Wife,* stay away from Yankees what want to put their arms around you."

"Why did you do this to us. I helped you, I...." She sobbed, feeling the tears begin to flow, hating herself because of them.

She sensed the smirk beneath his kerchief and heard the sarcasm; "After seeing you and China Sigrid surrounded by that gaggle of Yankees in the park today, I hunted me up a fire-cracker left over from the celebration of our country's birth and decided to explode it, tonight." Then his eyes went flat like the sudden monotone of his voice. "You weren't supposed to know it was me. But seein' as how you do, I reckon it don't make no difference. You don' care nothin' 'bout me. Never did. 'Specially, since you got your Yankee beau livin' here." He pushed her harder against the wall. It hurt.

"You're crazy!" She spat at him and tried to free her hands to scratch at his eyes, but he had his body wedged against hers like a vice.

He slapped her. "Don't you never call me crazy, again, woman. I know all about your so-called cousin, puttin' his hands all over you."

She tasted warm blood on her upper lip where he had struck her. As thoroughly as the smoke was beginning to engulf them both, terror swept through her body. At any moment, she expected to see flames leap out into the lobby. Never in her wildest imaginings had she thought sweet Hy Wilcox capable of brutal violence. Moody he had been and at times disturbingly so, but to stoop to this, she would never have thought it of him.

Before she could deny his accusation he hurried on, " As I was sayin' this here is only a warnin' 'cause you done helped us with the *White Star,* but your Lincoln lovin' Maw had better soften her tongue around town. She don't have as many friends as she thinks she does. And you, you better not be unfaithful to me!"

Franny opened her mouth to speak but he raised his fist again and she instinctively cowed. "Listen my pretty little *wife,"* he whispered in her face, his breath vile with sour rage, "you tell anybody it was me that fired this rat trap, I swear I'll come back for you and you'll be dead too."

With that, he knocked her head into the wall and fled through the smoke.

Stunned from the blow, for a full minute she couldn't breathe. She slumped on the bottom step gagging on her tears and gasping from the smoke. Then her mind shouted, *You dare not just sit here, Frances Margaret. You must find Josiah. You must find Josiah!*

Obeying an uncontrollable impulse, she staggered up the stairs. She ran into his room, then into all the rooms on the second floor, each one a searing den of smoke. She started for the third floor, but stopped and ran to the back of the second floor hall. The heat and smoke were worse than up front in the lobby, and she had to steady herself to keep from fainting.

Leading from the second floor into the kitchen and pantry in the basement, the narrow back stairs turned at an angle on the landing. She took off her wrap, tore out the sleeve, and tied this over her nose and mouth. It helped to filter out some of the smoke but did nothing to keep it out of her eyes. Stinging tears making it nearly impossible to see, wearing only her nightdress, she edged her way down the back stairs. Almost to the bottom she spied the door leading out onto the back yard and the porch. Tiny flames from the outside nibbled around the frame and little fiery

170

fingers poked beneath the solid oak. Next to the door sat the barrel Toby filled with water each morning.

Praying the fire would not burn through the door until she had searched the panty, she stepped down and stumbled over his body. Josiah lay face down, unconscious, bleeding from a wound on the back of his head, and barely breathed. "Oh, Josiah," she sobbed and pulled at this arms and legs, "please, please wake up." There was no way she could carry him, even dragging him more than a few inches seemed impossible. He was too large and there was no time to get help. How foolish she had been not to have Otto or one of the men come with her.

She swore, using curses she often thought but never uttered and ended her tantrum with, "Damn you! Wake up! I didn't come all this way only to have us both burn to death." She broke off because she saw the dishpan stacked against the back of the dry sink. Next to the sink stood the barrel. Had the day's use left enough water in the barrel? Could she make it across the kitchen, fill the dishpan with water and get back to Josiah before the fire burned through the door? She'd have to try.

She was back and pouring what little cold water the barrel held over his head before she drew another ragged breath. She knelt beside him and used her torn wrap as a wet rag to wipe his face turned to its side. As her lungs burned from the fumes and her eyes continued to water from the smoke, she kept shaking him. When, at last, his eyes opened, she fell on his neck, sobbing, and thanking God. He rolled over with a groan and his arm went around her, pulling her to him, "Franny?" he whispered.

Still groggy, he sat up, swayed, but remained upright. Suddenly, the back door burst into flames and a gust of fire whooshed into the kitchen. Consuming all in its path, flames bore down upon them. He lifted himself to his feet, picked her up in his arms and took the back stairs two at a time. Through the second floor hall and down the front stairs he ran. In the lobby flames leaping from the apartment nearly caught them, but he jumped aside, kicked open the front door, and staggered into the street.

The next day, after a speech offering any man the opportunity to forego the march south to join Sterling Price, Verboise led 51 men out of the Wilcox farmyard. Fifteen remained behind, deciding their families and farms needed them more than Sterling Price did. Through much soul searching, arguing with Hy, and fortified by several deep draughts of jug whiskey, Buster Cowles chose to be one of the fifteen. He reminded everyone that he was the only man at home and had five sisters and his maw to look after. Telling everybody to "kill a dozen Yankees for me," he sat on his horse a good while watching the men pack their gear, then wheeled and galloped out of the yard.

Hy and Chess watched him go. "Hell, he'll catch up before we hit the Osage," Hy said.

"Reckon?"

"I reckon." Hy turned to the younger man, added, "*Corporal* McDonald."

"Huh?"

"With Cowles gone, we need another corporal. I recommend you, McDonald."

Even up to the last minute Paw Wilcox tried to talk Verboise out of going. He stood beside the big chestnut, holding onto Verboise's reins. "Now, you don't know fer sure that my daughter-in-law will finger her own husband. And jest because that Yankee, Brady might still be livin' don't mean you all have to skedaddle."

"I'm afraid so, old friend. At least for awhile. Until tempers have cooled a bit. My informant learned that Scarborough is on special orders to find me and bring me before a firing squad. It wouldn't do to stay around and allow myself to be captured.

172

Even as you and I speak, Borenstein is planning to scour the county with over 300 soldiers. They've been reinforced by new troops from Colonel Stevenson who now commands all the river traffic. With the Confederate forces on the Arkansas border, the Federals control all the railroad and telegraph lines, too. I expect by tomorrow Home Guards will come here, asking about your son. They shouldn't hurt you; for as far as anyone knows, you are a peaceful farmer who has kept his mouth shut about his loyalties. On the other hand, I've heard tales from the northeast part of the state, the area around Hannibal and Palmyra, that troops under John Pope commit atrocities upon civilians they suspect of southern sympathies. Just the other day, a trainload of Federals shot at and killed a farmer tilling his field when the train rolled by." Verboise stopped, watched the old man stare back at him with a look of sour dismay, added, "You're welcome to come with us."

Paw's gaze shifted taking in his property, his barns, his home, before he said slowly, "I reckon I best stay right here. If'n I run, they'd know I was guilty, but if'n I stay, say I don't know where that damned boy of mine is, they'll jest have to believe me. But thanks fer askin' Cap'n." Wilcox wiped his brow with a dirty kerchief, continued, "Damn that boy, anyway. He knew better than to pull that dido—fool trick. I swear to you, Cap'n, if 'n he was younger, I'd whap his backsides 'til they bled."

Overhearing this, Hy moved into the shadows to stay as inconspicuous as possible. Just as when a child he had suffered his father's rage, all day long today, he'd suffered under the Captain's.

According to Verboise, he'd disobeyed orders. But Hy honestly thought the order to stay away from the hotel had meant, *don't go there openly anymore as Franny's visitor* - not - *never go there at all.* Stealing the silver pitchers from the dining room sideboard and other pretties

173

from the vacated rooms, even firing the hotel, Verboise hadn't minded. Nor had he seemed overly concerned that Hy's gun had jammed and he'd only knocked Scarborough out instead of putting a bullet through him.

That Hy had stupidly let Franny see him and had rowed with her was the flash point of Verboise's fury. Regardless of Hy's earnest attestations that his wife wouldn't give him away, Verboise believed she'd yell, "Hy Wilcox" at the top of her voice, even if it meant implicating herself in the *White Star* incident. So angry had the Cap'n been that he threatened to make Hy ride into town and give himself up! When Hy pleaded with him, the Cap'n then decided to shoot him, for disobeying orders. For nearly an hour he had made Hy dance in the hot sun as he fired bullet after bullet at his feet. One had nicked his hand but Verboise hadn't stopped shooting, and his Paw had just sat up on the front porch and laughed.

Had it been worth it? Hy kept asking himself. Yes, he believed that at last he had shown Franny the depth of his loyalties for the South and his jealous rage because of her. If she had been a proper, lovin' wife to him, he'd have no cause to do what he did. When all this war business was over, he'd get her back and things would be normal between them.

Even as Hy thought these things, at the back of his mind, a nagging worm of doubt holed its way through his bravado. He had hurt her and hurt Erin House and he knew how much she loved that old hotel. And she probably loved this distant cousin of hers, too. Leaving with Verboise would prevent him from keeping an eye on her and killing him. He'd just have to deal with her when he got back.

A sense of hopelessness exploded within him then, making him feel powerless and impotent, and numb. For at the bottom of his shattered heart he knew he had lost her and that she would never forgive him.

"Lieutenant!" Verboise shouted to him. "Mount up."

"Yes, sir." Hy hopped-to, bawling the order to the men.

They were leaving at dark before the moon rose full, and soon, packs and accoutrements jingling, Verboise led the newly named company, Mounted Rifles, along the postal road headed for southwest Missouri. Along the way, Hy knew they planned on burning every bridge and destroying all telegraph lines and railroad culverts. By the end of the week, they planned to meet up with either Ben McCulloch or Sterling Price's forces and, for awhile, lay aside guerrilla warfare. As true soldiers for the Confederacy they would swear in and join one of the cavalry units. Hy planned on fighting with bravery and honor but only for awhile. Then, he'd come back to Cole County and have a reckoning with his dear little wife.

The next day's sun had barely presented its hot face over the horizon before Paw heard loud knocking at his front door. He heard Aunt Sukey calling out that she was "a-comin'," heard the door creak open.

"Jeremiah Wilcox. Get him, now, Auntie." The voice was one he knew. He hitched up the suspenders on his pants, pulled on his boots. Yep, Verboise had called it right. That little bitch had told 'em Hy done it. The old man smiled to himself; he was ready for them. He came down the stairs, feeling the anger burn again, the bile rise in his throat, his hands twitch, eager to hold his old Lancaster and put a ball through each blue-belly daring to stand in his doorway.

"I'm Jeremiah Wilcox," he said mildly. "Howdy, Brudge," he nodded to a huge, moustached man standing behind the lieutenant. Seeing Brudge there didn't surprise him. A long time neighbor, though not a friend, Jeremiah had suspected he was a Union man. In fact, Brudge's place was on the list of farms to burn out; Verboise just hadn't got 'round to it. Now, by riding with a Federal search party

175

Charlie Brudge was coming out in the open. Jeremiah wouldn't forget.

"Mr. Wilcox, I am Lieutenant Gorditch of the Cole County Home Guards. You are under arrest." The swarthy lieutenant had a faint "Dutch" accent and poked his revolver in Wilcox's face.

"And may I ask why?" He hadn't moved but stood blocking the entrance.

"Shut up!" Brudge yelled and swung on him. He tried to defend himself but the others at the door pummeled him, until bleeding, he fell inside to the floor. He heard the lieutenant's order.

"Search it. Wilcox's got an arsenal here. And find his son!"

If old Sukey hadn't helped him up, he supposed the soldiers would have trampled him to death getting into the house. She sat him in a chair by the door and brought him a cold cloth for his bleeding eye and mouth. Upstairs he heard glass breaking, drawers being pulled out, furniture over-turned, and things being ripped apart.

They searched from cellar to roof and found nothing. He knew they wouldn't. Throughout the night after Verboise had left, he had busily buried the cache of ammunition and the trinkets as yet unsold on the black market in St. Louis.

"Where's your boy?" Brudge yelled in his face.

"Where's that thievin' Rebel house-burner?"

"Don't rightly know." He was still bleeding from the nose and mouth.

"You're a lyin' son-of-a-bitch," Brudge hit him in the left ear, bursting his eardrum. The ear roared with pain and Paw Wilcox felt the warm blood flow down the side of his neck. The soldier-neighbor started to hit him again when the voice of the lieutenant stopped him.

"Brudge, never mind. His boy's not here. We've searched the place over. We'll take what we can and Mr.

Wilcox to town. He can sit in jail until he decides to tell us where his son is."

"But, you can't do that. I ain't done nothin. I ain't responsible for whatever you say Hy done!" Jeremiah hadn't expected this kind of treatment. But his arguments went unheard. Roughly, Brudge grabbed him around the collar, yanked him to his feet, and propelled him outdoors. The Federals pushed him face down into his own produce wagon and tied his hands around his ankles.

As he lay hog-tied on the planking that smelled of tomatoes and melons, he listened to the sounds of his farm being raided. The Federals rounded up all his stock, two milk cows, his saddle horse, three sows with piglets, and the chickens, and loaded up a commissary wagon with grain and produce he had stored. Then, the lieutenant poked his ugly face into the wagon and told him that the government would pay him for his provisions and stock, but Wilcox didn't believe it for one minute.

When he heard Sukey plead with them not to burn the house, he prayed that it would be spared. If it were, he decided he'd give the Sisters of Charity in St. Louis some of the money brought from his sales of purloined goods on the St. Louis black market. And all the while Jeremiah Wilcox was bargaining with his deity, he was plotting Charlie Brudge's death.

Lying on the bed in Sigrid's room, half-dressed in her chemise and corset, Franny was resting before she had to pull on her hoop and the green checked dimity over it. The dress was new; a gift from Otto since all her clothes had been lost in the fire.

From the looks of the charred kitchen, the colored's quarters, and the apartment, her mother said that Hy had wanted to burn the staff and the family to death. Doubting this was completely true, Franny, however, moved in a daze of terrified paralysis. She knew he would return to kill her, because he said he would if she told everyone it was him. But she hadn't heeded. Indeed, screaming his name out in the streets, she had told them without thinking, told them when Josiah had stumbled outside with her and both of them coughing up their lungs. She had babbled his name and sobbed, gagged, and wept some more and spoke his name once again. But she had not admitted she was married to him. She would rather die first. And this she thought she just might do before she got a chance to confess.

Never before in her life had she experienced prolonged fright. The day she had waved to the boat had been frightening. But her panic had dissipated almost as soon as she got home. And, though fearful in the beginning that she would be named in the crime, this feeling too had abated over the past month. But the fear she held now clung to her day in and day out, for the past two weeks, grinding down her energies until by dusk she was utterly exhausted.

With no hotel to help run, she slept until noon and napped in the late afternoon. She jumped at shadows, hated to be alone on the street or in a room, like now, and heard every creak and footstep made in the night. Only in Otto and Josiah's presence did she feel absolutely safe.

Josiah -she thought a lot about him, loved it when he rode over and took supper with them. With his head still bandaged, he had tactfully declined Otto's offer of boarding at the small Zimmer home with the rest of the family--a "family" of seven extra people that included not only Franny and Dee but also Colonel Potter, Sergeant Brady, Tycee and her girls. Dee's "darlin' godson" chose to quarter inside the Capitol itself, near the enlisted men who tented on the grounds, and he had taken an eager Toby with him to be a camp cook and his valet.

Josiah was expected tonight for supper but Franny was too tired to dress, much less to eat. A tear crept down her cheek. Her own willfulness had caused this mess. Once again, she tortured herself with the "ifs" of the situation. If she hadn't pushed him to marry her - if she hadn't encouraged his pursuit of her in the first place - if she had been more compliant to his needs and wishes afterwards - if, if, if. Her head ached with the wisdom borne on the wings of hindsight.

A light knock, "Franny?"

"Come in, Sigrid, please." She sat up.

Looking delicious in deep gold muslin with fresh lilacs at her waist and entwined in her smooth, ebony hair, Sigrid poked her head in the door. She saw her friend's dishabille, frowned. "For heaven's sakes. Supper is on the table and your cousin is already here." She gave Franny a wink when she said "cousin." Then, said as though to dismiss the matter, "And he's brought Lieutenant Werner with him."

Franny smiled. "And Lieutenant Werner, dear Sigri, is why you are looking so pleased with yourself." She jumped off the bed. "Help me finish dressing, if you please, and stop blushing. You might as well admit it, you're in love."

"I'll not admit a thing, Miss Moone, " she giggled while smoothing Franny's petticoat and dress over the hoop, "until you admit your affections for your dashing cousin."

Over supper of cold ham, fresh green beans, corn, soft biscuits, quince preserves and fruitcake, the men talked about the war and the women listened until the discussion turned to the search for the Erin House arsonist.

"Nothing yet?" Otto helped himself to another biscuit and slathered it with preserves.

"No sir," Josiah answered. "And we still have his father in jail. What puzzles us is that the son appears to have acted alone. Yet, from what he said to Franny," he flickered an approving glance over her face and hair, "he burned the hotel because of my godmother's politics; that's something a bushwhacker would do."

"And if Sergeant Brady, here, had not dragged me with him to visit that low dive, the Kentucky Saloon, I would have been at the hotel and been able to stop the scoundrel." Colonel Potter reached for a piece of ham from the platter Tycee had sat in the middle of the crowded dining room table, but glared at his sidekick.

"Oh go along wid' ya, Colonel, you'd been a-snorin' in yer bed when the lad came 'round and be burned ta death 'cause ya wouldn't get up off yer dead arse fer love nor money if it weren't fer me once an' awhile getting' ya out - pardon, ladies." Brady grinned, turned red, and started shoveling green beans into his mouth.

"Well, if'n ya both had been in yer beds, where ya belonged at that hour, 'tis the life of me godson wouldn't have been risked," Dee frowned at them both, added, "fer shame, on both of ya."

Otto grinned, allowing his eyes to rest on Dee's pretty scowl before he turned serious and said to Lieutenant Werner, "Night riders have terrorized, especially among the *Deutshvolk.*"

"Right you are, *Herr* Zimmer, here in Cole County and around the countryside near St. Louis as well." Gus Werner sat next to Sigrid. It amused Franny the way he always agreed with the older man and sometimes spoke in German with him. Only, just then, she wasn't thinking much about the romance budding between her best friend and the young German-American officer. She had pointed to Hy as the fire starter, but she hadn't opened her mouth about his activities with Verboise. Should she, now? Should she tell Josiah everything she knew about Hy's moonlight rides? But she kept silent, fear twisting her insides and freezing her tongue.

Until without thinking she blurted, "Naturally, you've checked the Wilcox farm and out buildings?" She stopped eating, a bite of ham caught in her throat. Why had she allowed such a stupid remark to escape her? Of course the Yankees had thoroughly searched the property.

"Why do you ask, Franny? Are there some hidden buildings on the place we don't know about?" Josiah raised his eyes from his plate and stared into hers. Lately, when he had done this, she found herself unable to stop looking into his bottomless, blue eyes that held her captive.

"As much as yer went out there, yer should know, girl." Dee frowned. "After all, you two were sparkin' most all the time." She never ceased reminding Franny that it had been *her* "beau" that had nearly killed them all and practically destroyed their livelihood. Her mother was right, but her mother's implication that she had loved Hy was especially annoying when Josiah was around.

Now, she held her temper, forced her gaze down to her plate, dabbed her napkin at her mouth, and said, "My mother is mistaken about any mutual affection she believes I held for Mr. Wilcox. He and I were friends in school, that is all."

Josiah's mesmerizing stare drew her back when he said softly, "It doesn't surprise me at all that someone of my sex would find you... um...worthy of great esteem." He peered at her the way he had on the boat. Catching himself staring, he blushed, said hurriedly, "And I would imagine that he knew you did not return his affections, or else he wouldn't have done what he did." Looking away quickly and driving his fork into an ear of corn, he asked impersonally, "But, you were suggesting that there may be other buildings on the property we don't know about."

"There was this old shed that was falling in but we played charades in it."

Years ago, she had gone out there with Toby, Sigrid and Clay and had discovered the dilapidated building in a grove of trees. "I remember doing that." Sigrid chimed in

181

brightly. "Hy was even nice to Toby that day. An old hemp storage shed, it was at the back of the property."

"We'll get a detail together and go out there tomorrow and look for it, right Captain?"

"Yes, we will, Lieutenant Werner, first thing in the morning. But, tonight, I feel we've discussed this unhappy topic enough. Shall we tell the ladies of our surprise?"

"Yes sir," He laughed, turned to Sigrid, "There's a concert tonight on the Capitol lawn. Acting Governor Gamble will give a speech. He's most anxious to cooperate with the Central government, now that Missouri's provisional legislature has been established.

"--And we would be honored if you ladies consented to be our guest," Josiah finished, letting his eyes linger on Franny. Then remembering her mother he bowed toward Dee as if to say he also welcomed her.

"Oh, Papa, may we go? It sounds like a merry time." Color rose in Sigrid's cheeks and her eyes shone like Franny had never seen them do before. Her friend's happiness caused tears to form behind Franny's lids, an aberration she immediately attempted to hide behind a polite giggle into her napkin. She thought Sigrid would probably marry Gus Werner and be ecstatically happy with him, and Franny would have wanted nothing less for her friend.

What hurt like a blister was the awareness of her own fate. The way she saw it she had three realities awaiting her: a failed marriage, prison, or death. She could never live with Hy Wilcox again even if Mary, Joseph, and the Almighty Himself pardoned him. Or, she would be found out and implicated in the *White Star* murders and spend the rest of her life in the penitentiary. Or, before fate decided either of these two things, Hy would come back and kill her.

Again fatigue washed over her causing her to say, "Oh, do go Sigrid, but I must please decline." She longed to go but what kind of company would she be tonight as tired, blue, and frightened as she was? Besides, Ma probably wouldn't want to go and wouldn't let her go either.

"Nonsense," Josiah reached over and took her hand, "my little godsister has moped around this house for over two weeks, and I aim to make her laugh." His voice softened, "After all, that's the least I can do for someone who saved my life." He turned to Dee, "And you, dear godmother, you need some gaiety, too." Mindful of the men at the table, he glanced an invitation at each of them.

"I'm ta bed," Brady yawned. "No politician's speeches fer me, but thank ya lad."

"I too thank you, Sir, for the invitation. But I think I'll take my evening constitutional and stroll up the street a bit then I too will head for my earned repose."

"*Nein, Danke,* but I must go to the Royal. Otto shrugged as though to say what else as owner could he do.

Dee laughed, "No, lad, 'tis best for ya to be goin' without old Dee, this evenin'. But, for the invitation I do thank ya, kindly." Then to Franny she said, "An you, girl, best be goin' too. Ya hardly have tasted a thing tonight, an' you're not sleepin'----"

"--Ma, I'm really--"

"--No, ye ain't "too tired," like ye al'ays be sayin' ye are. Since the fire, ya sleep most o' the day, so how can ye be tired?" She patted Franny's hand. "You go along, now, an' enjoy yerself."

The night promised to be balmy and star-studded with a full moon close enough to touch. But it hadn't yet grown dark. The last pink rays of the sun clung to the purple sky and only a faint moon and the first stars twinkled above. Bearing the fragrance of wild primroses, a light breeze had sprung up which kept the sticky, mid-summer heat at bay. Beside her sat the most dashing man she had ever known—everything should have been perfect, and if this were six short months ago, it would have been. But the war had come, and she had made the worst mistake of her life, and now nothing could be perfect anymore. Everything held a flaw the size of a bullet wound.

Not the least of which was her ambivalence toward Josiah Scarborough - or, worse, what she sensed as his ambivalence towards her. The attraction she sensed between them frightened her. Almost palpable at times, it went beyond the bonds of childhood, the blood-tie of kinship, and even the gratitude towards the other for saving their life. Yet, each of them seemed to be keeping the other an ocean apart.

Of course in her married state, she could in no good conscience do anything else but; however, moments arose when she was with her kinsman, when she longed to run her hands through his wild hair and wondered what a kiss from his sensuous lips would feel like. Then, her good sense would warn her that here was a common soldier, probably used to dozens of women fawning over him, who, distant cousin or not, could never be trusted with her heart - if she had any heart left to give. And she would treat him as the "older brother" her mother insisted on making of him.

As for him, she hadn't a clue of what he wanted from her, if anything. Granted, when she had first encountered him on the road and then, on the boat, his intentions had been embarrassingly obvious. However, since learning of their family relationship, his ardor had cooled. And, lately, except for the times she had caught him gazing at her, he had treated her, as she imagined would any protective, jolly big brother.

The men had ridden over in a carryall large enough to squeeze in six. Josiah drove while Franny perched on the seat beside him. Behind them she heard Gus's low baritone and Sigrid's giggles.

"You're awfully quiet," Josiah let the pair of dappled

grays walk at their own pace.

"I'm just tired, I guess." In her head she fought for conversation. A lady always kept her chatter sparkling and bright until a gentleman got his tongue going. What was it she had learned in Virginia? Ask a question that required more than a "yes" or "no" answer. Men loved to answer women's questions and the wise woman asked ones that she knew he could answer. The question should ask something about him, but not be so personal as to offend.

"Pray tell, godbrother how did you come by the carriage?" Not too "sparkling" but it would do.

"Werner bought it from a Sesech on his way out of town."

"Really?" she turned fascinated eyes on him. "Who was the man?"

"Some fella named, Clony. Used to own a store in town, I think." He quickly veered the conversation off course. "You know, Franny, this is the first time I've been able to see you alone since we left the river."

The statement caught her off guard. Here, she planned to keep him involved in impersonal discussion, at verbal arm's length, and he goes and says something that has her blushing. And she's not with him, five minutes! "We're not alone. You forget Lieutenant Werner and Sigrid Zimmer."

"They're not paying us any attention and don't want us paying them any."

She sat up straighter and slid side-ways away from him as far over on the seat as she could get.

"Why ever would you think that, sir?"

"*Sir?* That's being a bit formal between us, don't you think, *Ma'am*? He cocked an eyebrow at her and chuckled.

Not knowing how she should respond, Franny bit her lip in silence.

When she didn't say anything, Josiah changed the subject again and whispered in her ear, sending little tingly thrills down her neck, "I think we're even on all counts, pretty cousin."

The way his voice tantalized and this latest enigmatic remark infuriated her. So, she turned on him, "Will you please make sense when you talk to me, Josiah Scarborough. Whatever are you talking about?"

He looked straight ahead, said in a tone absent of humor, "I saved your life, you have saved mine. That was one brave thing to do, little girl. Whatever possessed you to run into a burning building after me? Nevermind, you don't know, just like I don't know why I wasn't afraid to run out after you on a storm swept deck."

After a silence she asked, "You said 'on all counts;' was there something else?"

"Yeah, but I don't know how to bring it up without seeming like a complete cad. In a way, both of us misled the other at our initial meeting. First, you on the road to Rock Creek, blowing me kisses and inviting me to come see you--"

Franny blushed but couldn't help herself, and laughed. "I was such a silly."

He laughed with her, became serious again, "And then on the boat flirting with you and not letting you pass." He coughed, said hoarsely, "I want to apologize. I was an idiot. I didn't treat you like a lady, and I'm sorry."

He sounded so stiff, so awkward with this kind of unfamiliar apology that Franny giggled. It struck her funny that this man who could probably get any girl in the world to fall in love with him would apologize to her for not being a gentleman. Then she laughed outright. She tried to stifle it but failed until she simply had to throw back her head and howl with mirth.

When she did, Josiah laughed in response, but asked, "What is so damn funny?" He laughed and chuckled with her while saying, "I'm trying to be very sincere and a gentleman and you're treating it as some kind of schoolyard joke!"

"Oh," she gulped for breath," if you only knew how you sounded, so.... So...." and they went off again, giggling and laughing.

While they laughed, somehow she was once again close beside him. So close she could smell the light aromas of the Bay Rum he wore and the whiskey he drank, the faint odors of a cigar he had smoked, leather, his wool uniform, and soap. Buried beneath these, she caught his scent, the gentle musky odor that signaled his masculinity. He kept himself immaculate, she knew, for when he had lived at the hotel, she made up his bed and noticed the neat order of his toilet articles placed on the wash stand.

In a far better mood than when she had ventured forth, she enjoyed the concert. The German band played a mixture of martial airs and waltzes and throughout she tapped her feet. Even the speech by bewhiskered Hamilton B. Gamble was inspiring, urging all Missouri to back the acting legislature that was loyal to the Union. He claimed that the Jefferson City legislature was the real "voice of Missouri's people" and not the traitorous "rump and illegal" legislature meeting under Cleb Jackson in Neosho. Afterwards, the foursome strolled to the Capital Oyster House for a ginger beer. Going back, Lieutenant Werner held the reins and sat with his arm around Sigrid.

Finding herself snuggled into the rear seat with Josiah, Franny went shy. She went numb when he opened the conversation with "Tell me about Hy Wilcox."

"What's to tell?" she stammered.

"Folks who knew him before the war say he was crazy for you."

"*Folks*? Who, my mother! And people always tend to gossip about things they know nothing about." She felt his eyes on her, turned to him, saw he wasn't teasing, and added defensively, "Some *folks* shouldn't spread untrue tales."

"I'd say the stories are true. I'd say he must have been very much in love with you and you must have done something mighty mean to make him angry enough to burn you out."

She fidgeted with her reticule and lace mitts desperately trying to think. Then, "Why are you so interested in a demented man who wanted to be my beau? All you need to do is catch him." *Until you do,* she thought, the sadness sweeping over her again, *I'll pretend he meant nothing.*

"He didn't just *want* to be your beau, he *was* your beau. Your mother said you wanted to marry him and that she forbade it."

On this Franny almost fainted. Her head throbbed and she felt too warm. His body next to hers generated enough heat to withstand a winter blizzard. She wanted only to escape, but the moving carriage prevented her from jumping out and walking home.

"That isn't quite true," she coughed delicately into her hanky, "Mother never did understand that situation. He, well, he asked for my hand and I didn't really want to marry him, so, when Ma said, *no,* I could tell him that." She was rambling, she knew, but she had to say something. "And when I told him what she said, he became very angry." A sudden flash of insight made her add, "That's when he threatened me."

"Threatened you?" He sounded surprised. He had taken her bait.

Growing stronger as she fabricated the tale, Franny said, "Yes, even before General Lyon captured Jefferson City, he threatened to burn down the hotel if I wouldn't run away with him. I was trying to discourage him, kindly, so as not to set him off. I realized how dangerous he was."

"So, let me understand, you *didn't* welcome his attentions."

"No, I did not. He offended me." She managed to

conjure up a tear that trickled down her face and her voice broke, "I honestly didn't know who to turn to. Without a father, or other male relative to take care of her, a woman is almost defenseless."

Instinctively, she turned her face into his shoulder and shook with sobs. Very soft sobs they were, for she didn't want the lovebirds spooning up front to hear her.

"But, Otto would surely have sent him packing." His arm went around her.

"Yes, under normal circumstances that would have been true." She sniffed into her hanky, "But I didn't want to run the risk of having him burned out or hurt, too. Hy hated all Germans."

"Therefore, you had to handle this dangerous chap all by yourself and you felt you were protecting your mother and Otto Zimmer." His lips brushed the top of her hair as he murmured, "You sweet, brave girl."

When she turned a tear-stained face up to him the carriage passed beneath a street lamp and she saw the concern in his eyes. He had believed her. But there was something else in those eyes as well, relief. She said making a teary smile, "So you see, I really held no affection for that man, at all." In a way, this was true and had become more so after she had married him. But she decided not to tell Josiah this while he was apologizing for making her cry and kissing her forehead. His murmuring words of comfort and nuzzling in her hair sent shivers of delight throughout her body, but were all quite innocent until, as nature had ordained it, the two found each other's lips.

At once both seemed out of control, sparks suddenly ignited into full blaze. Josiah unfastened her bodice, kissed her neck, and ran his hands over her flesh. Husky with passion, his voice repeated that he loved her and would have died had she said she loved someone else. Whispering, "I've wanted you from the moment I laid eyes

189

on you," he suddenly pulled himself free and cast an eye to the backs of the oblivious couple spooning in front of them. Sloughing off his coat, vest, and cravat, Josiah caught her hands, and devoured them with kisses before he returned to her lips.

Franny's caged passion was set free and she clung to him, twining her fingers through his soft, raven hair, running her hands beneath his shirt, feeling his muscles tense beneath the smooth, firm skin and beneath the thick hair on his chest. She heard his sharp intake of breath when, with wild kisses, she covered his shoulders, neck, and face, opening her mouth and meeting his tongue, and feeling surge after surge of desire weld them together.

Ambivalence flown at last, Franny realized that what she felt for this man was ten thousand times greater than any hunger she might have imagined for her husband. She also knew that to be fair to Josiah, she should stop this romantic frenzy, admit her marriage, and beg his forgiveness. But she could not. Instead, caught up in the thrill of his kisses, she decided that tomorrow would be time enough to tell him. Tonight with the soft clip-clop of the horses echoing in the background and the round-faced moon watching them from above, she wanted to allow this rare, delicious moment of ecstasy to continue unbroken as long as possible.

The next day it rained. Even so, the fat drops of water seeping around the windows of his billet couldn't wash away the joy Josiah felt. Franny loved him. Franny Moone, the most gorgeous creature he had ever met, loved him. A lady she was also, but a passionate one, with real blood in her veins and kisses that had given him the most intense arousal he had ever known.

For the first time in his life he was in love. Prior to meeting Franny, women had only been sweet dalliances or sensuous teachers, bedmates to fondle and forget. Now, all those love poems and syrupy songs, all those mushy letters men wrote their wives and sweethearts made sense.

She had melted in his arms, but had also been able to subdue passion before their friends overheard them. Remembering, he laughed, and swung his feet over the side of his cot. He'd marry her before the month was out and tonight, he planned to speak to Dee about that very thing.

Josiah bunked on the third-floor in one of the Capitol's offices cleaned out hurriedly when Jackson had fled the city. In the basement languished Rebel political prisoners. One of these unfortunates was run-away Governor Jackson's son. Another was the produce farmer, Jeremiah Wilcox.

The old boy was screaming bloody hell about his "rights"; that the United States army had no right to keep him prisoner without charging him with a crime. The Provost Marshal told him that had changed since Lincoln had suspended Habeas Corpus, an individual's civil rights. Now, evidence wasn't necessary. Anyone even suspected of being a rebel traitor could be jailed until the military courts said he could go free. That didn't stop Jeremiah's curses whenever somebody went near him.

Josiah debated with himself whether or not to interrogate Wilcox before Werner and him, with 20 half-trained men, searched the farmer's woods - what Gorditch had not. Then, decided not to question the man, now. Since Gorditch had dragged him in, all Wilcox had done was complain about his son without giving any information as to his whereabouts. Josiah needed to find something first, then see if he'd talk.

As he stood before a cracked mirror hung over the wash basin, performing his morning ablutions, his mind turned to Gorditch. A local merchant, the company of volunteer home guards had voted Gorditch in to be their First Lieutenant. But, if leaders were also supposed to be gentlemen, then the rank and file certainly had shown poor judgment.

Something about Gorditch bothered him. Josiah speculated he stole from the county farmers suspected of southern sympathies. When he had brought in Wilcox, the lieutenant had also carted in a lot of provisions and several head of valuable live stock. Gorditch claimed that Wilcox was willing to sell them. This, Josiah doubted. He suspected that the ambitious lieutenant would get the money to pay Wilcox, all right, but the money would "disappear" somewhere between army issue and Wilcox's pocket, falling instead into Gorditch's. Also, Gorditch chose the worst bullies he could find from the troops for scouting parties. As his captain, Josiah knew he'd have to watch him more closely. Taking civilian property the Gorditch way violated regulations even if this was the way of the Kansas Jayhawkers like Lane, Montgomery, and Jennison. If Josiah could prove theft, he'd have the man court martialed and sent to prison.

He dried his face and hands on a piece of ragged toweling, remembered the soft, clean ones at Erin House, and looked forward to its rebuilding. Nothing beat his bed there or the home cooking, not to mention that he'd be that much closer to Franny.

Whistling, Josiah bounded down the stairs to Toby's breakfast made from army provisions - hard biscuits and gravy, maybe some side meat. Waiting for him were Werner and several other officers from Erin House forced to quarter in the Capitol building after the fire. Because the two prettiest girls in the city no longer were hostesses at the breakfast table, the men ate their meal and drank their coffee with scant gaiety and terse conversation. And, each one rushed off to his duties - on time. He and Werner detailed the men to go out to the Wilcox place.

Josiah's detail found the colored woman, Sukey alone and terrified of what she suspected they might do to the house. That he as squadron commander gave strict orders to the men to touch nothing and that Lieutenant Werner enforced it when one tried to slip a china cup in his pocket won the old woman's grudging confidence. She showed them where the collapsed shed was in the woods. Buried beneath the rotten timbers, the men discovered a cache of arms and ammunition large enough to outfit a company and barrels of stolen goods. A trooper found a canvas bag with silver candleholders and silverware and brought it to Werner who brought it to him.

"Captain, look at this." The Lieutenant displayed several knives and forks.

"It's got Erin House's initials on it."

"Right you are." Josiah turned them toward the light to clearly read the insignia. "Wilcox must have stolen this the night of the fire. Mrs. Moone will welcome its return." The cool rain was settling into a mist, the kind that drenched the earth and made digging that much easier. Feeling a chill, Josiah walked back to the house. Sukey's yellow turbaned head and walnut face watched and waited in the doorway. "Pardon me, Auntie, but you wouldn't happen to have a swallow of hot coffee, would you?" He smiled, touched the brim of his hat. "This is a cold and peculiar rain for mid-summer."

"Yas Suh." The tiny woman, bent with age, nodded soberly and motioned for him to follow her into the house.

"Awfully nice of you," he said, stomping the mud from his boots and entering the Wilcox pantry. "What did you say your name was?"

"Sukey."

As she sat him at the kitchen table and busied herself with pouring him a cup of steaming coffee and setting out a plate of molasses cookies, she maintained an

193

unwelcoming, solemn manner. It struck him that between this dour old bondservant and the free colored folks earning wages at Erin House yawned worlds of difference. Her back to him, she stood at the window over the dry sink, apparently watching something in the distance.

He'd try to talk to her. "You seem to be by yourself out here, Sukey. A farm this size should have any number of hands. What happened to the rest of them?" He savored the sweet smell of the coffee before he took a sip.

"Mostly, Mr. Jeremiah, done sold 'um all off." She said without emotion but turned to face him.

"Really? Do you know why ?" He reached for a cookie.

The old woman stared at him for almost a full minute before she spoke, apparently deciding whether or not she could trust him. Knotting her soiled apron in her hands she answered, her voice as flat as before. "One by one, de hands be sold in de pen." She paused, looking down at her knotted hands, "My old Jim, and li'l Samuel, too."

He didn't know much about the "peculiar institution," coming as he did from New York and serving mainly in the west before this war, but he'd heard of farmers separating Negro families by selling them off. He heard her pain, asked, "Jim? Samuel? Your husband and child?"

She nodded, said stoically, "He say he has to. He say he got no mo' money to take care ob 'um." Snorting with contempt she added softly, "He ain't got no money ' cause he poured it down on de jug and threw it 'way on de card tables."

So Wilcox was strapped for cash. That might explain the collection of valuables buried under the shed. He must have been selling these things on the black market, probably in St. Louis. But how had he gathered so much? Surely, he and his son, alone, couldn't have stolen it all. He'd find out.

But before he could ask she burst out, "He be gone."

194

"Mr. Wilcox?"

"Mr. Hy, 'ah means."

Josiah set his cup down and stared at her. "Where is Mr. Hy? Do you know?"

"Shore, I knows. He be my baby when his own mammy died."

He settled back, began munching a cookie, and waited. He'd listen.

"What you want to know for?" She asked.

"Just curious, I suppose. Strange, a man's son wouldn't come around and try to get his old father out of jail, don't you think?"

"He ain't 'round here to get his Paw outta jail."

"Where'd he get to?"

"He gone wid' dem bad mens he rides with." She folded her arms across her chest, settling her face into a scowl. Obviously, she didn't like her baby's choice of friends.

As Josiah quietly took another cookie, encouraging her to venture forth with more information and sipped at his coffee, the scowl suddenly crinkled into tears. Wiping her eyes with one end of her apron she groaned, "Seemed like he be caught, like a fish in de net, by de man. I done tole him and tole him dat he be 'ob de Devil. But he rode off wid that Cap'n Verboise anyway."

At the name, Josiah almost choked on the bite of cookie, gulped his too hot coffee too fast, and felt the burn all the way to his stomach.

Confronted by the evidence collected at the farm, Jeremiah Wilcox still denied knowing anything about it and steadily swore to his innocence. About Jacques Verboise, he again claimed no knowledge, but when Captain Hawk, the new provost marshal assigned to Jefferson City, read Sukey's statement to him, he erupted into vile oaths and threatened to beat his bondservant to death when he saw her.

Watching the interrogation, Josiah thanked heaven he'd been able to talk the old woman into moving into town with a family of free coloreds. Remaining alone on an isolated farm wasn't safe for any woman, white, or black. He doubted, though, if she'd ever have to return, for it looked like Wilcox was on his way to prison for the duration of the war.

Hawk shoved his cadaver-thin face into Wilcox's. His soft tone covered an icy rage. "You might as well tell us, *puke*, where your thieving, arsonist son went and who else rides with Verboise's murderous cowards that call themselves soldiers."

When Wilcox merely looked down at his tied hands, Hawk leaned his tall, emaciated figure over his victim whispering, "Tell us, old man, and you might save your farm. Don't, and by tomorrow this time, the house and land will belong to the United States government." Then he struck him, open palmed across the cheek. Josiah winced, noticed the trail of dried blood from Wilcox's left ear, and saw it bleeding again. He reached out to stop Hawk, but not before Hawk hit the old man again.

He knew this provost marshal, being from Kansas, despised Missourians, calling them all "pukes," and openly declaring that not one of them possessed a loyal heart. Josiah might not approve of the way Hawk treated suspected Secesh, but he did get the wanted information.

Wilcox rattled off the names of neighboring farmers, some of whom Josiah recognized as having sold horses to the U.S. Army and who walked the streets, pretending Union loyalty. They would have to be rounded up and herded in, questioned, property confiscated, court - martialed, and imprisoned.

But for Josiah's purposes, the information was only partially helpful as far as the *White Star* incident was concerned. Verboise and young Wilcox, with a number of the other participants, were still loose, had cleared out to meet up with the Confederate forces massing a 100 miles south, close to Springfield For all he knew, they were well nigh there by now. That accounted for the reports of the destruction of bridges and the cut telegraph lines south of town.

Major Prince, now, commanding officer at Leavenworth needed to know this, and, if necessary, Josiah needed fresh orders. Should he follow after Verboise or stay in Jefferson City? As he left the provost's office to send a telegram to Fort Leavenworth, he overheard Wilcox whimper. "N' I wanna tell the widder Moone how sorry I am fer what my son did. I need to tell her that." His raised voice stopped Josiah at the door. "You, sir, Cap'n Scarborough - ain't that yore name? Ain't you kin to the widder? Would you tell 'er I need to see her ?"

"Tis no good, that dirty, old man is up to." She sat on the haircloth sofa after supper and snorted with outrage. "I'll not be goin' to see Jeremiah Wilcox."

All through supper Wilcox's arrest, confession, and wish to see Dee had been the topic of discussion, pushing to the rear conversation about Werner and Sigrid's formal engagement announcement. Josiah hadn't been able to slip in five minutes alone with Dee to discuss his and Franny's new-found relationship. Now, he sat across from his godmother, listening for the umpteenth time to the pros and cons of her visiting Wilcox, wondering if he ought to stay any later, wishing he could coax Franny outside onto the porch for a few minutes before he left.

Franny looked delicious in a black and white gown that brought out her milky complexion and accented her bosom. He yearned to touch her again, to smell her rosewater scent, to nuzzle her wild hair - tonight drawn up into ringlets at the nape while two flirtatious curls danced at each side of her neck. With each toss of the curls, her

197

pearl earbobs danced too, catching the gleam of the small fire in the grate. Last night he had nibbled on those small, perfect earlobes. Remembering, he sighed.

Dee heard. "An what was yer groanin' fer, godson? Are ya tired, then, ov hearin' us jaw on about Mr. Wilcox?"

He straightened up his chair from its position leaned back against the fireplace and glanced at Brady and Potter half-asleep in matching haircloth chairs. Wrapped up in their happiness, Werner and Sigrid talked softly at the dining room table. "Well, Dee, you know what I think. I think you should see what the man has to say," he stifled a yawn.

"I don't think you should go." Franny said forcefully, not looking at him, but at her mother. It occurred to him that throughout the evening, Franny had avoided catching his eye. He put this down to maidenly shyness and perhaps embarrassment. After all, last night passion had reigned and they weren't formally betrothed.

Still, he wondered why she was so adamant about her mother not seeing Wilcox. "Why do you say that, Franny?" He smiled lazily, allowing his eyes to play over her face, hoping they told her how much he loved her. Her reaction startled him.

Turning on him, she spat out her words, "I say that, dear godbrother, because it is a cruel thing to ask of my mother! The disloyal rascal's son nearly destroyed our lives as well as our livelihood. And now, he wants to beg her forgiveness! That, sir, is an insult to her and to all of us caught in the fire." And she turned her stiff, little face back to her mother, taking great care to ignore his hurt surprise and to lovingly pat her mother's hand.

But Dee had noticed. Her eyes glanced from her daughter to him. Finally she cleared her throat, said, "Tis Mr. Zimmer I'll be askin' when he comes in from the Royal, tonight." She seemed to dismiss the topic with a dainty yawn. "I'll not make me decision, 'till Mr. Zimmer's has his say." Otto had suppered at his gambling house and wasn't expected until nearly midnight.

Bewildered and hurt, Josiah stood to go. "And I must bid you ladies good night. It's been a long day, and tomorrow promises more of the same." While Franny stared at her hands, which puzzled him further, Dee's face was wreathed in smiles as she stood and looked up at him.

"Good night, son. Beholdin' we all are that ya at least know where the dirty scoundrel Hy Wilcox is. An' sure as me word, me girl 'n' me had no idee he was an outlaw ridin' with that Verboise, fella."

This statement Dee had repeated throughout dinner and Franny vehemently supported. He believed them. It seemed natural that although young Wilcox was supposedly dying of love, that given the politics of his love's mother, he wouldn't want his sweetheart to know of his marauding.

He glanced again at Franny still seated on the couch, pulling nervously at her fingers. "Good night, Franny," he said softly. Suddenly, he remembered that he still had not asked Dee for Franny's hand and she might be thinking he had purposely avoided doing so. Why not now? It wasn't too late in the evening for something so important!

He opened his mouth to ask Dee if he might have a moment alone with her, but Franny looked up at him. And the look on her face - a look that spoke of profound sadness that went beyond their romance - stopped him cold. Tears stood in her eyes. She gave a subtle shake of her head as though to warn him off, said, "Good bye, Josiah."

On the way back to their quarters he sat beside Werner in the carryall, silent, ruminating over his sweetheart's apparent reversal of affections. Josiah felt an emotion he had never before experienced - heartbreak. And he'd never had a chance to ask her why. So, while he tortured himself with self-doubts, Werner prattled on about his wedding plans with Sigrid.

"Well, Missus," Brady said over a yawn, "if'n an old cavalryman's opinion ye be wantin', I'd say ye should go. I agree with me boy," referring to Josiah. "If'n ye don't, you'd always be wonderin' what it were Wilcox wanted ta say." He nudged the colonel, "Come on, sir, time ta fall out. Taps is sounded."

With a grunt, Potter stood, stretched and yawned, said, "Madam, if you would please, hear the seasoned opinion of a field officer, late in the service of his country. I would have to agree with the sergeant - with one modification, that you are chaperoned by one able to protect you from any malodorous word or deed the scoundrel might have in mind." He cleared his throat, bowed before Dee, "And of course, my dear Mrs. Moone, I stand ready to offer my sword in that endeavor."

"Oh fer pity's sake, Colonel, the lady don't need the likes of broken down old war horses like you to pertect 'er. Now, come along with ya." Immediately, the colonel protested that he was indeed still capable of fending off any miscreant who might harm Mrs. Moone. But Brady's firm grip pushed the old soldier out of the room and the two stomped off, each to his own couch in the attic.

Sigrid chatted for a few minutes, her cheeks glowing with happiness, her eyes filled with excitement. She couldn't stop herself from sharing that she and Lieutenant Werner planned a Christmas wedding. Then, she too excused herself for bed.

When the parlor had grown quiet at last Dee took up her embroidery, saying to Franny standing at the fireplace. "You don't have to wait up with me, child, for Mr. Zimmer ta come home. But, tis glad I am that ye are here, alone with me."

Franny poked up the low fire in the grate. Although

mid-summer, she felt a chill. Her back to her mother hid the tears that rolled unchecked down her cheeks. She had sent her beloved Josiah away, thinking that she had changed her mind about him. Tonight had been like planting an ice pick in her own heart, for she'd rather have died than to hurt him. She loved Josiah Scarborough, had loved him as a child, and wanted to love him as a woman. But she knew that until she had settled with Hy Wilcox it would be grossly unfair to encourage him. Last night she would have to put behind her and pretend it never happened. The immediate problem was Paw Wilcox's desire to see Ma.

She suspected Paw Wilcox wanted to reveal her secret wedding to Hy, offer it as an explanation of sorts for his son's outrageous behavior. With all the other men counseling Ma to see him, why would Otto's advice be any different? And her lone voice of protest would not prevail. Surely, Ma would go and find out and there would be hell to pay.

Would Ma send her away? When she was growing up Ma was always threatening to send Clay and her "back to Ireland." She had even said this once in a pique when displeased with something or other Sigrid and Toby had done. She remembered them all children collapsing into giggles at the images of either black Toby or the Chinese-German Sigrid being vagabonds in Ireland. Oh, if she could only pull back those days, to be a carefree innocent again.

"Franny, are ye listenin' ta me?"

She dabbed at her face, swallowed her tears, and turned to face her mother. "Yes, Ma."

The piercing look she gave Franny read her soul as well as knew her heart and Franny could contain herself no longer.

Dee said softly, "Now, ye've been cryin,' what on earth for? I kin see the boy loves ya, though the way ya

201

treat Josiah some times, I can't see fer the death o' me why. When ye were bairns, playin' on the lawn at Scarborough Hall, his dear mother and I often said we hoped ya two would grow up and marry some day. I have a wee bit o' unsettlement now about that, but..."

"Oh Ma," her voice came out high and squeaky. The flood dammed behind her eyes broke free, and she thrust her head into the lap of the matriarch who had ruled her life. "I've done the most terrible, ghastly thing. It doesn't matter if you do feel disquieted about Josiah loving me. I can never marry him because I'm already married to somebody else."

For a long while, Dee held Franny in her arms and listened to her cry. She crooned a lullaby she'd sung when Franny was a baby and stroked her daughter's hair. Franny thought at first that Ma hadn't heard what she said. But, when her sobs had turned to sniffles the lullaby ceased. For a long moment, the only sounds in the room were Franny's hiccuped breathing and the ticking of the grandfather clock in the corner. She clung to her mother, praying she wouldn't erupt.

But, her mother gently disengaged Franny from her lap and walked to the mantle. With nary a word she poked up the smoking embers and placed a small log on the hearth. Then, although she turned a scarlet face to Franny, she stood composed and serene with her hands folded before her and her back to the newly blazing fire. "Hy Wilcox." she said.

"Yes," Franny whispered, so ashamed she could scarcely raise her head.

"When?"

Franny told her.

Although the men folk surrounding her kicked up a ruckus, with each one insisting she take the offer of his gallant services, the next day Dee eluded them all and visited Jeremiah Wilcox alone. She figured there'd be enough guards around to protect her honor and her safety. She stood before him in a private room, damp with drain water and reeking of human filth. In the corner, a Federal corporal dozed over a rifle nearly as long as he was tall.

Arms and legs shackled, Jeremiah sat at a wooden table. "Cuse me fer not risin,'" He looked her over, smiled, exposing rotten teeth, "Even if you have gotten a tad plump, you're still a mighty fine figure of a woman, Dee."

Although it had been only twelve years since she had sent him packing, in the light of the small lantern flickering from the center of the table, he looked like he'd aged twice that. And she saw bruises and dried blood around his face and mouth. "Tis me wish that I could say the same about you. I remember ye as once cutting a handsome, manly figure but tis slovenly habits and the drink, I see that's got to ya. What is it you want to say to me, Jeremiah Wilcox?"

"My, ain't you still the firecracker, though." He chuckled, turned serious. "I jest wanna say, I'm sorry, Dee. Fer, Hy, fer ever'thing. I never tole that boy to do what he done."

"Is that all?" The overpowering stench caused her to hold her hanky to her nose.

"No," he drawled, "I s'pect you might want to help me."

"Why, for the love of Mary, would I be wantin' ta help the likes of you?"

He looked at her steadily, moved his bloodied mouth into a horrible smile, "What'll folks say if'n you don't lend a Christian hand to the paw of yore daughter's husband?"

She breathed into the hanky, "Yes, I know all about that. Franny told me, last night."

"She were skeered to tell you, afore now."

"Well, told me she has, and I ain't gonna help ya. 'Tis

203

an annulment she'll be gettin'." She turned to go.

"I wouldn't be sashayin' outta here so fast, Dee. There's more reason than that to be helpin' me."

Her back to him, she stood wondering what else her old lover wished to say.

When he told her of Franny's involvement in the *White Star* murders she hadn't understood immediately and he had to explain. But she didn't believe him. "You're a liar," she said, and again started to go.

And again his raspy voice stopped her. "No I ain't. And when I start to tell who she be married up with and they see the color of her hair, they'll believe me."

Panic hit her. First the horrible news last night, now this. *Oh Franny, Franny,* she thought wildly. *I should ha' sent ye back ta Ireland, after all.*

Finally, she turned back to him, asked, "What is it ya want me ta do fer ya?"

"Thought you'd listen when you heard what I had to say." Glancing at the guard, he dropped his voice to a whisper. "First, I want you to swear in court that I'm a loyal Union man."

"Upon me life! I can't be doin' that. Ya know ya ain't!"

"But you will, if'n you wanna keep that little tramp of yourn outta trouble. And then I want some money. Enough of it to git me the hell away from Cole County as long as this war lasts. I reckon I want 'bout $1,000." Satisfied, he leaned back and placed his shackled hands on the table before him.

If the stone floor had been cleaner, Dee thought she might have crumpled to it in a swoon. Instead, she stood her ground and breathed into her handkerchief. "Jeremiah, you've turned into a loon, a drunken loon, with the liquor softe' yer brain."

"I ain't goin' soft in the head. People know what a Lincoln lover you be. And that damn Dutchy you're carryin' on with is one of Mayor Bruns' aldermen. All you got to say is I'm a respectable man who's tole you 'bout his loyalty to the Central government."

'N' folks would think I'd gone daft. I'll not do it. Besides they found stolen goods buried on yer property." She added pointedly, "And some it was Erin House silverware!" She drew her tiny frame up to its full height.

"You're gonna tell 'um that I knew nothin' 'bout that. An' you're gonna say that I tole you I was afeerd of Cap'n Verboise and had no control over him or his raidin' in the county."

"I'll not be believed. Some there is has heard me speak ill ov' ya." She thought of Josiah, Brady, and others. "Why should I be testifyin' fer ya, now ?"

"Cause you're a Christian woman who wouldn't want to see even a dog get kicked around like they been doin' to me, 'specially if'n that dog was innocent. You tell 'um you done read me the wrong way, and know different now." He sighed, leaned back on the stool, and wiggled his hands inside the heavy iron chains attached to his wrists.

Without giving her a chance to respond, Wilcox blurted, pointing a dirty index finger at her. "If'n ye'd married me, woman, when I asked you the first time instead of takin' up with that damn Zimmer none a this would a happened."

Rage flew over her at the insult and she felt herself flush. "'Twas al'ays a fool ye were, Jeremiah. I didn't marry ye, 'cause ye didn't want me. Ya wanted only Erin House fer yer own. Ye even had that paper drawn up and tried ta trick me in ta' signin' it. Here I be with them four little bairns ta tend to, not knowin' the ways of business, battlin' the town ta keep the hotel open. If'n ye recall, them old-line families didn't take kindly ta a poor Irish widow-woman fresh off the boat openin' a fine establishment like Erin House. And here came yerself, prosperous farmer Wilcox with his smooth ways and promises of undying love. 'Tis the blessed Mother I have thanked everyday, that Otto Zimmer was around ta read over the paper and warn me that it was a deed o' transfer - from me to *you*!" Her chest heaving, she waited, loathing him as much now as she had then.

"Reckon you don' wanna be my character witness, then."

"Fer sure, that poor dog I'd help first afore I'd help you."

"What 'bout the money, at least?" He squinted up at her. "I might be able to post a bond and get free - please, Dee, I really cared fer you—"

She snorted in protest and suddenly without warning her eyes filled with tears. Indeed, once, he had meant a great deal to her. That was before he had become the filthy, besotted, old scoundrel now watching her with grey, cat-like eyes - before he had proven himself false.

"Oh, do what ye must. I'll not be givin' ye one penny." she threw her words at him, turned on her heel and strode away from the damp, fetid smell and from Jeremiah Wilcox.

With the air turned muggy in the hot sun after yesterday's rain, she next went to the Cole County courthouse, asked to see the marriage records. Sure enough, under the hand of the Reverend Horace Olmstead was recorded the marriage of Frances Margaret Moone and Hy Ebenezer Wilcox, May 5th, 1861. Looking at the undeniable written page, once again regret washed over her. If only she hadn't been skylarkin' with Zimmer in St. Louis and left Clay and Franny alone. Clay's escapade at Camp Jackson had been bad enough, but it paled beside Franny's. Then, there was that awful business about the *White Star*.

Her heart in her shoes, she paid the visit that she hated most making and caught Father Walsh in St. Peter's rectory.

The telegram from Major Prince offered Josiah a chance to rejoin his old regiment, now massing near Springfield and serving General Lyon. However, because he had raised two companies of Volunteers, technically, he could remain where he was. McClelland's original order, to protect Missouri's capitol, was still in force. The idea of getting back to actual fighting against real soldiers appealed to him. On the other hand, if he rode the hundred miles or so south he'd have to say goodbye to Franny for a while. He knew his duty was to rejoin his unit, but his heart wanted to stay in Jefferson City, even if it meant his chief task was the dreary hunting down of Secesh farmers - turned-partisan rangers.

Franny's coldness last night had given him a jolt. Frantic, he had spent the night tossing and turning, trying to determine just what it was he had or hadn't done that would have caused her reaction. But, after a few hours of fitful dreaming he awoke and saw the day had brought the sunshine. And the sunshine had chased away his doubts.

It was a Saturday, inspection of the men's quarters and gear, a short morning drill session and then he was free. He'd take his noon dinner at the Zimmers and straighten the mess out with Franny. Then he'd report back to headquarters for evening dress parade. After his obligatory talk with Dee, who he figured would be delighted, he'd put a wedding ring on Franny's finger - the sooner the better. Company C of the First would have to wait.

The morning flew by and the men remarked that Captain Scarborough, normally never gruff with them, seemed in unusually good spirits. Werner stood as Officer of the Day, so Josiah rode his personal mount over to the house. On the way he thought he spied Dee at a distance bustling out of the County court house.

He entered Zimmer's after a knock to find the house nearly deserted. Tycee's turbaned form greeted him with her usual grin.

"Where is everybody?" He looked around the parlor, strode into the kitchen, and picked up one of Tycee's butter biscuits, cooling on the table. Opal saw him slip it out of the plate, laughed, but shyly continued her chore of shucking corn ears.

"Dey all be gone," Tycee playfully slapped at his hand, "'cept Miss Franny and she still in de bed. She feelin' poorly today."

He bit into the biscuit and winked at Opal. "She's ill?" Of course, that was the answer. Last night she had been coming down with whatever had materialized today.

"Oh, she ain't ailin', like folks be when dey is callin' fer de doctor. She's got de melancholies. But I knows when she finds out you're here she'll perk right up. Opal, go fetch Miss Franny. Tell her Mr. Josiah be here."

He waited in the parlor, smelling the savory odor of dinner wafting from the kitchen and picked up the latest *Harper's Weekly*. On the front page he read about a bad fight occurring a few days ago on the 21st at a creek in Virginia called Bull Run, near the railroad junction of Manassas Junction. McDowel's boys had skedaddled all the way back to Washington City in the face of the Rebel charge. He knew this latest Confederate victory would lower morale and that the rebellion wouldn't be "over by Christmas," as he had been hearing since it started. With a whispered curse he threw the newspaper aside just as Franny entered the parlor.

Pale, haggard, she had thrown on one of Sigrid's work dresses, an unattractive dark cotton, which she had to tie up at her waist because it was too long. Her hair, she had unsuccessfully tried to subdue beneath a snood. It didn't matter. For all he cared, she could have been wearing a nun's habit and still seem utterly beautiful. He rose at once, went to her, and took her hands in his. He stared into her eyes, as usual struck by their misty green beauty, glanced to see if anybody were around and bent to give her a kiss.

When his lips brushed hers she pulled back, whispered, "Don't."

He stood in the middle of the room holding her hands, "Tell me what's wrong, sweetheart. What did I do?"

"It's not what *you* did. It's what *I* did." And she burst into tears.

Suddenly, Dee burst through the door. Behind her came Otto looking grimmer than he'd ever seen him.

"Hello, godson. Tis glad I am that only us are here now. We've got ta talk to ya."

Wiping her tears away, Franny whirled on her mother. "No, Ma, please, let me tell him. I should be the one."

With a nod, Otto led Dee outside to the porch, leaving Franny and Josiah alone.

She told him, without preamble, offering no excuses.

"Let me understand," he felt the wind go out of him, as though a horse had kicked him in the stomach, and he sat down, "all that story you told me the other night about protecting.."

".. Was a lie," she whispered, looking down at the floor.

"Did you love him?"

"No." Weeping anew, she put her face in her hands. Through her muffled tears, she said, "Not like I love you. Otto says I can probably get an annulment."

Emotions whipsawed through him. On one hand he wanted to take her in his arms and tell her it didn't matter, that he loved her anyway. The other demanded he lay a horsewhip on her backsides. She had lied, deceived, teased him into loving her as he had never loved any woman. But something else more sinister than a foolish elopement bothered him.

Things began to add up. Things that had been nagging

the periphery of his thoughts ever since he had learned that Hy Wilcox rode with Verboise and that Hy Wilcox had been in love with Franny. So, like a punch in the nose, the truth slammed his mind. Without calculation he said, "And you - you were the red-haired girl who lured the *White Star* to the bank."

"Oh God, Josiah," she raised her face to him, "You've got to believe me, I had no idea those men would get killed." She began to cry again and sniffled, "I am so sorry. Please, Josiah, I truly love you."

Too dumbfounded to move, he sat staring at her, taking in every line of her face and figure, remembering how she had felt in his arms, remembering that it was she who had saved his life. More, however, was at stake than personal gratitude and romantic feelings. The ghosts of 14 murdered men cried out for justice and now he must think rationally, like the officer he had been commissioned to be.

He spoke more harshly than he intended. "I'm sorry, godsister, but I have a duty to turn you over to the provost marshal for trial." He heard the military tone in his voice, couldn't help it, and hated himself for it. "You're little better than Jeremiah Wilcox. As you knew all along, he was sheltering Verboise and by so doing, aided and abetted treasonable enemies of the Central government."

The girl flung herself on the sofa, once more burying her hands in her face.

"You wouldn't enjoy being interrogated by Captain Hawk," he barreled on, "and you could go to prison for the duration of the war, if not longer." Her tears bothered him. He wanted to put his arms around her and tell her that everything would be all right. But, he knew nothing between them could ever be the same. How could he ever trust her again? His sweet cousin had proved to be sweet treachery and yet, he craved her like opium. If forgetting this vixen were possible, it wouldn't be easy.

Listening to her sob, his mind sneered: *Serves you right, Scarborough. You fell in love too soon without knowing balls about her. You trusted your instincts, which led you so far afield you'll never find equilibrium again. So much for instinct. So much for love.*

He noticed her snood askew, the loose knot of frantic curls at the nape of her neck coming undone and he knew he would always desire her. When the sun's rays streaming through the window behind the sofa caught her curls, turning them into a fiery halo, he could bear his pain no longer. He leaned forward, said softly, "But, you needn't worry; I couldn't put you or Dee through that humiliation. Besides, because you're a woman, Hawk would probably be easy on you." He abruptly rose, "Good bye, Franny."

On the front porch, he found Dee sitting beside Otto on the swing with her face in her hands while Otto tried to comfort her. The couple looked up as soon as he stepped out the door.

"Godson, Josiah," her voice pleaded with him.

His back to her, unable to look at this woman who in the space of a short month had almost taken the place of his own dear mother, he asked, "How long have you known?"

When Dee told him he turned to her, "And about the *White Star*?"

"Only this mornin', from Jeremiah Wilcox."

"Have *her* tell you about it," he said brusquely and strode to his horse. Without looking back he galloped away, Tycee's butter biscuit turning to a lump of dough in his stomach.

CHAPTER FIVE
August

Friday the 2nd--Dug Springs

Totten's cannons fired a round of canister into the rebel sharpshooters and suddenly, Scarborough heard the bugle call. "Charge," he yelled as he with 200 other cavalrymen raced down the incline to meet General Rains' cavalry massed against Steele's infantry.

Cutting and slashing their way through the rebel lines, Josiah's company, with the rest of Stanley's cavalry, found itself in hand-to-hand with seasoned horsemen who gave as good as they got. Metal met metal, clanging and crashing, saber against saber. The sharp *thwack* of gunfire caused the churning, dust-filled air to take on the acrid smoke from gunpowder, creating an eye-stinging, blinding haze obscuring vision until their sabers sliced and stabbed at victims they could not see. Leading his men into the thick of the battle, his black hair and uniform soon painted with grey dust, Scarborough tore at the enemy with a fury that the men he commanded sought to emulate. Bit by bit they drove the rebels back.

Around him arose an incomprehensible roar - of men cursing, horses screaming, carbine and pistol fire, and the most unholy, eerie wail he'd ever heard coming from the throats of the enemy. This rebel yell sent chills down his spine. Not even the savage war whoops of the Comanche and the Cheyenne had instilled the kind of choking terror, as did the caterwaul coming from the horse soldiers clad in butternut and home spun.

This kind of savage fighting he'd only dreamt of, but now, with a rebel Captain coming at him through the smoke and the dust, his saber raised to strike, Josiah

212

wished he still dreamt.

Within an hour after leaving Zimmer's porch he had been drinking at the Kentucky Saloon with Brush Arbor and looking deep into her black eyes. He had been late and a bit tipsy for dress parade. That night he informed Borenstein of his decision to rejoin the First Cavalry, and turned the command of the two companies of Volunteers over to Lieutenant Werner. Within 36 hours he had secured a sorrel mare, and rejoined his regiment. It didn't matter that he had to give up the comforts of garrison life, taking up the gritty life of field and tent. What mattered, was that he was away from the town that had brought him the love of his life and the pain of knowing he had loved unwisely.

Now, on this scorching hot day twelve miles out of Springfield on the Wire Road at Dug Springs, he was fighting for his life. As he sought to wheel the mare to the right the enemy captain locked with him. Of equal height and strength the man forced Scarborough's terrified mount to dance first to one side and then to the other, always moving backwards, being herded until the mare could move no further. Cornered, several horses rubbed rump to rump and nose to nose with other chargers caught in the rebels' killing box.

A great whinnying and snorting arose as the trapped animals began to buck and rear. Their riders were unable to maneuver from the jam, while Rains' men circled the deadly trap, keeping it closed, shooting and slashing at will with bloody zeal.

Although blocked from escape by bloodied horse-flesh and wounded men, sweat stinging his eyes and his arm gone numb with pain, Scarborough held his opponent tight in a deathly stalemate. His sabre refused to unlock the captain's, preventing the rebel from leverage. To do so would allow the captain to circle his arm around Scarborough's either to give a mortal thrust or to yank him from the saddle. With him unhorsed within the trap either the captain would shoot or sabre him or the horses would trample him to death.

With a hideous grimace, his pointed jaw and lolling tongue protruding between blackened teeth, his long gray hair made more pallid by the dust and his black, killer eyes bulging from exertion, the rebel's features reminded Scarborough of a gargoyle. Just then, the captain took a surprise blade from Sanders. For an eternity of moments before his body fell, the captain sat his horse while a fountain of blood burst forth when his head went flying through the thick air and rolled upon the ground.

But Josiah had no time to reflect on the hideous sight. For an old horse soldier with snow-white hair was leveling his rifle at Sanders. Before he pulled the trigger, Josiah managed to run his saber to the hilt through the man's chest. Blood gushed down his shirtfront and onto his saddle as he slumped and slowly slid off his horse.

Then he heard the boom from Totten's artillery and another shell fell into the Rebs. They galloped off continuing to yell their unearthly cry and left 200 horses tied in the ravine and twenty wounded soldiers.

"Let's get them horses boys," Scarborough shouted leading his company down to where the horses were tied. Around them rattled musketry fire as Rains' sharpshooters hid behind the rocks and brush on the slopes of the ravine. They were almost where the horses were tied when a cavalryman galloped up.

"Sorry, Sir, but General Lyons has ordered that all of us are to get out of the ravine, at once. He fears the sharpshooters will pick us off like fish in a barrel."

"He's lost his mind. We need these horses."

"Don't argue with me, sir, tell it to Cap'n Stanley. He's mad as hell about it too." The trooper galloped off to deliver the word to the other company commanders down the line.

Furious at the lost prize, Josiah reluctantly called back his men. Halfway out of the ravine a soldier crawled out of the bushes in front of him. Blood covered the dusty homespun jacket and when he looked up at Scarborough he held out one hand, as though to beg for help.

Josiah stopped. The man was hurt, not a threat, and he would take him prisoner. He offered him his canteen of water and noticed the youth of this trooper. He had heard about the boys, some as young as 12, lying about their ages to get into the army. To them it was action, excitement, and glory. In his own company last winter an overgrown 14-year-old had been unknowingly accepted. Three weeks into training, here had come the kid's father. He had jerked his son by the ear, leading him out the gate, to the hoots and catcalls of the other troopers. But who was he to judge? He had been underage, scarcely 17 when he had finagled his way in.

"Thanks," the boy tried to smile, but tears stood in his eyes.

"You've taken a hit in the arm. It'll be all right once the surgeon looks at it," Josiah's practiced eye looked his captive over. "Stand up."

He tried to stand, but toppled over on his backsides again. "Can't. My leg is bad hurt, too."

Josiah examined the leg; it was broken. He waved over two troopers. "This man is a prisoner. He's got a broken leg. Use your blankets to make a sling and carry him out. Make sure our surgeon looks at his arm, too."

Back at the Federal lines, he ate a half-cooked dinner of stale beef, hardtack and coffee, and tried to wash up before he moseyed over to Stanley's tent to discuss the issue of the lost horses. Congregated in a holding pen near headquarters, he ran into nearly 50 prisoners under guard. And there was the boy. The wounded arm was held up in a dirty sling and his leg in a splint. The surgeon had done his duty.

The boy called out to him as he rode past. "Captain!"
He stopped, curious. "Yeah? What?"

"I want to thank you. You saved my life. I was a-
dyin' out there fer some water."

Up close, Josiah noticed the curly brown hair and the
wide brown eyes that gave the rebel the look of a wise
deer. And now with the dust at least partially wiped off,
his face seemed familiar, as though he had seen it in a
tintype, somewhere. He studied the boy, asked, "What's
your name, Reb?"

"Private Clay Monihan, Sir. Company B Rains'
Cavalry."

A week went by during which gossip about the
combined numbers of Price and McCulloch's armies,
including all cavalry, armaments, and location fluctuated
from hour to hour. Refugees fleeing the Rebel army
poured into Springfield and reported upwards to seeing
40,000 men. However, cavalry scouts came back with
figures of around 15,000.

During this turbulent week, Josiah had been called up
to Lyon's headquarters to serve as adjutant's aide and
courier while Stanley's C company pulled escort duty for
the 20 wagons of supplies approaching Springfield from
Rolla, 25 miles away. And, although he had misgivings
about re-involving himself with his new found "family,"
good conscience demanded he personally see to
Monihan's parole.

Until now, St.Louis department headquarters, John C.
Fremont commanding, had dilly-dallied around, ignoring
for over a month General Lyon's urgent pleas, and not sent
the basic needs for an army on the march. Nearly non-
existent were reinforcements, food, clothing, ammunition,
weapons, and medical supplies. Thus, the minie ball had
been dug out of Clay's shoulder and his leg reset without
anesthesia.

"Ok, Monihan," said Josiah, who felt very tall,

standing over his fuzzy-cheeked cousin, "You can go home. But let me make myself perfectly clear. I never want to encounter you again in this man's war." Being his most intimidating self, Josiah glared down at this child-man relative of his. "If I do, you will think the pain you've gone through with that leg and shoulder was only a passing headache."

"Yes, Cousin Josiah. I do believe I've seen all I want to of fightin'. I done seen enough of the elephant." Clay grinned sheepishly.

"Stop grinning. I am quite serious."

Clay glanced at Toby preoccupied with frying bacon for the officer's mess, said, "Yes sir," and hung his head.

"Report to your Aunt Dee the minute you get back to Jefferson City. She needs you, especially now that Toby is with me as officer's aide and cook. And one last thing, I want your word upon your honor that you will stay there. Because, if you do break your parole, and try to sneak back into the lines, I will- I repeat- I *will* know of it and *will* be able to find you. Do you understand?"

"Yes sir." He looked up then, asked, "Sir, is there any message you wish me to deliver to Aunt Dee or Franny ?" Clay leaned on his crutch.

After a flicker's hesitation Josiah growled, "No, now, clear outta here. The wagon is waiting to take you home."

When the ambulance wagon pulled out taking Clay and several other wounded north, Josiah and Toby howled with laughter. Pushing his cavalry forage cap to the back of his head, Toby said, "I'se reckon I ain't never seen that boy so scared." Then, with his attention fixed on the frying meat, he asked, softly, "Mr. Josiah, why you don't send a message to Miss Franny ?"

Toby was the only man on earth who realized how much in turmoil Josiah was about Franny. Over the past weeks Josiah had confided in him. Since Toby had grown up with her, Josiah hoped he'd have some explanations

217

about Franny's reckless behavior. All his attendant had done was to shake his head and remark "Miss Franny, she always be goatheaded."

Josiah didn't answer Toby's question. He didn't have to. Toby knew he was still angry and heartsick. The ache wouldn't go away, no matter how fiercely he fought, how many scouts he volunteered for, or how much whiskey he drank. So, beneath the hickory and jack oak trees he ate his supper in silence while evening drew nigh and shadows like inky carpets spread around the pink limestone rocks.

By midnight, Lyon was on the march again down the Little York Road advancing towards Wilson Creek. An hour later the head of the column came in sight of the enemy's campfires. Orders went down that everybody was to rest on their arms, sleep in readiness to fight, until further notice. Lyon's staff bivouacked between the rows of corn in a field by the roadside. For Josiah it meant his horse remained saddled and he intended to roll up in his blanket beside the mare.

With an infantry lieutenant assigned to headquarters staff like himself, Josiah crouched beside a low fire and cradled a cup of coffee, laced with a splash of whiskey. Several yards away Lyon and his chief of staff, John Schofield, conferred in whispers over a flickering candle jammed into the dirt and shared one rubber-coat for ground cover between them. The commanding general seemed intent on showing his chief of staff where he planned to attack in the morning.

"How many do you think we're facing?" Josiah whispered.

The campfire flickered over the young man's face revealing a blonde curly beard. "From all reports looks like around 13,000. Add 800 cavalry."

"Jesus," Josiah inhaled. He eyed Lyon and Schofield before he passed the flask to the other officer, said, "What did we muster - 4,000? And with Sigel 's brigade moving up south of the Cassville road we've got maybe 5,000 all considered, less than half Price's numbers. Not friendly odds. Still, you've got to admire Lyon." He took back the flask, poured some more of the liquor in his cup, and sipped at it a while. He watched the fire dance, working its enchantment over the night around them. The man asked whispering, "You were there. What you think of that meeting with the higher ups last night?" He referred to a meeting Lyon had held with the top-ranking officers beneath him.

"He laid everything out for Sigel, Steele, and the others." Again, Josiah surreptitiously offered the flask, watched him take a swallow, and said, not to be overheard, "Thanks to three months enlistments being up and deserters, we've got a fast dwindling army with no supplies and fewer arms. Should we quietly strike tents and run for the rear, or should we make a big enough hit to hurt the Rebs before we skedaddle? You've got to admire the General. He'd fight rather than retreat, take the offensive instead of wait to be attacked."

"Well, Scarborough, it's going to be one hell of a hot little fight, I'd say." With that the officer yawned, handed back the flask, rolled up in his blanket beside the fire, and within minutes was snoring.

Watching him sleep Josiah's mind imagined the battle that would ensue on the morrow and felt a sadness sweep through him with such intensity that he felt unbidden tears rise through his lashes. Choking back the unexpected flow, he wondered how many would die tomorrow? Then, said softly to no one, for the camp slept and he heard gentle snores coming from the shared rubber-coat, "Will I die tomorrow? Do I give a good God-damn?" He downed his cup of whiskey.

Sitting there staring into the fire and breathing in the pungent smell of the burning wood, suddenly he was back at Erin House, waking up to Franny smacking him with a

219

wet cloth while fire swooped down upon them. He drank straight from the flask, remembering, and whispered, "Damn you, Franny. Why did you have to tell me you love me?"

Soon, he felt the comforting buzz the liquor always brought. Then, he staggered over to his horse, checked the mare's tether, saddle, and tack, rolled up in his blanket and felt the warm night ooze around him. Just before he dozed off he thought he heard distant gunfire. Then, during lulls, he heard the call of a dove.

For a moment the juxtaposition of the two sounds didn't make sense. What was it Monihan had said, something about "seeing enough of the elephant?" That he'd seen enough of blood and death? Josiah had sent home a distant relative who the higher ups called "the enemy." Who was the enemy ? Not that boy, surely. Not even the old-timer who had taken Josiah's sabre into his chest, nor the man whose gargoyle head rolled into the dirt. The enemy wasn't supposed to be people who spoke your language, looked like you, or claimed blood-ties. Everything seemed a paradox. Gunfire - doves; war - peace. Nothing about this set-to had made much sense so far. And not much about his own life, either, for that matter.

Saturday the 10th-Wilson Creek

Hy was trying to get a piece of burned chicken out of the camp fire when the first shells sent grapeshot and canister exploding into their camp. He checked the timepiece he had taken from a Cole County farmer some months before. "Hell, its only half-past five o'clock in the mornin'!" He exploded like the shell, spilling hot coffee down the front of his dirty shirt.

"Lyon's here." Verboise sipped his coffee and munched from a loaf of bread he had stolen the day before. He had committed his company,   The Cole County

Mounted Rifles, informally known as "Verboise's bunch," to Cawthorne's cavalry, of Rains' brigade. Around the giant, his Cole County men prepared for battle. The bugle blew "To Horse" and each man fled to his mount, except for Jacques Verboise. He continued to calmly finish his breakfast.

"Let's go, Cap'n Verboise," Hy wondered at the insolence Verboise got away with. Time and again he had clashed with the captain commanding and even talked about pulling his men out to serve in another unit - under McCulloch instead of Price. But the men had talked him out of it. McCulloch was a Texan, leading a pack of Arkansas men and Verboise's boys were all Missourians, like Price.

Another shell shattered into the ground, into a camp-fire several yards from them. Jumping out of the way, Verboise shouted orders. "The field we're camped in is too open. Get yourselves to the thickets and bluffs, yonder." He pointed to a ridge overlooking the valley of Wilson Creek. But the Federals kept on coming and soon, all of Cawthorne's men from both sides of the creek were riding or running pell-mell out of there, leaving behind breakfasts smoking on campfires. But they dismounted and reformed under the bluffs at the foot of the hill. The order to "Take the hill" came down the line and Hy found himself loading and reloading his carbine, and engaged in the fight of his life. He was trying to take Oak Hill, named for the plethora of jack oaks that grew on and around it.

Through the smoke and dust he tried to see Verboise, Chess McDonald, Horton, and others he knew, saw no one, and realized he'd been separated from his company. But that didn't matter, Federal bullets and canister whizzing over his head he was approaching the crest of the hill when he saw a blue uniformed officer astride his horse as though welded to the animal.

Damned if it weren't that Josiah Scarborough, trying

to pick his horse's way through the dense thickets and marshy fords. If Hy stood still a few minutes, he figured he could get the bastard in his gun sights. But the dust and smoke were too thick. Only occasional glimpses of blue could he see as the man he suspected of having his wife's true affections rode through the battle, going where, Hy couldn't guess. Suddenly, the smoke cleared long enough for him to clamp down Franny's Yankee. He fired. With great satisfaction he gave the yell that he had learned since joining up when he saw Scarborough take the hit and fall from his horse.

Grayness, darkness, booming sounds, musketry rattle, shouts of men, the sun, all flowed into each other and around Josiah as he lay in a thicket. When he came too, the lieutenant with the blond curly beard leaned over him. He wore a head bandage soaked in blood.

"Here, some water," the young man, poured tepid liquid down Josiah's throat, who coughed, tried to sit up. But the stab of pain in his side immediately flopped him back down.

"Can you tell? How bad is it?"

The officer ripped open Josiah's shirt, his pale eyes widened in surprise. "Not much of a hole, but looks deep."

"Minie Ball," Josiah gasped. It hurt to breathe and to talk. "Its shattered inside me. I'm a goner."

"Hell no!" his friend grinned. "The surgeons will dig it out of you in no time. You'll be fine."

The message I was carrying from Lyon - it's in my pocket. Make sure Sigel gets it, if you can find him." He referred to Franz Sigel commanding a brigade of St.Louis Germans.

The lieutenant looked at him gravely. "Lyon is dead. Nobody knows yet what happened to Sigel. Some say he left his own troops behind to get slaughtered and captured while he hightailed it back to Springfield. We're

222

retreating. I'm back on the field under a flag of truce to help gather up our dead and wounded."

"Jesus, what happened?" Josiah whispered just before he passed out again.

When he awoke, he was in a hospital tent. He knew that's where he was by the sounds and the smells, mostly by the smells. Humanity in all its fleshly decay assaulted his nostrils. Blood, urine, and feces mixed with the odors of sweat, grime, and rotting meat from dismembered limbs thrown aside under the hot August sun. Beneath the incessant buzzing of flies, his ears picked up the sounds of men either screaming in pain or moaning in death. And another sound, the sound of a surgeon's saw cutting through flesh and bone. He lay near the cutting table, dripping with blood from the operations and amputations, done that day. Waiting for his turn atop that table of agony he wanted to die.

But before he could, strong, smooth hands laid a cool cloth on his head and offered him a drink of water. Gulping the water, he looked up and saw a woman. She looked familiar. The dark hair pulled into a neat bun at her nape, the dark eyes, the round body, and he muttered, "Hello Patsy." The laundress, obviously pressed into the nursing corps by the emergency, stopped what she was doing, stared down at him before she whooped, "Joey!" She would have hugged him and planted a kiss on his dry lips if it weren't for his wound.

"Oh, Joey, you been shot up really bad." Her eyes grew dark and he saw their alarm.

"Yeah, I know. I'm gonna die." He closed his eyes, hoping for death.

"No you ain't," Patsy planted both hands on the sides of her ample hips and repeated, "No you ain't 'cause I'm not gonna let you. So there, Scarborough."

"How…. How are you, Patsy ?" He tried to grin, fought the blackness that was encroaching upon his peripheral vision.When she looked at his wound tears started in her eyes but after a pause said shyly, "I got married. He's a corporal with Sigel's brigade. We met after I got to St.Louis from Fort Smith."

He was truly happy for her. "I wish you a barrel of happiness, Mrs.-what should I call you now ?" He tried to reach for her hand, but just as he did and before she could answer, an orderly stood beside them.

"We're ready for him, ma'am. Surgeon wants you to help keep him calm."

Orderlies laid him on the surgeon's befouled table. The hands and apron of the doctor were stained with blood. Worse, he didn't know the man. Panic seized him and without warning, Josiah knocked his fist into the orderly standing next to him. He fought hard. And blinding pain rushed over him and roared in his ears. Suddenly he went deaf and the people struggling with him moved their lips but he heard nary a sound except a scream—his own. With the compassionate look of an angel's, Patsy was trying to say something. Suddenly, it wasn't Patsy at all but Franny, gazing down at him with serious, misty green eyes that dripped with tears. And the tears were being caught in a towel pressed over his nose and mouth

"He comes around." The masculine voice sounded foreign. Josiah lay in that grey realm between sleep and wakefulness trying to make up his mind who was talking to him. *English? No, German.*

"*Guten Abend Herr* Captain Scarborough." A short man with a fat, grey bearded face peered down at him over spectacles that kept sliding down his nose. Quickly the little man took his pulse and placed his hand on his brow. "You will live, *Herr* Captain." He smiled showing crooked teeth and turned to the nun standing stiffly by his side. It wasn't Patsy. "He's feverish, Sister Evangelina. See to it he gets plenty of water."

"Yes, Doctor."

The doctor bustled off and Josiah stared up at the older woman who plumped his pillow and offered him a sip of water. "What happened to me?" He asked.

"You have a wound in your side. They operated." She was tall and thin and her lips, while not harsh, looked like they hadn't smiled in years. She seemed to be picking lint off his coverlet.

"Who are you, Sister, ma'am if I may ask?" When he talked he hurt and a stab of pain made him wince.

"I'm the head night nurse, the only one on this ward. But you must hush and not talk at all. Take some more water before I go." She still hadn't smiled.

She held his head up slightly so he could get the water. When she did he caught a whiff of strong lye soap about her person; indeed, the ward seemed to reek of it and molding bodies. Well at least it was clean. He smiled his thanks, but as she left his side her sorrowful face was still unbroken. He lay staring at the dark above him. From the flicker of an oil lamp turned low, burning somewhere in the darkened room, the ceiling's rough beams dissolved into shadow. He turned his head to the left and saw a man in the cot next to his with a bloody bandage covering his entire face and head. "Jesus," he whispered and quickly turned his head to the right. Sporting a heavy black beard, there lay a fellow with both hands and arms in bandages.

The man returned his stare. "All our nurses is Sisters of Charity. She ain't so bad onst you get used to 'er." He whispered.

"Thanks, I'll try to remember that. What happened to you?" It still hurt to talk, but not as bad.

"Got m' hands mostly blown off."

There was nothing he could say. The thought of losing one's hands was too terrible to contemplate. He nodded understanding and turned his head back center.

"M' name's Getz. Master Sergeant, artillery, Company A, Sigel's brigade

225

Josiah gave his own information and asked, "Where are we, what is this place?"

"Gen'l Hospital in St. Louis."

He was about to ask his ward-mate why General Sigel disappeared from the honorable field of battle when Sister Evangelina reappeared.

"No talking, boys." She shook a stern finger at both of them causing Josiah to think of his mother and he grinned. "And those dimples you're so quick to show, Captain, won't get you my permission to chat the night away. You men must get your rest."

"Yes ma'am," both men said in unison, looked sheepishly at one another and closed their eyes.

Unable to fall asleep Josiah lay in silence until the shadows of the night deepened and the grayness of dawn stole into the hospital ward. Vague memories of how he got here surfaced. The last face he had seen that he remembered was Franny's. But how could she have been there? No, it was Patsy's. She said she got married. He had fought the doctor who wanted to probe his wound with his fingers, hit somebody, then, blackness.

Broken memories following the operation crowded his mind. The rush to get the wounded further to the rear because Price was marching on Springfield; the pain-racked jostling he took during the 100 mile ride between Springfield and Rolla, in an "avalanche," the two-wheeled bone shaker used for an ambulance wagon. In Rolla orderlies hoist him on the train for St. Louis

The head day Sister smiled more and when she did sunshine filled her face. Middle-aged, and rotund, dressed in her order's dark habit, she roused everybody up at dawn, washing faces and hands when the wound permitted and got the men their breakfasts. Everybody called her Sister Brigit Mary and spoke in reverent terms of her kindness.

The poor chap with the bandaged face died a day after

Josiah arrived and he hadn't gotten his name. Sergeant Getz and he became friends, chatting, playing whist, with the help of a "handed" boy who had lost his right leg.

And war news claimed that after Price's victory at Wilson Creek, he hadn't been able to get McCulloch go with him in an attack on the retreating Federals. So, the former governor of Missouri had taken it upon himself to leave Springfield and start marching his troops north through a state that was wide open to him. Along the way, he gathered men and supplies. His goal was to join with a southern army trapped north of the Missouri River and unable to cross because the Federals held the river.

CHAPTER SIX
September

Sunday the 8th

After nearly a month's recuperation, Josiah had his first visitor. Hat in hand, Toby stood over him, eyeing him soberly. "How you Mr. Josiah?"

"Toby," Josiah struggled to sit up. "I reckon you might say I've been better."

"Yas suh," Toby twirled the forage hat and looked down at the floor. He seemed troubled.

"How are you?"

"Well, suh, since you be shot 'n' all, I'se goin' back to Erin House. I suppose it's near 'bout fixed up, by now. Most a Lyon's army bein' let go anyhow."

Josiah's ears perked up. "The army's being let go? What do you mean?"

"Well, Suh, you heard 'bout the changes in the cavalry." He referred to Congress authorizing the formation of new cavalry units, and renaming the cavalry regiments already existent within the Regular Army. Josiah's beloved First, now carried the name the "Fourth U.S. Cavalry." Josiah nodded.

Toby continued. "The Regulars bein' sent north of the river to Hannibal under Gen'l Pope and the Volunteers be goin' home. They was three months men. Their enlistment be up. And dat means Toby's out of a job. Besides, I don' wanna stay 'lessin' y'all's there. I'se yore boy, not somebody else's." The young Negro scowled when he said this last.

Looking around, fearing they'd been overheard, embarrassed that others might think Toby was his slave, Josiah said quietly, "You're nobody's boy, but your own.

You're a free man. I was happy when you agreed to serve with me. But you're free to make your own choices." Realizing Toby still looked up to him for direction, Josiah continued, "Tell you what, Toby, old friend, take a furlough. Go home. And when I'm recovered I'll send for you. How's that?"

Toby left grinning and Josiah never gave another thought about him until the following Sunday, a week later. He heard the brogue before the speaker entered the ward. Dee rustled her petite grey silk beside each patient. "Howdy-do, boys," she smiled and greeted each man. In addition, she gave each patient a fresh rose, laying the flower on a man's chest if he couldn't hold it with his hands.

"Thank you ma'am. God bless you ma'am." The whispered voices followed in her wake.

When she finally came to him she placed a rose in his hands, gave him a withered once over, and pursed her lips. "A-'N' how might me only godson be fairin'?"

He didn't smile. "The Sanitary Commission that over-sees war hospitals came in last week and looked this one over, gave it a "commendation." We've got excellent food here. The ladies of St.Louis keep us well fed with lots of eggs and cream. And the Sisters of Charity keep my bed clean and comfortable, thank you, godmother." He knew he sounded stiff. Still, he couldn't help but feel joy that she had come to see him, and at last he smiled. So audacious was this woman who reminded him of his own mother.

She removed her hanky from her sleeve and dabbed at her eyes. "I can't thank ye enough godson fer sending Clay home."

He nodded, watched her sniffle, moved to a sitting position in his bed, and changed the topic "The doctor was in here this morning. Said I was getting well. The hole in my side is deep, but no organs were hit."

229

"Aye, we spoke with him before comin' in here."

"We?" He prayed Franny hadn't come up to St.Louis, too.

"Ah sure, now, ya don' think I'd be comin' all alone to this big city, do ya ? Mr. Zimmer came with me and he bought the roses for the boys."

When he only stared back at her, she blurted. "Well, the war news ain't good. There's this Colonel Mulligan's marchin' ta meet Price at Lexington at the river. But Mulligan's only got 3,000 boys and Price's got over 10,000. Mulligan keeps beggin' Fremont fer more troops he does, but they ain't been sent and the new post commander at Jeff City, don't send him troops, either."

He had already heard this news, but nodded to be polite. Again conversation ceased between them. He lay back down, resigned, and exhausted. "Toby, must have told you I was here."

"Aye." Looking at him steadily she added, "Don'cha wanna get out of here, mebbe come home?" She wrinkled her nose in disgust, "Smells like they've tried to cover up a dead cat with lye soap."

"No, Dee, I don't want to go back home. Maybe when I'm well. But right now I'm too sick to deal with anything that .."

"----Oh hush," she put her pudgy finger over his lips, exploding into conversation. "Now listen, ev'rything's been solved. Captain Hawk's, he's been very.." she exhaled, "understandin' with Franny. Father Walsh has filed for an annulment with the St. Louis diocese, a "matter o' form" he's callin' it. And Hawk is doin' the lawyerin' fer her annulment in the district court and got her a pardon for her misbegotten part in that steamboat affair."

Not surprised that Franny had gotten off the charge so easily, he watched his godmother while she prattled on. "After all, boy-o," she cocked her bonnet framed head back as though to say Josiah should have understood the same way, "*he* realized she had nothin' ta do with them murders and believed her when she swore under oath she didn't know anybody would be killed. Besides, a witness she'll be against the men who did do the killin' when their military trial comes up."

What bothered him about this story? That Franny hadn't been punished at all for her involvement? Or that Cyrus Hawk seemed to be taking such an interest in the family - no, correct that – interest in the girl that he'd act as her attorney in circuit court?

"Why is Captain Hawk helping Franny get her civil annulment?"

Her eyes grew round as she couldn't look at him, and she inhaled deeply, "Well, now that ye be askin' he's been payin' court to our Franny - your *godsister*," she ended emphatically, turning back to him.

The room began to spin. "And you are allowing this?" he whispered. "He's over twice her age." He tried to sit up but the effort taxed his strength and he fell back on his pillow.

Trying to calm him, she patted his arm. "Aye, older and settled he is 'n' our little Franny, you agree, needs a firm, gentlin' hand." When he said nothing but only stared back at her, she rattled on. "Ya got ta consider, Josiah, not many decent, eligible men would even consider Franny now fer a wife." She cleared her throat, "I mean…" She stammered, turned beet red. "After she had eloped 'n' all. She's ruined, don'cha know?" She finished in a whisper, staring at her hands making useless gestures to smooth his unwrinkled blanket.

Suddenly he was furious - furious at the morals that would deem a beautiful young girl "ruined" because of one impulsive act - furious that Franny was being encouraged to allow Hawk's pursuit - furious at himself for walking out on her the way he had. Yes, there it was. All along that

231

had been the root of his anguish since he fled Jefferson City in a rotgut-induced haze. He should have understood - even to why she felt she had to lie. He should have stood by her, told her that day he loved her.

Maybe it was the fever that still wracked his body or the room that seemed to whirl faster than before, but the whispered words flew out of his mouth before he could stop them. "You're wrong, Dee, about Franny being *ruined*. I love her. I want her to be my wife."

Looming over him the tiny woman gazed down with eyes that had all ready seen too much pain. "Aye, that I can see ya do. From the time we first met ya on the road, I knew. 'N' I didn't want to tell ya 'bout Captain Hawk." Her tone became gentle, trying to get him to see the folly of his love. "'Twouldn't be a good match, now, Josiah, between you 'n' me girl. Before, in the days at Scarborough Hall when yer two was bairns frolickin' on the lawn, yer sainted mother 'n' meself often would declare how nice 'twould be if the two of yers would grow up 'n' marry. *Born fer the other*, Lady Caitlin would say. 'N' agrees I would. But, now, all that's gone, starved away by the famine. Ye have no more houses or lands and who knows if the English government would bestow back yer title. Tis, in America we are lad, 'n' yer subsistin' on army pay. I'll not be havin' me only bairn married to a penniless soldier boy."

Throbbing, head and wounded side ached afresh. Weakness washed over him and he said, "You seemed to accept me, godmother, acted like you cared for me. I don't understand. And what about Cyrus Hawk. He subsists on an officer's pay." The effort to speak exhausted him and he lay too weary and heartsick to say more.

She reached to hug him but he turned away. "Oh, son, tis tears I have in me own eyes, you'd see if only you'd look at me." He felt his arm stiffen beneath the blanket when she reached out to pat him. "Even if ye hadn't raced away like ya done, come ta me 'n' asked, I wouldn't consent to ya marryin' Franny. I love ya, I do, like me own son, but I couldn't accept ya as me son-in-law. Cyrus Hawk, now, comes from a fine, wealthy family from Topeka. His father earned his fortune tradin' in the hemp market. He also, practiced at the bar-lawyerin' and tis to the family fortune and law-business Captain Hawk will be a-goin' when this wretched rebellion is over. He's talkin' 'bout politics, maybe runnin' for governor of Kansas, and hints that he's eyein' the presidential chair, he is. Tis a lucky girl, Franny, that such an accomplished gentleman would be interested in her."

After she thankfully left, Josiah refused his supper. Instead, he lay on his back watching the night creep into the room and letting the tears flow down his cheeks.

Friday the 20th Lexington, Missouri

Hy poked up the campfire and poured himself another cup of coffee. After Wilson Creek Verboise had mingled his men with "Old Pap" Price's cavalry riding first with Raines then Rives. All the men called General Price by the affectionate nickname, but not to the face of the jowly, bewhiskered veteran of the Mexican War.

All the way up the state they had experienced a high old time, living off the generosity of the southern people. The women came out in droves to meet and feed them--the men to join the southern cause. A week ago at Warrensburg, 35 miles south of Lexington, Hy had met a girl there who offered herself to him and he took her up on it. He remembered the brief encounter as he looked into the bottom of his cup. "What the hell," he muttered feeling the bitterness he'd carried all summer well up in him again. "My dear little wife refuses to be a wife. I got every right."

Blowing on his cup to cool it, he noticed the wiry

fellow in the bright red shirt moseying through camp on his horse. It was suppertime and everybody was in a good mood resting themselves and talking about how they had penned up Mulligan's Yankees in the town's Masonic College and cut off their water supply. But this man seemed to be alone and seemed to be looking things over, turning to look first at one cook fire then another. Hy said nothing, set his cup down, watched the stranger stop, observe Verboise from a distance, and start to ride over to them. At once, Hy was on his feet, his Navy drawn.

"No need to worry about me." The stranger, armed with four Navy's tucked in his belt and a Sharpe's carbine, and wearing a fancy plumed hat, fanned his empty hands out to his sides and smiled at them all.

"Sit down, Wilcox," Verboise growled and offered, "We have coffee, light bread, and chicken; you're welcome to share."

"Thank you," the young man fastened them with blue eyes set within even features and beneath light brown hair. "Just the coffee will be fine." Chess McDonald poured him a cup.

"Saw you leading the charge over the bridge," Verboise said admiringly.

"Figure if Old Pap can ride the front lines when everybody's tellin' him to go to the rear, I reckon a young fella like me can do it, too." Everybody laughed. They remembered the 52-year-old General, heavyset in his saddle, leading the men forward with raised sabre and shouted orders. A grape shard from Yankee cannon had shattered his field glass, but the General had gone on unperturbed, riding up and down the front lines.

"Y'all at Dry Creek?" The man referred to the hot little cavalry fight on the second of the month at a place 12 miles east of Fort Scott, Kansas.

"We were," Verboise answered, "enjoyed every minute of it. None of my boys took a scratch. Drove those blue coats right back to Kansas."

"Interesting isn't it," the man's eyes glowed with an intense hatred, "how they got the uniforms and we have to depend on our own selves. They got Government Issue muskets and most of us just shooting with whatever we were using to hunt with. Every rag-tag farmer in the surrounding country has come over to Price and every last one of 'um wearing his own canvas britches and carrying his own shotgun. Even our officers have to pin cloth to their shoulders so the men can tell 'um apart. On the other hand the prosperous Federals have raped Missouri and will ravage the south, if we don't stop them." He looked around at the numerous campfires flickering around the town's fair-ground and smiled, "But by God, I am proud of us. Look at these men here. And more are joining up everyday. We've swelled to almost 20,00 men."

"That's so." Verboise said mildly, "Mulligan's boys are pretty well dug in behind their earthworks and trenches around the College. But we've got 'um surrounded. Think they'll be able to make a stand and get out?"

"Don't think so, Captain, they're out of water. Soon they'll be so thirsty they'll be begging us to take 'um captive just to get something to drink."

"By the way, friend, we didn't catch your name," Verboise sat back on his haunches and observed this talkative, intense fellow.

"Sorry, got so interested in our conversation. Name's William Quantrill. Most folks call me Bill or Will." The two shook hands and Quantrill then shook hands all around.

The talk was easy and Hy liked this Will Quantrill with the easy laugh and a burning passion to defeat the North. He talked about forming his own guerrilla army deep behind the lines of the Federals, going to Richmond and securing a real commission. He wanted revenge.

"Jennison, Lane, and Montgomery's Jayhawkers are

tearing up western Missouri. They murdered and robbed Judge Younger from over near Harrisonville in June, and he was a Union man."

"We heard about that," Verboise said, looking at the rapt faces surrounding him.."Jayhawkers prey on anybody, political persuasions make no difference." He offered more coffee.

Quantrill took it, said, "Farmers who've done nothing, wives and children, beaten, homes burned - -it's got to stop."

"I agree." Verboise nodded. "The Federals under John Pope have committed atrocities in the northeast, around Hannibal every bit as bad as any Kansas Jayhawker. The Union command in Cole County, though, takes a softer approach to hurting Confederate sympathizers. Those boys are known to confiscate every valuable, every head of livestock, down to a man's last chicken and sell these on the St. Louis black market. This was starting to happen just before we left. My boys, though, struck hard against the Union farmers and shopkeepers in the county. And of course the railroad and telegraph lines."

"That's good. Y'all struck first and early." He put his cup down and rose. "Well, if you want to join up with me, keep your command as is and be a separate unit riding with my boys, y'all are welcome." He nodded a pleasant farewell, mounted up, and ambled out of the area, supposedly to his own campfire.

"What you think, boys? Want to ride with Quantrill, maybe get a really large bunch together ?" Verboise asked around. Everybody knew he'd make the decision.

Cyrus Hawk sniffed the air in the fast darkening room. "O'Shay, close the door. There's that abominable smell again." He watched the pudgy second Lieutenant close the door to the Provost Marshal's office, but it didn't do any good. The stuffy room seemed to hold all unpleasant odors, from whiskey to tobacco to unwashed bodies. The odor of human filth that drifted into his office, now, was coming from the dungeons below, crammed with three months worth of southern traitors awaiting trials.

"Have you looked into the city jail about taking the prisoners off our hands and out of the state Capitol's basement?"

"Yes, Sir," O'Shay faced him.

His youth, his eagerness to please, his physical awkwardness, an irritant, Hawk snapped, "And what did the city constable say? The legislators of the provisional government are starting to complain about the assembly chamber becoming nearly intolerable on warm days."

"He's looking into it, Sir. Something about paying him for feeding the prisoners."

"*Looking* into it—*something* about paying to feed the prisoners—what is this *something* to which you allude? Have you no particulars in the matter?" He'd have to go over there himself and straighten out the mess that his aide had obviously created.

O'Shay looked crest fallen. "I don't know, Sir, he didn't say."

Feeling his patience fast ebbing, with undisguised sarcasm, Hawk said "Haven't I trained you to ask *questions*, Lieutenant O'Shay? If the constable didn't say what the *something* was that bothered him, why didn't you open your mouth and ask ?" He exploded on the final word. O'Shay had come to him as aide at the end of July when his very Irish regiment under the very Irish Colonel James Mulligan had marched into Jefferson City and sent Borenstein's Germans home to St.Louis. And after nearly two months of working for him the boy still hadn't learned his job. He wished now he had encouraged him to go with Mulligan at the end of August when the "Irish Brigade" had marched out to confront Sterling Price. Hawk didn't know whom he despised more of the two classes of immigrants - the Germans or the Irish.

He waved away O'Shay's explanation. Feeling bilious Hawk flung open his roll-top desk, pigeon-holing the day's correspondence he had neglected and announced, "Lieutenant O'Shay, I'll be at Erin House should anyone need me for *urgent* business."

Walking the three blocks from headquarters towards supper at Erin House, Captain Cyrus Hawk grumbled at the inability of younger folk to understand simple instructions and weighed his chances with Miss Frances Moone. A misted rain fell, causing puddles that he had to avoid, but he didn't mind the rain. In fact, he rather enjoyed it. It helped calm him, helped him think.

Yes, technically, she still carried the odious married name of Wilcox but the annulment he had pushed ahead on the court's docket would soon become official, and so he never thought of her other than by her maiden name. However, "ruined" by all standards of decency, a maiden she was no longer. Instead of seeing her as tarnished, he chose to view his prey as he would a widow. And what a plump-breasted beauty, she was. She would, indeed, serve his purposes.

The civilian attorney, turned provost marshal, had almost arrived at the age of 39 unscathed by even a close romance. Having a woman "in love" with him, seemed such a remote reality that he no longer worried about it. The most he had ever stimulated in a woman had been a tepid friendship with a shy, pale spinster he had met at church - when he still attended Episcopal services in his Kansas parish. That had been ten years ago.

Mother had thought her unsuitable. From his mind he pushed away the image of the hatchet-faced New Englander with cold, black eyes, the woman who had borne him, raised him with strict discipline and a riding crop applied to his backsides. Who, when he had been seven years old, made him watch as she shot his puppy because it had gotten away and soiled the parlor carpet. He never owned another pet.

Not marrying the spinster, after all, hadn't really mattered too much. Although at the time he had felt keen disappointment for within their friendship had blossomed not passion but tolerance. She would have been patient with him, he remembered thinking at the time. But, one day mother had tea with the woman and then sent her away. She never again appeared in church and when he inquired at her lodgings the landlady told him she had moved to California - address unknown.

He walked slowly, pensively, lost in his thoughts and memories, feeling the mist cool the skin on his cheeks and hands that burned with fever. They always did when he anticipated putting them on the girl. Something about her deeply stirred him, making him edgy and tense. It was perfect that she was somewhat experienced and unspoken for. Officer gossip had hinted about the big Irishman, Captain Scarborough, being in love with her. But the fool had drunkenly marched off to the "real fight" he had jeered, and left her with no promises. But, Scarborough had fought his battles and gotten his just desserts. According to Mrs. Moone he lay gravely wounded in a hospital in St.Louis. Perhaps, he wouldn't recover; that would be nice. Hawk smiled to think of the veteran's possible demise.

How Franny might have felt about Scarborough, he didn't know. She didn't share intimate details of her feelings about others. It made no difference, but it might be helpful if she had been in love with him and he were to die. Then the door would be wide open for him. With deep satisfaction he imagined the moment. She'd weep for her dead love on his shoulder and he would be attentive. A tender thing like Miss Moone needed attention. Then with her squarely in his hands he'd begin the discipline process.

That ill-concealed temper of hers would have to be brought under control. Like a fine horse, she needed gentling, achieved by a firm hand and a sharp whip, if necessary.

He sighed remembering her behavior in his office the day he had brought her in to face charges of aiding raiders. Sullenly she sat before him.

"Miss Moone you are here because—"

"I know why I'm here." Her face in a scowl Franny refused to look at him.

He refused to be interrupted; "You are here because—"

"... I told you, I know why I'm here." She flashed deep emerald, angry eyes upon him and had the audacity to give *him* an order. "Don't repeat yourself." He heard the sharp inhale from O'Shay standing behind her.

She then whirled around and confronted his aide, "And I don't need the likes of you lurking over my shoulder. I don't have a revolver up my muff or a knife under my hat. Now, you go stand over there. "And without even a nod from him to give permission, O'Shay had scooted away and stood by the door.

One other time, a few days later, she had shown an obstinate nature.

"Miss Moone, if you will agree to testify that these are the men you saw boarding the *White Star* I can suggest leniency."

"Why leniency with me?" she thrust out her little chin. "I'm the cause the boat stopped in the first place. And Verboise treated me like one of his riders." Suddenly, she screwed up her face and wept. So loudly had she set up a wail that James Mulligan, Post commander at the time, looked into the office asking if everything was as it should be.

"Now, now darlin' girl. 'Tis cryin' I see you are." The young Colonel swept his tall, slender self into the provost's office taking no notice of the provost's authority. He helped the girl to her feet and led her from his office, saying over his shoulder, "Come, Provost Marshal, surely a wee slip of a girl like this couldn't have done anything so terrible to cause you to make her sob like a spongy cloud. Confine your harsher tactics to the unruly troops creatin' havoc in our streets and the bushwhackers shootin' at our trains."

Only Mrs. and Colonel Mulligan's interference had saved her from house arrest and a military trial. When Mulligan, a Chicago politician before the war, had suggested a pardon because she actually hadn't killed anybody and she eventually promised to name at least two of the men involved - Hy Wilcox and Verboise -at first he balked. He wanted the names of *all* the men involved.

But she had adamantly refused and he had ranted to O'Shay without remembering that his aide was Irish himself: "Those damn Irish, may every last one of them slide into hell stuck together like the slippery eels they are." Looking around Jefferson City, he sometimes wondered where all the real Americans had gone. He had been delighted when three weeks into August Brigadier General Ulysses Grant had taken over the command.

Squat, taciturn and cigar chomping, at first he had been a man after Hawk's own heart: disciplined, decisive, and deliberate. He had cleared the Capitol lawn of troops sending them to encampments outside the city and had closed down what had been one of Hawk's chief headaches - the recruitment of troops from downtown street corners. These recruitment stations often filled with rowdies loitering about the sidewalk. Arresting these drunks had created a problem and had taken up too much of his staff's time. Grant had ordered rations be brought in and strengthened fortifications around the city.

At first, Hawk had liked him. But Grant had taken a dim view of the practice of Federal reciprocation of goods

241

from peaceful southern sympathizers as a "tax" for their disloyalty, and had reprimanded Lieutenant Gorditch. This had interrupted the flow of a nice little side income the provost office had enjoyed receiving from Gorditch. But Grant stayed only one week in Jefferson City before promotion on and Colonel Jeff C. Davis and his 22nd Indiana volunteers had taken over the city. At the end of August Mulligan had marched out for Lexington. Gorditch and the provost office were waiting to see the measure of Davis before quietly renewing their "tax" gathering procedures.

Hawk looked up from his reverie, noticed a hennaed haired woman motioning to him from a doorway. With barely a glance he passed her by and heard her coarse laughter at his back. His mind turned again to Franny.

Miss Moone, even with all her sass fit his criteria perfectly: young, very pretty, educated but not overly so, certainly not one of those boring, brilliant females who wanted the vote, wore bloomers, and gave public speeches against slavery. Best of all, this child brought up in a boarding house by a widowed mother had no father or brother to check his past and take umbrage at his pursuit of her. And best of all she needed him. He doubted if she'd find another suitor as worthy as himself who would marry her, after her sordid past. And telling Mrs. Moone about his family fortune had immediately warmed that old bawd to the idea of him paying court to her daughter. If he was to marry before his 40th birthday to claim his inheritance, he had found just the one.

Whether she loved him or not was unimportant. All he wanted from her was a marriage where she stood by his side and greeted his guests who would further his political ambitions. With her he fulfilled the stipulations of his father's will. He admitted that he had allowed time to slip away and his court of other more socially acceptable women had come to naught. Everyone had refused him.

242

Perhaps they sensed his lack of passion and his o'er weening greed, traits he readily admitted. One had flung at him "you're cold, Cyrus Hawk, like a spent fish."

So, he had laid out the money for one seasoned damsel after another until they tired of him. He had forgone marriage and thus mother's objections about any ladies he might have had her meet. But time now grew short. He had only a little over a year left. Frances Moone would be his by then and he would be nearly 500,000 dollars richer.

Breathing deeply the moisture-laden air, Cyrus looked up into the dark, clouded sky, allowing the mist to fall directly on his face. Then he indulged himself; he began to whistle. Normally he liked to give the impression of a sober man of importance. Only Jack-o-napes smiled and grinned about others like drawing room monkeys. Solid men, powerful men, rarely took such ones seriously. That's why it seemed so important for him to have a beautiful wife who would shine next to him.

He had inadvertently wandered into Hog Alley. A cesspool for sure, and as Provost he had thought about making it off limits but knew if he tried the men would riot. Now it yawned before him, empty because of the rain except for a bedraggled cat skulking along the side of a building. A thought from nowhere entered his mind and he laughed, "Oh, how I'd love to introduce Frances Moone to my mother." Chuckling and talking to the empty ally he continued, "Mother, without your approval I have taken a Missouri Puke to wife - immigrant Irish to the core - and I want you to meet her." He threw back his head and belly-laughed. The image of the strict, dried-up old woman meeting the tousled -haired, busty, redhead, as his wife made him laugh hard enough to bring tears.

Followed, another thought equally funny. And if meeting Frances Moone doesn't give the old biddy heart failure, wait until I introduce Mrs. Moone! He laughed so hard, now, that he wheezed and bent double holding his fleshless middle. "And mother," he gasped for breath, "I want to present my... My... Bride's mother, owner of a boarding... *Boarding house*, Mrs. Deirdre Moone, right off the boat from the *'eld countree, don'cha know.*" So heartily did he laugh at this phantom scenario that he stopped and leaned against a doorway to catch his wind.

Everything smelled new and freshly painted and Erin House seemed as lively as it had been before the fire. But as Franny bustled to serve supper to the officers and other guests, she struggled to maintain a merry, polite exterior. For her smiles and gay chatter only masked the turmoil inside. There, she was dying. She did not want to marry Cyrus Hawk and she still feared seeing Hy Wilcox around every dark corner. Not to mention her heartbreak over Josiah's abrupt leave taking. When she thought of him, which was nearly all the time, she vacillated between still being in love with him and hating him. When Ma had returned from the hospital, her comments hadn't helped a bit. According to her mother, Josiah had said nothing; offered not one objection, when she had told him the Provost Marshal was wooing her daughter. Too, he had been gone nearly two months and not one word sent by letter, Clay, or Toby.

She sat a platter of ham on the table in front of a group of officers new to Erin House just as Cyrus Hawk entered the dining room. Watching him make his silent way to the table of a group of officers as sour and taciturn as he, she couldn't help but spot the difference between him and Josiah. When her godbrother had entered the room a dozen voices had risen at once inviting him to one table or the other. And Josiah had given a jocular word to each, always laughing, always time to talk, never in a hurry. On the other hand, Hawk's entrance never failed to quell and subdue laughter and he didn't stop to talk to anybody.

Oh well, she thought ruefully, maybe Ma was right. No respectable man will want me after my escapades. By now everyone in town had heard of her - the *infamous*, Franny Moone Wilcox - eloped with a notorious bush-whacker, helped him to waylay the *White Star*. And she had heard the whispers behind her back about the annulment. With resignation she accepted her notoriety as part of her punishment, her comeuppance. Indeed, she had received no more invitations from any young man since her story broke in full a week after Josiah left. She noticed the young officers still ogled her, but kept their distance. Only the presence of Lieutenant Gus Werner in the dining room prevented her from being insulted. Dear Gus, he treated her as a friend and a lady and insisted the others do the same. *Maybe skinny, old Cyrus Hawk with his stiff ways and sweating hands is the best I will ever do for myself*, she thought, sighing and making her way over to him to set out his plate and silverware.

"Good evening, Miss Moone," he smiled up at her. She wished he wouldn't try to smile. He looked uncomfortable doing it. "May I have a word with you after I've eaten my dinner?"

Reluctantly she nodded. She knew this would mean yet one more discussion in the hotel's common parlor while she did needle work and he bored her to death about the beauties of Kansas. All she'd ever heard about Kansas as far back as a child was that it was arctic cold in the winter and blistering in the summer and that the people hated Missourians. She remembered Hy going quiet and his face flushing with anger whenever anyone mentioned the state.

Just then, an officer covered with rain and mud, and who obviously had ridden a good ways burst into the dining room, announcing to all present, "Mulligan's surrendered to Price at Lexington. All our men are prisoners and all the guns and provisions taken. The Rebs hid behind hemp bales they pushed before themselves as they walked forward to take the college."

Thursday the 26th

No more debate with himself; he'd leave for Jefferson City. He must talk to her, apologize for abandoning her the way he had. If she didn't want any more to do with him, he could understand. But at least, he'd have it off his conscience. On his heart he'd bear forever the results of his behavior.

Josiah swung his feet over the side of his cot and stood up. Dizziness overtook him and he sat back down, his head in his hands. After a few minutes he stood up again, and swayed from side to side, feeling as though he had just downed a quart of *Bininger's*.

"Captain Scarborough, Sir, what do you think you are doing?" Sister Evangela scurried towards him, alarm written all over her face and Corporal Badder limping by her side.

Sister Evangela had taken over day shift. The change hadn't made her more agreeable. He eyed them both, hoped Badder wouldn't try to stop him. Right now, he was no match for skinny Sister Evangela, much less the Corporal. "I'm going to Jeff City." Josiah stood up refusing the faint that threatened him.

"You certainly are not, Sir. You are in no condition to get out of bed, certainly not to travel." She stood at the foot of his bed, her hands on her hipless sides glaring at him. "I'll ask Mr. Badder to restrain you if I have to."

Corporal Badder was the attendant the Sisters used for heavy lifting, and keeping the peace. As a former flatboat river hand brawling had taken up much of his time and he'd lost an eye years ago indulging this passion. Usually set in a menacing glare his one good eye had been dubbed by the patients "the evil eye." Barrel chested, wispy red hair, over six feet, his well-scarred face reminded Josiah of the New York plug-uglies he'd left behind. Although one-eyed, Badder had joined one of Lyon's units and at Boonville last June he'd suffered a broken ankle that hadn't healed right. Now, he served as hospital orderly and "guard dog." This morning, though, Josiah saw that the "guard dog" couldn't whimper much less bark and was in no condition to "restrain" anybody. That worthy attendant had been nipping at the jar again. And the "evil eye" rolled around in his head as though it was a loose marble although it couldn't be eight o'clock in the morning yet.

"Where's my trowsers Sister Evangela?" He felt foolish standing in his long drawers before this stern, competent woman. "And I want to see the doctor."

Wearing pants and waiting to be discharged, He parted with Getz who was on his way home, too, as soon as his wife could come in from Ohio to get him.

"Well, friend, we part. Both of us still alive anyway." His few belongings in a canvas sack over his shoulder, Josiah stood at the sergeant's bedside.

"Right you are Captain. But you'll fight again. My war's over." Getz waved his bandaged hands in front of him, added, "Don't know which one of us is the luckier man - you or me."

An hour later, a warning in his ears to go immediately to bed when he got to Jefferson City and a medical leave in his pocket, Josiah breathed the air of freedom. He supposed he knew how a slave felt once he'd crossed into the north, escaped from servitude. A block from the lavish headquarters for the Western Department of the U.S. Army, John C. Fremont commanding, he found a room and for the first time in six weeks slept without the stench of rotting bodies and laundry soap filling his nostrils.

Now that he had been discharged from the hospital, if he wanted to receive his pay or his mail he'd have to trot over to headquarters and report his official status and new address. The army liked to keep tabs on their officers - even ones on medical leave. But, the next morning so grand was the three-storied villa surrounded by a walled garden that for a while Josiah simply stood across the street and watched the cordon of sentries parade on the sidewalk in front. He couldn't imagine Fremont's family making it their home, as they were, or why the army couldn't have found a less expensive and imposing structure for headquarters.

He had trouble getting inside because the guard at the gate didn't speak English. Couldn't read it either. When Josiah held his medical leave paper in front of the man's nose the corporal muttered something unintelligible and brought his musket to ready. Nor did the man speak German for Josiah used what little German he had picked up earlier in the summer to no avail.

"Dammit, soldier. Let me pass. I am a captain in the United States Fourth Cavalry, wounded in the service of his country, and I will knock you down if you don't," Josiah yelled and raised his fist. The trooper cocked his musket.

"Don't worry captain, he won't shoot you." A graying, heavyset officer, wearing on his coat impressive oak leaves and fancy braided cord, shouted to the guard in a language Josiah hadn't heard before. Without further ado the head of "Fremont's Hussars," Major Zagonyi of the Hungarian cavalry escorted Josiah inside and through the bureaucratic maze, then took great delight in showing a fellow cavalryman around the downstairs rooms of the opulent headquarters - once the finest mansion in St.Louis.

The aide-de-camp doing Fremont's paper work was Polish and a member of the "Benton Cadets." Other household soldiers detailed to Fremont's personal service were called "Jessie's Rangers," the names of these units conceived to honor Fremont's wife, daughter of Missouri's first federal senator, Thomas Hart Benton. Josiah further learned that Fremont by-passed state and national military channels and issued his own commissions. Nearly all officers he personally commissioned - mostly Poles and Hungarians - held the rank of "Captain of Engineers." Even the bandmaster held the rank of "Captain of Engineers."

In the hospital he had heard that Fremont had started building up his own cadre of toadies and yes-men. Now that he saw it in earnest, he didn't like it. He had also heard of the lavish parties and expensive carriages, furnishings, and favors, bought with government money. How did the government expect to pay for all this wasteful administration? In Josiah's opinion, at least half these men detailed for Fremont's "personal service" should have been shouldering muskets and marching to battle.

As Josiah was leaving, Zagonyi effusively shook his hand, saying in heavily accented English, "Hope you haf' a speedy recovery Captain Scarborough. With your distinguished record, General Fremont will certainly wish to make your acquaintance. The General goes today to Jefferson City with a trainload of troops. Ride in the officers' cars if you wish. Wounded veterans always welcome and stop back when you are ready for duty assignment."

Josiah rode the train back with several "Captains of Engineers," sharing several bottles of whiskey. Since over the past six weeks he hadn't had anything stronger to drink than a sip of brandy ordered occasionally by the doctor, the whiskey hit his stomach and head with a sledgehammer. Thus, by the time the train arrived at 3:30 in the afternoon, he needed to find a place to sleep it off. He knew he'd never approach Erin House in his condition and would have been mortified for Franny to see him, reeling and lurching down High Street.

Waving goodbye to his friends preparing to encamp

back of the city, he made himself very straight and tall and hoped he could walk his inebriation somewhat off by the time he reached the Capitol. He remembered the back entry where the delivery wagons parked. There, snickering together over a postcard sized paper book, their muskets thrown carelessly aside, he found two young sentries. As they lounged against the wall they were oblivious to his standing a few yards away watching them, his arms folded over his chest. He recognized the men as being part of the Home Guard unit he had recruited in June and decried the obvious deterioration of discipline on guard duty. Apparently his faith in Werner's training abilities had been misplaced. Sounding his most military Josiah barked, "Kinzler, Hobrecht, look alert. Stand at attention!" When the boys dropped the French pictures to salute and sprang to shoulder their guns he couldn't help himself from stifling a laugh. But he fixed them with a half-stern eye. "The entire Rebel army could have snuck up on you two and you wouldn't have known it. Besides, you shouldn't be looking at naked ladies."

"Well, I reckon i's Captain Scarborough, ain't it?" Kinzler ran up and began pumping his hand. Grinning just as large, Hobrecht shook hands, asked, "Are you back with us, Sir?"

"Maybe, I should be the way you boys have gone to seed. Whose commanding here, now?"

They chatted about Wilson Creek, Lyon's death, Josiah's wound, new camp gossip, and the recent post commander, Jeff C. Davis, the wiry, black-haired colonel from Indiana.

Inside, men he didn't know passed him with a nod, and unnoticed, Josiah made his way upstairs to his old room on the third floor. The door was unlocked and the room stripped except for the camp bed he had slept on. His head resting against the blue-ticked mattress, devoid of blankets or pillow, Josiah passed into sleep.

The big, grey ledger book saved from the fire showed the hotel's debits and assets. When Franny scrawled the figure from the day's receipts on a line, as if to punctuate her efforts, thunder clapped like cannon fire and made her jump. At first in soft, slow drops came the rain, then harder until the window panes rattled, making her tedium all the harder to bear.

She wondered about her boredom, knew it didn't stem from being back in the rebuilt hotel these past three weeks. If anything, although smelling of new carpets, furniture, and paint, the place burst with excitement and guests. Her malaise came from having to endure the mooning stares and proprietary manners of Captain Cyrus Hawk. She had escaped these upon the pretext of "settling up the books" and as Franny labored over her figures, Ma was in the dining room giving a "Thank You" party for Captain Hawk, his provost staff and Colonel Davis. If she had to listen to her mother gush one more time about how grateful she was for Hawk posting a night time guard around Erin House, she thought she'd scream.

And now, dressed in a green silk dinner gown, hair loosened from its ribbon and curling down her back, Franny bent over the desk in the drafty lobby, absorbed in her chore. From the registration she copied the names of the current guests and their room numbers onto six slips of paper - one each to Tycee, Opal and Ruby, Ma, Toby and one for herself. Each guest would be served a cup of hot coffee in his room first thing in the morning, before they came down to breakfast. Ma called it "carryin' coffee to the bed," and most guests delighted in this small, extra service.

She started to tally up the receipts from dinners sold that night to non-boarders when the door opened. A swoosh of cool, wet air brought her goose bumps and riding on the air was the scent of whiskey, a lot of it. She didn't bother to look up. But, from the corner of her eye, she spied high muddy boots capped by light blue, kersey trowsers with the yellow cavalry stripe running down the outside seam.

Just another drunk Yankee, she thought and didn't bother to look up when the boots strode to the desk and stopped. She'd let him wait until she was through, then tell him to leave. His kind was exactly what Dee Moon did not want staying at Erin House. As she had heard her mother say time and again,

"There'll be no besotted scoundrels lurching' 'bout me hotel 'n' befoulin' the air. 'Tis a clean 'n' genteel, respectable homey atmosphere we're keepin' here, dearie."

Slowly, she wrote down every dinner ticket, taking special pains to inspect each one as to specific charges for specific items. When finished, she placed these in another pile and started to redo her calculations to see if she would tally out with the same amount.

The Yankee stood directly before her, fumes from his whiskey soaked clothing thick as morning mist, but said nothing. She became self-conscious of her low cut bodice that showed off her ample bosom but thought, *I'll refuse to acknowledge him. Right this very minute his impudent self is probably looking down my décolletage. I don't care. I've faced his kind before. I'll throw down my pen, frown, look him in the eye, and tell the cur there are no vacancies tonight and to clear out. If he becomes a problem there are 20 Federal soldiers in my dining room that will relish throwing him out into the gutter where he came from.* On second thought such a scene, while amusing her as it danced in her head, she knew would spoil the atmosphere of quiet, stuffy elegance so artfully achieved by her mother.

As she placed a dot at the bottom of the TOTALS column in the ledger, suddenly, a strong, rough hand drew up her chin until she was almost nose to nose with the bluest eyes she'd ever seen. "Josiah!" she whispered and a warm rush flooded her body.

He grinned, joked in his husky baritone, "I caught the kiss you blew me that day on the Rock Creek road. Thought I'd come by and return the compliment. Only, I don't blow kisses away on the wind, Sugar; I give 'um to stay." Then to her dismay he kissed her, a slow, lingering, wholly improper kiss, like the ones he had given her in the carryall, ones that sent jitters up her spine and now, made her spill the ink pot. India black ink flowed onto the ledger page.

Reflex raised her hand to slap him; turbulent emotion lowered it. "Look what you've made me do!" She looked for paper to blot it up, found none, took Josiah's proffered handkerchief, and dabbed at the stain. "I hope I can salvage these figures. It's a night's work, Josiah, It would serve you right if this handkerchief of yours never gets clean again."

"You might say thank you." Gentle laughter underlie his sheepish tone.

"And you might at least say you were sorry!" she flung back at him.

Finally she stopped scrubbing the page, satisfied she'd salvaged most of her work, threw down the blackened handkerchief, and folded her arms across her bosom. His appearance shocked and saddened her. Sallow skinned and much thinner than when she saw him last, there, he stood, this Yankee kinsman, ill, seemingly half-drunk and half-undressed. His hair, as usual, curled uncombed over his brow beneath his wide-brimmed hat, a hat pushed carelessly to the back of his head. His wet coat hung open and the top two buttons of his shirt gapped apart allowing her to see fingers of black hair curling on his upper chest. His deep-set blue eyes were puffy and blood-shot. Furthermore, he had abandoned her, discarded her like so much old baggage, when she had needed him to put his arms around her and understand. And she had shed buckets of tears over him. However, his emaciated, careless condition made her heart go out to him and she knew she was still enchanted by this rascally man.

"I'm sorry, Franny," he put his hands on the desk and looked at her steadily. The time for teasing past he seemed totally serious, now. "I want your forgiveness." Then, apparently embarrassed, he dropped his gaze and stared down at his fingers curling on the counter top. "Although I know I don't deserve it, I'm asking for your forgiveness. I should never have left you in the fix you were in the way I did."

"My *forgiveness,* is that all?" She blurted, caught herself, blushed, "I mean, is that why you came here, tonight?" Lead weights formed in her heels and there tumbled her heart. She thought, He has come only to right the air between us as Irish relatives and the kiss meant nothing more to him than his normal playfulness. He doesn't love me.

"That would be a start, at least." He reached for her hand. Took it, then swayed against the desk.

"You're drunk!" she hissed at him, jerking back her hand, feeling the anger and humiliation she had carried for two months whip through her again. He had trifled with her heart but she had wanted him to. In the carriage she had thrown herself at him, and naturally he had kissed her the way a lover would. She had mistaken his glances for those of a sweetheart's because that's what she wanted them to be. Silly fool that she was, she had done what countless other cupid-struck females probably had done over him, cried before him and actually told him she loved him. Her histrionics that awful day must have embarrassed him, that and the facts of her crime. No wonder he rode away and never looked back.

As these thoughts swiftly turned in her mind her cheeks felt hot. Ma was right. "Only like an older brother does he care for ya," she had said when back from visiting him in the hospital.

"You come here in this state to ask my forgiveness?" She glared at him.

He gripped the desk and winced in pain. "No, not drunk, was drunk this morning on the train. Spilled some whiskey on my coat." He grinned weakly. "Not now, but sick. Doc said I had to go to bed as soon as I got here. I wasn't supposed to leave the hospital, but I had to see you, tell you in person how damned sorry I am for being an ass."

Immediately she realized he was still suffering from his wound. And whether or not he wanted to be her lover made no real difference in the situation she faced with him tonight. He was still her godbrother and she must show him familial charity. Anger left as swiftly as it had come to be replaced by concern and her tone softened. "Now you've said your piece, godbrother, you'll go to bed at once. Come on, I'll help you up the stairs. Then I'll tell Ma you're here."

Within the shadows of the oil lamp flickering in the hall, Franny found his room. Groaning with relief, Josiah fell on the bed, popped up immediately, pulled off his damp coat, and gave it to her to hang on a peg next to the door. She lit a bedside candle and noticed his muddy boots. It wouldn't do to have him stretch his tall frame over the clean, white counterpane with those things on. She stooped to help him take them off. The whole way up the stairs he had leaned heavily upon her and she had filled him in on the Erin House renovations, her annulment soon to be heard in circuit court and her dealings with Hawk about the *White Star*.

"But I'm only going to testify against Hy Wilcox and Captain Verboise," she said, grunting as she bent over facing away from him and pulling off one of his boots. "I'll not say a word about the other men who rode with

Verboise. I grew up with most of them."

"Can you testify against your own husband?" He mumbled.

"When the trial is heard, Hy will no longer be my husband." She pulled off the other boot. "Have you eaten today ?" She stood over him, her arms akimbo.

"I'm not hungry. I had some oysters at a restaurant before I came."

"Good night, then. We'll talk in the morning. I'll tell Ma you're here," and Franny turned to go. But, before she could leave he stood up and caught her around the waist. She nearly fainted at his touch. Caressing her face with his hand, he whispered, "I wanted to say thank you for all you did, tonight," and he kissed her - not teasing, not like a brother, but like a lover. Although startled, Franny closed her eyes and stood very still within the warm cocoon of his arms, succumbing to the rhythm of immediate ecstasy that coursed through her body. This was not the time to think, evaluate his motives. Once again the sparks between them instantly ignited. With that, she forgot her doubts and gave herself to the moment.

Feverishly, he helped her out of her overskirt, bodice, hoops, and corset, letting them lay where they fell and yanked off his own clothing. Then he pulled her down on the bed with him. His hand found its way beneath her chemise to her neck, then to her breast, and his soft, hungry lips followed. One hand caressed her ankle and removed her slipper then moved slowly to her garter. He unrolled it with a stocking and gently pulled them off her leg.

Driven by her own desire, she arched her back to allow him freer range over her body and played her hands through his hair twining and untwining her fingers through its thick, unruly mass as she pressed her breasts into his lips.

But, like a firecracker exploding in her head, she

heard a loud laugh from the party below, several "hurrahs," and the clinking of glasses. The party was ending.

What on earth am I ever thinking of? What am I doing? Holy Mary! She was about to give herself to a man who had promised her nothing. One who desired her but who failed to mention marriage or ask for her love.

Again, Ma's voice separated itself from the babble in her mind and after the disaster of her elopement, a voice she had decided to heed. "'Tis not by blood, so much that the two of ya are entwined, but by memory, chains of the heart and family. 'N' it's not surprising that ya find him beguilin', a handsome Mick like him. But yer godbrother's a typical Irishman who takes his grog and his women as he finds 'um, and being a horse soldier doubles them lacks o' character." Franny heard herself telling Sigrid months ago that a man like him was "not husband material." That he would "tire of me in less than a year." At least a sorry rogue like Hy Wilcox had married her.

She tried to move but he had her penned with his body while his tongue met hers and he fondled her breasts. Now, his hand pulled at the tie on her dainties beneath her chemise. She knew that in seconds he would have her stripped bare.

"Stop it," she whispered, "I've got to go."

"No, you don't," his words muffled within the flesh of her bosom. She felt her dainties give way to his touch.

"I do. The party's over. They'll wonder where I am!"

"Let' 'um wonder." His lips returned to reclaim hers. She struggled against his weight. "Please, Josiah, let me go. I shouldn't--"

"--You can't leave me like this, Franny. Let me show you how much I love you."

While he pressed her close with his hips his hands possessed her, stroking, caressing, gently kneading her buttocks, her stomach, her thighs. Never had her body felt so wanted; never had her body so wanted to give in return. He had succeeded unleashing a passion within her that was altogether foreign. And it frightened her. His own need urgent, yet, he paused, holding her, seeming to sense her fear, whispering, "Don't be afraid. I won't hurt you. I could never hurt you."

"No!" she shouted and with a mighty shove that surprised even her, she flung him off. In doing so one of her feet accidentally jerked up and planted a kick in his groin.

"Son-of-a-bitch!" He swore and rolled away, grabbing himself and moaning in pain.

Horrified at what she had done, terrified of what he might do, Franny sprang from the bed, grabbed up her clothing, and scooted out of the room. She raced down the dark hall and down the back stairs, peeking to make sure she was unseen, so she could slip into the apartment and tidy herself before the guests took their final leave.

In the apartment and hastily dressed, she sat before her mirror. Heavily perspiring as she ran a quick comb through her tangled hair, she sat thinking and noticed her rumpled dress, loosened bodice, a deep red place on her neck where he had kissed her with lingering force, and her over bright eyes. Inside, she raged with fever; outside, her skin tingled with electricity. She felt alive! Churning with a desire she did not understand, she dropped the comb to sit stock still, stare at her disheveled reflection and listen to the thump of her heart. Feeling very wicked and ashamed, unbidden tears coursed down her cheeks. *He said he wanted to show me how much he loved me.* "Oh Josiah," she whispered aloud, "if only I believed that you did."

After a sleepless night Josiah came down to breakfast determined to square things with Franny. He hated himself when he remembered that he had almost forced himself on her, something he'd never do to a woman. And this particular woman was Franny, the girl he loved, the girl he intended to marry as soon as possible - but she was nowhere to be seen. Gus Werner saw him, though.

"Captain Scarborough, Sir," Gus bellowed from across the room when he entered. He arose at once and soon was pumping Josiah's hand and grinning like the prodigal had returned. Proudly, he introduced him around to the new officers billeted at Erin House. When Brady and Potter walked in a few minutes later they practically fell all over themselves welcoming him back. But later in the apartment alone with Aunt Dee he sensed a less cordial welcome.

"So why are ya back, then?"

"My original orders were posted here," he explained, "thought I'd take up where I left off as soon as this side of mine stops giving me trouble."

"Is that yer only reason fer coming back?" They sat on the settee in the apartment, still reeking of fresh paint and partially unfurnished. Aunt Dee had put in a large arched bay window overlooking the back garden and apologized for it not yet being draped. "We're having trouble getting the velvet fer it. What with the war on, everything's going fer the effort. It'll be along, presently."

"To answer your question, honestly, Aunt Dee, no. My orders have nothing to do with me being back here. On medical leave, as I am, I can go pretty much where I please. Most men go to their homes on such leave. You had said, once, that because I have no family left except for you, Franny, and Clay, I should think of Erin House as my home." He stared at her, feeling slightly hurt, but knowing the reason for her reticence. Well, he'd shake her up a bit more. "I've come here to ask Franny to marry me."

With a snort, Dee threw up her hands. "Well-a-day, ye can't stay here. Won't have it. No. You two moonin' around each other—"

"...Then she does care for me," he cut in.

259

"Don't be getting' yer hopes up, dearie," she said quickly, "the lass don't know what she wants. 'Twas her heart ye broke when ye went off in a snit."

"Where is she this morning? I need to talk to her." He reddened, remembering the mess he'd made of things last night. He'd face her, once again, with another apology and hope she believed him when he said he loved her.

She left early for Zimmers. She and Sigrid had shoppin' to do fer the weddin'."

"Oh, yes, the wedding. Josiah smiled. Gus had been elated telling him about the wedding the first week of December. He had promised to be Gus's best man. Perhaps, her mother's blessing or not, if he moved swiftly enough on Franny, they might just make it a double wedding. Her annulment would be final by then.

Aunt Dee prattled on. "I told ya in the hospital, no penniless soldier boy is gonna marry me only child, no matter how much I might think of him." She peered at him, drawing her lips into a narrow line.

Franny does that when she's upset, too, he thought and hoped the similarities between them went only that far. Dee's money-grubbing attitude irritated him. Perhaps, he had expected too much, a larger, more generous soul. On the other hand, who was he to judge her? If he had worked as hard as this widow had, had struggled in poverty and famine, he might be the same way. And, if he had an only daughter would he really want her to marry an army man, someone not making a whole lot of money and who was getting shot at all the time?

"Aunt Dee, I've decided to resign my commission when Franny and I marry."

"And what would ya be doin' if ye ain't drawin' army pay ?"

"I'm trained in engineering and horse doctoring, or I imagine I could do most anything I wanted to. I was first in my class." He grinned at her. Now was the time for him

260

to be his most charming.

"Stop showing them dimples, Josiah Scarborough. Rakehell handsome ye are. But you're still an Irishman, a Mick. And ye likes yer grog 'n' I imagine yer women as well. 'Taint nothin' about ya that makes me think yer a settled man, a serious man o' business. Perhaps in ten years—"

"Ten years! Good Lord, Aunt Dee, Franny isn't going to wait for me for ten years while I make my fortune. Besides, I want us to make it together." Dee waved him off with a condescending shrug, causing Josiah to become even more emphatic. "With Franny, I would never need another woman. And as for my fondness for grog, as you call it, I can swear off anytime. I promise you. From this day forward, I will never take another sip of whiskey." And in his heart he meant it.

Apparently tired of his attempts to convince her she said, "I'll be talkin' it over with Zimmer, who likes ya, but thinks yer not settled enough for marryin' anybody. Now Gus Werner is. His family has a nice leather works in St. Louis and the boy will do well. He'll provide an immediate home for Sigrid."

Irritation swelled to anger. "So it's still that I have no ready money now, no "family" to back me, no good name to trade upon, isn't it Aunt Dee?" He abruptly arose, feeling his anger close in around him. "As I am unworthy of your daughter's hand and you think so little of me, I'll move out immediately."

"Wait," she held out her hand. "Ya can't be traipsin' off like this. 'Tis sick ye still are and look at yerself, skin 'n' bones. I've changed me mind. Ye can stay here 'n' ye'll get the care ye need. Doctor Bruns will look around to ya. 'Tis a-worryin' I'd be 'bout me godson's health 'n' I would if 'n ya was ta stay someplace else." Apparently irritated with herself because she did care deeply about him, Dee rose and held his arms at his sides. She smiled

261

when she said gently, "I promised yer mother I'd look afta ya. But ya have ta know, 'tis Captain Hawk, who's asked fer her hand and I want her ta have the chance ta get ta known the gentleman. And you, boy-o," she waggled her finger beneath his nose, "can't be takin' up all her free time."

In light of his godmother's open opposition to him, normally, his pride would not have permitted him to stay. Normally, he would have left in a dignified huff and sought out other ways of seeing and wooing Franny. But the reminder about his health made him realize that at Erin House he would receive superior nursing care, food, and the company of friends - not to mention the close proximity to Franny. This surely would strengthen his efforts to win her. Dee's warning meant she'd not permit Franny to accept invitations which might throw them alone together - walks, talks, or carriage rides. And, she'd tolerate no overt attempts on his part to court her daughter. But, he reasoned, nothing could prevent them from bumping into each other on the stairs, in the garden, in the dining room - and Dee Moone's watchful eye couldn't be in every corner every minute. She had to sleep sometime. So, not at all ashamed of planning such clandestine meetings, wherein he would convince Franny to elope with him, Josiah remained at Erin House.

It wasn't until after supper that he managed to see Franny alone for five minutes. She was seated behind the lobby desk and no one else in sight. "I need to talk to you." He said, leaning against the desk and removing the black, lace-up slipper from his pocket. All day he had carried it, lovingly running his fingers over its satiny softness, marveling how dainty it was. Now he laid it before her. "I found this in my room this morning. It doesn't fit me."

Her eyes round, her cheeks flaming with embarrassment, she grabbed for it, but he snatched it back. "No, no," he grinned, "I want to see if yours is the tiny foot upon which this slipper fits." He dangled the slipper by a tie beyond her reach and toyed with one of the curls that bounced beside her ear.

"Give me my shoe," she hissed, moving out of his reach and looking around wildly to see if anyone observed them.

"No, you've got to try it on first. And if it fits, then I'll turn into Prince Charming and take Cinderella away from all this drudgery."

"Oh," she heaved a sob, put her hands to her face, and turned her back to him.

"Franny ?" he asked, trying to see if she was crying, but she kept turning away, preventing him from seeing her face. As suddenly as she had turned from him, she wheeled around and faced him. She was struggling not to cry.

"Prince Charming, indeed! You love to taunt me, don't you?" She spat at him, her eyes turning slate green. He had never seen her so angry. Baffled, feeling vaguely as though he had achieved another upset between them before righting the first, he could only stare at her while she plunged on.

"You are the most conceited man I have ever known. You are so accustomed to women throwing themselves at you that you take everything with a shrug and a grin. Can't you ever be serious about anything? You have played false with me, *godbrother,* and trifled with me and I have let you because I am no better than all the other dalliances you've enjoyed. But, a man who would try to make a...a...conquest of a cousin, no matter how distant, his own *godsister,* who lives beneath the same roof, is a mudsill and lower than worms —"

"—I love you!" He blurted, hoping this admission would quell the hysteria he saw building in her and would have told her more but--

"Well, well, me two favorite youngsters." Brady came

out of the dining room picking his teeth. "Takin' Potter down to the Kentucky for a pint 'o ale." He winked at Josiah. "Wanna come, along?"

Sunday the 29th

Mrs. Fremont peered down her long, elegant nose at Franny and wreathed her aristocratic features into a warm smile. "Welcome, Miss Moone to our little concert tea."

So thrilled was Franny at being in General John Fremont's pavilion tent with all the top officers and top city and state officials that she could think of no response. In three minutes, three years of Virginia schooling failed her. Her tongue became soggy cornbread and she could only mutter, "Thank you, ma'am," as she clung to Mrs. Fremont's outstretched hand like a lifeline. Then, Franny bounced a little curtsey that she knew immediately made her look ridiculous. But Mrs. Fremont, *the* Jessie Benton Fremont, daughter of the state's first national senator and now wife of the great "Pathfinder," smiled over her head and greeted Otto Zimmer and Deidre Moone in the same hospitable manner.

"For heavens sakes Frances watch what you are doing." Captain Hawk whispered and took her firmly by the arm, leading her away to their seats near the band. Settled in her chair, so excited was she that when Captain Hawk asked if he might bring her refreshments from the table groaning with every kind of delicacy imaginable, she could only nod absently. While he was gone, she noted the huge lanterns, the lavish furnishings of the large tent, and the 75-piece band tuning up their instruments. Captain Hawk had told them, when he had invited them, that the bandmaster a "Captain of Engineers" led the finest theatrical orchestra in St. Louis. And Mrs. Fremont planned to give this concert tea every night for as long as her husband planned to make Camp Lillie in Jefferson City his headquarters.

One side of the tent was thrown open and she saw the campfires of Fremont's 20,000 soldiers encamped in the fields and hills around them. She wondered if they were as thrilled with seeing all the elite and hearing the music as she was at being here. This, she knew, would probably go down as one of the most elegant occasions of her life.

"Stop gawking about at people," Captain Hawk muttered, returning with a plate of cucumber and butter sandwiches and petite-fours. Behind him trailed his fat aide, O'Shay, carrying two cups of tea, poured into the thinnest, daintiest china she had ever seen. Ma and Otto took seats behind them. In the crowd coming inside she spotted Sigrid and Gus. "Sigi, Gus, we're over here," she raised her voice over the din and waved excitedly, hoping to get their attention and that they'd sit with them.

"Frances, I've told you before, don't call attention to yourself," Hawk reprimanded loud enough to make a head or two turn and look at her.

She went hot. Lately, Cyrus had taken to calling her behavior to her attention as though she were a five year old, and she hated it. So flustered did she become that she spilled her tea in her lap. Jumping up, trying to brush it out, she spilled the plate of food into Hawk's lap. He cursed, not loudly, but enough that those closest to them overheard. By now, humiliated, near tears, she excused herself to tidy her dress, and in her haste to leave tripped and fell into the lap of a stout city official whom she vaguely knew, upsetting his refreshments and causing his wife to hiss something about "clumsy manners." By the time she had reached the comforting shadows outside the tent she was weeping with embarrassment.

"I saw what happened." Suddenly beside her whispered Josiah. They had exchanged no more than a "good morning" in the two days since he had dangled her slipper under her nose and claimed he was Prince Charming.

265

Neither had he returned the shoe.

But that didn't matter now. She looked up from her sniffles into his eyes and saw not lust, nor teasing, but something she hadn't expected to see—caring acceptance. At that moment, he was her friend, one who stood beside her to give her comfort although she thought she had committed the worst faux pax ever seen in the state of Missouri. Never again would Mrs. Fremont welcome her to any of her social gatherings. To the state and city politicians and their wives she would irrevocably and forever be that ill-bred young woman who had drawn such unseemly attention to herself. And she lay her head on his chest and wept. When she did, his arms went around her and she sighed with relief as the hateful world around her slipped away. From inside the pavilion the band struck up a march, *The Colonel's Daughter*.

She clung to him through another military tune, as she calmed herself and the first stars began to flicker in the darkly blued sky. Then, the band struck up the rowdy favorites *Old Rosin the Bow* followed by *Oh Susanna*. As people inside the pavilion began singing and hand clapping he said, trying to be heard over the noise, "If its any consolation, not as many people as you might think saw your exit, particularly Mrs. Fremont."

"Really ?" She yelled, cocking back her head to look up at him.

"Really." He grinned, made a gesture at his ear signifying that the music was too loud and began walking her away from the tent.

"How is it that you are here, godbrother?"

"All commissioned officers from Lieutenant grade up are invited and I made some friends on the train coming to Jeff City from St. Louis. I was sitting with them over by the far wall when you came in. That's why you didn't see me."

They strolled arm and arm in silence, Franny lost in

thought wondering what her mother would say about her departure from the tent, especially if she knew she was with Josiah. What would Captain Hawk say? Thoughts of the Captain always made her angry. Daily, Ma told her how lucky she was to have him interested in her, to be helping her, to have asked for her hand. And she should feel gratitude for his lawyering of the annulment and securing a pardon. Hawk had gone to great lengths to tell them how he, personally, had convinced Colonel Mulligan that Franny should not endure a military trial and deserved a pardon for her involvement in the *White Star* affair. But, if now she barely stood his stifling, boring company, how could she stand marriage to him?

The band changed tunes and from the pavilion lilted one of the new Viennese waltzes. Suddenly, Josiah stopped, bowed before her, said, "Ma'am I would be most honored if you consented to have this dance with me."

Before she realized it they were waltzing beneath the stars, taking small steps to avoid being overly noticed, and she was blurting "Am I such an unladylike creature, like Ma says, that no man will have me unless it's some dried up old thing like Cyrus Hawk? And all he wants to do is…. change me."

He didn't answer for awhile and she wondered if he'd heard her. When he spoke his tone was soft, "No darling, you are not so unladylike. You're irrepressible and impulsive and I wouldn't want to change a thing about you. I love you."

"What did you say ?" What she thought she heard seemed to have slipped out as though he meant to say "I like peas." She held him away from her looking up at him, still moving in time with the music. "What did you mean by that?"

"I said I love you. I've been trying to tell you that for days but either I've been interrupted or you wouldn't let me close to you. And what did I mean? I mean that I love you, Franny. And I want us to marry. But I'm not sure of how you feel about me."

She saw he was sober and dead serious. His avowal of love she had prayed for, fantasized over, still, how much could she believe it? She asked, "That I eloped with someone and committed acts of treason against the government doesn't bother you? It did once and you left. Don't career army officers have to marry ladies above reproach?"

"Can you forgive me for abandoning you and then almost forcing myself upon you? And sweet, girl, you are a thousand times above reproach - besides, I'm not going to make the army a career."

She went tingly all over like someone had showered her with gold sparks and suddenly the music and the stars were one and she and Josiah were one, floating in each other's arms. She was opening her mouth to tell him how she felt about him, when a harsh voice stopped their dancing and her tongue.

"So this is where I find you. Out in the dark with another man when I am your escort. How dare you humiliate me this way." Hawk grabbed her wrist.

"Just a minute Provost Marshal," Josiah said, "you touch her and you answer to me."

"And who might you be to Miss Moone, Captain Scarborough? Come along, Frances."

"I'm her godbrother and Franny isn't going anywhere with you." Josiah pulled her away from Hawk and stood in front of her.

"Does that make you speak for Miss Moone?"

"Yes, it does. You are rude and harsh with my god-sister and I won't allow her to go with you."

"We'll just see about that!" Hawk reached around Josiah and jerked her by the arm making her trip and fall to her knees. By now, the corporal on guard, moments before enjoying watching two lovers dance in the moonlight, moved forward. The few men who had left the tent to see the reason for the raised voices joined him and saw her fall.

"You bastard!" Josiah spoke as he swung, smashing Hawk in the face. Then he picked up the skinny figure by his coat collar and hit him several times in the chest and stomach until Hawk lay on his back, bleeding from mouth and nose, holding his stomach, and moaning in pain. He had tried to defend himself but he was no match for superior muscles 18 years his junior coupled with jealous rage. By now, the concert had been thoroughly disrupted as spectators poured outside to see the fight. It took four men to pull Josiah off the battered, bloodied provost marshal.

An officer from the crowd said, "He's drunk again, like he was on the train coming out."

General Fremont himself had come outside to see what the melee was about, became livid when he heard the remark and barked, "Arrest Captain Scarborough." He gingerly approached Josiah who stood quietly now, rubbing his chin from the one connecting punch Hawk had thrown. "Captain, your sword. And you are hereby ordered to be confined to your quarters while papers are being drawn up for your court-martial for profanity, drunkenness and striking another officer."

"But he caused my godsister to fall. I was defending her, General Fremont, sir."

"The court will hear your side of it. Your sword please."

And Josiah handed over his officer's sword.

When a smirking O'Shay stepped forward to arrest him, saying, "I'm going to enjoy this," Josiah raised his fist and snarled, "Get away from me, West Point, unless you want what the Provost got."

Heartsick she watched two other provost guards take Josiah away as Hawk whimpered for a doctor and Ma pushed her way through the crowd.

"Come along, Frances Margaret." With all the Irish dignity she could muster, Ma propelled them both through the crowd until they stood before Mrs. Fremont.

"Tis a lovely evenin' you provided fer us, Mrs. Fremont, and me daughter and meself wish ta thank ye-- Frances ?" Ma prompted.

But Franny couldn't lift her eyes from the ground. The world had suddenly gone black around her and she wished only to die. When she looked up it seemed that Mrs. Fremont had grown six inches since she had earlier greeted them. "Yes, thank you, ma'am," Franny mumbled and her mother poked her again.

"Thank you for coming, Mrs. Moone — Miss Moone." But whereas the welcome had been decidedly warm, the unsmiling goodbye seemed glacial and Franny noticed beneath the well-lit lamps of the pavilion, that a flush had spread across Mrs. Fremont's high, delicate cheekbones.

As Otto helped them into the carriage to take them home, the band struck up the *Star Spangled Banner*, the sign that the soiree was at an end. All the way back in the Zimmer brougham Dee talked about how she would be sending Josiah's luggage to his new boarding house as soon as she learned which one.

CHAPTER SEVEN
October

Sunday the sixth

"Why search Erin House? Nobody boards here except legislators and officers." Franny addressed six soldiers who had just stomped into the lobby in the golden fall afternoon. All the boarders gone on Sunday outings, Clay larking around town, God knows where, the colored folks visiting friends, Ma carriage driving with Otto, Sigi and Gus spooning somewhere, Josiah - her heart stopped to ache - kicked out to a shabby boarding house across town, and she all alone.

The corporal in charge looked uncomfortable but said, "We're under orders, ma'am to search every house in the city for cut wire and wire-cuttin' tools. We're trying to find those that cut the telegraph line from Jeff City to General Fremont's camp last Wednesday night now that he's on the march. And uh," embarrassed, he ducked his head, "to search for weapons."

"Oh, this is so silly!" She exploded. Damn Thomas Price, the acting post commander now that Davis and Fremont were marching out. She remembered when the post commander before the war had been mayor of the city. He had been plain old rich, Mr. Price then instead of General, and no relation to the Rebel general Sterling Price.

"We put off searching y'all, ma'am, until we was sure we was supposed to."

"And when did you find out we were on the list to be searched?"

"Just today ma'am. Everybody else in town already submitted to the search."

"Who ordered ours, specifically?"

"Lieutenant O'Shay, ma'am."

271

"O'Shay? The Provost Marshal has his own guard around this place to protect it from harm, corporal. It doesn't reason that his aide would order a search."

Again the young corporal looked grieved. He cleared his throat before he finally spoke. "All due respect, ma'am, but he said that you was the cause he wanted to search the hotel."

"Me!" She couldn't believe her ears.

"Yes, ma'am, uh, well, the General figured it were somebody who lived inside the city and seeing as how you once rode with that bushwhacker gang, and now that your kin laid out Captain Hawk—"

She slapped him hard across the face. Immediately, two privates grabbed her, held her in place while the corporal collected himself, passed his hand through his whiskers. To his credit, she saw he wasn't angry. "I'm sorry, Corporal, I struck you. Forgive me. But it's upsetting when others won't let the past be the past."

"Yes ma'am."

"Go ahead with what ever you have to do." She knew she couldn't stop them. They searched every room, looked under every bed, even banged around in the kitchen and the apartment. Finding nothing after an hour, they marched out without further ado, leaving her again, alone.

Late that same night, dressed for sleep, Franny sat on the edge of her bed listening to the wind and knew sleep was impossible. Maybe if she had something on her stomach. She slipped into the parlor of the apartment. From Clay's room she heard snores. Gentle breathing came from Ma's. Both had gone to bed early, leaving her to close up. On the table in front of the huge new window overlooking the back garden sat a flickering oil lamp, its wick turned low but providing just enough light for someone needing to arise in the night. A new touch Ma had wanted in the newly rebuilt Erin.

Taking a candle, she headed through the lobby and

272

the dining room. In the kitchen she went to the pie shelf where Tycee had put the extra apple pies, removed one, set it on the table, and cut herself a small piece. Thinking of Jefferies on duty she thought he might like to share a late night snack before he returned to his post.

She threw open the door. The cool fall wind rushed into the kitchen, nearly blowing out the candle in its holder on the table. "Corporal Jefferies?" She called, softly. But no stalwart soldier answered her call. Odd, where was he? Usually the provost's sentries rested and probably dozed in the porch swing for all anyone knew. But he was nowhere to be seen. "Corporal Jefferies?" She called again and stepped out onto the dark porch. The wind caught her hair and nightclothes and she hugged her arms to her breasts against the chill.

Suddenly, from behind, a cold callused hand closed over her mouth. A strong arm around her waist penned her arms to her side and in her ear rasped the voice she had dreaded for months to hear.

"So now it's him, you're callin' fer, ain't you, wife? What a li'l whore you've become."

Struggling, kicking with her feet, trying to bite the hard clamp over her face, she couldn't break his hold.

In her ear Hy whispered as he kept her arms penned while he moved his hand from her waist to her breast, "Don't seem you're glad to see me." He chuckled and groped her body with his hand. He inhaled sharply, said, "Don't matter, none. You're still mine and I aim to take what's mine. If I can't, then what's mine maybe shouldn't outta breathe air. I think you get my drift."

He whirled her around to face him, catching her hands and holding them over her head while he lashed them swiftly with a leather strip to one of the posts supporting the porch roof. He wore a Federal private's blue sack coat, devoid of any insignia. Only the curled bugle on his cap told her the former owner had been an

273

infantryman.

With his revolver stuck in her mouth Hy bent into her face, "You eyein' m' uniform. I figured since you been lovin' with them Yankee's you'd like me better dressed as one. But, don't worry, darlin', I ain't changed sides. This boy gimme his duds just afore he died. Seein' as how he was so gen'rus, I ended his misery quick.". He chuckled, nodded indicating the area in the black yard, "Like I done yore Corporal Jefferies." He took the gun out of her mouth, holding it to her lips, then snickered, "What's the matter - get tired of your Yankee cousin, or whatever kin he was, that why you callin' for Jefferies?"

In the clouded moonlight she saw spatters of the corporal's blood drying on his face. Immediate sympathy for the young soldiers who had given up their lives to protect Jefferson City and Erin House swept through her and tears filled her eyes. Through these she said, "If you've come back to kill me, then do it."

"Oh, my, what a brave li'l woman I married." He moved the gun over her face to press on her left eye. "I should. That's what I said I'd do if'n you tole anybody were me set this rotten timber on fire. How you want it, sugar in the eye with my Navy? It's done it's share of killin' I reckon. Or maybe you'd prefer a knife, don't make no noise that way." Hy stuck his gun in his belt and brandished his Bowie over her. She noticed the fresh blood on its hilt and closed her eyes. "Or maybe, if I sliced into your soft white throat, like I done Jefferies, you'd prefer that? Look at me, sweetheart, when I'm talkin' to you."

Her eyes popped open. Every nerve taut with fear, she said a silent prayer and suddenly her brain went clear. She knew what to say to this insane boy.

Whispering she gazed into his eyes, eyes maddened by jealousy, heartbreak, ungratified lust, by the demon that now possessed him. "I'm sorry I hurt you, Hy. I truly am. You deserved so much more in a wife then I could give you. I've filed for an annulment. When it becomes final you'll be free of me. You'll go on and see –"

"—No!" he raised his voice, lowered it again to a whisper, "No, there ain't gonna be no annulment. I already heard about it in town and that's why I come tonight. This thing you've got built up between us ever since our weddin' day, is comin' to a stop. I believe the preacher said 'til death us do part,' and that's exactly the way it'll be for us." He moved in closer, pressing her into the post until it hurt and placed his hard lips upon hers.

When finished, he raised up, said hoarsely, "'nough jawin'," and fished a dirty kerchief out of his pocket. Although she resisted, he wadded it up and stuffed it into the back of her throat. Before her choking could spit it out he had tied a second kerchief around her mouth. "Now, breathe through your nose," he said and waited until she had demonstrated that she could. Having effectively gagged her, he put the knife to her throat, while he loosed the leather from the post, partially freeing her hands that had gone numb. The leather still remained tight on her wrists and he quickly pulled these behind her, looping the binding several times and leaving an end, like a leash. Holding this he pushed her forward. "Move, down them stairs. My horse is in the side yard."

He propelled her into the backyard with the knife pressed between her shoulder blades. When she moved into the blackness, she almost stepped on Jefferies' corpse. With a stifled scream, she shrank back and felt the blade jab against her. "I'll kill you when I'm good and ready," he growled softly, "Right now, I'm doin' what I should a done the day I married you - take you back home with me and tell your ma to suck eggs."

Tycee's screams woke everybody up. "I goes out the back to de coop to get de fresh eggs fo' de mawnin' breakfast, 'n' there he be - layin' all frozen 'n' blood

275

every-where." The weeping cook was talking to the grim soldier-boarders gathered in her spanking new kitchen. And all assembled knew layers of whitewash and shining new pine floors couldn't dispel the fear that crept like insidious dust into the room.

But Dee's unsettled nerves took on near hysteria when she discovered Franny's disappearance. Clay, still recovering from his wounds, nevertheless rode over to the Zimmers to see if she had gone over there. Sergeant Brady supervised a detail to remove the corpse from the backyard while Colonel Potter gathered others to search the hotel. After calling her name and searching in vain, Dee had to admit, Franny hadn't slept in her bed all night and was no where to be found.

Brady found his landlady weeping inconsolably in the guest parlor and flanked by Otto and Sigrid. "Um, Ma'am?" He nodded to Otto, gave him the message instead. "The remains of Jefferies have been removed and the boys have, uh, tidied up the yard." He meant, of course, that all signs of blood had been covered over by dirt.

"*Ja, gutt*, Sergeant. Dank you."

" If you please, ma'am, ah, Mr. Zimmer, but, I think your god-son should be told about this."

She raised a tear stained face. "Josiah Scarborough?" Then tried to dismiss the suggestion and all the implications that arose. "Whatever for, Sergeant Brady? He'll have no news. I'm sure."

"Pardon me, Ma'am," Brady persisted, coughed realized he tread on delicate ground, "but, he - uh - they did care for one another a great deal at one time and she might be..."

"Mr. Sergeant Brady!" Deidre Moone rose as though to strike him, "Have ya no decency? How dare suggest, and in front of Miss Zimmer, too. Tis ta Captain Cyrus Hawk me daughter is intended. And he, fine gentleman

276

that he is, half-dead from the beatin' me drunken disgrace of a godson gave him, home bein' tended by his dear mother. I'd give me soul if he were in town at this instant. Me daughter may be headstrong and spirited, but respectable she is and would never... " She flung herself back onto the sofa and for all Brady's troubles he got glares from her and Otto and an icy stare over his head from Miss Sigrid.

"But, ma'am that ain't what I was suggestin' I was only sayin.."

"—Not now, man, for der love of *Gott*. Can't you see the tears flowing from her eyes? Leave the godson out of this." Otto waved him away.

But Brady was not to be deterred. Colonel Potter sat in the lobby helping Clay keep as much order as possible. They had been busy with nosey neighbors stopping by, asking questions, and with Hawk's sissy aide, O'Shay, dropping by to hear Tycee tell the story yet, one more time. "Come on Colonel, we're gonna tell me boy. If she ain't with him, he'll mebbe know how to find her." He noticed the eager face on young Monihan. "No, boy, somebody must tend the desk. Stay to yer post."

Folks were just coming astir at Swain's and although they hadn't heard Captain Scarborough arise no one thought it odd that two older military men clanked down the hall and knocked on his door. Wasn't the reclusive Captain awaiting a military court martial? Swain's wasn't known for keeping tabs on roomer's guests whether they be male or female.

"Who is it?" The speech sounded slurred, the voice thick.

"Get yer randy self up, lad."

"Brady, I told you to leave me the hell alone. That's an order!"

Brady pounded at the door. "No, this time I ain't goin' away. I'm insistin' I am ta see ya. There's been a murder and the woman yer love has disappeared."

"Really, Sir, but you are impertinent," sniffed the Colonel. "What a suggestion -'the woman yer love'- Totally improper."

"Might be improper fer me to mention it," Brady whispered, "but 'tis true and 'tis high time to harvest that somebody started talkin' about it."

Suddenly the door cracked open presenting an unshaven, puffy-eyed, very hung over Josiah Scarborough with hair wilder and blacker than usual. An involuntary sigh of pain escaped Brady to see how much the once handsome young man had gone to rot in the week since he'd last seen him. He seemed thinner than when he had arrived from the hospital, and the smell hanging around his former protégé of sour whiskey a week-old brought water to his eyes. The Colonel honked into his kerchief.

Dragging the colonel into the room with him, Brady barged through the door-crack and the smell. Lighted by a trickle of sunlight struggling to enter by way of one heavily draped window, the room was unoccupied, save for the paying lodger - a very half-dressed one at that. Over his underwear he had thrown on a checked shirt, which hung open, and a pair of cavalry pants, unbuttoned and held up only by their suspenders. Both were filthy. Ah, the poor boy-o, he thought sadly. He'd watched too many other officers skid the same way because of an over fondness for the drink.

"I do apologize for awakening you Captain Scarborough, but this former sergeant of yours..."

"—It's ok Colonel." He turned on Brady, "What the hell are you blatherin' about now, you dumb Mick? Murder? My *sweet-heart* disappeared?" he shuffled behind his dressing screen and they heard him urinate in his chamber pot.

"Yer girl, the one you told me you adored." Brady raised his voice and eyed the miserable room. The Widow

Moone would have never permitted a boarder to live like this, paying customer or not. In the gloom it looked like a week's worth of dirty dishes lay scattered on the table and the floor. And sure enough, cockroaches fed from several of them. Blankets and sheets probably hadn't been laundered in months. Why, he'd seen cavalry camps in the field in cleaner shape then this. And never had he known Scarborough to tolerate slovenliness in himself or in the men under his command.

"I've adored a lot of women, old friend." He rejoined them, winked at Potter, brushed the roaches off a chair attacking some dried food, and sat at the table.

He motioned for them to draw up chairs and join him. Brady and the Colonel eyed the roach infested furniture and declined. But when Scarborough reached for the nearly empty bottle of whiskey left from last night, Brady jerked it away.

"Now, you listen ta me, Laddy. Tis no lark that old Potter and me is here. 'N' I want ya to straighten up outta your cups for serious business is afoot." Brady leaned forward, feeling the urgency to get through to this wayward boy with all the talent in the world to be the finest officer commanding cavalry he'd ever seen. "Tis a filthy disgrace ye are. Leavin' yer billet get this way and sleepin' 'til mid-day-"

Causing roaches to scatter, Josiah reached for the timepiece thrown carelessly on the table with his wallet, grinned, said, "--Its only half-past seven in the morning."

"—'N' drunk ya are most o' the time when ya know ya should be eatin' healthy food 'ta get over the wound ya took at Wilson Creek. —"

"—I'm on furlough!" He laughed out right and tried to grab the bottle from Brady.

"No, ya ain't havin' no more o' this rotgut, today anyway." He held the bottle out of Josiah's reach and turned to Potter, who also seemed appalled at the debauched squalid to which a fellow military officer had sunk. "Colonel Potter, Sir, see if you can shag some coffee and mebbe a biscuit or two with some jam, fer me boy. And Colonel, make sure the plate is clean and tell the landlady to get off her arse and get in here and scrub down this pig-sty." Then, making a disagreeable face he offered Potter the whiskey, "Oh, and get rid of this." To hear himself talk, anybody'd think he was still First Sergeant Brady.

An hour later a bathed, shaved, sobered Josiah appeared at Erin House. With Brady and Potter, he had left his landlady and two colored girls with scrub buckets and mops sloshing out his room. Inwardly, he squirmed at having to come back to the place where a little over a week ago, his own godmother had pitched a violent scene and thrown him out, and where he had lost his heart. But he sat at attention in the private apartment on the stiff new haircloth sofa smelling the new paint, hoping he gave the impression of a young man in complete charge of himself. Dee seemed as uncomfortable about his presence as he felt at being there. She sat rigidly across from him, avoiding looking at him directly, staring at her hands or the oil painting of pink roses that hung over the fireplace. Sigrid sat in the Boston rocker beside the fireplace. He sipped at the coffee and nibbled at the apple tart Tycee had brought him.

"The death of the sentry was out and out murder, Aunt Dee. Jumped from behind - guerrilla style. Lately, several pickets patrolling bridges and railroad trestles have been found the same way." He stopped, eyed Sigrid before he continued, realizing she might take his next remark as being indelicate, "Their throats slit, their bodies stripped of uniforms and valuables. The outlaws used the uniforms to slip into the city unnoticed." Sigrid hadn't blinked an eye. He turned back to Dee; "These are the same men who probably cut the telegraph wires a few nights ago."

"Night ridin' is back, bad as it was last summer," she murmured, still refusing to look at him.

He waited a beat, then brought up the one name other than his own that might cause his godmother to go into a conniption fit. "That could mean Hy Wilcox is back."

"So, what if he is," she snapped. "Franny's got nothin' more to do with him."

"As far as we know—"

"—What d'ya mean?" She glared at him, "She would have no truck with that rotter a'tall."

He spoke as gently as possible, hating the thought, having to voice it anyway. "Who else would she have gone off with?" *Maybe with me,* he didn't add. *If I hadn't been confined to quarters and in a drunken stupor all week.*

"Tweren't nobody me Franny went with of her own accord, boy-o, no matter what yer been thinkin'," she shouted and wangled her finger in his face.

"You don't know that. Maybe she sent for him."

"If you'll permit my opinion, Captain Scarborough, but I don't think she would have done that," Sigrid broke in timidly, "She held only contempt for him as she expressed to me many times."

See," Dee nodded triumphantly, "Like I told ya, she didn't go away willingly."

But like a loose tooth he had to work the pain back and forth. He smiled at Sigrid, "Franny's been known in the past to keep her true feelings about people a secret, even from you, Sigrid. Isn't that so?"

The girl dropped her gaze and looked into the low fire burning on the grate. He turned back to Dee, feeling anger mount towards his godmother who had hurt him so. And now he wanted to hurt her.

"Franny been talkin' to any strangers lately ?" he asked.

"What do you mean, *strangers*?" She answered, again

281

taking umbrage, just as she had at nearly everything he'd uttered since entering Erin House this morning.

"I mean, have there been any strangers, maybe in Federal uniform, hanging around the place?"

"Nearly all me boarders is Federals, as ye well know." She sniffed.

"Perhaps you didn't notice him, dressed in a Federal's uniform - a stranger, dropping in for dinner or supper, hanging around outside." His voice rose and he pursued the thought with relentless vengeance. "Or she saw him in town when she went shopping, talked to him then."

He thought someone had shot her. Dee clutched her heart, turned pale, and alarmed Sigrid so that the girl sprang to the woman's side. "Aunt Dee, are you going into palpitations, again?"

Dee gasped and nodded her head, pointing towards the water pitcher in the corner.

"Palpitations?" He asked, watching Sigrid from the corner of his eye.

"Been going on for a week, ever since you moved—" she remembered, blushed, whispered, "out."

Gasping, still clutching her chest, Dee managed to speak. "Dear Captain Hawk posted guards around me place to keep the likes of Wilcox out of here. Put on every night. And I can assure you, Captain Scarborough...." He noticed she had not addressed him as "darlin' godson" or by his Christian name since he entered the door ".... Tis not a speck of communication has my Franny had with that terrible, terrible man."

"I don't agree, Mrs. Moone," he would address her formally, as well. "My bet is that she's with Wilcox right now, and the reunited lovebirds are hell-bent headed south out of Missouri so he won't be arrested by our army." He had spoken as if it were no concern to him. Yet, inside he bled, his heart severed, at this possibility. When Dee stared at him, fear written across her face, he continued not trying to mince his words to protect Sigrid's innocence. After all, the girl was due to being married in a little over two months. Time she knew a few things about life, if Werner hadn't schooled her already.

"She probably did go with him willingly. After all, you're pushing her to marry Cyrus Hawk." His tone hardened. "Maybe she decided that since you refused my suit of her hand she'd rather go home with her husband than get an annulment and marry a man she doesn't love. He's closer to her age, *don'cha know*?" He had spared her nothing, down to mocking her accent. His plain speaking had meant to be brutal, but he also wanted to get to the truth. Yet, watching her emotionally crumple under his onslaught remorse struck him. Unsettled and embarrassed, he shifted in his seat, crossed his long, booted legs before him, and couldn't bear to look at her. He didn't want his godmother to know how ashamed of himself he was.

Dee burst into sobs and abruptly arose.

"Captain Scarborough, how could you be so hurtful?" whispered Sigrid glaring at him as she went after Dee who ran into her bedroom, slamming the door behind her. Sigrid knocked softly, called, but Dee didn't open her door. When she didn't, he decided he'd wait a decent interval, then stroll back to his room, finish out his eight days of confinement. His side ached like his head and along the way he'd buy a bottle and kill both pains with it. Thanks to Brady and the Colonel he'd return to a clean room.

"You're wrong about Franny," Captain Scarborough. Unsuccessful in getting Dee to open the door to her, Sigrid returned to her place in the rocking chair by the fireplace. She settled her luscious raven-haired self and frowned at him, an expression that made her eyes even more heavy lidded. Watching her scold him, he'd wished he'd been able to conjure up the kind of passion for her, he had felt for her best friend. She was, indeed, lovely and Gus

283

Werner a lucky man.

"I happen to know the truth about Franny's affections. We had a habit of sharing confidences with each other. With the one exception that she never divulged to me that she and Mr. Wilcox had eloped. I thought he was her best beau and never dreamed she had already married him. In fact," she bowed her head ashamed, "the Sunday she joined him to way-lay the *White Star* she told me she was going to the Wilcox farm for a family picnic and I promised to cover-up for her. Her mother and my father believed she and I spent the whole day together." Gathering her poise before she spoke, she said, "But afterwards, she was completely honest with me about her feelings for…. certain people." She looked away from him, again.

He waited, expecting a deluge of girlish secrets. When Sigrid merely tightened her shawl around her shoulders and rocked gently to and fro, in silence, he prompted, "Well?"

"It would demonstrate a lack of Christian character if I were to share her secrets with anyone."

"Miss Zimmer, you've already demonstrated your lack of Christian character by admitting your duplicity about lying for Franny, you might as well take it a step further and say whatever it is you want to tell me." He hoped his grin softened the harshness of his words.

She faced him but no playful manner met his own. "Let me just say, that Franny held no affection for Hy Wilcox. Thoughts of him terrified her."

He couldn't resist asking, "What about Captain Hawk? Looking forward to all that money he could shower her with, was she?"

She observed him carefully, then glanced around the room to make sure ears hadn't sprouted in the shadows, and whispered, "She despised him. But after you….I mean…. after the *argument* you and Captain Hawk had

284

she despaired, fearing that you had ruined yourself and that in someway, she was at fault." The clock ticked twice before he mustered up the courage to ask, "Me? Did she feel anything but pity for me after the fight and after her mother threw me out."

Sigrid blushed, making her skin even a deeper ivory and looked at her hands. Finally, "I'd rather not say, Captain Scarborough and I would ask you to please not to press me on it."

He exploded, "God…!" then he quickly remembered where he was and that he was having a delicate conversation with a delicate, young girl, and allowed the oath on his lips to die in time. He stood up, paced the floor gathering control and running his hands through his hair.

"But I'll tell yer, godson, how she felt about yer." Neither of them had observed Dee quietly listening from the shadows of her bedroom door. Her hands held a small, flat book. Gone was the brittle control, the contentious attitude. In their place stood humility and if he was right, a silent plea for forgiveness.

"She loved ya with all her heart. If that girl ever loved anybody or anything, 'twas you, Josiah." She walked with dignity to the fireplace and stood with her back to him. "But I kept her from ya. 'Twas me own misgivings 'bout ya that made me keep the truth from her about how you loved her. When I got back from the hospital after visitin' ya, the girl asked me, tears in her eyes, for she'd been weepin' and moppin' all over the place after ya when ya left like ya done, she asked me if you'd expressed any objections to her marryin' Captain Hawk. And I lied. I told her, you'd not raised an eyebrow, but smiled and wished her well." She turned and faced him. "I never thought, you'd be comin' back, here. About all I ever expected from ya was maybe a letter or two."

Suddenly, she strode briskly back to her room. On her way she thrust the book into his hands. "Take it, it's her diary. It's all there. Just try not to hate me."

Once again he found himself alone with Sigrid. For a startled moment the two could only stare at one another. It was as though a great drama had just unfolded on a stage and the curtain had gone down before the play was over. Embarrassed that she'd probably heard more than she ought, Sigrid stated for the door. "Excuse me, I must see to getting the noon dinner up and served."

Left alone, Josiah thought, that, like Dee, Sigrid too had made a theatrical exit. It reminded him also of another theatre tradition: that no matter what, the show had to go on. Regardless of murder, heartbreak, or possible abduction, life at Erin House would go on.

He slumped on the sofa. He supposed he'd be as welcome as anybody to eat dinner. But he wasn't hungry and the last thing he wanted to do was make light conversation. He'd made enough conversation this morning to last a lifetime. His mind teamed with Dee's admission. So much of it explained Franny's nearly frantic clinging to him when he had first returned and her subsequent coldness. He had been correct to surmise that Dee had poisoned her against him. Catching the light from the as yet, undraped, high arched window overlooking the backyard rose garden, he opened Franny's diary.

He smiled at her precise hand, the childish, occasional misspellings, her poor knowledge of geography. *He says he's from New York City,* she had written about him. *It must get really cold there because it's pushed next to Mayne.* Before he read more, it occurred to him that he was snooping into a young girl's most intimate thoughts, and perhaps would be indelicate of him to read further. Feeling guilty, he closed the little rose leather diary, embossed in gold script with the words *My Diary,* but unable to contain himself, after looking about to see if he were still alone, opened it again. He blushed over her descriptions of him, blushed even more when she described their behavior coming home in the carryall after the band concert, felt his own tears as he read about hers over the hurt he had given her when he had stormed out that day. Sensed her fears when she wrote...*I know Hy Wilcox is only toying with me, waiting to kill me. He hates me now and is probably watching me write this, even now. I wake up at night. I listen to the wind, to the blind clatter and the dogs barking and think that Hy Wilcox is sneaking up beside my bed to put his hands around my throat or to smash my head into the wall like he did the night of the fire, to kill me. If only I could tell Josiah.* "I wish you had told me, sweetheart," he murmured, feeling the rage and the tears load behind his eyes, again.

Then it hit him. Last night the wind had blown up a duster. He looked up saw the rose garden and went to the window. From the window he saw on his left the back porch configure with the garden, saw the spot where the corporal's throat had been slit. On his right he saw the end of the side driveway leading to the hotel's livery stable, the drive way - an unnoticed place to leave a horse on a dark nigh. He swung his vision around to the left again. The back porch led off the new kitchen, taken out of the basement and built on level with the dining room. That explained the pie found lying out on the table. He was starting to think the matter through and spoke aloud to himself. "If she was afraid of Wilcox and if it was he who appeared here during the wind storm, then she may not be with him at all by choice.

The lobby was empty. Clay he found in the dining room seated with Sigrid and eating with Potter and Brady. After first seating himself Josiah broke into their conversation. "Clay, did Franny roam around the hotel at night by herself ?"

"Only on nights she couldn't sleep, Captain." The boy looked up from his chicken wondering why he asked.

"She must have been up last night. The wind was blowing. And the wind frightened her." Josiah shook a silent "no" to Sigrid's offer of eating dinner.

Everyone gave him blank looks for answers. He hurried on. "Did she sometimes sneak into the kitchen and get into Tycee's pie keeper?"

The boy blushed, grinned to admit it, "Yeah, we both did. But we never told on each other. We made a 'cousins' pact."

"Here's the way I think everything happened here last night…." Josiah described the scenario, naming Wilcox as the abductor. But Brady corrected him. "Naw, the corporal wouldn't ha' come inside to eat his pie, she'd a brung it to him. He might snooze a bit on the guard duty he was a-pullin' but leave his post all together - Naw, never."

"Brady, I do believe you are correct, for a change." Potter began. "Now, then, Captain Scarborough, I see the scoundrel Wilcox lurking in the back watching her through the undraped window that looks directly into the apartment as you say. But before he can do that, he first has to dispose of the sentry, which he does, forthwith. He is thinking about entering the hotel, and now that he has the new room arrangements in mind he schemes to enter through the kitchen and make his way to the apartment. But, he sees her leave the apartment. He waits. He sees a candle flicker in the kitchen and is about to enter when low and behold the young woman steps outside--"

"--Callin' ta the corporal ta have a piece o' pie."

"That's when he grabs my cousin from behind." So rapt in the story had been the men, no one had noticed Sigrid's growing anxiousness. Suddenly the girl put her face in her hands and ran from the room, sobbing.

Conversation at the other tables ceased. Unsympathetic eyes turned to the three men and the half-grown boy huddled at the corner table. Every pair of eyes accused them of some gross, ungentlemanly behavior. Not waiting out the awkward moment, all four rose as one as Josiah said, "I think I know where he's taken her and she didn't go willingly, as some of us may have thought at first."

Giving the appearance of any soldier on a spree, he had made her sit astride in front of him in the saddle, his knife at her back, her gag off, but her bonds hidden by the night. With her naked knees in plain view, hair loose, and dressed in a nightdress and wrapper, she looked like any Hog Ally whore drunk with her soldier boy. With Hy singing bawdy songs at the top of his lungs like he'd had too much to drink, but not enough to be arrested, they drew only a jaundiced eye and a smirking leer from other rowdies still on the streets at that hour.

At the first picket, he was "too drunk" to remember the password, but when he mumbled the name "Lyon" the sentry had let him pass.

"Takin' the lady to camp, are ya?"

"Thought I would."

"Think she'd like to play with me, some, before you take her on through? I got some of m' pay left over. You can watch my post."

Hy laughed, "Naw, I'm about all she can handle. Ain't that about right, honey?"

When he had spoken to her he tightened his already firm grip, pressing her back against his shoulder with his knife concealed in his palm. "She agrees with me. You can find her in the Kentucky, name's Lorna. Well, gotta go, much obliged."

The other defenses posed no problem for Hy either. The two sentries posted near the fair grounds were deep in discussion and Hy took a little known path avoiding them. Even further out, almost to the ferry across Boggs Creek, the third sentries were asleep. Also, he avoided Mr. Robinson's little steam ferry and rode three miles down creek where it was fordable.

When he passed the third post and hit the St. Louis road, he picked up to a gallop. By the time they reached the Wilcox farmhouse every bone in her body felt broken and she was freezing with cold. Dismounting he roughly pulled her off the horse and marched her towards the darkened house. Not a word had he spoken to her the entire way out after the exchange with the first sentry. He broke his silence when they reached the porch and he pulled her up close to him and whispered at the back of her neck. "One word, one itty bitty noise from you when I take you inside and you will be sliced up like a side a beef."

He entered the musty front hall, black except for the sliver of moonlight coming from beneath the front door. He opened and closed it so softly, she wondered who he was trying not to awaken. His father was in prison, moved to the facility used by the state penitentiary. She had seen no other horses tethered in the yard. To her left she remembered the parlor. On the right one entered the dining room and on through to the back was the kitchen. Beyond the kitchen lay the woods. She'd offer to cook and find a way to escape, she plotted as he pushed her before him up the stairs. But before she could escape she'd have to find something to wear. Maybe, go to the attic to see if any of Mrs. Wilcox's old clothes had been left to rot in the trunks stored up there.

The bedrooms were on the second floor. They reached the landing, lit only from the moon coming from a small triangular window. Mixed with the smell she had noticed in the entryway, came an odor like an animal had died and been left to decay. But Hy didn't tarry on the second floor, instead he pushed her quickly on to a narrow staircase at the back of the hallway.

At the top, windows opened out on all four sides and the moonlight seemed intense as it streamed into the little room. He tied her hands to one of the four posters of the bed, posts too high for her to lift her hands over them, and lit a lamp. With the lamp and the moonlight she saw clearly the beautiful old furniture that seemed to have been lovingly cared for. Too, it was clean! The unpleasant odors from below failed to waft this far. Instead, there lingered the very faint smell of paint, like oil paints used to paint pictures on canvas. Sure enough, propped in a corner she saw an artist's easel.

"This was my mama's room. The Yankees didn't bother lookin' up here when they took Paw away and tore up the house. Her "studio" she used to call it. She'd come up here and paint pi'tures before I was born. I done cleaned it real good and fixed it up pretty, just for us." Hy stood behind her caressing her hair. "Remember what I done tole you. I may not want to, but I will kill you if'n you holler out. You can talk but you got to talk in a whisper. If'n you cooperate, then I'll leave the gag off, but if'n you don't I'll either put it back on or I'll jest kill you."

She took a deep breath, whispered, "They'll come after me, you know."

"Who? Yore husband-to-be, old man Hawk ain't in town. 'N' your cousin Clay is too little and whipped by the Yankees. Who else gonna give a care or even suspect it were me? That stupid dutchy lover of yore ma's? Hell, he's so fat he can't sit a horse." Still keeping her tied he embraced her from behind and nuzzled her neck, whispering, "But I suppose you got a hundred of them Yankee boys just creamin' in their sleep over you after the way you wiggle yore self in front of 'um."

"Hy, you are mistaken. I have never been unfaithful to you." This was true, if she didn't count the night in the carryall with Josiah. Even that had been only heavy kissing. She closed her eyes, remembering, yearning, regretting it would never be anything else. Doubtful, she'd ever see him again.

His tone turned cold and his hands playing over her body mauled instead of caressed. "You lie, woman. I've seen you m'self prissin' around the 'new' Erin House that ever'body's callin' it, smilin' and flirtin.' Not to mention that old geezer who's lickin his chops wantin' to marry up with you when yore so-called annulment is final." He turned her to him so he could face her squarely, "Have you done lost yore mind, girl? Hell, he can't bed you. He's too old!" Then, added slyly, "But I ain't."

The realization that undetected, Hy had been able to watch her as she went about her daily business at Erin House sent new shocks of terror through her frame.

He chuckled and was trying to kiss her when she said, "It is my duty to be a welcoming hostess to Erin House's guests and I did nothing improper. If you were watching me as closely as you say, then you would have seen that. And as for Captain Hawk, he helped me to get my annulment from you and once he gets back to town and discovers my abduction, he'll come out here so fast the fleas want have time to jump off a dead dog."

"What abduction, sugar?" he fumbled with the tie at her throat. He clearly meant to undress her while keeping her tied to the bedpost. "There's not a sign of a struggle. 'N' remember, no body recognized 'twas li'l Franny Moone astraddle that drunk soldier's horse tonight. Lorna--have to admit that was quick thinkin.' Bet that boy heads fer the Kentucky and asks fer Lorna and everybody's gonna think him nuts." He stifled a laugh while he slowly unbuttoned her nightdress.

"There's somebody you failed to mention who might care very much, smart enough to know I was abducted and by you, and who will come after me."

"I ferget' somebody?" He had the gown unbuttoned below her waist and he slipped rough, warm hands inside, around her body. "Good Lord," he whispered hoarsely, "I've wanted you." His hands playing over her nakedness, he bent to kiss her.

"Josiah Scarborough."

Immediately, he dropped his hands and raised his head. In is eyes flickered a peculiar glint of fear. "Not unless you be talkin' 'bout a ghost. He's dead. Killed him m'self." And he told her about Wilson Creek.

It was all Franny could do to stop herself from screaming. But with tears streaming down her face, she hissed, "Oh, God, how I hate you." For pure spite she added, "If I were going to be unfaithful, that is the man I would have. I love him with all my heart. And he's still alive! So there." She sobbed unable to wipe her face, her head pressed against the bedpost and at that moment cared not a whit whether or not her insane husband killed her by knife, gun, or rope just so he killed her. How her dearest Josiah had suffered, because of her.

He stood away from her watching her cry. Quietly he said, "Yeah, I knowed all the time 'twas him you really cared about. I knowed from the day Paw come home and tole us 'bout him puttin' his arm around you on the street. I had a feelin' 'bout him. I've tried to kill him twice and twice, it seems he comes back from the dead. Reckon, I'll jest have to wait and try a third time. Third time's the charm, they say. Then, after he's finally dead and gone, I guess I'll jest have to give you time to love me."

He untied her and left her alone sobbing on the bed.

Sunlight streaming through the windows and shouting from men's voices awoke her. It came from the second floor landing.

"You will take the girl home. That's an order." *Verboise. He knows I'm here.*

"No, I ain't. She's my wife and she belongs here." *Hy, sassing the Cap'n.* She crept closer to the locked door and listened.

"How long before every Federal in the county gets out here? You fool, you've jeopardized every man that rides with us."

"For all anybody at Erin House knows she done run

of ... of her own free will."

"Don't be even more stupid than you are. First firing the hotel, now abduction. And you killed the guard Hawk put on the place to get to her. Have it your way. Keep your wife here, but you stay with her. We're through with you, Wilcox. The men and I are headed for the bush, without you."

She heard Verboise's heavy boots stomp down the stairs and Hy's right behind him. "Wait a minute Cap'n. Now, listen." Although fainter, she could hear him clearly. He was begging. "Aw, goddamn it. Other boys have their wives and sweethearts with 'um. You're the only man in the outfit that don't have female companionship. Maybe if you did, you'd understand!"

Suddenly she heard a thump, a scuffle, and Hy's scream of rage and pain. She guessed Verboise hit him. Good, maybe he'd kill him. Then, she wouldn't need to go through the humiliation of an annulment, barely less scandalous than a divorce in her case.

As quickly as it had happened the fight seemed to be over. She heard the front door slam and moved quickly to the windows that provided a panoramic view of the entire Wilcox farm. In the yard below a half-dozen of the gang rode up as Verboise strode out to meet them. She thought she recognized them all, these men and boys whom she had refused to turn over to Hawk. Every one of them she had known as a schoolmate or he had done business at Erin House. Before the war the only things she knew about these men killing had been squirrels.

The morning shone with glorious light, and around the farm nature had outdone herself in painting the trees with the deep reds and golds of autumn. The remains of a cornfield sloped off towards the creek. The stalks brown and withering, she supposed the Yankee's had taken the harvest. Below her Verboise talked and gestured towards the house. A dozen or more men rode in and she knew most of these as well. Amazing, she thought, watching the numbers in the bare earth yard climb until she counted nearly 50 riders. So intent on counting the numbers of raiders congregating below, she didn't hear Hy unlock the door.

She jumped, startled, when she saw his appearance. His eye was fast closing shut; he had a bruise on his face, and kept putting his finger to a cut on his lip. He threw her a pair of pants, a man's shirt, a rough farm jacket and a slouch hat—all of which were filthy and stunk of Paw Wilcox. "Get dressed. We're ridin' out before the Federals get here and you're comin' with me."

"No, I'm not going with you. And these clothes are filthy," she yelled, throwing the clothing in his face and backing away from him.

His hand flew in an arc catching her up side the head while his other grabbed her and began tearing off her wrapper. She screamed and he slapped her again, ripping off her nightdress. While trying to hide her nakedness she struck back and got in one good punch on his nose. It began to bleed and he charged her like a maddened bull. Shrieking, sobbing, she tussled with him on the floor but he managed to sit astride her and began choking her with one hand while rhythmically slapping her from side to side with the other. She couldn't breathe but through her sobs she heard heavy boots pounding up the stairs. And, like a rag doll Hy was tossed into a corner of the room.

"Touch her again, Wilcox, and I'll rip you apart with my bare hands." Verboise stood over his former lieutenant. He turned towards her, saw her curled into a naked ball and threw a bed-quilt over her. Then he reached down for her hand, but she was stricken with fear and sobbed harder. He crouched down beside her, seemingly uncaring of Hy, lying in the corner, watching them. "Come, Mrs. Wilcox, I will help you. I have no wish to harm you." To Franny's ear his voice seemed as calming as a mother's but she was hysterical. Then, large gentle hands were sliding under her body, wrapping the quilt around her and lifting her into his arms where she lay, still sobbing like a small child. Immediately, Franny felt that this is the way her own father - Eddie Moone, who had died the year she was born - might have comforted her.

She realized that for all her life she had yearned for a father's protective love and she wept all the more for being denied. Then, Franny felt disloyal to dear, Otto Zimmer who had tried as surrogate, but she knew it wasn't the same. She missed her own father.

As she cried against this stranger's broad chest she noticed he wore a crucifix beneath his shirt. Odd, she wondered, this man of violence carried the emblem of the man of peace, and she thought of God. Filling her mind were the faces of the suffering Christ hanging on the cross in St. Peter's and Father Walsh consoling her about getting the annulment. In a whoosh the guilt she had carried since the elopement washed over her afresh, making her cry even harder. And she asked herself, If God is the heavenly father, did He comfort people by holding them in His spiritual arms? Even terribly sinful people like her?

Unable to answer this question, she decided that if she ever got back home alive, she'd put all of this behind her, try to forget Josiah Scarborough, and marry Captain Cyrus Hawk - the dullest man she knew. All she wanted was to be left in peace with a life that had no seams or ripples, no danger, no rushing emotions, no ecstatic passions. For now, all she wanted to do was lay her head against his broad, muscular shoulder and feel herself calm while being rocked gently to and fro.

When she did, the state of her nakedness before this strange giant became acutely embarrassing. But she remembered in those moments before he had covered her with the quilt that his eyes had never strayed from her face. And in those eyes, now void of coldness, she noticed a light, one she'd not seen there before.

"We must find you something to wear, Mrs. Wilcox." He smiled a little and pushed her hair out of her face. "Unless you'd prefer wearing only a blanket."

"Wilcox!" he barked and she started, "get some suitable clothing for your wife."

Throughout the time Verboise had held and comforted her, Hy never took his fierce, angry eyes off them. "I done brought her some. But she wouldn't wear 'um," he said, preferring to lie in the corner rubbing his injured shoulder.

"Excuse me, Mrs. Wilcox." With that he put her down. Wrapping the blanket more tightly around herself, she shivered from the tension in the room and with the cold. One giant hand scooped Hy from the floor, making that man yelp with pain, "What the hell you doin', you crazy son-of-a-bitch?" The blow from the other made Hy cry out and again his nose bled. "She's my wife 'n' she does like I say. I brought her up some riding clothes. There ain't no more clothes in the house, 'less you want her to wear a Yankee uniform."

The second punch, Franny heard a bone snap and Hy sprawled on his back. Groaning, holding his ribs, he tried to sit up. His blows of self-defense had fallen on muscles made of iron and stone and he desperately scooted backward on his tail bone trying to get away from the ogre looming over him and delivering blows to his head, face, and neck. Watching them, Franny thought it curious the way Verboise seemed to be only mauling Hy, at worst like a teacher with a recalcitrant student, boxing his ears. No, that wasn't it. Suddenly, she saw the murderous intentions of the Captain. He was toying with Hy, toying until he decided to deliver the lethal blow that would kill her husband. Good God, she groaned inwardly, *I might want to see Hy Wilcox dead, but not murdered before my eyes*! "Captain Verboise," she called out, "wait, please, Hy may not remember that his mother's old trunks are in the attic."

"You know this to be a fact, Mrs. Wilcox?" His fist raised in mid-air, Verboise pulled back.

"Yes, we played here as children. I'll go up there myself and find something to wear."

Limping, Hy led the way as the three climbed the narrow rickety stairs to the attic, brushing away years of cobwebs and sending elderly spiders scurrying into musty corners. There they were. Under layers of dust the trunks stood as sturdy as ever. When Verboise opened the largest, she fished out underpinnings and an old, blue velvet riding skirt. With it came a riding jacket, a blouse, and a knitted sweater. Beneath all of these lay a black velvet hat with the plume still attached. And luck of all luck all of these delightful garments had kept themselves hidden from the moths. If the beating she had suffered from Hy hadn't caused her face to hurt she would have laughed aloud in pure joy at the find.

Oblivious to the men watching her from the attic doorway, Franny examined first one piece of clothing then another. Finally Verboise spoke. "When you are dressed, Mrs. Wilcox, please join us in the front yard." He grunted a command and pushed Hy ahead of him as the two clumped down the stairs.

Outside, she noticed the men loading up a wagon with equipment and supplies while Verboise stood in the middle of the yard shouting orders. Watching the activity, huddled against the chill in the morning air, Hy sat in his Paw's rocking chair. He had bandaged his head but his puffed eyes squinted up at her as she came onto the porch. Seeing him caused only revulsion, and she whisked past down the stairs.

"Franny," Hy whispered behind her. "Please, listen to me."

She paused at the third step, kept her back to him, waited.

"I never meant you no harm. I jest went crazy, there, fer a minute."

She said nothing, continued to wait.

"He would a killed me sure, if'n you hadn't remembered them old trunks of Maw's and mentioned 'um."

"I know."

"So, I reckon I should say thank you."

Her back still to him she asked, "Is that all you wanted with me?"

"Will you turn around and look at me, please?"

Remaining on the step she turned. This second look at his battered condition brought her a quick pity for this boy. The thought came to her that here was a warrior who had loved the wrong woman, followed the wrong commander, and for all she had been told, the wrong cause. When he didn't speak she asked, "Is there more you wish to say to me?"

"Verboise's takin' you with him. Says he'll get you home. I want you to forgive me."

She dropped her gaze, unable to look at him any longer and pulled on a pair of buckram gloves she had found in one of the other trunks. Struggling to hold back tears she asked, "But will you ever be able to forgive me?" Then, she saw Verboise watching them. He beckoned, and with a sigh she joined him at his waiting horse.

Hy watched Horton lead his horse up to the porch. His friend squinted in the early morning sun making him look older than his 20 years. He gestured towards Hy's bandaged head, "Whipped you good. He made me Lieutenant. You're really out?"

"That's what the chief says."

"Why's he takin' your woman?"

"Franny? Hell, she ain't my woman. She's leavin' me. Ain't you heard? Gettin' an annulment."

"Jeez, boy, Naw, I ain't heard nothin' 'bout no-body,

'cept old Buster, shut up in that Yankee dungeon in the jail with them other boys who didn't ride south with us."

Hy didn't say anything, observing as Verboise helped Franny onto her horse. His ex-commander was entirely too friendly for his taste - dusting off and adjusting the stirrup, holding her foot until it got placed, fussing with her reins until they were just so. And Franny, not quite what he'd say "friendly" with Verboise, but sure enough hell enjoyin' his attentions.

"Looks like, only me left of us three who started with Verboise last April." Horton grinned, "Remember the Liberty Arsenal and how we was all scared of him?"

"Most of the men still are," he said dryly. Verboise's hand rested on Franny's thigh and he was saying something to her, laughing up at her. Verboise wasn't known as a big smiler much less a laugher. But then, Hy hadn't seen Verboise in the company of a woman before. He thought he lived like a monk, taken a vow or something. No doubt about it, his Captain was the spookiest man he'd ever known.

"Horton, mount up the men!" Verboise yelled as he moved to his horse.

Hy watched as every man and wagon pulling camp equipment rode or rolled out of the dirt yard. A few glanced his way as they rode out, their faces wondering, but not asking. Most of them knew by now. No sooner was the yard quiet then the scraggly chickens reappeared to peck endlessly into the barren earth.

He sat, staring after his vanished army, forbidden to follow or be shot, feeling his guts churn with anger. Worse, he felt an empty chill fill his heart. Franny had gone with Verboise, to go home, to go back to her Yankees, back to her Yankee sweetheart. He took a wad of Missouri Bootheel from his shirt pocket, bit off a chaw and felt the numbing bitterness wash over his tongue and throat. *Never, ever should a hit her that way*, he thought.

300

Never should a ripped her clothes off. The image of her naked body shivering under him as he had choked her came to mind and it drove him crazy with guilt, lust, and hopelessness. Suddenly, Horton's question drove him off the porch.

He had asked, *Why was Verboise takin' Franny?* He remembered Verboise holding her in his arms and rocking back and forth. He said he'd get her back to town. But how was he plannin' to do that? And when? Right away? Today, in broad daylight? Or would he keep her overnight with him in his big officer's tent, encamped in the woods. Up to now, Verboise had exhibited no interest in the fairer sex because of - what Hy put down to - religious reasons. But a monk could lose his religion.

If what he suspicioned was true, he'd kill Verboise himself, put a bullet through him like any other man. Powder and ball could drop even Verboise. His cracked rib hurting like hell, Hy saddled his mare and followed the tracks out of the yard, heading towards the woods.

Lieutenant Werner and Clay galloped out to call together the Home Guard. Josiah, Brady, and Potter strode up the hill to the Capitol and into the office of the Provost Marshal. O'Shay pushed a quill across a document before him, looked up after they walked in, sneered. "Well, hello, the officer who's not a gentleman. Do you have permission to be here, Scarborough?"

"*Captain* Scarborough to the likes o' you, laddie, 'n' don'cha be forgettin' it."

"Nevermind, Brady," Josiah motioned the sergeant still, asked O'Shay, "Have you posted a detail to look for Miss Moone?" From the corner of his eye he noticed Potter staring at several documents lying loose on top of Hawk's desk.

" No, why should I?"

"She was abducted by the one who murdered

Jefferies, your own sentry."

"The murder of the sentry will be looked into." Then, O'Shay snorted, "Abducted, ridiculous. She went with the murderer willingly."

"What makes you think that?"

"A woman, who rode with bushwhackers, as loose as she is—"

"That's enough!" Josiah made for him. Brady pulled him back.

"Go on, hit me Scarborough. That's the way you always handle your disagreements, isn't it." But O'Shay stood up and scooted out of reach behind his desk, smirked, "Yes, the Provost himself was courting her, but that didn't make her a lady. It just made the old fart look foolish."

A coiled spring ready to pop, Josiah remarked sarcastically, "I see you're a loyal staff member to your superior officer. Teach you that at West Point, did they? And for your information, Miss Moone is a lady above reproach. One more word dishonoring her, and I'll tear you apart, O'Shay, something I should have done when we left Ft. Smith. I have nothing to lose. Might as well face a court martial for whipping two pricks instead of one."

"Get out!" Hawk's loyal underling glanced around at them all - Potter by Hawk's desk standing with his hands in his pockets, Brady grabbing Josiah's arm and standing in the sight line between O'Shay and Potter, and at his former cavalry mate poised to strike, "All I have to do is call the guard. You, Scarborough," he pointed a stiff arm at him, "are to be in your quarters, and you other two I can have arrested for loitering where you don't belong, retired out or not."

A quick shove from Brady and Josiah, reluctantly, left the office. Potter nodded, "Good Morning," and tipped his old-fashioned, bell crown broad-brimmed hat to the lieutenant. Outside, they stopped to talk over their next plan. Obviously, post command didn't think it important enough to chase after a murderer and a girl.

"Werner can detail around 20 men. That will have to do. God knows how many we're facing. Wilcox could have acted alone and the first place we'll go is the Wilcox farm. But I doubt if he's alone. I have a hunch that Verboise is back with Wilcox and a whole bunch more came back with him." Josiah punched Brady's shoulder, laughed, " We just might bag Verboise after all, old man. You two can keep things quiet at Erin House. Dee needs all the calming she can get, right now."

"No yer don't boy-o. I'm goin' with ya."

"Yes, and I as well. I can still sit a horse with ease."

"Get-along, now, Colonel, you never could sit a horse with ease. You was infantry."

"I beg your pardon, Sergeant Brady, but I had a particular charger that carried me through the Mexican war with aplomb."

"No! Neither of you is going," Josiah interrupted. "I wouldn't think of having you along."

"And why not? I was along plenty besides yer and not so long ago, neither. But I can understand yer reluctance about the Colonel, here."

Potter drew himself up to his full height, about Josiah's chin, swelled out his chest, sucked in his gut and bellowed, " I will go on this exercise. I was a full colonel in the United States Army, cited for valor at Veracruz, and I will not be put on the shelf. I will engage the enemy." He dropped his voice for suddenly his eyes misted, "Besides, I watched little Franny grow up into the charming young lady she is now." Before he left Erin House to come with Josiah and Brady to the Provost Marshal's office, Potter had put on his old army uniform. Standing there now, wearing the old fashioned blue swallow tail coat and yellow vest he had worn in the Seminole and Mexican Wars, he looked formidable enough to take on every guerrilla in the state.

By noon, flanked by Werner and Colonel Potter, Josiah led a column of 25 men past the sentries and onto the road headed for Wilcox farm. Sergeant Brady rode behind them and Clay behind Brady. "Never thought I'd be soldering with a company of Federals," he quipped taking his place in line.

"'Tis lucky ya are he let ya be along a'tall. Yer, under age," Brady growled. In field uniform, once again, Brady was First Sergeant, taking command over the sergeant and two corporals serving the volunteer Home Guard, commanded by Lieutenant Werner.

"Werner, did you tell post Commander, Tom Price, you were taking a detail of the Guard out?"

"No sir," he grinned.

"That means you're doing this without authorization. Could be trouble for you," Josiah grinned back.

"I'll just say it was a drill, sir."

Josiah sobered, "I hope it turns out to be little more than that, Lieutenant. Let us pray so."

At the Wilcox farm, the men surrounded the house, then waited. Seeing no one about, no horses tied in the corral or the yard, Josiah dismounted, petted the toothless old hound that greeted him on the porch, knocked. When no one answered he motioned for Werner, Brady, and Clay to follow him into the house and had Colonel Potter shift a dozen men to the outlying buildings.

A cold pot of coffee on the stove and two dirty cups told him that the place had been recently occupied. Guns drawn, they carefully went upstairs, found beds lately occupied and the flight of stairs up to the studio. Brilliant with noon sun, the studio revealed the blood spilled that morning and Franny's torn nightdress and wrapper. On the bedposts clung a cut leather tie.

"They's hers," Clay said softly, picking up the ripped garments still redolent with her fragrance.

No one else spoke. Too choked with fear for what may have happened in that terrible room and feeling his rage mount, Josiah ordered them all out.

His mind in a whipsaw of emotions, he stumbled into the yard gasping for breath. Colonel Potter showed him the tracks towards the woods he had found. "If you notice the number of hoof prints and the wagon tracks rolling off into the brush, one could surmise a considerable force of men and equipment rode this way."

"They took 'er with 'um, Cap'n," Clay squinted into the dark trees.

Each man instructed to stay silent and "look sharp," by twos the column rode into the brush. They followed the trail of scuffed earth and broken tree limbs without difficulty until they came to Boggs Creek. There, it ended. Brady and a corporal scouted nearly a mile in both directions up the creek's side and found nothing, no place where they might have veered off. " Here's where they forded the creek," said Josiah, and he gave the order for the men to do the same.

The country around the creek was swampy and burst with foliage so thick that the horses had a tough time breaking through. Rolling hills and convoluted ridges ending in sharp ravines, laden with marshy undergrowth, made the party wind back and forth, until one of the men wondered if they weren't going in circles. But once again they had picked up the trail.

As he picked his way along with the rest of the troop, Josiah's mind couldn't erase the images of the ripped clothing, cut leather ties, and blood. Was Wilcox so crazed that he had tortured Franny? Maybe murdered her and buried the body? He should have taken a closer look at the grounds before he went tracking after the gang. These chilling thoughts made him sick with despair and nausea churned his stomach. He needed a drink. That would stop the burning, help him face whatever inevitability lay ahead of him. He started to reach for his flask, eyed Brady, and thought better of it. The old sergeant would know at once what he was doing and would make him put it away, then on some pretext get him out of earshot of the men, and give him hell for bringing it along in the first place.

The small company of Home Guard rode the better part of the day, the sun hanging low and unable to pierce the density of thickets and hardwood forests. A slight chill in the air broke the day's Indian Summer warm. Suddenly, Colonel Potter who had taken the lead stopped them all with the silent order to halt. Down the line went the whisper.

At first not a sound came in the thickening gloom, then they heard it away far off - the chop, chop, chop of ax on wood. Somebody was cutting firewood. "We'll run into their pickets, soon," Josiah whispered to Werner. "Have the men dismount and advance on foot, staying low, carbines at ready. Leave the horses here."

Two recent recruits stayed back with the horses while the rest of Werner's detail crept forward in what seemed like inches. When they got to the first picket he was so surprised that he dropped his weapon and ran. Swiftly caught, he was dragged back to Josiah.

"Biddle, that's my name. And I'm a farmer over in Cole County. I never meant no harm to nobody, Sir. But he tole us that we couldn't quit once we got started."

"How many does Verboise have?"

"Mebbe 50 of us."

"Where's the next sentry?"

"Up ahead, eighth of a mile."

A large, blond private dispatched Biddle to the rear. The rest of the company fanned out, moving forward and using the undergrowth for cover. The next guard was asleep. He joined Biddle at the rear. By now they could hear men laughing and talking, smell bacon cooking over a fire. "I'm hungry," Clay mumbled.

"You lads can earn yer suppers," Brady whispered in return.

"On signal, we'll charge making a lot of noise, make them think there's more of us than there are. And gentlemen," he pointed out Clay, "imitate this young man. Give us that yell, Mr. Monihan, you Rebs were hollering at Dug Springs."

Clay went crimson. But at Josiah's signal he rushed forward with the screeching yell that had sent terror into the hearts of the proud First Cavalry. Soon the others had taken up the cry as they rushed the camp. So taken by surprise was the gang that few had time to scramble for their guns or skedaddle for their horses. Smoke from gunpowder quickly obscured the scene, filling the air with its acrid smell. Men dove into the thickets. One of the bushwhackers brought his britches to blaze when he ran through a campfire and screamed as flames rose around his body. He beat frantically and ran, until another man, threw a blanket over him and pushed him to the ground. Both were captured. Suddenly, from out of a grove of trees Verboise galloped through the camp followed by what seemed like over half his numbers. They held their reins in their teeth and fired Colt revolvers with both hands.

Scarborough stood up, fired point blank at the half-breed as he screamed by, missed, took aim again, and missed again. Verboise whirled around, galloped back. Stopped for an instant before his former charge, yelled over the din, "I knew you'd come after her," and galloped away.

The gun in his hand didn't fire again. Franny was *alive*. She *was* here. Suddenly, nothing else mattered. Capturing the bushwhackers, bringing in Verboise - nothing but finding her and making her safe. Bullets flying around him he ran to the far end of the camp for he had spotted earlier an officer's wall tent. That's Verboise's tent, of course. But where would Wilcox's be? That's the tent she'd be in. Not many tents were up, only two small ones. He ran to these to find them empty. By now, the battle was winding down. Who hadn't been captured had ridden out with Verboise. He returned to Verboise's tent. He found her, hands in prayer, tears streaming down her face, and kneeling in a corner praying.

"Franny!" He rushed to her and lifted her into his arms. Immediately, he noticed the bruises. "Oh my darling girl." He held her to him. "What an ordeal for you to go through."

She sniffled against his chest. Then, although tears still glistened on her lashes, she smiled. "I told him you'd come."

"Who hit you?" Josiah gently rubbed his thumb over her bruised cheek.

"Hy Wilcox." She said trying to turn her face away from him.

"No, let me see," he turned her to him, studied the marks on her cheeks and chin. "If you're going to engage in fisticuffs I must show you how to duck a punch, darling." But he wasn't laughing. Instead, he scowled, vowing to himself that if he ever got his hands on Wilcox, he'd kill him.

"I bloodied his nose," she said proudly.

"Captain," the young sergeant of the Home Guard poked his head inside the tent, "you better come out here. We caught one lurking in the woods on the far side of the camp. When he heard you was commanding he insisted on seeing you."

His arm around Franny, Josiah stepped outside. There confronting him was a fighting, lunging prisoner, so angry that veins protruded from his neck and oaths blued the air. At his side he felt Franny freeze.

"You dirty, wife-stealin' son-of-a-bitch." With that, Hy Wilcox managed to break free from the burly corporal that held him and ran to Josiah, several feet away. No one caught him. The private raised his pistol, aimed, but the gun misfired. By then, Wilcox rose up, seemed to fly through the air, and tackled him, throwing him into a muddy trench. The smell identified it as one dug for the sinks, the camp's toilets.

Schooled by the best brawlers New York City could produce, Josiah did everything he knew to throw off his assailant. Eye gouging, ear biting, he even clamped down on Wilcox's nose until he tasted blood, to no avail. Over and over in the stinking trench did the men roll. Wilcox seemed to have a rage empowered strength of 10 men. It took five privates and Werner's shouted commands that he would put a bullet through him the first chance he could, to subdue Franny's enraged husband.

There was one other thing Captain Scarborough had to look at. Reeking from sink scum, Josiah followed Brady over to a rotund figure lying on the ground. Colonel Potter stared up at him. "I believer, sir, I've taken a wound."

A dark stain began spreading down the front of the old coat. "Don't talk, Colonel. Let me have a look."

"No, boy, just listen." The old man waved Josiah closer and he coughed. His voice hoarsened. "There isn't time. Look in my left pocket. Get the papers."

"Colonel, let Josiah help you. He knows a bit about doctorin'-horses, mostly but... "

"... No, dear friend," he grabbed Brady's arm. "If you hadn't come to Erin House I would have spent the rest of my days in that wing chair beside the parlor fire." He coughed again, this time blood. "We had a good time at the Kentucky."

"That we did, Sir." Brady sniffed very hard, spit into the ground, and looked away. His eyes brimmed with tears.

"The papers, Josiah," he whispered, "they show Hawk and his staff are crooks of the worse kind. Stealing....from the people....the government." His eyes

309

began to glaze and with his last breath Josiah thought he heard him say, "I have served well."

Along with one dead Werner's report listed one horse killed, three men slightly wounded, and the capture of eight prisoners. Brady was going to bury the Colonel there in the woods. But Franny wouldn't hear of it. Grief stricken, she insisted on bringing the body of Colonel Potter back to the city for a "decent Christian burial." Thus, Colonel Potter rode home stretched out on the floor of the gang's supply wagon. Seated around him were eight bushwhackers and Privates Kinzler and Hobrecht, their carbines very much at ready and, for the moment, French pictures forgotten. Brady led in the Colonel's saddled and bridled but riderless horse.

"If you notice, sir, the papers document that Hawk was acting as liaison between the procurer of stores and buyers of same." Josiah stood before Colonel T.L. Price showing him the receipts Colonel Potter had stolen from Hawk's office. Outside, the rain beat a tattoo against the windows, adding to the gloom. Lieutenant Werner and Sergeant Brady crowding into the room, making the Colonel's office at post headquarters seem smaller than it was.

"Hum," the Colonel at this desk studied the papers before him. "Who is this Lieutenant Gorditch whose name appears here?"

"He was under my command, sir, before I left to join General Lyon." Josiah sensed a vast integrity about this new Post commander. He hadn't blinked, when Josiah had requested a meeting without following protocol, had inquired if Josiah felt prepared to face the court martial and offered assistance.

Were you aware of his pillaging, then?"

"I suspected them sir, but had no proof. Had I stayed I would have taken responsibility as his officer commanding and ordered him to stop unlawful procurement from civilians, under Articles of War numbers 30 and 32, sir."

"Yes, of course. Who took over your command when you left, Captain Scarborough?"

"Uh, I did sir." Werner spoke nervously. Yesterday, he had been severely reprimanded by the Colonel for going on a scout without authorization and with a man facing a court marshal. "But when I verbally objected to the way he treated civilians encountered on patrol, he transferred to another unit, now at Tipton with General Fremont."

His white shaggy brows knotted in concern, Tom Price, stared up at them.

"It appears that this Gorditch procured hay and fodder—"

--"*Stole*, sir, stole hay and fodder," Josiah corrected.

Price glanced at him, continued, "Stole, if you insist--then sold it back to the army for a profit, and Hawk used his staff to wagon the goods to the buyer."

"Yes, sir, it would appear that way."

Price exhaled and leaned back in his chair. "My God, look at this three month total, over $30,000. And the money going in the pockets of Gorditch and Provost Marshal office." He stood up abruptly, pushed past them, called out to the sentry on duty. Get Captain Grover in here, now."

"Thank you, gentlemen, for this information. Gorditch and O'Shay will be apprehended. An arrest order for Captain Hawk will be sent at once over the telegraph to his home in Topeka. What unit did Gorditch transfer into?"

"The 3rd Missouri, sir." Werner relaxed.

"That will be all. Except for you Scarborough, I want to speak to you, privately."

After the others had left, Price once again sat down,

folded his hands, and stared up at Josiah. Finally he spoke, "You realize, sir, that bringing these incriminating documents to me at this time makes it look like you are doing it to discredit the Provost Marshal—the very man who has filed charges against you."

"I can't help that, sir."

"How long have you had this information?" Josiah told him.

"Good," he nodded when Josiah had finished the story. "Then no one can claim you sat on them until now." He drummed his fingers on the desk, stared at the rain coming down outside. When he spoke it was low so as not to be overheard. "Listen to me Scarborough the charges against you are enough to cashier you out of the military. Assaulting an officer, even one as odious as Hawk, is serious, and then of course there is the fact of your drunkenness."

"Beg pardon, sir, but I had not been drinking that evening. Not a drop. My teacup had been filled with fruit punch - unlaced fruit punch," Josiah emphasized. "I intend to call witnesses to attest to that fact. And, my record will show that I have never been cited for drunkenness while on duty, sir." *That's only because you haven't been caught with the flask to your lips, you hypocrite*, his conscience reminded him.

"I have the written statement of your side of the argument before me." He opened a drawer and took out a file. "You claim to have been protecting your sister—"

" - Godsister, sir."

"Godsister - Miss Moone. I've known Franny since she and her mother came here to Jefferson City. Hard working, lady, Deidre Moone. Too bad about Franny's, uh, unpleasantness." His voice took on strength. "But I must congratulate you, sir. You did a bang-up good job out there, bringing back Miss Moone and the murderer, Wilcox." He scowled and smiled at the same time making

312

him look like a benign ogre. "Nevertheless, you are technically still under confinement to quarters. However, you are on medical leave and as such I suppose allowed to live and go where you please." He smiled outright. Unofficially, I will square what I can with General Fremont. When I've told him the whole story, in light of your valor yesterday, he may rescind the orders for the trial. After his arrest Hawk will be brought back here and jailed with O'Shay and Gorditch in that filthy hole he keeps in the Capitol's basement. Then, *his* will be the court martial and the disgrace."

"The marriage between Frances Margaret Moone and Hy Wilcox is hereby, annulled." The circuit judge turned to Franny sitting next to her mother in the courtroom. "And you are henceforth to resume the surname of your birth."

Although she thought she would have felt elation, she didn't, only numb. Ma took her home and with Clay, Otto, Josiah, Sigi, and Gus held a quiet "celebration" in the apartment. Home over a week after her abduction, her outer bruises had mostly healed, but her mind and heart had been irrevocably scarred. She prayed she'd never again feel the abject terror she had felt or the sense of utter helplessness while in Hy's hands. Naturally, she didn't mention this during the gathering, a gathering, she thought, should have been a wake instead of a festivity. Didn't anybody but her find it sad that the marriage had been stillborn?

Ma called her out of the gray world of introspection. "Tis, time to propose a toast," she poked Otto. He came in on cue. "*Ja*, a toast to *fraulein* Franny Moone and Captain Josiah Scarborough. An announcement they make, tonight." He beamed at Josiah and while Ma didn't exactly "beam," she seemed accepting of the inevitable.

Shyly - a new mien for Josiah - he gave his

devastating grin and raised his glass of Madeira to her. "Franny has consented to be my wife."

She sat quietly, accepting their well-wishes, pretending joy when she felt fury. Only two days ago, had he made a formal plea for her hand. Then she had cried and kissed him passionately, and told him what she hadn't had the chance to say when she was waltzing with him. That she loved him with all her heart, had loved him all her life, but hadn't known it. And as lovers will they had talked into the night, seated on the back porch swing out of the chilly, October wind.

"Oh, Franny you and Josiah can get married when we do," Sigi squealed. "It will be a double wedding." Grinning, Werner was slapping Josiah on the back and shaking his hand and the babble around her rose until she thought she'd scream. Didn't anybody understand?

"Perhaps, it best that you have *your* day, Sigi," she smiled into her friends excited eyes. "After all, a woman's wedding day is so very, very special." Franny almost choked on the words, remembering her own. "And something that you and your husband should treasure for the rest of your life." She caught Josiah's eye. He was frowning at her. She shot him an angry glance and turned back to Sigi.

"Hold on, Franny, why can't we all share a double happiness and a double wedding would make the occasion even more memorable." Gus didn't understand either.

The room fell silent. Glancing around at the baffled faces surrounding her, Franny drew a deep breath before she spoke. "I think…..that if Josiah and I were to marry so soon after….this unpleasantness ….that the condemnation and whispers about me would mar what should be Sigi and Gus's happiest day."

Her mother exploded, "Ain't no whispers, I—"

"—Ma, please, I've heard them behind my back, seen the look in the eyes of women I've known nearly all my life when I bump into them out shopping." Feeling close to tears she continued. "I guess, I'm what you'd call an *infamous* woman. Some are convinced I rode regularly with Verboise's gang." She turned to Gus. "On the night I was abducted a detail of soldiers came here to hunt for wire cut from the telegraph line. The Corporal in charge said, I was to blame--that because I 'rode with that bushwhacker gang,' Erin House came under suspicion.

"Got his name?" Josiah muttered. Gus nodded.

"Today I got an annulment." She dropped her head and her voice dropped to a near whisper as Josiah moved beside her. He stood with his arm around her shoulders as though to ward off the invisible blows she was giving herself. "I have earned more notoriety because of the abduction and soon, I will earn even more when I have to testify in a court against that boy I was once married to." With her hanky she wiped at her eyes, sniffed. "So, now you see, Sigi, dearest friend a girl could ever have, why I won't court any more scandal and spoil your wedding day."

Comprehension of what Franny had said began to show on each face. Josiah murmured comforts in her ear. She turned her face up to his, pleaded, "And why we mustn't let our announcement leave this room, just yet. After their wedding, then we can announce ours. By then, perhaps enough time will have elapsed."

Later on the porch swing, Josiah whispered in her ear, "We could elope, get married in St. Louis."

She broke free, pushing away his hands. "How dare you suggest such a thing!"

"Sweetheart, I was only thinking about having a wedding where we wouldn't be noticed, that's all." He reached for her but she avoided him.

"I'll never marry again in a heady fly-by-night manner. When I marry again it will be a proper wedding in St. Peter's and Father Walsh will have said our bans every

315

Sunday for the three weeks. He will officiate. I will wear my prettiest dress, and my mother and all my friends will be there even Toby, Tycee, and her girls."

Only when he showed he was willing to wait, although reluctantly, did she consent to have him kiss her.

CHAPTER EIGHT
November

Friday the 8th

The army continued building fortifications around the city, begun during the early days with Borenstein and intensified under Grant, Davis, and Fremont. The old trees lining High Street died by axe, becoming abatis. The trees laid on their sides; the roots served as a line of defense for the Capitol. When Franny ventured outside the hotel and saw block after block of felled oaks, she burst into tears.

The daytime weather cooled. The army tried Hy Wilcox by military court a month after his capture and included Buster's trial with his. For Franny, knowing in advance the probable verdict for the boys added to her misery - mitigated only slightly by the favorable ruling her case received from the judge advocate. A no-nonsense major from St. Louis headquarters, he upheld her pardon, determined that she had been innocently duped, and didn't see the murders - a contention Franny held all along.

But with Josiah and Brady the court called her, too. All three would appear for the prosecution.

"Ma, I can't do it! I can't sit before all those men and tell them how he.... he...manhandled me.... And....and beat me.....and killed that guard. Besides, I didn't actually *see* him kill Jefferies." Her shame drove her to her pillow, weeping for release from the burden of appearing in a public trial. How many more indignities would she have to suffer for bringing disgrace on herself, her mother, and Erin House?

Try as she might, Dee couldn't soothe her. Only Josiah could. Once more ensconced at Erin House and on somewhat better footing with his prospective mother-in-law, Josiah would hold her close, telling her, "You won't be alone. Brady and I will be there, too. You don't think we'd let anything terrible happen to you, do you? You have nothing to be ashamed of. You did nothing to cause his viciousness and everyone there will know that."

Then her mind would shrink to a pebble and in wicked whispers tell her, *Oh, he's wrong; you were the cause, Franny girl. If you had merely tried to be a wife to him, perhaps lived on the farm when he wanted you to...* But these recriminations had rattled around in her head since almost the day she married Hy.

The day of the trial she awoke with flowers from her monthly visitor. Ma brought her biscuits and warm chamomile tea and let her miss serving breakfast to stay in bed until it was time to dress. Headachy and cramping, reluctantly she pulled on a heavy muslin caped dress, without ruches or ruffles, that did nothing for her except make her look more weary than she was. Even better, for her purposes, it was drab brown almost a Quaker woman's "goin' to meeting" dress. Her hair she yanked back plastering every wispy curl with pomatum to stick it down under her equally plain bonnet. Satisfied that she looked respectably subdued, as well as wan and unwell, she set out with Dee, Josiah, and Brady for the capitol. The sky had turned a bright blue and a crisp breeze curled and fluttered autumn leaves before them as they made their way.

The three-man board called Brady in first. Tired, still grieving over Potter, and suffering from a cold, the old veteran entered the Capitol's chamber set aside for military trials. He had told the prosecutor he would testify that Wilcox and Cowles had been two of the four who stormed the main saloon and shot 14 unarmed men on the *White Star*. After his testimony Brady said farewell to Dee and Franny with a courtly bow and pumped Josiah's hand.

"I'm off, Lad, just got time to make the 11:30am for St. Louis. Goin' ta stay with me sister that I was supposed ta see in June."

"I'll miss you, old man." Josiah shook his hand then embraced him like a son would his father. "But, I know where to find you; you gave me her address."

Brady looked over at Franny then winked at Josiah. "She'll settle ya rascal self down aplenty or me name ain't Oliver Brady. Think mebbe I should stick around and tell her about some of yer didos, boy-o? Might change 'er mind about you."

"Get along with ya, now, Brady." Imitating Brady's accent, Josiah blushed, grinned and shook Brady's hand one last time.

"Plenty o' stories I got about this big Mick, Miss Franny."

"—Brady, you're going to miss the train." Laughing, Josiah saw him to the street.

The court called for Josiah. She had asked him not to testify that her testimony was damning enough. But he had told her "It's my duty, sweetheart. I must report what Wilcox told me when we finally ungagged him. He bragged about killing Jefferies and torching Erin House." Praying no one would bring up his unauthorized sortie or his pugnacious behavior towards the former provost marshal, Josiah did his duty.

Waiting in the outer room for her name to be called, she felt disappointed in Josiah. Why didn't he just leave well enough alone and let her be the one to drive the nail in Hy's coffin? She might as well take on that blame, too. She ached for Hy. When, shackled, he had limped into the courtroom, his skin's pallor, his thinness, startled her, and he hadn't bothered to glance in her direction. He was only a boy, really, barely 20 years old. Why couldn't they see that he, too, had been duped by Verboise as she had, as all the gang had? Made to feel that no matter what evil they did, they were still, all righteous warriors. That's what she'd say to the court. She'd plead for mercy.

319

Trailed by Ma as her chaperone, Franny entered the court. Three officers, all busily taking notes, looked up when she entered. One whispered something in the ear of the man next to him and they both smirked. She went crimson. Finding her mind filled with glue and her tongue stuck to the roof of her mouth, the idea of fainting appealed to her. Perhaps if I fainted, she thought, then I wouldn't have to testify, today. I could go home. Rest and think about what I would say when they made me come back.

But she calmed herself enough to be duly sworn in, give her name, age, and place of residence.

"Miss Moone, you were Mrs. Hy Wilcox before your annulment, were you not?"

"Yes, " she whispered staring at her hands.

"How long have you known Mr. Wilcox?

"About 10 years off and on."

"Off and on? Could you explain that, ma'am?"

"We were in early school together. Then, he went off to Kansas with his paw for a spell when I was around 12 years old, let's see," she did the mental arithmetic quickly, answered, "around 1856 and came back the same year and I went away to the female academy in Virginia a year later."

"One could say, you had known the defendant most of his life?"

"Yes."

"You would then, be able to give a statement as to the character of Mr. Wilcox."

Here was her opening. "Yes, Mr. Wilcox, Hy," she met his eyes, "was one of the sweetest, kindest boys in my school. His class was ahead of mine, but he never teased us and always showed proper respect and courtesy to my mother—"

"—Miss Moone, please." The judge advocate peered at her as though she had grown a wart in the center of her forehead. "How Mr. Wilcox behaved in school is not the inquiry of this court." He got up from his chair across from Hy and Buster and walked up to her with his hands behind his back and a rattlesnake smile on his face.

"Would you please tell this court why you sought an annulment from Mr. Wilcox?"

She swallowed, stared at the middle-aged major bristling with military starch and preening before the panel. Furious, knowing she'd have to incriminate Hy with her answer, she said nothing.

"Miss Moone?" He waited. "If Mr. Wilcox was all that you have painted him to be then why did you seek an annulment from a person of such sterling character?"

"I'd rather not answer that question, sir, if you don't mind."

From the corner of her eye she saw Hy's glare turn into wonder.

"Miss Moone, your answer will tell his board the immediate character of the defendant."

"I'll tell yer boy-os why," Ma, who had fidgeted since taking her seat in the corner, jumped up, waving the umbrella she always carried. She bustled to the front of the court and confronted the three jurors, too startled to object. "Too young was me Franny. I'm to fault. I'm the one who wanted her annulled from him. Slavers were the Wilcoxes 'n' we aren't."

The president of the board banged his gavel. A heated discussion erupted between the major and the jurors.

Taking the opportunity, Dee plopped herself in the chair next to Franny's. "Now, I ain't through, talkin', so yer boys better listen to me." She yelled over to the blue huddle. "What she's wantin' to say to yers is that when she eloped with this little fella, she thought he was still the proper young man she had always known. And I'd agree, the lad was always most respectful ta me. But he changed, yer see."

"Madam!" the President banged his gavel but Ma barreled on like a charging bull.

"Got under the spell o' Satan himself, he did. His pappy, too. Ya hauled him off ta jail last July." The more the President banged his gavel the louder Ma talked. "Verboise's the cause o' all these troubles all summer. He drove the boy crazy, crazy enough ta burn down me hotel and shoot them men and in love with me daughter enough ta abduct 'er."

The judge advocate motioned for the sergeant-at-arms to remove Ma from the room. The young soldier approached, warily eyed Ma, and gingerly reached for her. "Touch me, sonny," snarled the matronly owner of sedate Erin House pushing her umbrella at him, "'n' I'll ram me umbreller through yer chest! Now as I was sayin', the boys went mad with fever, with war fever and if this damn shootin' hadn't started they'd be home plowing a peaceful field 'er two."

Nothing she or her mother said made any difference. Nor did Hy and Buster's personal defense that they acted as legitimate, Confederate soldiers engaging the enemy. By the end of the next week, after scrutiny by St. Louis, the verdict came down. Josiah and a *Harper's Weekly* reporter attended the sentencing. It was no surprise.

"For Hy Ebenezer Wilcox and Buster Arthur Cowles, having once been pardoned for the crime of taking up arms against their Government and having once taken a solemn oath not again to take up arms against the United States, have been taken in arms, in violation of said oath and their solemn parole. These prisoners have committed crimes that unlawfully violate the civilized rules of war. Your souls are stained with crimes, which no right-minded man can view except with horror and disgust. They are therefore ordered to be shot to death three weeks hence on Friday, the 29th of November, between the hours of 10 o'clock a.m. and 3 o'clock p.m." The President of the board banged his gavel to dismiss the court.

The day before the execution she went alone to see him confined to the filthy county jail at the corner of Monroe and McCarty streets where the army had moved all prisoners but officers convicted of crimes. These were still housed in the basement of the Capitol. They shackled him and she visited him in his cell. His skin had even more pallor than when he was in court and he had developed a cough.

She stood before him, fighting back her tears. "Hy, I just wanted to tell you, I am so…." Her voice broke… "sorry."

Hy leaned back on his cot and watched her stifle her sobs and wipe her eyes. "Yeah, so am I. Reckon you'll be a widder, soon."

"I don't know what to say. The trial wasn't fair. None of this has been fair to you or to Buster. How is he? Has his mama come to see him?"

"Buster's ok, puny from being kept shut up in here all this time." He coughed, talked through it. "Bunch of soldiers went out to his house and 'captured' most of his corn crop. That's what they called it, 'captured.' Left his maw and sisters with next to nothin' to eat." Hy brought up phlegm from his chest and spit into a corner of the room. "Said because they was Secesh they owed it to the government. But to answer your question, yeah she and the oldest girl come by during the trial. I expect they'll be by before the shootin' starts." He bent double coughing.

His last remark again made the tears form beneath her lids and she waited until he sat upright. "Is there anything we can bring you, do for you?"

"Some decent food. We're tired of them ole hard biscuits they give us an' the bad pork. Even the coffee taste bad." He wiped his mouth with his dirty sleeve. "By the way, what you said 'bout me in court, that was mighty nice of y'all. But your maw sure surprised me, hoppin' up

323

that way and defendin' me."

"Sometimes Ma does things like that, and she knew you and Buster weren't getting fair treatment."

"Verboise lied to us, Franny." He sat forward and folded his hands.

"How?"

"He told us in St. Louis when we all signed that pardon after Camp Jackson last May, he told us that it weren't no good, meaning it weren't legal 'cause we had signed it under 'duress'. That's the word he used, meaning we was forced to sign it. And that means the court shouldn't a brought it up in considerin' our case. But when I tells this to the judge advocate he just laughs and says, "Boy, that was the most legal paper you ever did sign."

"So you signed the pardon and felt safe."

"Yep. And afterwards, as soon as we got back from the raid on the Liberty Arsenal, he done swore us all into the Confederate army, real formal like and told us that we was now soldiers fighting under the flag of our country and had all the rights and privileges, forthwith. But, Hell, he didn't have no right to swear us in...." A fit of coughing broke his thought. When he finished his face had the sour cynicism of one who has discovered his idol 's feet of clay. "He didn't hold a commission in the Confederate Army 'till we all done rode south and got sworn in agin when we met up with Price."

"That's why, then, the court saw you and Buster as plain old murderers instead of as soldiers fighting for your cause."

"And you mark my words, girl, it's gonna get worse for Missouri. The Yankees won't let a man hold his own convictions. He's gotta come out 'n' swear a loyalty oath to the goddamn Lincoln government. Even if he's signed his parole 'n' is tryin' to live peaceful, they're gonna make him enroll in the Federal army to 'prove' his loyalty. Right now, things ain't so bad, but hear me, Franny, things'll get so bad that all a man has to do to get his self shot is to have a neighbor who don't like him and tell the Feds he's Secesh. No proof needed. Just on the say-so of some angry farmer who don't like you."

She left as she had come, weeping. Before she left, however, she had tried to embrace him but the guard wouldn't let her. Nevertheless, by nightfall she returned with Tycee and Toby carrying a large tureen of chicken and dumplings, pans of corn bread, sides of sweet potatoes, and a pot of Erin House coffee. They stood by and watched the starving men devour the food, then collected the dinnerware and pans. Buster wept when he thanked her. She asked Tycee and Toby to wait for her outside, leaving her alone with Hy.

Rubbing his very full stomach, he smiled. "Hot damn, but that were some eatin'."

"Hy, I must ask you," she began timidly, "but I want your forgiveness."

"What for?" He looked surprised. "That's what you said goin' down the steps at the farm the day you rode off with Verboise."

She told him and then burst into tears.

"Now, Franny, don't take on so." He rose, his shackles clanking as he did so, and moved to embrace her, but again the guard waved his carbine and shook his head no. So he stood a foot away from her and became the gentle boy she had known so many months and years ago. "We wasn't meant to be married in the first place. You always was a lot better than me, with your schoolin', 'n' all. I knowed better than to run-off 'n' get married the way we done, and then not tell yore maw. You wasn't ready 'n' neither was I." He paused, watching her, then with only the slightest of edges in his voice asked, "You gonna marry that Yankee cousin of yorn?"

Josiah - so wrapped up in Hy had she been all day that she scarcely had given her sweetheart a thought. How was she to answer this former lover, husband - this condemned man's question? Should she wound him further by admitting her love for another man - have him go to his death knowing she had encouraged Josiah's attentions less than two months after their wedding day? Confess that with Josiah she had found the ecstasy she craved that she hadn't found with him? "I don't know," she mumbled not looking at Hy.

"He wants to marry you, don't he? The son-of-a--," he caught himself, "better."

"Please, don't blame Josiah for any of my wrong doing towards you. He had nothing to do with it. He didn't even know I was married for a month or more after I met him."

He smiled, a warm gentle smile, conveying his understanding. "It's ok, sugar. I needn't know. Just make me feel worse, knowin', wouldn't it?"

Just as she turned to go, saying goodbye one last time, Hy called to her.

"Franny, was you plannin' on being there?" He meant was she going to his execution.

"Of course not," she said softly. "I couldn't stand it."

"It'd mean a lot to me to find you in the crowd and look at you, one last time." He bowed his head, almost ashamed to admit, "I'm scared, Franny. Mebbe with you there, I wouldn't be so scared."

"Please, Hy, don't ask me to be there."

"Just this one last thing," his voice became urgent, pleading, "Please, be there, sayin' one of them prayers you know. Please ask God to forgive me."

He was frightened; she could see. Her heart breaking she said, "Alright, Hy, I'll be there if my presence would be a comfort to you."

"Promise me, Franny!"

She hesitated, knowing to give her word would lock her into the reality. Whispering, "I promise," she fled the

326

room and Hy Wilcox's specter of death.

Friday the 29th

The day dawned clear and bright but by noon, black clouds had formed in the sky and it threatened rain. The execution was scheduled for three o'clock in the afternoon, giving the condemned the opportunity to breathe as long as possible on his last day of life. No one else from Erin House planned to go, even Clay refused to go with her and spent most of the day shut up in his room. She would go alone, she thought. Ma shut herself up in her room for the afternoon with the tearful statement: "Ye promised the boy, then, go along. Get it over with."

She was halfway out the door when she met Josiah coming in from headquarters, after clearing up statements he was to make at the up-coming Hawk court martial. "I'm going with you." His look was grave as he took her elbow and guided her along the street.

"No," she stopped, in mid-sidewalk. "How would it look if we were together watching my former husband be shot to death?" Her resolve, so strong in the morning not to shed anymore tears, broke and the tears rolled down her face. Grabbing for her handkerchief she dabbed at her eyes.

"You shouldn't be alone, sweetheart."

Josiah was right, of course. But he was the last person who should be standing next to her when Hy searched the crowd and found her. Sighing, wishing he could wipe away all of her unhappiness, but realizing it was her cross to bear and hers alone, she gave him a little push away. "No! If you come with me it mustn't look like you have. He can't die watching you and me standing together …knowing about…us…the way he does." With that she took off at a dainty run down the street.

Blindfolded and paraded seated on his coffin through the streets from the old rock jail, Hy wore a clean white

327

shirt and had been permitted a bath. Buster also had been given a clean shirt and a bath and his oldest sister walked beside him to Price's Flat, a grassy field on Jefferson Street. Father Walsh trailed after them, saying his prayers and rattling his beads. Anyway, that's what Hy thought of religion, just a lot of Psalm singin', bead-rattlin' hypocrites. Like Paw, he'd never gotten acquainted much with the church. God had let his maw die and those people at Pottawatomie. Now, God was letting him die. Nevertheless, suddenly he very much wanted this modest priest to say a prayer for him. He would die first, then Buster. So the priest should be praying for him, now, not for Buster.

He pulled off his blindfold and spoke to the rifle-wearing corporal walking beside him. "Can you have Father Walsh talk to me, too?"

"Thought you didn't want to see a clergyman, Wilcox. We asked you this morning."

"I was wrong. I want to see one, now."

"Sure you do. With hell fire lickin' at your tootsies any minute now, I guess you would want a priest." The lanky Iowan motioned for another guard to take his place and he went back and spoke to Father Walsh.

Ahead of Hy marched a company selected by the post commander. Next came Hy and Buster, their hands shackled. Behind them came the 12 men in the firing party, six men to a prisoner, each man chosen by lot, the unlucky ones getting the job. Behind these marched the rest of the post command. Every soldier had been ordered to attend. When they came to the execution grounds, these formed a three-sided square facing inwards. On the open side the guard ordered Hy to sit on his coffin, which had been brought up with him. Facing him, the firing party positioned itself 50 feet away. Only one of the six muskets facing him carried the blank powder charge and no member of the party knew which one it was. Each man hoped it was he. Before they bandaged his eyes again, Hy saw Father Walsh pushing his way through the crowd, for a dense mob had gathered.

"You wish to confess, my son?" He opened his prayer book.

"Yes, Father Walsh. What do I say?"

"Just say whatever is on your heart that God might want to hear you say."

Hy looked into his eyes and saw kindness and compassion. He wished he'd gotten to know this priest better. He wished he and Franny had waited and married in this priest's church, like she originally wanted to do. He wished...

"Father I done killed some people and hurt my wife. Only she ain't my wife no more because of all the bad I done." He bowed his head and wept. He heard the words of pardon "...in *Spirituous Sanctum*..." When he looked up he saw tears in Father Walsh's eyes.

Somewhere in the crowd he heard somebody crying. Then he spotted Franny standing, weeping quietly to one corner of the crowd. She had come and she had come alone. She had promised and she had come. He couldn't let her see him bawlin' this way. If he couldn't have lived like one, at least he could die like a man. He scanned the crowd once more before they put the bandage over his eyes and saw Scarborough on the opposite side of the field from Franny, standing at attention with a company of Home Guards. Suddenly, he didn't hate him anymore.

"Ready!" Hy sat upright on his coffin. "Aim!" His body went rigid with anticipation. "Fire! " He heard the command and the caps go off their muskets. Then a sledgehammer ripped into his chest, and he didn't feel anything anymore. Weightless, he floated through a dark tunnel with a bright light at the end. But out of the darkness rode John Brown his savage hair blowing from the hot breezes of hell, riding towards him, keeping him from going into the light. Suddenly, a mighty arm reached down, lifting Hy above Brown's lathered charger. A voice that both rolled like thunder and tinkled like music said, "He is mine." And Hy Wilcox entered the loving light.

As the volley blasted Hy back over his coffin, Franny thought she felt their impact upon herself and she sagged to her knees, sobbing and holding her arms across her chest. Through her tears she saw blood spurt from Hy's clean, white shirt, staining it crimson. In her ears she thought she heard Hy's mute scream as he might have called out to her, and she knew that she would hear its roar in her mind the rest of her life.

Before Buster could be brought up before his firing squad, from High Street came pistol shots. Then from different parts of the downtown came more gunfire and a high pitched wail, like a thousand demons from hell had escaped to riot for a season upon the earth. Commands were issued; soldiers readied their arms. The crowd began pushing and running in every direction, women and children screaming, falling down, being trampled by the crowd suddenly gone berserk. From a store on Madison Street flames shot into the air and the bell in the court house began to ring. Franny found herself being pushed and shoved in every direction. She looked frantically about for Josiah but didn't find him and she began to run.

Within minutes, what seemed like an army rode across the lawn and pulled Buster onto a horse. Although his hands were shackled, he could still ride, and leading it all was Verboise. Yelling, "Yesterday, the Confederate States of America recognized the rightful, elected leader of this state, Governor Claiborne Jackson, forced into exile by tyrants of the lowest order, and added Missouri to her sister states fighting against such tyranny. We fight, here, today, against your drumhead courts and unfair punishments." He then lapsed into incoherent profanities and prophecies of doom upon the city, and stormed the Federal troops, in disarray and running to get away as hard as the civilians were.

High Street seemed blocked with soldiers, Verboise's gang, and civilians all jumbled up together. So, half-blinded by tears, she ducked into Hog Ally. Strangely, this place of sordid vice seemed deserted. Pausing only a minute as she looked down its shabby, muddy, corridor, she set out on a dead run to its end, to the Kentucky saloon. Expecting it to be filled as usual with soldiers, hard drinkers, gamblers, and women to whom she wouldn't dare speak, she braced herself as she pushed open the door. The emptiness of the place made her catch her breath. Only Brush Arbor sat at a table, smoking a cigar and drinking a glass of whisky.

"They all went to the shootin', honey." She curved her lips in a painted smile but her black eyes remained wary and hard. The eyes swept Franny's figure, judging her. "You'll have to get another dress. That one don't do nothin' for you." She had worn the plain brown muslin. "I might have one you could borrow until you make your poke."

"I'm...I'm not here for that." All Franny could do was stare at this raven-haired woman, so infamous that, according to Otto, the city council had talked about running her out of town.

Brush laughed. "Oh, you're not. Then, pray tell, why are you in here, honey?"

"Listen," Franny ran to a window and looked through the dirty glass. "Can't you hear all the shooting?"

When Brush didn't answer Franny turned and caught her eyeing her with a shrewd look. "You're that Irish Widder's gal, ain't you? Moone--You're Franny Moone." And she threw back her head laughing. "Hell, kid, the way you're going I expected you before now. Lots of ...conversation...about you, lady." And she pealed out again, laughing in short sarcastic bursts.

Although the gunfire seemed to be coming closer, she hadn't seen anyone enter the ally, not yet. So, in her iciest tone Franny said, "I'm not sure to what you refer, Miss Arbor.

"Oh, yes you do." Brush waggled a finger at her and fixed her with a knowing grin. "And you think in time all the talk about you is just going to go away - just evaporate -go poof." She waved her hand before her as though pushing aside the unseen. "Jesus, you're stupid."

"In time, people will forget."

"People never forget, honey. And they don't forgive. A woman slips once, and that's it." She leaned forward and whispered, "She's ruined."

"She can still marry. I intend to."

"Oh, you are? Well, congrats and all that bull." She sipped at her whisky. "It don't make no difference who the man is who'll marry you. Your past will follow you wherever you go - even if your man turns out to be President of the United States. Remember Rachel Jackson? Married Old Hickory?"

Franny vaguely remembered the story, that Rachel had married very young a man who flew into jealous rages. She left him thinking he would file for a divorce and then married Andrew Jackson, only to learn after two years of marital happiness that her first husband hadn't gotten a divorce at all. Finally, a divorce was issued and the Jackson's remarried. "Why do you bring up Rachel Jackson, Miss Arbor?" She hovered by the window, daring not to venture closer to Brush Arbor. Other than being profane and coarse, something sinister about her, repelled Franny.

Brush blew a smoke ring and sipped her whiskey. "She died before Andy Jackson took office, some say the slander of being called an adulteress and a bigamist finally killed her. They was married in the 1790's and she died just before he took over the presidency." She thought for a moment, said, "1828. That's the date she died. My mama was from Tennessee before she moved to Kansas and she told me the story. So how many years is that? Damn near 40 years of puttin' up with snide remarks, snubs, and whispers about you when you enter a room." She peered around the smoke from her cigar and grinned. "That's gonna be your story, Franny, no matter how long you live or who you marry."

Before Franny could retort, for Brush had made her angry, the door swept open and Verboise lurched inside. He slammed and bolted the door, then crouched to the floor, waving his revolver before him.

"What the hell? Verboise, you can't come in here and lock my door. I'm always open for business, you know that." She rose to confront him, but the look of evil on his face caused her to slowly sit back down.

Franny tried to duck down behind a table near the window, but Verboise spotted her. "Mrs. Wilcox," he smiled without mirth, "we always seem to be meeting under the oddest of circumstances." Swiftly, he walked over to her, glanced out of the window, and pulled her up to him. He reeked of gunpowder and death. And she didn't like the light she saw in his eye.

He bent and kissed her, hard enough to make her gasp for breath. "There, I have done it," he said, relaxing his hold. "I have at last foresworn my first love." He bent to kiss her again but she fought - beat at his huge chest, kicked him in the shins, and did all she could to squirm out of his grasp. Shocked and surprised, she was appalled at this bully touching her. "Surely you sensed how I've felt about you," he said.

"Looks like the lady ain't interested in what you're offerin', Verboise," Brush snickered.

"Shut up!" So vicious was his anger when he wheeled on Brush, Franny thought he might shoot her. And this he threatened to do. "One more word from your filthy, painted mouth and I'll put a bullet through you. You're not a woman, you're a parasite and exterminating you I would enjoy." He turned back to Franny still struggling to be free, sighed, and released her. But hemmed her in so she couldn't pass or go around him. His eyes held hers. "You're afraid of me, aren't you?"

"That goes without saying, Captain Verboise. Let me pass." She stared hard, up into the depths of those odd gray eyes and felt every inch of her body tighten with fear.

"A moment, please, Mrs. Wilcox, Franny, if I may take the liberty of addressing you by your Christian name. Just hear me out and then give me your decision."

"I already have my decision. Let me pass and leave me alone!"

"Ah, but I truly love you."

Utterly shocked she could only stare into the eyes that held hers captive and seemed to be getting closer.

"Yes, I think I have loved you from the time you went with us to the *White Star*. In that room at the farm house when I held you naked and shivering wrapped in a blanket, rocking you gently to soothe the injured little girl you are, I knew I loved you then."

She barely whispered. "I never did or said anything that you might believe I wanted your attentions or affections, sir."

"True, but a woman doesn't have to do anything. Just by her *being* a woman draws a man to her, and she doesn't have to indulge in flirtations or utter a word. Hear me out, Franny." He put the revolver next to her face, not so much to frighten her-which the move did - but to rest his gun on something as he talked to her. "I have been faithful to my dead Nina for nearly 15 years. Like eagles mate for life, so she and I made that pledge to one another. And so, like the eagle left without the mate, I have flown alone, remembering her, yearning for her. But now, it is time for me to take another mate. That one is you, Franny." He bent to kiss her and she pushed him away.

"No! I don't love you, at all. In fact, there are times when I despise you."

He laughed showing perfect, white teeth. "I can make you love me and promise you the ecstasy of the flesh that you so desire."

Mortified, she blushed and looked wildly over at Brush for help. But none was forthcoming from that quarter. The whore sipped her whiskey, smoked her cigar, and watched them with a smirk on her face. His hand turned her chin up to him, forcing her to look directly into his eyes.

"Yes," he said softly, "Yours is a body that demands fulfillment. And I can give you that and children and you will learn to love me as my wife. Besides, I am a very rich man, and Scarborough is penniless."

"Why do you mention him?"

"Because, he loves you, too. Stop pretending to me that he doesn't. I know all about your little affair with him. He's my true rival for your affections. I could have killed him today but his back was to me and it wouldn't have been an honorable killing."

"Hey, gal, better take the offer. He says he's rich. Remember what I said about Rachel Jackson." Brush smiled into her whiskey glass.

" I don't want to speak to you again, Miss Arbor, is that understood?" He didn't turn around but held Franny under the spell of a hypnotic gaze.

"Ok, Chief, just tryin' to be helpful."

Franny heard Brush's soft laughter but the longer his eyes held hers, felt her own will slipping away. "You're an outlaw, a killer. If I went with you I'd be fleeing the rest of my life."

"Oh no, little treasure," he gathered her to him again. "With my money we can live anywhere in the world we wish. And with you by my side, I'd have no reason to kill. Besides, I am a commissioned officer in the Confederate Army."

"But my mother—"

"—Out of that dreadful boarding house she's scrimped so hard for. With us, if she wishes, living a life of indolence and plenty. Seeing sights she's always wanted to see but hasn't. The pyramids of Egypt, Franny, are magnificent. And the music halls of London and Paris are lively with laughter and filled with beautiful women and well-dressed men. I shall buy you the finest of Parisian haute couture, and you shall be my beautiful little treasure."

Gunfire in the ally drew his attention. He let her go and crouched by the window, giving Franny the opportunity to spring out of his reach. Brush arose and joined him at the window. "Look's like the whole Federal army's headed this way, Chief. Better get out while you can, out the back."

"Yes, on this one, Miss Arbor, you're right," he scowled, looked around for Franny who watched him from a safe distance hidden beneath one of the tables. Calling to her, he said, "Come with me, Franny. I can get us to safety and by nightfall be married."

"Yeah, kid, you should go with him. You stick around this town, you're gonna get the same frozen shoulder that Mrs. Jackson did." Brush too, craned her neck, looking for her.

Outside Franny heard the sounds of soldiers approaching and a knock at the door of the saloon and a voice call out, "Brush, open the door."

Brush went to obey, but Verboise grabbed her arm. "No," he whispered. "Tell them you're closed for the execution." Then called again for Franny, "Frances, this is silly. Stop hiding from me. Brush is right. You have no future in this town. You'll be ostracized the rest of your life, here, and anywhere you move within the United States, your past will follow you. Come, live abroad with me."

The knocking came again. "Brush, come on open the door. This ain't no social call."

"Let me go, Chief. I gotta unbar the door. They'll break it down!" and Brush managed to break free. Before she unbolted the door Verboise started for the back. Then, he spied Franny. Jerking her from under the table, he dragged her along with him. Brush unbolted the door and a swarm of Federal soldiers charged inside. Franny heard Brush call over her shoulder as she ran away up Hog Ally, "Just don't break nothin' lookin' for the chief, but he's here and he's got his sweetie pie with him."

"Please, I don't want to go with you!" Franny wept trying to free herself from Verboise's steel embrace. They hid behind a tall stack of whisky barrels in the storeroom at the back entrance. Inside the saloon soldiers were yelling and looking in the rooms upstairs.

"Don't you, Franny? Not in the least?" He asked gently, putting his arms around her waist and drawing her to him. He cradled her in his arms and pushed her head against his chest. "Liar. You do want to go because it is the adventure of a lifetime for you, and you, little treasure, crave not only ecstasy but excitement." Like a feather he brushed soft lips across her brow.

The thought struck her that maybe this violent man, who at times could be as nurturing as a woman, knew her better than she knew herself. What if she did run away with him? Back at the farm she remembered thinking that if she lived through the experience she'd marry Cyrus Hawk because he was the most boring man she knew. But maybe she was thinking that way because she was just frightened. She hadn't hesitated a minute to accept Josiah after he brought her home and that was before everybody learned that Hawk was dishonest and stealing from the

337

government.

"What makes you think you know me, so well?" She gazed up into the mesmerizing eyes looming over her and no longer felt fear, in fact, she admitted to the attraction that she hadn't known lay within her. She remembered Josiah. She had thought she loved him, wildly desired him, but did she really? Furthermore, what would married life be like with him? An army Captain's life was hard with barely adequate pay and while he was posted here with orders she would have to remain in Jefferson City. After her marriage to Josiah, the whispers about her would intensify. Maybe Brush Arbor was right, people never forgive or forget when a woman has slipped. And if Verboise were a man of his word, as she sensed him to be, then she would be able to take Ma to Paris and London and Egypt and all those wonderful places she'd love to see. She raised her face to his and his lips hovered inches from her own.

"Verboise!" Josiah stood in the storeroom six feet away, his revolver pointed at them both. When he saw it was her locked into Verboise's arms, in quick succession the looks of utter surprise, dismay, pain, and rage fleeted across his face. It hardened into anger but he lowered the gun.

"She's coming with me, Scarborough" Verboise said mildly, keeping his embrace around her waist. " You refused to do so when I asked you. Only, of course she is coming in another capacity. She'll be my wife."

Josiah caught her eyes, his so filled with pain and anger that she couldn't bare to look at him. The spell Verboise had worked vanished and shame swept over her as she tilted her head back and saw the man she was considering in a moment of truth. As though awakening from a trance she saw that his eyes held the look of a savage wolf waiting to tear its prey apart. His mouth, only moments before smiling with tenderness, was a line set in

338

hate, and she remembered Hy--poor Hy with his sunshine and rain moods who had blindly followed this man unto his own death. Verboise might possess all the wealth in the world, might be dashing in his way, be able to spell-bind her into going with him, but beneath all his appeal still lay a vicious, blood-soaked killer--a beast that might in a fit of rage one day turn and devour her. Josiah's presence made her all the more aware that, after all, her heart truly belonged to him. She would have a bushel of explaining to do to her sweetheart once this was over, but now she had to concentrate on extracting herself so as not to cause the beast to growl.

"No, I'm not going with you, Captain Verboise." She spoke softly and brushed her hand across her eyes, clearing away the last of the trance under which he had held her. She realized the dangerous situation they were in and used the only weapon she had - Verboise's love for her - to try to break through the heavy tension in the room. "But you sure do give a girl a persuasive argument why she should." His hands relaxed from around her and she turned, shielding Verboise with her body and holding down at his side his gun hand with her own. This prevented him from drawing his weapon and she figured that he'd shoot Josiah the minute he freed his hand from hers. Also, with her standing dead in front of the guerrilla she knew Josiah wouldn't shoot. Then, she would be able to pay her debt to Verboise. She faced her love. "Leave him be, Josiah."

Angrier than she'd ever seen him, Josiah shouted, "Move out of the way Franny."

"No." And she stood her ground, feeling the heat coming from the giant behind her, feeling his gun hand break free from her grasp.

"You don't have to be a shield for me, little treasure." And Verboise moved to get Josiah in his sights. "Now, I can shoot you, facing you, man to man. I could have shot you this afternoon, but your back was towards me." He pushed Franny aside, but as his finger pulled back on the trigger she threw herself forward into the stack of liquor barrels piled up next to Josiah. The stack fell and caused whiskey to spew over the room as the bullet hit the barrel that glanced off Josiah and knocked him to the floor. And Josiah's bullet skimmed the side of Verboise's head.

The soldiers had heard the crash and she heard voices coming their way. "Get out now, while Captain Scarborough is stunned." She picked herself up, her clothing wet from the whiskey seeping from the hole in the downed barrel and pushed Verboise towards the back door. Blood poured from the bullet's scratch and made a rivulet down the side of his cheek. He seemed not to notice, then with his hand wiped the blood away.

Verboise hesitated only a moment, heard the soldiers tramping towards the back room, and nodded. "But, I'll be back for you, little treasure," he whispered, touching his wound, and vanished. Outside she heard a horse gallop by.

Fallen barrels barred the door. "Captain, you in there?" A voice called out.

Groggily, Josiah answered, scrambling to his feet. "Yes, Sergeant. I'm in here." And added, when the men tried to force the door, "But, just leave me alone a few minutes."

She faced him then, and she would have rather faced a dozen of Verboise's guns then the flinty blue of Josiah's eyes.

"Hope you realize what you've done. You've allowed the worst killer in the state to go free." He looked away and began checking his gun.

"Please, Josiah," she went to him and he tensed, not wanting her to touch him. So she stood near, but apart. "It wasn't what you think. He was about to kill you and he may have saved my life at the farmhouse."

Interested, he looked at her then, waiting. Until now,

she hadn't told him what happened in the studio that morning, hadn't wanted to relive the shame and terror she had felt. Even after she told him the horrible story he seemed unmollified, again playing with his army Colt, checking the load, twirling the barrel, finding any excuse not to look at her. Finally, his tone, still flat with anger he said, "From what I saw you were thinking to go with him."

Had she? But said, "No not really."

His cynical grin broke her heart. "Bull, you were in his arms and he's about to kiss you. Didn't look like to me you were having any problems with which one of us you wanted. If you hadn't wanted him you would have rejected him out of hand."

"No, I did immediately reject him, then—his eyes, --" She stopped in confusion.

"His eyes?" Josiah's sharp, cold tone cut her to the quick. "What, he promise you the moon, the universe? That's the same tactic he used to get those foolish boys to follow him. Today your Romeo shot up the town and freed a condemned man and fifteen people are dead—three of whom are civilians and one of those an immigrant German woman caught in cross fire. And you're as foolish as Verboise's followers to think the man speaks the truth." He holstered the Colt and raked her with his unsmiling eyes.

"Why didn't you go?" He asked softly.

"Why do you think?" She felt her chin harden, her mouth set itself in it's stubborn line, that she stunk of whiskey, and became aware of a stray curl falling over her brow. Josiah Scarborough sometimes could be the most thickheaded man in the world. "Well, why do you think I didn't go with him?"

"But you would have gone if I hadn't come upon you two, just now, wouldn't you?"

Frannie realized the power Verboise had; yes indeedy

she had been entranced. Perhaps, if Josiah hadn't burst in when he did, she would have gone, but how could she explain this to him. So she said only, "I'm thankful that you came when you did." Not able to bear the coldness and tension between them another moment, she flung her arms around his tense shoulders and looked into his face. "Oh, for heavens sakes, Josiah Scarborough. I love you."

"You helped him get away." He gazed down at her and she saw a flicker of love in his eyes.

"He perhaps saved my life, I told you that."

He stared at her for a long moment, then suddenly his arms were around her and his lips on hers. He lifted her off her toes and whispered softly, "A life for a life. Is that it? I suppose I should be grateful to him too. But one day, little girl, I'm going to catch up with him." And he kissed her again and again and again.

EPILOGUE:

January 28th, Tuesday, 1862

On this date along with war news, three articles of local interest appeared in the *Jefferson City Examiner*.

Jefferson City

At a marriage held at St. Peter's Church Captain Josiah T. Scarborough and Frances Margaret Moone were united in the holy bonds of matrimony—Father Walsh officiating. Captain Scarborough is the son of Lord and Lady Peter Scarborough, of Westmeath Ireland and New York City. Miss Moone is the daughter of Edward James Moone, deceased, and Deidre Monihan Moone also of Westmeath Ireland and proprietress of Erin House Hotel in the City. Of the wedding party were Mrs. Gustave Werner (nee Sigrid Zimmer) as matron of honor, First Lieutenant Gustave Werner as groomsman, City alderman Otto Zimmer stepping in for the deceased father of the bride to give her away, and a host of friends and well wishers. Out of town guests included First Sergeant Oliver Brady, retired from the U. S. 4th cavalry and who holds citations for bravery and General David Hunter. Colonel Thomas Price, Governor Hamilton Gamble, Mayor Bernard Bruns, Aldermen King, McCarty, Campbell, and Wollencraft, and Police Constable Brudge, with their wives were among the military and civilian dignitaries in attendance.

The bride wore an ivory gown of satin, with insets of baby pearls on sheer silk around the neck and throat. Her hair had been brushed into a coronet of curls that encircled her head beneath an ivory silk veil. She carried a bouquet of mixed winter greens, taking into the wedding the festivities of the Christmas tide, just past. All guests and friends were invited to the reception held at Erin House.

343

News from Jackson County

Fearless raider and guerrilla, William Quantrill has struck again at Federal forces near Independence. Reported to be riding with him are former residents of Cole County, named herein: Buster Cowles, Horton Davies, and Chester McDonald. Also in their company is seen a tall half-breed who appears to wage control over a part of the Quantrill gang.

News from Topeka, Kansas

Former provost marshal of Jefferson City, Captain Cyrus Hawk has been jailed for his attack on the editor-in-chief of the *Topeka Kansas Freeman*. At a court martial heard on December 7th ultimo, Captain Hawk and Lieutenants Clarence O'Shay and John Gorditch were found guilty of fraudulent dealings with the Government. All three men were subsequently cashiered in disgrace from the United States Army and their commissions revoked. In addition, Mr. Hawk and Mr. O'Shay were fined and Mr. Gorditch has been confined to prison in St.Louis for the duration of the war. The nature of their offenses and the verdicts were wired to their hometown newspapers, in keeping with Article 85 of the Articles of War. The offenses of John Gorditch appeared in the December 20th edition of the *Jefferson City Examiner*. *The Chicago Tribune* received notification of the offenses of Clarence O'Shay. Cyrus Hawk filed a legal action against the *Topeka Kansas Freeman* barring the paper from publishing his name and offense. When the Circuit Court of the district of Kansas ruled on January 20th against Mr. Hawk's motion to bar, Mr. Hawk thereby entered the newspaper's editorial offices and drew his pistol on the editor-in-chief, John Turley. During the ensuing scuffle, Mr. Turley received a broken shoulder and bullet wound to his left leg. Mr. Hawk then fled but fell down a flight of stairs exiting the building and was easily taken in hand by Topeka police, called to the scene.

FINIS

Fact From Fiction

Obviously the fictional characters of *Righteous Warriors* rubbed shoulders with persons who actually lived during that time. To help the reader who may be unfamiliar with some of these people I have composed a brief after-look of these true personages.

Colonel Heinrich "Henry" Borenstein

At age 56 this Prussian immigrant and editor of the German language newspaper *Anzeiger des Westens* took up arms under General Lyon. After his stint commanding the Jefferson City post and resumed editorship of his newspaper. However, towards the end of 1862 the paper had failed and he returned to Europe. By 1873 he was living in Vienna and is presumed to have died shortly afterwards.

John C. Fremont

Fed up with Fremont's inability to follow orders and his administrative inefficiency, Lincoln relieved him of his command, replacing him with General David Hunter on November 2, 1861. In March of '62 Lincoln gave him the command of the Mountain Department, encompassing the Shenandoah Valley, where he unsuccessfully met Stonewall Jackson's campaign. When in June of '62 he refused to serve under General John Pope, Lincoln removed him from the field and Fremont lived in New York City for the remainder of the war, "awaiting orders." In May of 1864, he flirted with the idea of running for president on the Radical Republican ticket but eventually declined their offer. Railroad building and financing engaged his time after the war. In 1873 the French government found him guilty and sentenced him in absentia for shady dealing in the proposed transcontinental line from San Francisco to Norfolk. He served as Governor of Arizona, 1878 - 1881 and was named Major General on the retired army list in 1890, the year of his death.

Jessie Benton Fremont

After Lincoln dismissed her husband from command and removed him from the field all together, she spent the remainder of the war in New York with her husband. There she wrote *The Story of the Guard: A Chronicle of the War* (1863) a book of her experiences in St. Louis during her husband's command of the Department of Missouri. She went on to write several other books telling of her life and defending her husband through his varied careers. She died in 1902.

Governor Hamilton Gamble

After two difficult years in office as provisional governor, on December 17, 1863 Gamble slipped on the steps of the State Capitol re-injuring an arm fractured in a railroad mishap a few months earlier. He died in St. Louis of pneumonia on January 31, 1864.

Governor Claiborne Jackson

The beleaguered governor moved the government from Neosho, Missouri to Arkansas. He died from pneumonia near Little Rock December 6, 1862. Thomas C. Reynolds the Lieutenant-Governor took control of the government-in-exile, moving it to various cities around Arkansas and relocating it again as Federal's threatened each place. Eventually after a short sojourn in Shreveport, Louisiana, the exiled Missouri government established its capitol near Marshall, Texas. It remained there until the end of the war.

General Nathaniel Lyon

The first Union hero of the war. Following his untimely death, his body was removed to the home of Federal Brigadier General John S. Phelps near Springfield. Mrs. Mary Phelps, wife of the general, ordered a local tinsmith to make a zinc case for the walnut coffin that held the body. She then buried the remains in the ice-house and covered it with straw. However, word got out, and a crowd cursing the General began to form in her yard. Fearing the General's body would come to harm, she asked General Sterling Price to send help. He promptly did and a Confederate detail buried Lyon in the Phelps' front garden. On August 22, Lyon's cousin, Danford Knowlton and his brother in law, John Hassler arrived by wagon with an iron coffin. They removed the zinc case, placing the wooden one inside an iron one and packing it in ice. By August 26th the coffin and relatives were back in St. Louis where Lyon lay in state for two days while thousands came to pay their respects. On August 28th the city saw an official military funeral, complete with flag draped coffin, accompanied by cavalry, infantry and artillery units. Lyon's horse that he had been riding when he was killed also accompanied the cortege. Free of charge, the Adams Express Company provided a heavily draped funeral car back to Lyon's home in Connecticut. Along the way the remains of General Lyon lay in state in Cincinnati, Philadelphia, New York and Hartford. In New York alone more than 1500 persons came out to view the coffin and pay homage to the fallen hero. After a funeral service worthy of his fame and sacrifice, he finally found his final place of rest on September 5, 1861, in his hometown of Eastford, Connecticut.

Colonel James Mulligan

After his capture at Lexington he was exchanged nearly two months later and went on to command as Brigadier General the 1st, 2nd and 3rd Division in West Virginia. He died from wounds incurred at the Third Battle of Winchester in September of 1864, after telling his men to "lay me down boys, and save the flag." He was only 34 years of age and left a wife and young child..

Major General Sterling Price

After the battle of Lexington, General Price retreated south to Arkansas to suffer defeat at the battle of Pea Ridge, Arkansas, and at Iuka and Corinth, Mississippi. In 1864, he staged a raid upon Missouri that took his army to Jefferson City which he failed to fire upon. He swung west toward Westport where his campaign dissolved under the onslaught of the Federal resistance. After the war he went to Mexico, but there his dreams of building a Confederate colony died with the overthrown Maximilian government. He returned to St. Louis a broken and disillusioned man and died September 29, 1867.

Colonel Thomas L. Price

Although owning many slaves and a Virginian by birth, he served throughout the war with the Union army, rising to the rank of General. One of the wealthiest business men in town before and after the war he was politically active trying to keep Missouri in the Union and after the war worked tirelessly to restore citizenship to former Confederates. He intended to endow a college and started building, but unfortunately he died when it was only one story high and the college was never completed. A true healing of both sides can be said to have occurred when, in 1867, the son of Sterling Price, Celsus, married Celeste, daughter of Thomas Price. He died in 1870 worth a half million dollars.

William Clarke Quantrill

In November of 1861, Quantrill went to Richmond and received a colonel's commission. Back in Missouri with a force of nearly 150 men he waged partisan warfare against the Federal and Union sympathizers throughout the summer and fall of 1862. He continued these activities, mostly in western Missouri throughout 1863. Federal general Thomas Ewing initiated a policy of arresting women and girls suspected of giving aid to Quantrill and his partisans and jailing them in the dilapidated Grand Street jail in Kansas City. When the building collapsed, killing and maiming several of the women, Quantrill and 300 outraged men sacked Lawrence, Kansas in August of 1863. During the winter of '63 he took his band to Texas and there gave up control of his command to Bill Anderson and George Todd. After Price's final retreat from Missouri, in January of '65 Quantrill with a small group crossed the Mississippi, heading east in the hopes of joining with Confederate general Joe Johnston. But in Kentucky he met up with Fedral troops and was wounded. He died a month later in a Catholic hospital on June 6, 1865 after taking confession in the Catholic Church.

The Author..

Meredith Campbell holds advanced degrees in English and United States History and has been a Civil War buff all of her life. With the writing of Righteous Warriors and doing Civil War re-enactments, she has enjoyed putting her interests and literary talents together. Currently she lives with her husband, Jack; Spaniel, Bridey; and enjoys her vintage Civil War garden in Richmond, Virginia.